Enticed

Enticed

Kathleen Dante

HEAT I NEW YORK

THE BERKLEY PUBLISHING GROUP
Published by the Penguin Group
Penguin Group (USA) Inc.
375 Hudson Street, New York, New York 10014, USA
Penguin Group (Canada), 90 Eglinton Avenue East, Suite 700, Toronto, Ontario M4P 2Y3, Canada
(a division of Pearson Penguin Canada Inc.)
Penguin Books Ltd., 80 Strand, London WC2R 0RL, England
Penguin Group Ireland, 25 St. Stephen's Green, Dublin 2, Ireland (a division of Penguin Books Ltd.)
Penguin Group (Australia), 250 Camberwell Road, Camberwell, Victoria 3124, Australia
(a division of Pearson Australia Group Pty. Ltd.)
Penguin Books India Pvt. Ltd., 11 Community Centre, Panchsheel Park, New Delhi—110 017, India
Penguin Group (NZ), 67 Apollo Drive, Mairangi Bay, Auckland 1311, New Zealand
(a division of Pearson New Zealand Ltd.)
Penguin Books (South Africa) (Pty.) Ltd., 24 Sturdee Avenue, Rosebank, Johannesburg 2196, South Africa

Penguin Books Ltd., Registered Offices: 80 Strand, London WC2R 0RL, England

This is an original publication of The Berkley Publishing Group.

Copyright © 2007 by Kathleen Dante.
Cover photo by Sydney Shaffer/Getty Images.
Cover design by Monica Benalcazar.
Text design by Tiffany Estreicher.

First edition: March 2007

Library of Congress Cataloging-in-Publication Data

Dante, Kathleen.
  Enticed / Kathleen Dante.
     p.   cm.
  ISBN 978-0-425-21491-6
  1. Intelligence Officers—Fiction.   2. Artists—Fiction.   3. Blind women—Fiction.   I. Title.
  PS3604.A57E59   2007
  813'.6—dc22   2006038201

PRINTED IN THE UNITED STATES OF AMERICA

10 9 8 7 6 5 4 3 2 1

Thanks to my wonderful agent, Roberta M. Brown, for her enthusiasm and encouragement; my editor, Cindy Hwang, for the lightbulb clicking on; and Shadow of Anne Amie Vineyards for the inspiration for Timothy.

CHAPTER ONE

A hot extraction barely sped his pulse these days. Things were bad when it took a massive boom to get the heart pounding.

Hell, no. Dillon Gavin rejected the thought with a sharp mental toss of his head. That was just lack of sleep and back-to-back missions talking. A bit of R&R, some sexual comfort in the arms of an understanding woman, and he'd be fine.

True, he'd been skimming along for the past few years, ever since he'd lost his partner. But leave the shadowy black ops world and its attendant adrenaline rush? Not even for that last message from Lantis.

Ready to be an uncle? Better yet, how about a godfather?

Stopping to adjust his collar, Dillon studied his reflection in the black marble framing the entrance to Walsen Galleries. Tall, though not as tall as his former partner. A male in his prime. Hardly the image of a godfather—at least not in his estimation.

His lips quirked at the absurdity. It didn't matter. Lantis and Kiera were both in excellent health. When Lantis got out of black ops, his best friend's life expectancy had to have doubled, if not tripled.

Just because the missions weren't as much fun without Lantis didn't mean it was time for Dillon to turn in his papers. He'd adjust to the difference even if it killed him.

Brushing back the wavy lock drooping over his left eye, Dillon dismissed this morbid line of thought. Retire? And do what? Plant his ass somewhere and watch the grass grow? He snorted quietly. He wasn't ready to hang up his spurs. Perhaps he never would be. Anyway, despite his imminent godfatherhood, there was no hurry.

He had a whole month to himself—thanks to the Old Man's stiff-necked insistence—and a wallet flush from the efforts of his investment banker and the last few months of spartan life in the field. Might as well spend some of it on art.

Smiling in anticipation, he sauntered through the gallery's tinted glass doors into the world of color and light.

When Kiera's assistant had informed him that his childhood friend and her new husband planned to attend the opening of a Jordan Kane exhibit tonight, he'd been delighted. As a longtime fan of the psyprint artist, he'd enjoy sharing her work with the two most important people in his life.

There was a dreamlike quality to Jordan's work, one that appealed to him at the deepest level, an optimism that refreshed his palate after all the horrors he'd seen in the field. It wasn't that her artistic vision ignored the harsher realities—such deliberate blindness wouldn't appeal to him—but there was an underlying message of hope: things would get better, good will prevail despite the odds, the light at the end of the tunnel might not be a deflagration spell lobbed by hostiles.

There had been times when that belief was all that had kept him going. After this last mission that had nearly gone to hell, he needed that reminder. He needed it desperately.

Neither Lantis nor Kiera was in sight when Dillon reached the wing housing the exhibit. It took only a single sweep of the first room to reach that conclusion. His best friend's towering stature was distinctive, to say the least, and as a supposed civilian he had no reason to conceal his presence.

Dillon didn't worry, confident that he'd catch up with the lovebirds at some point. He could use the time to get his head screwed back on right and tight.

He shook his head. *Should've known this funk was coming—what with ops palling almost as soon as Lantis retired.* It was nearly at the point where the adrenaline rush wasn't worth the static from higher up. The Old Man had probably sensed it, thus his refusal to send Dillon out until after a month off.

Needing the distraction, Dillon turned to the nearest psyprint—a moody sunrise over an anonymous old town. The rooftops in the picture reminded him of Rotterdam, where Lantis and he had first pretended to be lovers to throw the arms dealer they'd been surveilling off his guard.

Dillon grinned. He could still see the patent disbelief on Lantis's face that had met his suggestion, one of the handful of instances in their long partnership when Dillon had succeeded in shocking his friend. But Lantis hadn't dismissed it out of hand. And the rest was history. They'd used the pretext successfully countless times since that sunny day in the Netherlands.

That's what had been missing in the past few years: the sense of fun. Sure, black ops was serious business—but that didn't mean you shouldn't enjoy yourself. The other agents Dillon had worked with since Lantis's retirement just couldn't match his friend's open-mindedness. Together, they'd been hell on wheels.

He sighed, for a moment wishing for a return of the good old days before giving himself a mental snap kick in the butt. That was the past and quite selfish, considering Lantis was supremely happy with present conditions—especially Kiera's current condition. It was up to him to adjust, to find something else that brought the pleasure back to the job. Nevertheless, he took note of the price on the psyprint; it would make a nice addition to his Jordan Kane collection.

Almost every piece Dillon saw reminded him of his defunct partnership with Lantis. Good memories for the most part. But it probably wasn't wise to see the lovebirds while he was in this mood. Lantis could read him as only a former partner could, and Kiera knew him like the sister he'd never had. He didn't want them to pick up on his melancholy. For some reason, it felt like he was closing a chapter in his life and had to conduct a final retrospective before he could move forward.

Reluctantly amused by his whimsy, Dillon looked around for something to divert his thoughts. Some incidents were too gut-wrenching to relive. They hovered like specters in the back of his mind, just waiting for a lapse in his vigilance.

A bright pink shock of hair caught his eye, aided by a cheerful wave of a slender arm.

On a surge of relief, he threaded his way through the crowd, sidestepping a clump surrounding a well-known model, to reach Kiera's friend. Tatianna Jones—Shanna to everyone who knew her—was a free spirit who ran the gallery with a sharp capitalist's eye for what pricked the public's interest and changed her hair color as frequently as her underwear or so it seemed. And she knew she had a guaranteed sale in his person.

"I didn't know you were in town," Shanna burbled happily as Dillon bent down several inches to brush a kiss of greeting on her cheek. "Anything grab you?" She raised pink brows a shade or two darker than her hair in teasing inquiry; below them her normally hazel eyes were a sparkling green.

Dillon laughed, forcing easy cheer into his voice as he struggled to bury the trenchant scenes of his lost partnership. "You know me too well. There are several, actually. But I haven't decided which ones to buy yet."

She dimpled a smile at him, the sharp glint of determination beneath her darkened lashes warning him of a coming sales pitch. "Maybe we can help you decide." The doll-like gallery manager turned to a slender woman in a long-sleeved cream sweater dress that hugged understated but delightfully feminine curves.

He stared, his attention snared by the oldest magic in the world. Damn but she made his mouth dry. One would think he'd never seen a woman before. Jealous of the soft wool hiding her body from his gaze, he feasted his eyes on the svelte lines of her figure, regardless of propriety. What wouldn't he give to explore that virginal territory with his own hands?

Dillon's heart conjured rolling thunder as he studied her fine features. Here was someone who could distract him from his nostalgia and the darker memories lurking in the recesses of his brain. Over the roar in his ears, he heard Shanna's high, clear voice as she addressed her companion in a bantering tone: "Jordan, this rogue is something of a fan of your work."

Jordan Kane, the artist herself.

A few inches taller than Kiera's diminutive friend, with short, shaggy, honey-brown hair feathering her pale cheeks, the other woman radiated a pool of exquisite calm, apparently oblivious to the excitement around her. Her even demeanor made him wonder what it would take to banish it. His imagination conjured all sorts of carnal incentives he might offer her for the privilege of finding out, the sensual images crowding out the ghosts of missions past clamoring for his attention.

He latched on to the diversion gratefully, having wanted to meet the creator of the evocative psyprints he'd bought. Now was an excellent time to make her acquaintance—and perhaps more? Given her composure, she didn't seem the type to jump into bed on first acquaintance, but perhaps she could be persuaded?

"Dillon Gavin," he introduced himself, taking her delicate hand between his much larger ones. He'd bet his cock would more than fill her hands. Heat flooded his veins as he savored the contact, using the silken sensation to force back the lingering specters that threatened to spoil his enjoyment. How would her hands feel gliding over his bare skin? "I'm honored to meet you."

Her pale blue eyes seemed to look straight into him, a penetrating glance that saw things he kept hidden from the world. A flurry of emotions flashed across her face, then her eyes widened suddenly as she gasped, her hand jerking in his grasp.

Jordan had noted him long before their introduction. A muscular, black-haired man, he reminded her—oddly enough—of Timothy. She'd nearly giggled in amusement. Most people wouldn't have considered the comparison a compliment, but it was. Silent, thoughtful, in perfect control of his well-proportioned body, and totally at ease with his surroundings—very much like Timothy. He wore his self-sufficiency like an invisible cloak that made people give way instinctively. A man among men.

Her arms prickled with sensual awareness at the thought.

He'd drawn her attention like a soft melody that teased her ears into listening, dominating her senses with his mere presence, so much so that the others in the room faded into faceless blurs— her clairvoyance responding to her interest. His deep-set black eyes had turned dreamy or glittered in slitted response to some thought as he stalked among her artwork. A strong chin, slashing brows, an aristocratic—almost Roman—nose, high cheekbones, and well-formed lips her fingers itched to trace. The exceptional combination tempted her to bend her rule on portraits.

His light baritone caressed her ears, sent shivers tripping down her back, and made her core clench with a rare hunger. Her toes curled reflexively as he laughed in response to Shanna's sally, something primitive inside her stirring at the sound of the low chuckles. Surely it was simply an automatic female response to the presence of an exceptional male?

Jordan sniffed delicately, hoping to find something to mitigate the unexpected attraction, and nearly frowned when she failed. Unlike many of the other men in the room, he didn't soak himself in a dissonant clash of cologne and aftershave, content with citrusy soap and his own clean scent.

He probably smelled like that all over. Her nipples tingled in speculation, her breasts firming as she failed to rein in her suddenly lusty imagination. *Would she find that intriguing scent all over him?*

Her core clenched once more as desire pooled in her belly and a moist heat gathered lower. She bit her lip to suppress a groan at the unfamiliar sensation.

A most unusual man. He intrigued her enough that she was willing to brush her fingers over his own, to allow that rare physical contact, to risk the flood of visions that came with triggering her psychometry.

When his rough, warm hands enfolded hers, a dizzying kaleidoscope of images flashed before her mind's eye, disorienting, even though she'd braced herself for it.

A stocky, brown-haired man pried open a wooden crate with quick efficiency. The top panel, covered with strange writing—all straight lines and circles—and unintelligible numbers, slid away. The top layer of contents was pulled aside to reveal boxes stamped with the universal symbol of hazardous materiae magicae.

Dillon Gavin leaned in, a string of silver medallions draped between his hands. The metal ovals glowed purple for a single heartbeat, then disappeared in the batting between the boxes. With a brief gesture at a tall man, he moved to another crate filled with mottled green cylinders.

From a black bag, he took out a gray block and started kneading it between his hands like so much putty. He formed the gray substance into a thread, hiding it around the cylinders.

Working smoothly, he and several other men opened and resealed rough crates, then exited the speeding railroad car, wind clawing at their bodies. They leaped off—into empty space.

From somewhere high, Dillon and his companions watched a locomotive trundling along a bridge spanning a deep ravine. Distance reduced the conveyance to the size of tiny ants. A haze of virulent yellow-green energy suddenly rose from the valley floor, engulfing the train. Purple light sparkled over a few cars, then the train vanished in a powerful blast that shattered the bridge and leveled the surrounding trees.

Before she could gasp, the setting changed.

Explosions ripped through the night, the darkness punctuated by short bursts of light. Men in black jittered in halos of blue power, fell limp and deathly still to the ground.

Scene after stark scene followed, some of such explicit violence her stomach lurched.

A gun swung into her face, its muzzle filling her vision just before it hit. Going to shoot her— No, it was going to shoot Dillon Gavin!

Dillon knelt beside a badly injured man as healers worked, a knife held at ready, his face a cold mask of determination.

Jordan flinched. *He's a killer!* Something rose up inside her in denial, arguing for accuracy. He's killed before but not out of malice or enjoyment. But still . . . the first man to pique her interest in ages and he was too dangerous to have in her bed. The realization was like ashes on her tongue.

A bearded man with an elaborate tattoo on his cheek sprang out from behind a tree. Dillon pushed someone down, then was thrown back as bullets slammed into his chest.

Jordan gasped, shock plunging her body in ice and leaching blood from her face. Her stomach dropped and lurched, her knees threatening to fold under her. *Not just a dangerous man, but one with a dangerous job.*

"Are you alright?"

Slamming her shields down on her vision, she withdrew into herself, desperately blocking all input to stop the invasion of Dillon's waking memories. It left her isolated in the ever-present darkness, the blindness she'd learned to live with closing in on her. The ground swayed under her feet.

"Jordan?" Shanna asked from somewhere beside her, warmth close by Jordan's shoulder suggesting a hand in midair, uncertain of its welcome.

"I-I'm sorry, I—" Jordan broke off, yanking her hand free. Welcome heat flooded her cheeks as she clung to the shreds of her composure. "I got distracted." She pressed her fists against her belly. She wasn't her mother. She refused to collapse like her mother had, over so much less. With sheer desperation, she forced her lungs to work and her knees to hold. With her palms safe from physical contact, she felt secure enough to open herself to her vision. Her clairvoyance showed Dillon staring at her in puzzlement, his black eyes narrowed in speculation.

"Jordan's blind," Shanna confided in a whisper with the swift delivery of discomfort, as if to excuse her strange behavior. Dillon Gavin had to be a good friend—not just a favored customer—for Shanna to share that. She knew Jordan preferred to keep her blindness to herself.

Dillon's eyes widened, clearly taken aback by the revelation. Jordan wasn't surprised; she'd worked hard to foster an appearance of normalcy. Her clairvoyance usually allowed her handicap to pass unnoticed.

"Well, look who's here." A deep voice cut through the din of music and polite conversation around them.

To her relief, Dillon's attention shifted, pure delight lighting his face as he grinned up at the speaker, hardly the image of a man with blood on his hands. "There you are. I thought it'd take a search party to find you."

Jordan drew a sharp breath as her clairvoyance showed her the newcomer. *Dillon's comrade in arms.* He'd looked every inch a warrior in her vision but here he cut a devoted figure, standing with a solicitous arm around a beautiful and very pregnant redhead. Shanna had introduced them earlier: John Atlantis and his wife, Kiera. She'd never have suspected such a gallant man could have taken part in the violence she'd witnessed.

———— ∞∞∞ ————

Lantis met Dillon's gaze with the slightest arch to his brow, then slid his eyes sidewise to indicate his wife meaningfully. Kiera appeared radiant, evidently contented with life in general and enjoying the exhibit. But if Dillon knew his heart sister, she'd put in a full day in the office despite the advanced state of her pregnancy, running the toy company she inherited from her father. Lantis probably thought she needed to rest.

"You look like you could use a day off." Dillon leaned over to kiss Kiera's proffered cheek.

She grimaced at him, obviously sensing a double-team in progress, then admitted ruefully as she rubbed her back, "Putting my feet up would help."

"Well, then. I won't keep you standing around." Dillon exchanged a look of satisfaction with his former partner, ignoring a stab of disappointment at their early departure with the ease of long practice.

Reflexively, he put the best light to the situation: this would give him the opportunity to try charming Jordan out of her reticence. While her blindness might explain her initial lack of response to him, the way she'd jerked her hand free nettled his curiosity, immediately identifying her on his mental radar as a challenge. What was she like when making love? Would her air of calm shatter or dissipate like a fog bank before rising wind? He dearly wanted to find out.

Reading his carnal intentions like an open book, Lantis gave him the barest quirk of his lips. There were few things Dillon could keep hidden from his best friend. A brief fling while on R&R wasn't one of them.

"Drop by later, after you've seen everything?" the taller man suggested in a murmur. He evidently didn't think much of Dillon's chances of getting into Jordan's bed tonight.

"Tomorrow." So Kiera wouldn't wait up. Dillon grinned, suddenly filled with good cheer; his former partner had an uncanny habit of being right. Well, he wanted a diversion. It wouldn't do if he had it easy. Deprived of eye contact, he'd just have to be more creative in wooing Jordan.

The look Dillon and his teammate shared held a library of meaning, speaking to Jordan of shadowy deeds and hidden danger. And a secret capacity for violence that sent a perverse frisson of sweet excitement through her body. Her unthinking response made her shiver. How could she even be attracted to such a man? Yet despite her knowledge, something inside her melted at his proximity.

"Do you do portraits, Jordan?"

Dragging her attention from the oh-so-intriguing yet dangerous Mr. Gavin, Jordan turned to the willowy blonde in a short black dress talking to her. A popular fashion model—or so Shanna told her—Lindsay Thorpe was a patron of Jordan's work. Shanna would never forgive Jordan if she ignored Shanna's directive to socialize and cultivate buyers.

Tilting her head toward the woman's flat voice, Jordan smiled ruefully to soften her answer and kept her hands clasped together at her waist. "I'm afraid my muse keeps me too busy for portraits." The last thing she wanted was to risk a client triggering her psychometry. That run-in with Dillon merely served to reinforce the wisdom of her stance.

Unfortunately, some people had a difficult time accepting "no" for an answer. The model appeared to be one of them. "I'm sure something could be arranged," Lindsay countered, her wide lips stretching in a smug smile.

If the other woman hadn't bought her work before, Jordan

would have thought it was the cachet of a Jordan Kane portrait that was the main attraction. In fact, Lindsay didn't strike her as someone interested in the arts; the model had spent more time holding court than looking at the psyprints on display.

"I rarely accept commissions." A tug on her sleeve drew Jordan's attention to Shanna. She turned to her agent with relief, hoping to avoid a scene.

The rescue proved to be worse.

"Dillon has a few questions about your landscapes. Why don't you go talk to him?" Obviously a rhetorical question since Shanna pushed her in his direction.

Jordan made her escape while her agent diverted the blonde's attention. Dillon was at her side almost instantly, an expression of solicitude on his face as he drew her away, his large hand like a hot brand on the small of her back. To her dismay, he was alone. "What happened to your friends?"

"They had to leave," he explained, giving her a sharp look that had her nipples tightening with unwanted awareness. "Kiera was getting tired."

"That's too bad," Jordan murmured politely, swallowing her reluctance as Dillon cupped his warm hand under her elbow. It wouldn't be wise to irritate such a dangerous man unnecessarily. Perhaps she could slip away later.

Tingles of pleasure radiated up her arm from where he held her. How could she still be responding to him? He was a man of violence, one who frequently risked his life. That alone made him off-limits. Now if she could only convince her hormones of the wisdom of avoiding him. "Which landscapes interest you?"

"Actually, I haven't had time to go through the entire exhibit yet. Care to join me?"

Jordan's heart sank. Since Shanna had facilitated her escape, she suspected her agent wouldn't object if Dillon monopolized her. This late in the evening, the important sales pitches were done. There was no way she could avoid spending time with him.

She accompanied him through the exhibit, intensely aware of his scent and warmth at her side, the pleasant timbre of his voice evoking an ineffably carnal response from her body. His thumb drew teasing circles on the tender skin of her inner arm—nothing objectionable, except the gentle friction had her core fluttering in delighted anticipation.

Despite her inexplicably insistent libido, it was a rare pleasure to hear the opinion of a man who didn't try to impress her with his knowledge, to impose his own interpretation of the rightness or wrongness of her work. One who didn't dismiss it as overly indulgent fancies. Yet it was surprising to hear it from someone of his violent line of work. An appreciation of art wasn't something she'd expected in a killer, especially one whose polite attentions were making her come undone.

"I was wondering about your inspiration for this sunrise." He waved his hand at a psyprint, then caught himself in midgesture, obviously remembering her handicap. A look of discomfiture flashed across his face, one Jordan suspected he was unaccustomed to wearing. "It's the one with a purplish haze over an old town."

As Dillon studied the psyprint, his strong features softened, losing the edge that hinted at knife-ready reflexes.

Her clairvoyance persisted in showing her the curve of his kissable lips, the sparkle in his dark eyes, the firm line of his jaw. She cursed it even while she wondered what his features would feel like under her fingers.

Somehow, she gathered enough wit to provide a sensible answer. "There was something in the news about escalating racial tensions in Europe." Hate crimes and rising incidents of vandalistic magic. "I wanted to acknowledge the reality yet point to a brighter future."

He nodded, evincing no surprise at her words. Did his job require him to keep abreast of such news?

"It reminds me of Rotterdam."

Startlement rendered Jordan speechless. The indistinct skyline in the psyprint played across her vision. She hadn't incorporated any landmarks, leaving it a nameless town at twilight, pierced here and there by valiant sparks of light. With all the tourist havens in Europe, how had he unerringly identified the city?

"That's very specific," she finally managed.

"It's the roofline, I think. I haven't seen its like in Italy, Spain, or France." Whatever his thoughts were, they gave his features a devilish cast, a warning to whomever might think to cross him.

Edging away from Dillon, Jordan laced her fingers together in self-protection, preferring not to risk triggering her psychometry, in case he was thinking of battle. Men seemed to enjoy the bloodiest things. "You sound well-traveled."

"I've done my share of traveling, seen some sights." Dillon grinned at his understatement. He knew his way around most of the hellholes in developing countries although he'd had missions in Europe. But that had no bearing on his current hunt.

"What do you do?" Jordan's brows drew together in gentle interest—contrary to the wary tension of her body and the two surreptitious half steps she'd taken away from him, but she didn't go so far as to free her arm from his grasp. Obviously, the pretty artist had picked up on his desire and was uncertain what to do about it. He was tempted to assure her he didn't bite . . . much, though he'd bet she'd make a sweet mouthful.

Maybe later.

"I'm a troubleshooter," Dillon replied, tongue in cheek. "My company sends me where there are problems with ongoing projects and I do my best to fix things."

She blinked several times, as if she were batting her lashes at him, except she wasn't—couldn't be—looking at him. "It sounds rather stressful."

Remembering his last mission and the deafening exchange of

gunfire and offensive magics that had capped it, Dillon shook his head. She had no idea! "It has its moments." Which he didn't want to think about right now, not when he had the undivided attention of the woman he wanted in his bed.

"Do you like it?"

"It keeps things interesting. It's also widened my horizons considerably." He forced himself to survey the psyprints near them and not the gentle curves swaying near the back of his hand; yet he couldn't resist stroking the delicate skin under his thumb. Just the friction sent a tingle through his cock that he couldn't help but relish. "That's part of the appeal your work has for me, I think."

"What do you mean?" Jordan stepped closer with some reluctance, giving him a better view of her soft lips and the intriguing whorls of her ear with its bare and vulnerable lobe. Were they sensitive? How would she react if he licked the velvety nub? If he took it between his lips and sucked on it?

"This orchid scene, for example. I've seen something like it in my travels but never quite like this." Dillon stared blindly at the almost-photographic image, the way her mouth puckered, as though inviting his kiss, filling his mind's eye. It took some doing to drag his thoughts back to their conversation. "I like the effect of the light glittering on the petals and the raindrops clinging to them. The contrast to the darkness of the rain forest's foliage is stark, but at the same time very hopeful." It cast a different light on his own experiences. The jungles he'd hacked, crawled, and sometimes swum through really hadn't been all bad.

The beauty in her art was amazing, made more so by her blindness. How had she been able to conceive it, much less depict it?

Jordan tilted her head to one side, almost as if she were studying the psyprint. "I don't know why I did it that way. I'm not even sure it's right." Her hands traced patterns in the air, the graceful motions seeming to sketch the exotic flower in the picture. She rubbed the tip of her nose, frowning. "Do orchids shimmer?" She fell silent, the pensive expression on her face making him think she'd forgotten his presence.

Dillon spoke to draw her back from wherever she'd gone. "Actually, some do."

Her head jerked up. "You've seen this?" She leaned toward him, her hands folded together at her waist, her knuckles turning pale. There was a strange urgency in her voice, as though she needed confirmation of the reality of her artistic vision—enough to temporarily overcome her wariness of him.

"Several times." His curious brain wondered at her intensity, poking at her question for hidden meanings.

The brilliant smile Jordan gave him almost made Dillon forget what he was saying. His cock twitched at this sign of her interest. Perhaps he'd prove Lantis wrong this time.

She stiffened suddenly, her smile vanishing like faerie light. The corded tendons along her neck and slight cant of her chin told him her attention had focused elsewhere.

Following the angle of her head, Dillon shot a sidelong glance over his shoulder. The predatory fashion model was staring in their direction, making sharp, peremptory gestures as she spoke with Shanna. Apparently, the blonde hadn't yet given up hope of commissioning a portrait.

"Forget about her." He ushered Jordan out of hearing range of the woman's sultry demands. As much as he usually admired tenacity, anything that made Jordan uncomfortable was beyond the pale—especially when it impeded his pursuit.

Her back rigid under his hand, Jordan turned a startled look at him, then gave him a smile—albeit a grudging one.

Well, well. Things are looking up. "What is it?"

Her brows twitched at his question. "Huh?"

"You were smiling at me," he explained. "I wondered why."

She ducked her head and shrugged, a fine tension still quivering through her muscles; if it weren't too soon, he'd have taken her into his arms and stroked away her disquiet. "Nothing. You just reminded me of someone."

"Who?" Dillon prompted, inordinately disappointed that the look on her face hadn't been meant for him. His hackles rose at the hint of competition.

Jordan shook her head. "It doesn't matter."

Her demurral hardened his determination. "No, really. I'm curious."

"It wouldn't mean anything even if I told you." Her glossy pink lips curled up at the corners in a secretive smirk. Damned if it didn't make him want to give her something else to fill them.

"But, now, you've pricked my curiosity."

"Timothy." She kept her answer simple without any elaboration. Just that one name.

"Who?" Another man? *What else, dolt?* He could hardly have reminded her of a woman. At least he hoped not.

"See. I told you it wouldn't mean anything to you." She stepped away from under his hand. "Do you have any more questions? About my work, I mean."

Dillon accepted the hint and directed the conversation back to art. He hadn't wanted an easy hunt, after all. Courting Jordan promised to keep him well occupied. Suddenly, a whole month of R&R didn't seem long enough.

Jordan's knowledge of her companion's dangerous lifestyle did nothing to dispel her fascination with him. Her clairvoyance persisted in parading Dillon's body before her mind's eye. His shoulders were broad and well-muscled, no mere paper pusher. He had to work hard to maintain that physique—probably a necessity in his profession. He shrugged absently, the simple movement making his chest bunch and his shirt glide over his broad back. The ripple of muscle derailed her train of thought like a sudden decadent whiff of dark-chocolate fudge brownies. Fluid poetry in motion. Her fingers ached to touch him.

He'd be even better naked.

Aghast at the thought, Jordan licked her suddenly dry lips. *Dillon Gavin's off-limits, damn it!* The reminder did little to calm her racing pulse or the ardent hunger heating her heavy core. She needed to do something to distance herself and help her cool off. "All this talking's made me thirsty."

"Can't have that." With his solicitous hand under her elbow— *hot, rough palms stroking her body all over*, her hyperactive libido whispered—Dillon led her to the tables near the bar that was set up in a corner of the gallery. "What would you like to drink?"

Jordan fanned her warm face, grateful the air-conditioning kept her from overheating. "Anything but dry."

"I guess you get too much of that, talking about your art. I'll see what they have."

As Dillon left for the bar, Jordan reached back, feeling for the seat. While she knew there was a chair behind her, she couldn't tell how far it was. Her clairvoyance enabled her to get around in unfamiliar places, but it wasn't the same as not being blind. Her vision wasn't anchored to her perspective, allowing her to see all angles and distances. If she wanted, she could have a three-dimensional, close-up view of whatever interested her, but it also meant she had difficulty using it to judge spatial relations.

Her fingers finally found the hard edge of the bar chair. She patted it surreptitiously, orienting herself by feel. Soft leather brushed her fingertips.

A knife slashed down, cutting upraised arms. Blood splattered black walls, dripped on a dark floor. A mangled face trying to scream.

Jordan recoiled in horror, ramming her side into a table edge. *What on earth?* Her skin prickled at the vision, gooseflesh running down her arms. A murder? Was that what she'd seen?

Extending a trembling hand, she cautiously prodded the seat's rigid plastic. Nothing came to her. She touched leather.

A knife slashed—

Jordan slammed down her mental barriers. Pulled into herself until nothing from her sight could reach her. Only then did she explore, limiting her inputs to touch.

Soft, fine-grain leather. Small—she spanned the width with her hands—and strangely shaped. Tight seams. Narrow wedges. Like fingers? *Gloves!* Long-fingered gloves elegant in their simplicity and lack of adornment.

She shivered. These were witnesses to a murder?

"Is something wrong?" Dillon's soft murmur cut through the darkness, resonant with undeniable concern. His audible sympathy drew Jordan out of her mental fugue.

She smiled weakly in his direction, a chill running down her spine, her ribs raising a belated complaint. "Uh, no. I don't think so." The possibility that she'd found evidence pointing to a bloody crime in the middle of her own exhibit was preposterous. But her sight, the visions she received from her psychometry were never wrong.

Not wanting to think about the implications, Jordan tucked the gloves into her purse.

Automatically monitoring the conversations around him, Dillon studied Jordan as he placed the plate of cheese and crackers on the table. Fall fashion, stock market movements, oil prices—none of that interested him. They weren't what bothered Jordan. From the pallor of her face, whatever had happened to frighten her wasn't anything so mundane. Tamping down his arousal, he scanned their surroundings for the source of her distress but everything seemed normal, including the thwarted model frowning at them over the people clustered around her.

"I think you'll like this. It's a dessert wine." He set Jordan's white wine down on the table, the glass ringing with crystal clarity.

Despite her blindness, Jordan picked up the goblet without any awkwardness, possibly homing in on the sound. Raising it to her lips in a controlled motion, she inhaled absently, as though going through the motions of normalcy would make it so. Then her blue eyes widened, color returning to her cheeks. "Ooh!" She took a delicate sip, then smiled brightly.

Dillon hid his grin behind his own wineglass, gratified by his success at distracting her. The fruity bouquet reached his nose, reminiscent of lychees, melons, cherries, and orange blossoms. How much more delightful would it be with her sharper senses? "Too dry?" he asked, unable to resist teasing her.

She gave a gurgle of relieved laughter. "You know it's not. I'll have to get some for my cellar."

He sipped his own, relishing the burst of golden sweetness balanced by hints of pepper, hazelnut, and chocolate. "Have some cheese." He nudged the plate forward with a gentle scrape.

Jordan frowned—at him?—then extended a tentative hand toward the plate. Did she doubt the safety of the food?

He gave an impatient mental shake of his head at his professional paranoia. *Relax, man.* Maybe the sound just hadn't been loud enough for her to home in on.

Her fingers brushed the rim, then, with very little groping, she found a slice. She managed it so adroitly, he might not have realized she was blind if Shanna hadn't told him.

"Afraid I'll get drunk?" She sipped her wine, closing her eyes as she savored its taste with almost tangible single-mindedness.

Dillon clenched his jaw against a surge of lust, wondering if she brought a similar dedication to lovemaking. He could practically feel her legs clamped around his hips as she rode him to completion with the same absolute focus. "Actually, I'm hoping you'll join me for dinner."

She frowned at him—this time he was certain it was at him—as she nibbled on cheese, her lips puckering erotically as they enveloped the creamy slice.

His cock sprang to steel-hard attention with a throb of burning interest. Need knotted his gut, sending razor-edged desire stabbing through his body. Suddenly, he didn't care about challenges and diversions. He wanted her now, in his bed, any which way he could have her. He shifted in his seat, trying to ease the tightness around his fly.

"I'm sorry, I can't. I've already made plans for later." Damned if she didn't look at all regretful.

Dillon frowned inwardly, startled by a strong flare of possessive jealousy. Did she plan to meet this Timothy she'd mentioned earlier? He stopped himself from pressing for more detail. That would be so uncouth. *She's supposed to be just a bit of R&R, remember?*

By the time Dillon watched Jordan take her leave, he'd managed to rein in the uncharacteristic proprietorial emotion. She slid into the passenger seat of a scarlet sports coupe, laughing at a quip from Shanna. From his angle, he couldn't make out much about the driver through the tinted glass.

"It was nice meeting you, Dillon." Hesitantly, Jordan extended a polite hand in his direction.

"It was my pleasure." He savored the touch of skin on skin, promising her silently they'd meet again—and soon. He wanted to feel her smooth hands on his body, craved her touch like nothing he'd ever wanted before, and intended to do everything in his power to make it happen.

The hairs on his nape prickled suddenly, his battle-honed instincts warning him of undue—and hostile—attention. But from where?

Jordan freed her hand from his grasp and closed her door. With a final wave of farewell, she sat back and the car pulled away from the curb, merging smoothly with the late-night traffic.

Dillon turned back to the gallery, casually scanning his environs. There were too many people around, any one of whom could be his watcher. No one stared openly in his direction.

"So." Shanna looked up at him, a gleam of good-natured avarice in her eyes. "Which ones are you buying?"

Chuckling, Dillon shook his head in mock sorrow. "You know me so well." He accompanied Shanna back into the building. Despite careful scrutiny, he couldn't spot whoever had set his intuition jangling.

⸺⸺ ∞∞∞ ⸺⸺

Her palm still tingling from male heat, Jordan settled into the soft leather, shamelessly wallowing in a cloud of well-being. Excellent wine, creamy cheese, and lots of ego-boo were good for the soul. Even Dillon Gavin's dangerous company had been good. She closed her mind to importunate patrons and ominous gloves, refusing to allow any unpleasantness to ruin her mood.

"Enjoy yourself?" Dan asked softly, an undemanding presence beside her. From the smell of light sweat and floral perfume coming from her cousin, he had come straight from a date.

"Um-hmm." Jordan stifled a yawn with her fist. "Thanks for the pickup. Hope you're not hungry."

"No problem. I ordered takeout. It should be ready by the time we pass by for it."

She raised a lazy hand to stop him. "Don't tell me. I bet I can guess." *A clerk at one of their favorite fast-food chains slid a pizza topped with shellfish into a box and wrote their name on the cardboard. Drinks and a few side orders joined it.* "Seafood Delight plus cocktail prawns, chicken wings, and mashed potatoes with shiitake mushrooms."

"Wha— Oh. It's done?" Her cousin's nonchalant acceptance of her statement made Jordan smile.

"Um-hmm." Sighing, she kicked off her shoes and stretched, enjoying the absence of visual imagery bombarding her mind. In addition to the forbidden Mr. Gavin, the exhibit had been stressful as always. A necessary evil in her line of work, although it did make her more appreciative of the quiet times.

But as she settled in for the drive home, the memory of how Dillon Gavin's shirt caressed his chest and shoulders danced in her head. And her fingers itched with the need to experience the contact for herself.

The dream unfolded slowly in the formless darkness, impinging on Jordan's slumber with relentless unconcern and waking her body with its sensual imagery.

Stroking her hands across her lover's broad back, she strung kisses along his shoulder, the firm muscles slightly salty to her tongue. He groaned in approval, tilting his head in demand and giving her better access to the strong tendons of his neck. The control implicit in the motion fanned the flames of her excitement, dared her to drive him beyond it.

She intended to.

Nibbling gently, she swept her arms around him, her greedy hands kneading his steel-hard pectorals, laying claim to every inch of hot male flesh. She ventured downward in cautious swirls, her palms lingering over the etched slabs of his belly. So firm and resilient.

Strength incarnate.

All male.

And all hers.

His waistband posed no barrier to her exploration, yielding readily to her avid touch. His rampant sex rewarded her daring. He filled her hands to overflowing—velvet and silk over living marble. Hot and heavy. So thick she wanted to nibble on him and taste him, to feel him against her lips.

To claim him as hers—forever.

She skimmed her fingertips over him, relishing the proof of his desire. Below his erection, his furry sac hung low, promising a long, slow ride to ecstasy.

Her core clenched, its emptiness a nagging ache. Need pressed her, desire such a ponderous weight on her chest she could barely breathe. She wanted him that much.

Carnal hunger clawed her belly, requiring satisfaction. Now. She had to have him, couldn't wait a moment longer to hold him inside her.

She swung her leg over to straddle Dillon's narrow hips. Taking his thick penis in her hand, she set its broad head against her slick labia and—

"Prrp?" A furry paw gently patted her jaw again in an insistent request for attention.

Jordan grunted in confusion, the heaviness on her chest like a lingering wisp of her dream. She reached up, her fingers tangling with thick, silky fur. "Timothy?"

Her pet purred in confirmation.

She groaned. "It can't be morning yet." She flung her arm carelessly into the ever-present darkness, rapping her knuckles against the clock on her nightstand. Running her hand over its jagged face, she winced at the hour. She hadn't been asleep that long.

Shifting the muscular cat off her chest, Jordan sat up, struggling against the sheets snaked around her body, then flailed around to return her pillows to a semblance of order. "Why'd you wake me?"

Timothy whined, rubbing his cold nose against her arm.

"No, it wasn't a nightmare." She stroked his back in reassurance. He'd woken her from her share of those. But this time he hadn't. Not unless dreaming of hot sex with an extremely dangerous man was a nightmare.

Remembering the eroticism of her dream, heat flooded her cheeks. Evidently her subconscious hadn't received the memo that Dillon Gavin was unacceptable. Because of her sight, she'd never allowed herself to be attracted to men with risky occupations, not wanting the heartache of her mother. Her few lovers had all been safe—which couldn't be said of her companion from last night, despite his unexceptionable behavior.

Jordan reached between her legs. Her wet labia were swollen and aching, throbbing at the slightest touch. *Would he really be that—* She jerked her hand away, appalled by the reckless thought. Despite her body's frustration, she refused to compound her folly by deliberately fantasizing about him. That dangerous man wasn't going to be her lover and there was no point in contemplating the possibility.

Her core spasmed in protest, desire a turgid presence in her belly.

Groaning, Jordan buried her face in Timothy's fur. Such highmindedness! She was in for a long night of discomfort.

Chapter Two

A casually dressed Lantis let Dillon into Kiera's condo, his faded black tank top and shabby denim shorts attesting to an intent to spend the day relaxing at home. "When did you arrive?"

"Flew in yesterday afternoon."

"Changing hotels soon?"

Dillon raised his brows at the question. "Of course." SOP limited hotel stays to no more than three days, preferably two. It prevented staff from becoming overly familiar with an agent's routine—if one were careless enough to fall into a routine—making it harder for hostiles to set up an ambush.

"You're welcome to stay at my old place," Lantis offered, leading the way to the living room.

"You still have it?" That made sense. Dillon eyed his friend's muscular form. Despite a few years of civilian life, there wasn't much of a difference in the taller man's body.

His former partner had fitted his basement apartment with a

well-equipped gym and a large sparring area. Staying there would make maintaining his fitness easier. Taking some R&R shouldn't mean going to fat.

Lantis shrugged as he lowered himself onto Kiera's legless couch. "Have to keep my stuff somewhere until the house is finished."

Before Dillon could join him, Kiera appeared in the doorway from the bedroom. "Dillon!" Arms outstretched, his childhood friend and heart sister waddled to him like a runaway duck—a radiantly happy runaway duck—her golden eyes sparkling with precious welcome.

Dillon met her halfway, lifting her off her feet to twirl her in the air with a grunt. Her protruding belly made their customary welcoming ritual rather more difficult than usual. "Oof! I think I hurt my back," he joked, carefully setting Kiera on her feet.

He hugged her as she threw her head back and laughed, savoring the nearly physical aura of happiness surrounding her.

Kiera had been the reason he'd gotten into black ops. Her devastation when her mother was killed by a terrorist bomb when they were children had sparked his determination to fight such scum. But Lantis's friendship and drive were why he'd stuck it out despite all the aggravation from top brass. It helped that the job let him blow things up, although lately not as much.

They spent a pleasant morning catching up on one another's lives. Dillon had lost touch since his recent string of back-to-back missions had kept him incommunicado. It was a while before he could work the conversation to the local attractions and the latest places conducive to seduction, soliciting suggestions for his campaign to get Jordan into bed.

"Plotting the downfall of another woman?" Kiera wrinkled her nose, rubbing her ripe belly. "Do I want to be a party to this?"

"You're a pregnant woman!" Dillon protested. "There's no way you can claim ignorance. Not when you're married to Lantis!" He pointed an accusing finger at the blackguard sprawled beside her, who, after several months of marriage, had undoubtedly educated his childhood friend thoroughly on matters sexual.

Drawing his wife into his arms, his former partner huffed in amusement as she blushed. "Very convincing. The way you talk, one would think Kiera and I met by accident."

Watching his heart sister snuggle against Lantis, Dillon grinned. Last year, he'd deliberately brought his best friend into Kiera's orbit, hoping chemistry would take its course. The success of his matchmaking exceeded his expectations.

"Come on. What might prick her interest?" Dillon prompted, returning to his problem.

As usual, Lantis caught his wordplay, quirking a brow in approbation.

Kiera glared at Dillon, then giggled, finally smacking her husband's chest in reproof. "You two. Really."

Lantis caught her hand, lacing his fingers between hers. "Since she's blind, that's two strikes against your arsenal." At his wife's look of inquiry, he explained: "His face and that boyish grin of his."

Dillon grimaced in acknowledgment. That had been obvious from the onset. Not that it deterred him. He enjoyed a worthy challenge. The difficulty made success all the sweeter, and Jordan promised to be very sweet indeed.

Across the low coffee table from him, Lantis absently brushed his lips against Kiera's knuckles, his patent contentment raising a niggle of envy in Dillon. "Your best bet is an appeal to her other senses; they're probably extra sharp."

Kiera was nodding in agreement even before Lantis finished speaking. It almost made Dillon wonder what games they played in private. Almost. There were some things a brother—even if just one of the heart—was better off not knowing. It was enough to know she was happy and in love and had a strong man at her back.

His two friends exchanged a quick, unreadable look, communicating silently in some kind of marital telepathy. *What was that about?*

"There's also the basics." Kiera nibbled her bottom lip in thought, apparently still reluctant to aid in the seduction of another woman. "What are her interests?"

Dillon shrugged. "I've still to find out. But when Jordan agrees to go out with me, where would you recommend I take her?"

"Well, now, that depends." Kiera smiled, a speculative glint in her eye.

Dillon was hard-pressed not to warn her about getting her hopes up. While a little lust and a little romance were fine for R&R, he'd be gone soon enough, once he was recalled to duty. Whatever developed between Jordan and him was unlikely to survive that.

I'm leaving in a few minutes to blow up a bridge in another continent. He grinned at the thought. No way he could say that to a civilian.

After some more thought, Kiera came up with a list of places. Then her face lit up with enthusiasm. "Just Desserts!"

Lantis snorted, his lips pressed together, his deep-blue eyes narrowed with mirth.

Dillon raised his brows at his best friend in silent query.

"It's a restaurant near the federal courthouse downtown. She's been craving their Triple Chocolate Manslaughter for months."

Dillon's grin widened in reflexive amusement. "And you haven't?" His former partner had a thing for chocolate himself.

The bigger man returned his gaze steadily, one brow arched, his sardonic reply clear: There's a big difference between craving and *CRAVING*. As Dillon well knew.

"She's been demanding it all hours of the day. I tell you, this"—he patted his wife's belly—"is mostly chocolate."

"It is *not!*"

At Kiera's outraged expression, Dillon roared with laughter.

"It could have been worse," he offered between breathless chuckles. "At least it isn't ice cream with sardines . . . or with raw fish."

——— ⊗∞⊗ ———

The smell of salmon, up close and almost intimate, roused Jordan from slumber. She recoiled from its purring source, grimacing at its proximity. Sometime while she slept, her defender against nightmares had gorged himself on expensive fish. She drew the obvious conclusion: "Dan didn't feed you your cat food, did he?"

Her self-satisfied pet grunted in confirmation, his whiskers brushing her cheek. His bulk trapped her under the blanket, a familiar position from which he guarded her dreams.

Jordan had to laugh, pulling her arms from under the swaddling with some difficulty to stroke the plush fur behind his ears. He was such a good friend she couldn't begrudge him his occasional lapses in diet. It wasn't his fault her cousin chose to feed him fresh fish.

"Now keep that mouth away from me. You know I don't like fish breath." She dodged to one side as the odor strengthened. "Timothy!" she protested halfheartedly.

"Prrp?" Large paws closed gently around her wrist in an invitation to wrestle. He kept his claws sheathed, for which Jordan was grateful; though he rarely used them except on his scratching post, the half-inch-long talons were knife-sharp.

About to give in—she enjoyed the rough-and-tumble play as much as he did—the warmth of the day registered on her senses. The sun had apparently been up long enough to burn off much of the coolness of the spring morning.

"Not now, Tim. I think I'm running late." She'd promised to get back to Shanna about the charity auction before noon. She scratched behind the cat's ears in apology, freeing her arm from his hold with a well-practiced twist.

Brushing her hand across the face of the clock, Jordan groaned at the raised figures under her fingers. Since frustration had kept her up late, her body had obviously decided to make up for it by sleeping in.

She shook her head in incredulity, throwing off memories of last night's erotic dream that threatened to distract her. It wouldn't do to remember how her dream self had made free with Dillon Gavin's person. Such a topic had the potential to divert her thoughts for hours—a diversion she could ill afford.

Luckily, her cousin was around to fill Timothy's bowls, even if he persisted in pampering the muscular cat. That meant one less thing to delay her today.

Sitting up, Jordan oriented herself, finding the edge of the nightstand with her hand. At home where she'd memorized the placement of every piece of furniture, she preferred not to use her clairvoyance.

A shift of the mattress and a heavy thump announced Timothy's departure. She walked through the ever-present darkness to the bathroom, automatically extending her stride to accommodate her pet's weaving between her legs. Timothy was so friendly and social, it was a good thing he wasn't a fan of water, otherwise he might have joined her in the tub.

A quick breakfast of muesli, partly spent repelling Timothy's playful attempts at her milk-filled bowl, and she was ready to meet the day. She fished into her small purse for the memory strip Shanna had given her last night just before the exhibit opened.

Unexpectedly, her fingers brushed leather.

She frowned. In her purse? She took it out, exploring the supple material by feel. *The gloves from last night!*

Her memory jogged, the horrific vision she'd picked up flashed before her mind's eye. Jordan shuddered, dropping the gloves, repulsed by their proximity to murder.

"Prrp?" Timothy nudged her, his nose cool against her arm.

Picking up her pet, she stood to pace, his weight barely registering. She found it easier to think on her feet, a furry bundle tucked under her chin. Dan called the cat her security blanket; at times like this, she thought he might have a point.

"Was it really murder?" *A knife in the darkness, slashing down.* She shivered at the memory.

Timothy's response was noncommittal, a whine almost too low to hear.

"Maybe I'm wrong. It could have been a— A—" *Blood splattering, dripping, falling like a gush of dark tears.*

Timothy chirped inquiringly, batting Jordan's ear with a gentle paw. His prompting recalled her to her line of thought.

"A movie?" Jordan finished weakly. Said aloud, it was obviously ridiculous. She was clutching at faerie light, a will-o'-the-wisp—*ignis fatuus* by any name.

She rubbed her cheek on the cat's round head, knowing what she had to do. She wouldn't be able to concentrate on anything else until she laid to rest that nagging uncertainty.

Timothy purred loudly, seeming to approve her decision, a reassuring rumble against her chest.

Jordan returned to the kitchen table to confront the gloves. The wicker chair creaked under her weight as she sat down, lowering the cat to her lap.

"Come on. How likely is it you'd find a clue to a murder out in the open? At your own exhibit, for goodness' sake," she muttered to herself, trying to gather her nerve. Only Timothy's weight across her thighs kept her from fleeing the room. She gulped for air. "A murderer would have to be stupid to hang on to such a giveaway."

Timothy mewed in agreement.

Or arrogant. Had she met a murderer last night?

Her heart raced, her pulse pounding in her ears. She reached out gingerly, then flinched halfway there, her heart leaping to her throat. Stroking Timothy convulsively, she comforted herself with the feel of his thick, silky fur between her fingers. His fluffy tail flicked over her calf, a light tickle that seemed to say everything was fine.

She let out a shaky breath. *It's just a glove, damn it all.* "It's not going to bite." The tremor in her voice didn't sound convincing even to her own ears.

Timothy rocked his weight from side to side, his paws pressing down on her thighs, then pushed off, landing on the table with a thud. Perhaps sensing her equivocation, he ran his rough tongue up her cheek encouragingly, as though assuring her of his support.

"Right. Thanks, Tim." Jordan took a deep breath. "Okay, okay. I can do this." Snatching up the gloves—quickly to forestall any third thoughts—she opened herself to her sight.

The first scene was as terrible as she remembered. *A knife slashed down, vicious in its speed. Rising and falling with deadly intent. Over and over. Merciless.* Jordan flinched at the violence, her stomach roiling with revulsion. Her breakfast threatened to make a bitter reappearance.

Blood splattered the floor and trickled down the walls. She didn't know why she was sure it was blood—there was no color among the shadows, no scent—but she knew it was blood that turned the walls black. So much blood. She cried out in horror.

A growl answered her. A brush of fur snatched the supple hide from her hands. Things toppled over, rolled across the kitchen table, and crashed on the tile floor in a clatter of hard plastic and metal.

The scene vanished, the sudden loss a wrenching but welcome shock. Jordan gasped for breath, trembling in her seat. Chills ran up her arms. Dampness welled in her eyes, spilled down her cheeks to be licked by a whining Timothy.

Jordan wrapped her arms around her pet, cradling his familiar bulk. *Oh, that poor woman!* She didn't know how she knew, but she was convinced the murder victim was female.

Making himself comfortable in the roomy leather recliner in Lantis's old apartment, Dillon frowned at his PDA. "'Murder on the Waistline'?" That sounded like something he ought to try first. Kiera's description of rich white-chocolate cheesecake topped with true maraschino cherries was enough to awaken his sweet tooth. "That might be a bit much for an opening salvo."

He pondered Kiera's list, wondering what might tempt Jordan into spending a few hours in his company but wouldn't make too strong a statement. As much as his instincts urged him to sweep her off to bed, and take her as often and as many times as necessary to get her out of his system, he couldn't do that. Jordan Kane didn't seem the type to welcome such effrontery.

"Appeal to her senses, huh?" It was rather lowering to realize it had been a while since he'd needed to convince a woman to go out with him. He'd either been on a mission or sidestepping a couple of agents who wanted to add his notch to their bedposts. No wonder he was bored, males being hardwired for the hunt and all that. He smiled in anticipation. Jordan certainly promised to be a challenge.

Of course, all his plans hinged on finding her first.

"'Use whatever you need,' he said. Well, every campaign needs intelligence." Thankful for his friend's accommodation, Dillon switched on Lantis's computer and went online.

A quick search yielded Jordan's home address and phone number, a car registration for a red Sirocco—the same sports coupe that had picked Jordan up at the gallery—as well as some feature articles. It seemed she was something of a recluse, didn't grant many interviews, and those she gave focused mostly on her art. Dillon couldn't find any discussion of her personal life and not one reference to a "Timothy." Strangely enough, there was also no mention anywhere of her blindness.

He sat back, puzzled. Was it a recent affliction? She seemed to have adjusted to her handicap quite well, if that was the case.

———— ∞∞∞ ————

Jordan bit her lip against the cruel throb circling the base of her skull where a band of shamans had set up shop, drumming up a slew of death magic. She should have expected it after turning her sight on the gloves. After all, no good deed ever went unpunished.

The pounding was enough to make her wish she were merely blind. Bright illusory lights stuttered in the ever-present darkness, flashing in concert with the driving rhythm thundering in her head. Even at a whisper, her own voice added to her misery. "I know I said I'd have a list for you by noon . . ."

"What happened?" Shanna's concerned voice came through the phone handset with brain-rattling clarity. "You're usually such a go-getter."

"I've got a killer headache," Jordan confessed, choking back a moan when the shamans upped the tempo to apocalyptic proportions. "Can I give you the list later?" She'd wanted to finalize which psyprints she'd donate to the charity auction of the Spatha Foundation immediately. Unfortunately, it didn't look like that was going to happen.

Jordan winced as sparkling—head-piercing—laughter filled her ear. She moved the handset away in self-defense.

"Don't worry about it," her agent assured her. "Take your time. Fab doesn't need it until the end of next week. You're the one who set today as a deadline."

Gratefully, Jordan ended the call, sinking back into the couch pillows to rest her head. The back dipped as Timothy settled his bulk behind her. Purring in commiseration, he kneaded his paws on her shoulders.

She groaned as the rumbling set off another torturous drumroll. "Not so loud, Tim."

She paced her breathing, trying to relax the rock-solid coils of her neck. She had to learn not to take to heart what she saw in her visions. But who could remain unmoved by such horror? Yet she hadn't seen anything useful, nothing that could help identify the victim, much less the murderer. Nothing that was worth this agony.

"I'm home." Echoing off unseen walls, the ghostly announcement in her cousin's light tenor broke the soothing silence, startling Jordan. She hadn't heard the low growl of his car engine turn into the driveway. "Tim?"

She tracked Dan's progress through the house though the pounding in her head. His footsteps squeaked on the ceramic tiles of the kitchen floor, then were muffled when he crossed to the parquet of the hallway.

"You okay, Jordan?" The smell of sweaty male strengthened along with his voice. He must have come straight from his gym.

"How'd you know something's wrong?"

"Timothy always meets me, unless he thinks he's needed elsewhere. Maybe to provide comfort?" A chair cushion creaked in his direction.

"Killer headache," Jordan mumbled, pulling her pet down into her arms.

"Ah, I know just the thing." Another creak. "Don't move. I'll be right back."

"Ha. Ha." As if she could.

The scent of lavender oil reached her nose, making it tingle even before its cool bite registered on her nape.

Timothy's weight shifted, his paws pressing on her arm, his whiskers brushing her chin. Then her pet sneezed—which, thankfully, didn't set off more fireworks in the darkness.

"Not for you, Tim." Dan's fingers dug into her tight shoulders, rubbing them rhythmically in soothing circles. "Now, what brought this on?"

With the patience of long practice, her cousin coaxed the whole story from her as he reduced her headache to a lesser throb. Just recounting her vision threatened to undo the effects of his massage.

"I think you should go to the police." Dan paced in front of her, the legs of his shorts rasping against each other with every step.

Jordan remained sprawled on the couch to keep the migraine at bay, Timothy stretched out beside her like a purring afghan. "And tell them what? All I have are the gloves. There's no body. No murderer. Why should they listen to me?"

"There's your sight."

"But unless I get enough relevant detail, it's all 'These gloves give me the creeps, Officer.' They won't investigate just on my say-so. I have to give them more to work with."

Her cousin didn't dispute her statement. From his silence, she knew he realized she was right.

Jordan swam through darkness that night as she slept, not an unusual experience since her blindness made darkness a constant attendant that withdrew from her presence only when she summoned her clairvoyance. It was both bane and haven, separating her from other people and normal experiences yet sharpening her other senses and protecting her mind when the images brought on by her sight proved overwhelming.

It also served as a mental buffer, giving her space to work through issues she didn't want to face. Better yet, it allowed her subconscious to speak to her dreaming mind and stir her creativity with fantastic imagery.

That night it wrapped her in red.

The darkness revealed a distant speck of light that pulled at her like siren song, overpowering and irresistible. It took on color as she approached floating on the currents of her dream. Turned bright red and exploded. It left her surrounded by beautiful sparks of glittering red as though she were in the heart of a fireworks display. Then the sparks grew larger and darkened.

Blood splashed on wood, dripped down the walls, covering the floor in a tacky carpet. It rose inexorably, lapping at her knees and thighs with a sentient hunger. She tried to flee, but it clung to her, splattered her arms and breasts when she shielded her face from the viscid surf. In a violent surge of wetness, it rose to her shoulders, threatening to drown her.

The taste of copper flooding her throat, Jordan opened her mouth to scream.

Chapter Three

Set some distance back from the street, Jordan's two-story home wasn't what Dillon had expected, given her blindness. Its front walk meandered through a wild garden bursting with spring color, a frothing artist's palette run amok. Smooth rocks in interesting shapes were strategically placed beside the path, catching the eye like freeform sculpture.

The house itself was built along traditional lines, its weathered yellow bricks giving an impression of age. With its lush greenery, it fit easily into the residential neighborhood but wasn't what he'd have thought a blind woman would live in. Wouldn't the layout of a smaller structure, perhaps a cottage, be easier to memorize?

The wide front porch brought to mind family and laughter, and sultry summer nights spent smelling the flowers. The complete antithesis of his cold and long-discarded childhood home—not that it had been much of a home. It appealed to something deep inside him, rather like Jordan's art did.

A honeyed fragrance wafted over from a shady corner where a hammock hung waiting. Around it, thick gnarled vines spilled a dense curtain of purple wisteria, a good covert for an ambush. Dillon grinned at the thought. He might be on R&R but some things couldn't be switched off.

Tall chestnuts dotted the grounds, offering shade and privacy—and more cover for those who lived in the shadows that were Dillon's other life. From where he stood, he could barely see the street, much less the neighbors. The only commendation he could see, defense-wise, was that their branches didn't come within jumping distance of the roof. At least they didn't provide an easy overhead route for intruders.

Putting down the opening salvo for his seduction, Dillon pressed the doorbell, setting off a stately four-tone chime.

A short while later, Jordan's soft soprano came sweetly from behind the door. "Who is it?"

"It's Dillon."

"Dillon?" The lack of recognition in her voice didn't bode well for his R&R.

"Dillon Gavin. We met at the show the other night," he reminded her, quelling his nettled pride. *You wanted a challenge, right?* He shook his head at his miffed reaction. *Damn, you're spoiled, man.*

"Yes, I remember."

There was a long pause as if Jordan was debating whether to welcome him or not. Dillon reined in his impatience while she decided. In the end, perhaps the need to keep a longtime patron sweet tipped the scales in his favor.

Opening the door slightly, Jordan leaned out through the gap, her fingers curled tight along its edge. She made an extremely fetching picture, barefoot, her honey-brown hair rumpled as though fresh from bed, and wearing a large T-shirt of soft cotton that clung to her high breasts and dropped to the tops of her thighs, emphasizing her shapely legs.

Dillon stared, trying to stifle the erotic thoughts her dishabille inspired. Something told him he wouldn't get far today, but damned if he could think of anything else.

He wanted to grab the hem of her shirt and yank it up, to bare her to his hungry eyes and lay claim to the gentle curves that lay beneath. It would take so very little time to get Jordan naked and slung over the hammock in the corner. They wouldn't even have to worry about discovery; the trees and wisteria would guarantee their privacy. He could practically hear her cries of pleasure as he pumped into her, her wet channel gripping him firmly. The fantasy had his balls heavy and aching with need.

And wasn't that the damnedest thing? Sure, he was looking for sexual comfort, but there was no reason for the violence of his desire for this woman.

She frowned warily from behind her barricade, clearly not accustomed to entertaining guests. "So, why've you come?"

The challenge she posed to his seductive skills set his blood flowing. First, he had to lure her out into the open. "I remembered you wondering about orchids shimmering and thought I could help."

Crossing her arms under her breasts, her hands cupping her elbows, Jordan cocked her head toward him, her brows knit in puzzlement. Her eyes were also turned to him, staring blankly, almost as though she could see. "How?"

"Well"—Dillon checked the boxes he'd brought, wondering if he'd gone overboard—"I thought you'd like some."

"Orchids? You brought me orchids?" She pressed her hand to her chest, the gesture confirming her braless condition as the cotton stretched over her pebbled areolas and tight nipples. Hopefully, that meant she approved.

"Uh-huh." He left it at that, giving her time to consider. Rushing his fences might just frighten her into deep cover. *Don't worry. No pressure.*

Jordan drummed her fingers on the door, her eyes flicking about as she thought.

Dillon smiled to himself. It looked like he'd chosen the right bait. *Come and get it. You know you're curious.*

She took some time about it, nibbling her bottom lip while she silently argued with herself, but finally she nodded as though she'd come to a decision.

"Do you mind?" She extended her hand into the space in front of her at face level. Despite the polite phrasing, her crisp delivery and the peremptory tilt of her head made the gesture almost a command. The motion also lifted the hem of her T-shirt, revealing more smooth thigh. As far as he could tell, she wasn't wearing any shorts under it.

Grappling with the image his speculation brought to mind, it took Dillon a moment to understand what she wanted.

"Not at all." He stepped closer, raised her hand to his cheek, dangerously close to his eyes. He kept his muscles loose but ready. It was unlikely she'd attack him but he hadn't survived years in black ops by being careless.

With a thoughtful pout, Jordan explored his face, her fingers almost as light as butterflies, her cool palms like silk on his freshly shaved jaw. She measured his forehead, smoothed his brows, ghosted across his cheekbones and down his nose. Her touch made his skin tighten, drew an unexpected tingle from his nipples, had his cock springing to steel-hard attention.

Hell, he'd never responded that quickly before. And not even to a caress! The thought of her touching his body, giving it the same thorough examination, nearly had him shuddering.

When she reached his lips, he couldn't resist the impulse to give her fingers a quick kiss.

Jordan jerked her hand away with a sharp breath. Her lashes fluttered under a frown. Her shoulders tensed. Then—to his profound disgruntlement—she dismissed his advance with a simple shrug.

Her fingertips returned to his mouth, tracing it gingerly, as light as butterfly wings on his sensitized lips, but with incendiary results. The teasing pressure was like a live wire plugged straight into his cock. And she dragged out her exploration with barely there caresses that seared his nerves.

Dillon fought for control, his nails digging into his palms as he strove to keep still. No way was he going to scare his prey into hiding just when he was about to get her to lower her guard.

But it was damnably hard.

He was about to break out in a sweat by the time she gave him a reserved smile, removing her hands from around his neck. "So that's what you look like."

Determinedly ignoring his pounding heart, Dillon grinned. "Pleased to meet you, too."

"Sorry." Her smile turned bashful, a wash of pink tinting her cheeks. "I know some people don't like it when I do that."

"No problem. It goes with the territory." He shifted his weight from one leg to the other, trying to relieve the tightness of his trousers and grateful that she couldn't see the effect she had on him.

Jordan took a deep breath that showed her high breasts to advantage, pressed against the thin fabric of her T-shirt. Her nipples, Dillon noticed with congratulatory self-satisfaction, remained budded despite the warmth of the day. "Well, won't you come in?" After a heartbeat's delay, she pulled the door open wider, still hesitant about allowing him into her domain, the blush on her cheeks darkening.

Her fluster was quite endearing; he didn't get to see much of that with female agents. Too bad she quickly regained her composure. "This is Timothy," she added with a downward gesture to a spot beside her.

A large, black-and-white cat stood there, more than knee-high to Jordan, staring at him with curiosity bright in its round, blue eyes. Rising on its hind legs, it spread front paws the size of demitasse saucers on Dillon's hips, tipping its head back to maintain their eye contact. There was something almost human about the way Jordan's pet seemed to take his measure; it didn't help that the cat's eyes were the same shade as Lantis's.

Before that inquisitive gaze, Dillon's hard-on subsided.

"Prrp?" Timothy waited, obviously wanting something.

Dillon stared, startled by the rather doglike behavior of Jordan's pet. The cat's serviceable claws prickled through his trousers, warning of unpleasant consequences should he fail to decipher its wishes correctly.

He suddenly remembered her mysterious comment at the gallery. *This is Timothy? I remind her of a pussycat?* He didn't know whether to be insulted or amused.

"Pet him or pick him up," Jordan suggested, her body poised for flight. "He's very friendly."

When an exploratory pat and a scratch behind a large ear were greeted by a soft purr and a gentle butt from a furry forehead, Dillon decided to take Jordan's word at face value. Since the cat remained propped on his hips, blocking his way, Dillon picked him up. He lifted a brow at Timothy's weight. Hefty cat. Jordan's pet had to be at least twenty-five pounds.

The cat hung limp between his hands, evincing no discomfort. Wanting his hands free, Dillon gingerly slung him across his shoulders as he turned to Jordan. To his relief, Timothy contented himself with batting his hair.

As Dillon bent down for his boxes, a cool nose pressed into his ear. He hissed in surprise, fighting down a reflexive jump. The cat chirped, sounding suspiciously smug.

Dillon stilled, forcing the tension out of his body. *It's just a cat, man. Pull yourself together.* Considering his overreaction, the Old Man might have been right to insist he take some downtime.

"Is something wrong?" Jordan's face was bland, though she seemed more relaxed. If she sensed what was going on, it didn't show on her face. If she was silently cheering her pet on, it wasn't obvious.

"No—" His voice nearly cracked as something wet and rough lashed his ear. He jerked his head away from his purring assailant. He'd have sworn the cat was snickering at him.

Dillon gave Timothy a sidelong look, trying to be grateful the cat's presence gave him something else on which he could focus his attention. The distraction did help him maintain his self-control around Jordan.

Her pet met his gaze with such an expression of wide-eyed innocence Dillon expected to see bright feathers sticking out of his mouth. *Yeah, right.* As one predator to another, he didn't buy it for even a second. The cat evidently felt territorial and had no qualms about making his feelings known. Dillon could respect that. "No teeth," he warned his assailant in a whisper.

Timothy blinked, promising nothing.

Cautiously, keeping an eye out for another attack by his feline passenger, Dillon picked up his boxes, then followed Jordan into her home.

It was like stepping into an old photograph: a thousand shades of gray, black, and white, from ash to slate, obsidian to midnight, cream to snow. The few hints of color were dark wood and fat, unused candles probably kept for their scent.

Despite her blindness, Jordan weaved her way gracefully around the furniture without stumbling into anything, staying several steps ahead of him and out of reach. Headed toward an open doorway, she stopped abruptly, her face a picture of chagrin. "I don't have a vase!"

"You don't need one," he assured her with a smug grin. Looks like he'd called this one just right. Thankfully, he set down his lures on an oversized bench ottoman that—judging from its position in front of an overstuffed couch—doubled as a coffee table. Then he reached up to divest himself of his feline cargo.

With a deep rumble, Timothy flexed his paws, sharp needles pricking Dillon's shoulders through his denim blazer.

Bad move. He shouldn't have picked up Jordan's pet in the

first place. Mentally kicking himself, Dillon lowered his hands with greater caution. Fine. So long as the cat didn't do anything, he wasn't going to force the issue. Not when doing so might scare off Dillon's quarry.

"I don't?" Jordan joined him by the couch, but chose to sit in a flanking armchair, making it clear she wanted to keep some distance between them.

Dillon shook his head, then remembered she couldn't see the gesture. "Nope. They're still in their pots." Opening the first box unleashed a cloud of exotic fragrance.

"Oooh!" Jordan inhaled deeply, her eyes shuttering to pale blue slits. "They smell wonderful! These are orchids?"

"I brought different types, but they're both orchids." Dillon pulled out a pot with flamboyant white flowers the size of his hand and set it in front of her. "This one's like the one in your psyprint."

He watched as she bent close to sniff it, strange shadows hovering under her eyes like faint bruises. "And it does shimmer, like it's refracting light."

Relaxing a little more, she reached out a tentative hand and cooed, apparently marveling at the texture, exploring the blossom the way she had his face.

Timothy gathered himself on Dillon's shoulder. With a powerful thrust of his hindquarters, he launched himself at the ottoman.

Rocked against the couch, Dillon bit back a curse. He'd definitely felt claws that time. Checking under his shirt, he rubbed the red welts he found. No blood, so the skin wasn't broken, but that didn't excuse the cat. Raising a brow, he gave Jordan's pet a look of forbearance. One free pass only, his patience wasn't limitless.

Timothy yawned, countering Dillon's warning with indifference. He bared his fangs for a long moment, added an impertinent flick of his tongue, then turned away to wash his paws.

Finally, obviously having decided that his actions were sufficient to uphold his honor, the cat joined his mistress in sniffing the blossoms.

Dillon shook his head in disbelief, then decided to let it pass. There'd be time enough later to come to terms with the territorial feline. As it was, most of his attention was occupied with watching Jordan. He smiled, unable to deny a sense of delight in the pleasure she took in his gift.

When it looked like Jordan was done, he opened the other box and pulled out another pot. The long-leafed plant sported several arching sprays of brownish-red-and-creamy-pink flowers as large as his thumb.

"Chocolate?" Jordan muttered, tilting her head doubtfully. She seemed to forget her wariness of him, kneeling on the carpet to get closer.

"As soon as I smelled it, I knew I had to get it." He chuckled. "Go on. It's very different."

The look of wonder on her face was everything Dillon could have hoped for. Most women of his acquaintance would have preferred a bouquet of roses; he'd bought his share of those. But for Jordan, he'd wanted something different.

She sniffed extravagantly, showing every indication of enjoyment. "They're wonderful. But I'm not sure I can keep them alive." Her hands twiddled with the pot as if she were torn between refusing his gift and giving it a place of honor.

Dillon grinned, glad he had an answer ready. "You don't have to worry about that. There's a shop in town that lets you trade them in, when they've finished blooming."

"Oh. In that case . . ." Presented with no other option but to accept, Jordan bent down for another sniff, but Dillon caught a pleased smile hidden behind the masses of flowers.

The orchids broke through Jordan's defenses temporarily, enough that she offered Dillon snacks, giving him a reason to extend his visit. They discussed her works over chocolate éclairs but he could see the anxiety lurking beneath her polite manners, her barriers going up, as the food dwindled.

It was all there in her body language for him to read. The distance she kept between them. The way she perched at the edge of her seat ready to take flight. The slight stiffening of her shoulders after she licked her slender fingers. Her relief when the cat tried to steal a pastry. Her resistance only served to heighten his predatory interest.

"Care to join me for lunch tomorrow?" he invited, watching her face closely. "I know a restaurant that specializes in fabulous desserts. It's the sort of place that's better shared."

Something that looked strangely like fear flashed across her face. Twisting her fingers together, Jordan shook her head in wide-eyed rejection. "I'm sorry, I'm not really comfortable going to public places."

Or perhaps not going with strangers? No, that didn't quite mesh with the tension radiating from her. There had to be more going on than Jordan's not wanting to drive off a patron of her art. Something he didn't know.

"So it's not the desserts you object to?"

Jordan shifted her weight, rather like a skittish horse. "Obviously, I have something of a sweet tooth." She gestured at the now-empty plates between them, then pulled Timothy onto her lap, a furry barrier that bared sharp fangs at him smugly.

Respecting her withdrawal, Dillon took his leave before her disquiet drove her away. He wanted to enjoy his month of R&R, not wait out a siege. Which meant he'd have to prick her interest a bit more to draw her out from behind her defenses.

As he drove away, he banked his lust with an inner sigh of satisfaction. Not much progress though he could tell Jordan wanted to spend time with him. But for some reason, she was putting a lot of effort into resisting their attraction.

No doubt he had a few nights of sexual frustration ahead of

him. Now that his desires had a focus, no other woman would do to provide him release, not until this overwhelming desire had run its course. But that didn't faze him. While there was much to commend the quick relief to be had in the arms of the female black ops agents of his acquaintance, this time he wanted the thrill of the hunt. He craved the added spice to the inevitable surrender.

———∞———

Closing the door behind her unexpected guest, Jordan bounced her head against the hard panel, trying to beat some sense into her hormone-soaked brain. "Idiot." How could she have been so foolish as to offer dessert? She knew he readily risked his life, but now she had to contend with his seductive laughter echoing in her head, inviting her to throw all good sense to the wind and play with him. And oh did she want to play with him!

At Timothy's chirped protest, she stopped, giving it up as a lost cause. She was relieved to have him gone, she insisted to herself. Relieved not to have his sharp-eyed, electrifying presence in her living room. Relieved not to smell his clean male scent or hear his easy laughter. Relieved to have the temptation of his firm, masculine body out of her home and far away. *Yeah, right.*

Done was done. She just had to remind herself he was like a big cat: all that feral beauty was better appreciated from a distance. A frisson of desire shivered up her arms. She rubbed her still-tingling fingers, her heart leaping at the sudden memory of his hard jaw and mobile lips beneath her hand. She couldn't deny she wanted to touch more than his face, to explore the hard body she'd dreamed of—and do more.

"It's such a crying shame. You know that, don't you?" She addressed her comment to the side of her leg where Timothy leaned. "I mean, here's a sexy guy, all sweet and thoughtful, and he's mixed up in Dangerous Things. As likely to get himself killed on some troubleshooting job." She shivered, goose bumps covering her arms, as the vision of Dillon getting shot played before her mind's eye.

Her pet stropped her leg encouragingly.

"Why couldn't he be an accountant, for pity's sake? Or a model? He's good-looking enough. With that stride of his, I'd bet they'd mob him on a catwalk." Making a face, she shook her head. "A shame, really and truly."

Timothy mewed in agreement.

She laughed at her bravado, knowing part of her vehemence rose from the need to distract herself from the nightmare that had troubled her sleep. Still, that didn't mean there wasn't a single note of truth in her words.

Jordan forced herself to return to her studio. After all, she'd committed to the charity auction and had a responsibility to fulfill—something she'd already had to put off once.

Sitting at her computer, she set herself to choosing the psyprints she would donate for this year's auction. With studied determination, she managed to dedicate a couple of hours to the effort. But the heady perfume of the orchids, which blended wonderfully with the sweet fragrance of the wisteria climbing the porch, eventually drew her back to the living room.

At the threshold, she pressed her hand to the little-used light pad on the wall and cudgeled her memory for the spell that activated the lights. When her palm prickled, indicating a successful cast, she went to the window with the southern exposure where she'd asked Dillon to place his gifts.

Dropping to her knees on the carpet, she took a deeper breath, immersing herself in the exotic scent as she opened herself to her clairvoyance. She touched a crisp, white petal gently, admiring the way its surface sparkled in the stronger light. Soft fur brushed her elbow as Timothy joined her.

To think Dillon had taken the time to find an orchid that matched the psyprint, merely because she'd wondered about the accuracy of her depiction. An extraordinary man.

He was even more magnificent than she remembered from the exhibit: his confident stride; that easy manner he'd adopted with Timothy; the heat in his gaze; the focused, nerve-ruffling attention he gave her words, as though hearing more than she said. Even his light baritone sounded much warmer away from the gabble of conversations that had surrounded them at the gallery.

And those eminently kissable lips!

Her hands clenched at the memory of learning his face and running her fingers over those lips. So firm and perfectly formed, like those she'd once felt on a Classical Greek bronze of an athlete.

Pulling a cushion off the armchair beside her, Jordan took another self-indulgent lungful of sensual perfume and lay back on the thick carpet, hugging the cushion to her chest, her sleep-deprived body welcoming the horizontal position.

What would he have smelled like if she'd pressed her nose to his chest or belly . . . or lower?

It was truly a crying shame he was off-limits; she couldn't learn his body, though she dearly wanted to. She could only imagine what delights his clothes concealed.

As Jordan relaxed in comfort, her pet purring soothingly by her ear, an inner voice raised an idle question. Floating in near euphoria, she hummed while she considered it. What was he doing right at that moment?

A vision drifted before her unwary mind's eye, of a place she'd never visited.

Sweat dripped down the side of Dillon's neck as he stripped off his shirt and wiped his face with the mottled brown fabric. She gasped at the broad expanse of chest he revealed and the pale, old scars that marked it—more proof of the danger he faced in his line of work. He must have been badly injured, without access to a healer. Her fingers twitched, wanting to trace the jagged lines and erase the memory of pain that marred his torso. But even the scars couldn't diminish the attractiveness of his physique.

Slinging the soaked shirt on a metal bar, he lay down on a bench, folding his brawny arms behind his head as he stretched and rolled his shoulders. The position threw his rippling abdominal muscles and the thick ridge that tented his cutoffs into stark relief. Sweat beaded the hollow of his throat, made dark lace of the light dusting of hair on his pectorals. It gilded his belly, drew her eyes to his erection, which was barely restrained by his shorts.

With a soft inhalation, he lifted a massive barbell off its rest, his biceps flexing and bunching as he raised and lowered the weight over his chest, moving with smooth efficiency. Poetry in motion. A male animal in his prime.

Jordan couldn't imagine the effort and discipline it must have taken for Dillon to regain peak physical condition . . . and she couldn't ignore the mouthwatering result. What would it be like to run her hands over those hard muscles? To feel that strong body cradled between her legs, moving over her, thrusting into her with all the power at his command? To have him inside her, pleasuring her with everything he had?

Instinct told her it would be unforgettable.

Still elated by the success of his initial foray, Dillon ended his last set and returned the weights to their holder with a gentle *clink*. He'd worked out to give the exhilaration flowing through him an outlet, something to do before he started bouncing off the walls. Despite his physical exertions, his mind continued to dwell on Jordan, preoccupied with the fresh intelligence he'd gathered.

It hadn't surprised him to learn that the house was her childhood home. It explained the flamboyance of the garden as well as the childproof styling of the furniture—its curves and rounded edges, well-padded against blind exploration, and lavished with textures. But it still didn't solve the mystery of her car registration.

He shrugged to himself, on his way to the shower. He had time to satisfy his curiosity. More importantly, the hunt was on and his skittish prey was a worthy target.

Stripping off his cutoffs returned Dillon's thoughts to Jordan; how she hadn't been wearing any shorts and his plans for seduction. So his pretty artist was a sensualist. Which made sense, given her blindness. Might that make her stomach the fastest way to her heart—or at least her bed? Maybe if he engaged her tongue with new tastes? His chuckle rose from deep in his chest. He knew one thing he wanted to feed her.

His cock was still hard enough to drill through concrete and had been since before he'd left her. He'd nearly swallowed his tongue when her T-shirt had ridden up, exposing the edge of a plain white panty, as she fled to her living room. Damned if that accidental glimpse hadn't made him feel like a Peeping Tom. Hard to believe it had made him hotter than a deliberate striptease could. He'd wanted to rip that T-shirt off her back right then and there, he'd been that turned on by the sight.

It occurred to him that it was a good thing Jordan was blind. If she'd seen her effect on him, she might have run away screaming or . . . maybe not?

Stepping under the shower, Dillon allowed a fantasy to play in his mind, one that embroidered on real life. As warm water sluiced over his body and caressed the aching length of his hard-on, he closed his eyes and gave himself over to his imagination.

They were alone this time, no cat at their feet playing chaperon. Jordan still wore that large T-shirt, its fabric so thin he could see the dark circles of her areolas when she crossed her arms under her high breasts.

But this time her nipples raised distended peaks under the white cotton, daring him to act on his urges. This time he could see the merest shadow of the delta between her thighs, barely veiled by the hem of her T-shirt—and she'd dressed that way deliberately, knowing he had come for her.

This time after she learned his face, she didn't stop at his neck. . . .

His hands slowed, the soap gliding over his chest a poor substitute for Jordan's touch that continued across his shoulders. *She trailed her fingers along his collarbones like inquisitive butterflies, lingered at the hollows at the base of his throat, then unbuttoned his shirt to trace his sternum, drawing light circles over the taut skin. Her lips followed the path of her hands, scorching to his awareness and branding him with that slightest of contacts. As the sweet perfume from the wisteria engulfed them, she explored the lines of his ribs, paying strict attention to the furrows of his abs, making such languid progress he wanted to howl.*

She knelt on the porch as her exploration meandered south, skating over his hip bones to arrive at his balls. She played with them, scraping her nails over their hairy pouch, weighing them in her palms like a woman in search of fresh fruit.

Dillon cupped his balls, imagining her fleeting touch exploring him intimately. Just the memory of her fingers on his face was enough to send a storm surge of liquid heat flooding his veins. With his other hand, he slowly caressed his swollen cock, trying to draw out his fantasy.

His insubordinate flesh paid him no heed, throbbing in time with the beat of his pulse. His fat balls were tucked up high against his body, equally engorged.

Pre-come trickled down his turgid cock, auguring his imminent release. Jordan followed the wet trail with an agonizingly laggard finger, all the way up to the weeping eye.

He groaned as she traced fiery rings on its head, brushing her thumb over the sensitive ridge of the crown and lighting off flares up his spine.

"Not yet."

Then she drew her hand back to lick her wet finger thoughtfully, tasting his readiness. The sight of that slender digit slipping between her pink lips made him shudder with hunger, with the need to feed her something more.

It was no use. His cock refused to subside, bobbing in the air and tapping his belly like a drumstick. The warm water raining down on his aroused body, stroking him with invisible fingers, only served to heighten his desire.

Dillon took his shaft in a firm grip, intent now on finding satisfaction. *He dragged the tail of her shirt up, revealing soft brown curls veiling her wet slit. He gathered her into his arms, pressing her against the wall. With his knee, he spread her thighs and stepped between them, sheathing himself with a quick thrust into her welcoming body. She was hot and tight—and oh-so-slick with desire.*

He groaned in longing, knowing Jordan would be hotter and tighter than any fantasy, eager and passionate, once he'd assuaged her fears.

She wrapped her legs around his hips, clinging to him and moaning in a low undertone as he drove home. He hammered her with short, brutal strokes, rubbing the crown of his cock over her pleasure spot, and exulted in her cries of pleasure. . . .

The look of raw passion on Dillon's face as his body moved under the pouring water made Jordan gasp, her body yearning for his. *What she would give to be the focus of all that intensity!*

Trying to soothe the insistent ache of carnal desire, she rubbed her mound against the soft cushion, her rhythm matching the pistoning of Dillon's hips. Her body ached to have him inside her, stretching her empty sex. Filling her as she hadn't been filled in a long time. Her hands itched with the need to touch him, to run her palms over his hard muscles, to pleasure him in every way she could.

Dillon turned to the shower jets, his eyes shuttered. His chiseled lips parted around unheard moans as he milked his thick cock, his fist pumping with feral urgency. He spent himself with a silent roar, his face a picture of primal delight.

Her own desperate moan of desire floated into the quiet room, thready and startling in its solitude.

Jordan jerked upright, need coiled tight in her belly, shocked by her response to the vision. *But it wasn't an ordinary vision, interchangeable with other visions, was it?*

Her empty core clenched as if in answer, demanding completion, craving Dillon's thick cock pounding into her body. Hot cream trickled between her thighs, scenting the air with her arousal.

Burying her face in the cushion, Jordan groaned, aggravated with her clairvoyance and her subconscious's insistence in giving her such intimate insight into that delectable, dangerous man— an image she could never erase. Why didn't her libido understand there was no future in such an attraction?

"Mew?" Timothy's curious query came from a distance. Had her restlessness driven him from her side? Warm breath gusted against her cheek as the cat came to nuzzle her, his damp nose cold on heated flesh.

The last thing she needed was more temptation. Dillon Gavin was off-limits. With the danger he courted and the many perils inherent in his "troubleshooting," only heartache lay in his direction and she'd vowed she wouldn't follow in her mother's footsteps.

The aching heaviness in her core pulsed, uninterested in such mundane concerns. Her body evidently disagreed. It needed Dillon now, and didn't care about tomorrow. What would it hurt? After all, giving in to their attraction didn't have to mean forever.

Didn't it?

CHAPTER FOUR

The phone rang as Jordan finished washing the breakfast dishes, before she could escape to her studio and work on the list of psyprints for the Spatha charity auction. To her surprise, it was her agent calling to discuss that very thing.

"I know the psyprints you're donating for the auction will all be previous works, but they're asking if you can do an original, just for them." Shanna's voice dropped to a confidential whisper. "I heard one of the donors backed out, so Fab wants to top last year's take. Maybe show whomever it was they're replaceable."

Jordan snickered despite herself. Fabian Merellyn, dubbed Fab by Shanna for his reported good looks, headed the Spatha Foundation. The scholarships funded by the auction helped many deserving teenagers—the children of soldiers and police—who otherwise couldn't afford to go to college. But from what Shanna passed on, the politics and infighting that went on in the background were unbelievable and Fab was a master at them.

"An original?" It would take time, preparation and—most

especially—inspiration, which Jordan wasn't sure she had available, not so soon after the rush to complete her last exhibit. "Do you advise it?"

"It'd make good publicity for you."

Running her fingers through Timothy's fur, Jordan weighed Shanna's statement. Her agent had a point. Also, an original Jordan Kane psyprint would likely bring in more money for Spatha than her current works. "I'll see what I can do, but no promises." Given the nightmares haunting her sleep, she wasn't sure she could come up with a psyprint she'd be willing to put up for sale, not unless she had a stroke of pure genius.

The restaurant was precisely where Lantis said it would be: near the courthouse, on the periphery of one of the shady downtown parks. Tucked between an arts-and-crafts shop and a store selling *materiae magicae*, it presented a demure face to the outside world.

Just Desserts: Specializing in Gâteau Aid. Dillon grinned reflexively at the discreet subhead, liking the place already. As might be expected given its proximity to police headquarters, it was lousy with cops. Even from outside, he could see that the line to the cashier was almost solid blue from uniforms.

Inside was even busier. Tables were full and several people were eyeballing a long bank of display cases.

Sidestepping a pair of lawyers debating between truffles and tarts, Dillon peered at the racks thoughtfully. *If the lady won't go to the pastries, then the pastries will come to the lady.* The bewildering array of desserts gave him pause. The restaurant obviously believed in truth in advertising.

He knew Jordan liked chocolate, but if the confections and cakes in sight were any indication, the knowledge didn't narrow his choices by much. He swallowed back temptation, reminding himself he wasn't here to indulge his own sweet tooth. So which ones might tempt Jordan's fancy?

After a stroll down the extensive display compounded his difficulties, he finally opted for variety over quantity, ordering the Chocolate Super Sampler. That plus a bottle of the dessert wine she liked should make a suitable offering.

Too bad they'd have her pet as chaperon. But if he couldn't outwit a cat, he had no business working black ops.

While waiting for his number to be called, he drifted to the windows facing the park, keeping his back to the wall. The chill in the air was refreshing, a welcome reminder that he wasn't in the tropics with his ass in a sling because a frigging newbie didn't have the spell control of a gnat.

Sensual motion in a secluded corner of the patio caught his eye, a couple engaging in a public display of extreme affection. Dillon grinned. That boded well for his planned seduction of Jordan, if the desserts inspired such activities.

Then he blinked, recognizing Rio Rafael as the male half of the amorous couple. His fellow black ops agent shared the outdoor table with a regal woman with a striking streak of white waving through her black hair. With Rio to refresh his memory, he immediately placed her as the cop who'd helped them last year with Kiera's espionage problem. It looked like he wasn't the only one on R&R.

Deciding to give his friend some privacy, Dillon returned to the counter to watch his order being assembled. He couldn't tell if any of the items was what Rio and his lady had ordered; the debris from their meal had been inconclusive.

"Oh, that's decadent," a familiar-looking blonde sighed, sidling over. She propped a copper-clawed hand on an out-thrust, bony hip that identified her as a model or otherwise fashion-fixated. He'd worked in Europe often enough to recognize the Continental styling of her short dress. "Don't tell me you plan to eat all that by yourself."

"I hope not to." Dillon watched as more chocolate pieces joined those already lined up in his box. His hackles rose as the woman invaded his personal space, pressing her breast against his arm.

"I haven't found a restaurant with quite the same selection in Milan. I'm going to miss it while I'm gone."

He smiled politely, ignoring her signals. Jordan was the only one who interested him now. But even if his focus hadn't locked on her, he wouldn't have taken the blonde up on her obvious offer. He rather disliked being a notch on someone's bedpost. Luckily, his order was soon ready, allowing him to pay and escape while the woman waited her turn.

With Shanna's call to reinforce her determination, Jordan managed to ignore her purse with its cache of ill-omened gloves. She didn't want to court another roaring migraine on top of the repeat of her nightmare. By the time the door chimes rang, she'd reviewed a couple of years' output. As the effort translated to dozens of psyprints and several hours at the computer—broken only by Timothy's polite insistence on lunch—she welcomed the unexpected interruption.

"Who is it?" she called out as she reached the door.

"It's Dillon."

The growled answer triggered a powerful rush of happiness and breathless excitement that caught her off guard. She tried to tell herself the sudden pounding of her heart was due to fear but couldn't entirely convince herself, not when it was accompanied by a flush of sensual heat. "Dillon?"

"Haven't we done this before?"

His bemused response broke the stasis that gripped her limbs. A laugh escaped her as she disarmed the security spells. "But that was yesterday!"

The gratifying scent of dark chocolate greeted her as she opened the door, mingling with the perfume from her garden and the subtler one of citrus and musky virility that called to her feminine senses like ambrosia. "More orchids?"

She dug her nails into the door, trying to ignore the glowing embers of desire his presence awoke in her. The memory of him in that titillating vision—all wet and naked and everything male—sent a dart of heat through her. How could she keep her distance when her own libido insisted on parading temptation before her?

Relaxing at the tentative welcome in her voice, Dillon grinned. "It's the real thing this time, plus that wine you liked."

He was disappointed to see Jordan wore somewhat more decorous attire this time. Though still barefoot, she had on a green—and quite opaque—tank top and short shorts that bared lissome legs. He eyed the pale, slender pair appreciatively. *Yup, definitely lissome.* He could hardly wait to have them tight around him while he rode her to ecstasy.

Leaning against said legs, Timothy returned his scrutiny with a blue-slitted glare of suspicion.

Dillon jerked his gaze back up with a guilty start, in time to see a peculiar, unreadable expression flash across Jordan's face as her eyes turned gray beneath fluttering lashes. Her hand dropped down to stroke her pet before she extended it to him.

He placed the wine bottle in her palm. Her smooth fingers brushed the back of his hand, light and delicate. He could imagine her touching his cock head in exactly the same way.

That member sprang to instantaneous aching fullness at the thought. *Pitiful, Gavin. That's just pitiful.*

She relieved him of the tall, narrow bottle, which suddenly looked rather dildoesque in her hands. She explored its gleaming length and raised label with a thoroughness he wanted directed at him—wanted it with a ferocity that bordered on pain. He'd never have thought he could be jealous of an inert piece of glass!

"Thank you." Though her back was poker-straight, Jordan invited him in. This time she led him down the hall to the kitchen, her pet threading between her legs.

Dillon took the opportunity to admire the way she filled her shorts and to envy the cat's freedom to flirt his tail along her inner thighs, gliding over silken territory. One day soon he intended do the same himself, to find out if her skin was as smooth as it looked.

"Chocolates, you said?"

Timothy leaped onto the table as she set the bottle down. The cat remained on all fours, ready to pounce, his head swiveling between the two of them as though following their conversation.

"Chocolate desserts," Dillon clarified. "And something for Timothy." He quickly opened a carryout container of Chicken Supreme and presented it to her pet. The eager growl that greeted the dish affirmed the wisdom of his tactics.

"Not you, too!" Despite her muttered protest, Jordan seemed more resigned than angry.

Still, the large cat hooked a paw around the carton and quickly dragged it down the tabletop, away from his mistress. Ears pricked in her direction, he buried his muzzle inside, consuming the bribe with due haste. Obviously an exponent of "Better safe than sorry."

Gratified by his victory, Dillon proffered the box of pastries to his quarry, wafting the chocolate aroma under her nose in temptation. "I hope I didn't interrupt anything."

Despite knowing she should resist, Jordan couldn't bring herself to refuse Dillon's offering and cut short his visit. "I was just going through my work." Trying to keep things impersonal, she took refuge in discussing her art.

After tucking the box of desserts in the refrigerator, out of Timothy's reach, she moved their conversation to the more businesslike confines of her studio. Through a fog of hormones, she explained the modifications to her psyprinter and computer that adapted them to her blindness, including the tact boards that augmented the video displays, automatically pressing the self-test button that raised the sharp metal pins of the psyprinter's tact board.

Through it all, she was uncommonly aware of Dillon's presence beside her, barely hearing the board's three-tone chime that indicated all was well—that certainly wasn't the case with her. All her senses were focused on her companion. His warmth. His musky, citrus scent. The laughter in his voice that invited her to share his delight.

His visit was a fearful pleasure, fraught with trepidation and excitement. Though Dillon presented an easygoing face to her, Jordan couldn't forget the snarling man of her visions, who fought with deadly skill . . . and had been shot and nearly killed in the course of his work.

Yet she also couldn't erase from her memory the image of that virile male who had taken his release with a ferocity that left her breathless with lust. What would it be like to taste him—to experience that—even just once?

Heat engulfed her at the thought. If only she could!

It took every ounce of willpower she had to not give in to her libido and flirt with Dillon, especially when he made it more than clear that he reciprocated her desire; the warmth in his voice and the way his electrifying touch lingered whenever they made contact left no doubts about his interest. The painful memories of her mother pacing the kitchen in endless circles and crying herself to sleep whenever her firefighter father was away responding to emergencies barely swayed her hunger.

Thankfully, it seemed Dillon's company was just temporary. "You're not based here?"

"No, though I did grow up around here. These days I fly in, as often as work permits, to visit Lantis and—"

"Lantis?" Jordan repeated, confused by the unfamiliar name.

Dillon chuckled. "Well, he hardly looks like a John. That's what most people say they notice the first time they meet him."

Oh, he meant John Atlantis. Indeed, the man she'd seen in her vision working beside Dillon at his violent trade hadn't looked anything as commonplace as a John.

She suppressed a shiver. *Never forget that, Jordan.* While Dillon might seem to be the answer to any woman's dreams, there was no guarantee his job wouldn't kill him. *Just like Dad.* Or that he wouldn't turn his lethal expertise on her.

The warmth in Dillon's voice when he spoke of his comrade hinted at a long-held friendship, tested through danger and battle, like steel tempered in the heat of mutual peril. Such ties were stronger than any chance-met attraction.

What would it be like to win even a fraction of such regard? Jordan stifled the need waking in her heart. Dillon was the last man who'd be suitable for a lover; why was she even entertaining such thoughts?

The familiar hum of Dan's car distracted her and Timothy. Her pet bounded out the room, his steady thumps fading into the distance.

The cat's sudden departure niggled at Dillon, preventing him from enjoying their unexpected privacy. It also recalled Jordan to herself, prompting her to shift away just when he'd nearly gotten her snuggled against him.

Even absent, her pet still managed to throw a spanner in the works. And he wasn't done, apparently having left to greet someone.

"Hey, Tim!" The newcomer didn't bother trying to hide his presence. A light tenor, crooning nonsense to the cat, preceded him as he approached.

It irritated Dillon to realize just how comfortable the other man was with Jordan's pet. Who was he? His hackles wanted to bristle at the prospect of a prior claim to Jordan's attentions.

A man about Jordan's height appeared in the doorway, accompanied by Timothy. Dressed in business casual, he had narrow shoulders but a wiry build that hinted at hidden strength. That, plus tousled, honey-brown hair and delicate features, and he could be mistaken for Jordan's masculine twin. His face was somehow familiar, although not because he looked so much like Jordan; Dillon couldn't quite place it.

"This is my cousin." Jordan tilted her head in the stranger's direction. The change the newcomer's arrival made in her was marked—her smile came easily, her tension eased, her shoulders relaxed.

"Dan." The other man extended his hand in greeting. "Actually, I'm also Jordan Kane, but that gets confusing." He gave Dillon's hand a firm shake, smiling all the while. "Since I'm the younger one, Jordan has first dibs on the name."

Well, that explained the mysterious car registration: As simple as two cousins with the same name. Recognition dawned. "You're with kidTek, right?"

Dan gaped, his light blue eyes, so similar to Jordan's, widening at Dillon's statement. "How'd you know?" His gaze dropped to his plain polo shirt, as though checking if the company's colorful logo were sewn on it.

Dillon shrugged. "Kiera mentioned you."

Various emotions streamed across the younger man's face as he absorbed Dillon's statement.

"Really?" Jordan asked, before her cousin could recover. "What did she say?"

Whoops! Now he was in for it. Dillon quickly considered his options. He had to tell Jordan something to satisfy her curiosity, but a full explanation would reveal the nature of his involvement in kidTek and only raise more questions than it answered. He immediately chose to sacrifice Dan. Every man for himself. "That he has a reputation among the ladies in kidTek."

Jordan squealed. "He does?"

"I do?" Dan echoed. Then he froze, his eyes rounding in a look of horror. "Kiera said that? She knows?" The thought didn't seem to agree with him.

"Yup." Dillon bit back a chuckle as Dan buried his face in his hands with a groan.

"A reputation for what?" Jordan prompted with a smile of lively interest, obviously quite taken with the topic.

"Ah . . ." Dillon cudgeled his brain for the details. "Apparently a lady friend described him as 'fabulous.'"

Jordan gave a shriek of laughter, collapsing on the couch in a fit of hilarity. "Dan's boss said that?"

"No, she's the president!" Dan snatched up a cushion to cover his face. "Why'd you tell her?" the younger man moaned, sending Dillon an agonized look that accused him of betraying some mystical brotherhood over the gray tassels.

Enjoying Jordan's mirth, Dillon spread his hands, silently disavowing any malice. After all, it wasn't as if he'd made up Kiera's comment. Giving in, he allowed his lips to stretch in a wide grin. If the other man didn't enjoy his reputation, he didn't have to maintain it.

Dillon's visits were the start of a sensual siege that left Jordan breathless and aching with sexual frustration. It was maddening how little willpower she had whenever he knocked on her door. He came almost daily, usually to invite her to lunch. She'd always managed to refuse, but hadn't been able to bring herself to turn him away completely, though she told herself she ought to. Unable to resist temptation, she'd spent hours in his tantalizing company.

And she couldn't convince herself it was merely good manners that made her do so. Just being in his presence heightened her awareness of her femininity, of the sensual potential between man and woman—more so than she'd ever been with any lover. It had been so long since she'd felt that way that she found herself anticipating Dillon's arrival, despite her better judgment.

The one time he hadn't dropped by, he'd still made his absence felt. She'd come to expect his visits and had worried when he didn't show up by late afternoon. For her troubles, she'd learned he slept in the nude—her clairvoyance had shown him in all his masculine glory, sprawled across an enormous, leather-paneled bed, her view unimpeded by blanket or shower spray. Even with his scars, he'd looked all that was desirable in a man.

That knowledge didn't help her resistance or her sleep one whit. If she wasn't having nightmares, she was dreaming of making love to Dillon, of running her hands over his chest and flat belly, of following the line of hair down to his penis and caressing him to throbbing arousal. She even found herself wondering what he tasted like.

Although she fought the attraction, Jordan could feel her defenses weakening with each visit. After a week, she found it increasingly difficult to remember why it wasn't a good idea to agree to Dillon's lunch invitations. Lunch was safe. It wasn't like it would be a date.

She was spending time with him anyway, why not eat? Certainly, it would keep his hands occupied and less prone to giving her those innocent little touches that were so seductive.

"What did you bring me now?" Jordan grimaced inwardly at the childlike anticipation in her voice. After that first visit, Dillon had made a point to bring little gifts, nothing as lavish as the orchids—desserts, potpourri, scented candles—but always something that teased her senses. His intentions were obvious but given the care he took to play to her senses, she couldn't help but wonder how he'd be as a lover. Surely a brief taste wouldn't start her down her mother's path to perdition?

He set his burden on the ottoman with much clinking of

glass. "I thought I'd go with something different, this time." His opaque hint was par for the course for the first part of his visits; he'd made a game of his presents, having her guess what they were.

Jordan enjoyed it enough to play along, using her blindness to keep them on a friendly footing. She didn't resort to her clairvoyance, not wanting to spoil the game.

The bag rustled as he reached in. There was a grating sound— two rough surfaces sliding against each other—just before something wafted past her nose.

Her nostrils tingled as she sniffed, then had to swallow when her mouth watered at the flavorful aroma. "You brought me vinegar?"

"Not just any vinegar, it's a selection." The grin in Dillon's voice as he handed her a small cruet of etched glass invited her to share his delight. "There's honey vinegar, sherry, apple cider, fig, raspberry, balsamic, tarragon and a few others I thought you might like to try." A tinkle of glass accompanied his words.

"Vinegar," she repeated in bemusement. "Maybe you'd better bring them to the kitchen."

The clink of crystal accompanied Dillon's motions as he unloaded the bag on the countertop. *How many cruets did he bring?* It was followed by a thud and a curious mew as Timothy arrived to investigate Dillon's largesse.

"I discovered this restaurant that does miracles with vinaigrette. They make their own vinegar." Dillon smacked his lips in exaggerated gustatory appreciation. "You have to taste it to believe it."

Well, why not?

Shaking her head at her weakness, Jordan smiled reluctantly and surrendered to the inevitable. "Alright, you win. You've tempted me."

"You mean to lunch?"

The surprise in his voice prompted her to tease him. "Don't tell me you've given up."

He accepted her surrender with gratifying haste, urging her to dress while he kept Timothy from underfoot.

———— ∞∞∞ ————

Keeping Jordan's pet occupied turned out to be as simple as a few games of catch and, when Timothy tired of that, an investigation into the contents of the refrigerator. Dillon was trying to get the inquisitive cat out of the main compartment when the clicking of heels on wood told him Jordan was about to make an appearance.

"Ready." She'd changed her T-shirt and shorts in favor of a casual sundress that covered up her lissome legs to just above her knees but bared her shoulders with a clinging halter-top. Creamy skin with just a smattering of freckles showed she didn't get out that much; Dillon looked forward to counting the spots and kissing them.

But not quite yet.

He had to consolidate his gains first. This was a risky stage of the hunt: Jordan was now out in the open but he hadn't managed to tempt her with a kiss yet—a matter that had been plaguing his daydreams. But, finally, his patience was bearing fruit. He'd have to watch himself and his sexual frustration, to make sure he didn't scare her back behind her defenses. She was bound to be skittish. Now that she'd taken that first step, he had to throttle back and give her some breathing space—if only it were that easy!

"You're nearly out of fruit. Want to buy some after lunch?" Pulling Timothy out by the scruff, Dillon finally closed the refrigerator door.

"Oh, no need." Jordan smiled. "I'll just order online. It's a local grocer. They have standing orders to deliver it to the hatch in the pantry."

"Convenient." He had to admire her workarounds even when they hindered his seduction.

"Uh-huh. And they do a good job of choosing fruits." She

dragged him to her studio and the computer, to show off her independence. It didn't take her long to access her grocer's website and fruit section.

"Now, what to get?" Jordan glided her hands over the computer's tact board—a smaller version of the one on her psyprinter—that repeated the monitor display in high relief, much like a three-dimensional image done in unblunted steel pins. "Hmm. Strawberries?"

"They have a sale on imported melons." Dillon leaned over. Close but not too close, enough to catch a hint of the fruity cologne she'd applied but not so close that she might take fright. He took it as a positive sign and wondered if her dreams the past week had been anything like his. He could only wish they were, hoping she shared his carnal torment—especially when cold showers didn't work and hand jobs left something to be desired.

She cleared her throat twice, faint color washing across her cheeks. "Too expensive."

"Huh?" *Her dreams?*

"Timothy would eat half of it. He has a penchant for cantaloupe and honeydew."

Oh. Finally understanding the cat's insistence in checking out the refrigerator's fruit bin, Dillon snickered. Jordan's pet had to be the most unusual of his kind he'd ever encountered.

Just then, Timothy joined them by the monitor. Staring at the melons, he tapped long, sharp claws on the flat screen suggestively. "Prrp?"

Jordan made a face in the direction of her pet. "And it doesn't help that Dan gives in to him."

Her look of long-suffering was too much. Unable to suppress his hilarity, Dillon doubled over, roaring with laughter.

She snorted once, then joined him in his levity, giggling as she continued through the site. "Ooh! Red Globe grapes." She stroked the raised pins depicting the large, plump berries with a loving hand. "They feel like a good size. Out of season but I can't resist."

Dillon's lungs seized as she fondled fat berries the size of his balls. The way she lingered over them as though savoring their heft and texture had his cock springing to turgid, painful attention. He had a feeling her actions would be front and center in his dreams tonight.

Chapter Five

"Don't expect me Friday night. I'll be *occupied*."

Jerking out of her half-doze, Jordan paused her audio book politely. Despite the narrator's droll delivery, the author's gastronomic adventures in the Philippines couldn't hold her attention as her body tried to make up for another nightmare-riddled sleep. "Hmm?"

Coiled around her feet, Timothy woke from his own nap.

She ran her cousin's words back through her mind. Dan had given the last word an intimate timbre that meant he intended to spend the night with a lover—or lovers—and not at home. He never brought any of his women to meet Jordan and had a revolving door on his love life; she'd long since stopped trying to keep track. His apartment over the garage meant he was independent, but he did her the courtesy of keeping her apprised of his plans.

"Maybe way into the weekend, so—"

The demure two-tone vibrato of the phone on the table beside her interrupted her cousin's announcement.

She answered it absently, smiling at Dan's easygoing lechery. Despite it all, he somehow seemed to remain on good terms with his lovers. "Hello?"

"Jordan."

Her heart skipped a beat at the light baritone that turned her name into a vocal caress. Just the very sound of it had her toes curling and heat pooling in her belly. Her nipples tingled as if he'd done more than just say her name. It made her want to purr.

"Dillon!" Thankfully, she managed a mild, even tone. "What's up?" Even after several friendly lunches, she still hadn't grown accustomed to her visceral response to him. Something inside her melted with every minute spent with him. She couldn't understand how she could be so attracted to such a dangerous man.

"I've got tickets to the Diuata Gong Orchestra concert for the day after tomorrow. I've heard good things about them and thought you might enjoy their music."

"A gong orchestra?" She frowned, trying to imagine the music such an ensemble would produce. "Is that like a carillon?" Whatever it sounded like, the medium certainly wouldn't be primarily visual.

Dillon's thoughtfulness in his choice of entertainments struck her once more. In the week since she'd succumbed to his invitations, he'd introduced her to different cuisines, taken her wine and chocolate tasting, and even had her sniffing perfumes in search of a birthday present for Kiera. Activities that didn't depend on sight. Ones she'd never dared try because of her blindness. Using her clairvoyance for necessary outings was draining enough.

But that hadn't been the case with Dillon. His presence seemed to imbue her with confidence. He had such control over his body—and by extension, the situation—that she didn't worry at all about her surroundings, because he was with her.

And through it all, his behavior had been unexceptional. If she didn't count thumbs circling and stroking her inner elbow and the back of her hand—friction she felt in her hungry core.

His chuckle warmed her ear and her cheeks. "Not hardly. It's Asian music, which is very different from a carillon. They use different scales."

Asian? An outgrowth of his travels? The chance to experience something of a different culture was enough to pique her interest—never mind the chance to spend more time with Dillon while he was in town. Sooner or later he'd have to return to his perilous line of work, then it would be back to her curtailed lifestyle.

"What do you say? It starts at nine thirty in the evening, so we can have dinner before the concert."

The time gave her pause.

"I'm not sure what my plans are for Friday, just yet." Worrying the handset with her thumb, Jordan mentally debated Dillon's invitation. He'd somehow charmed her into going out with him on several occasions. But lunches were one thing, this concert bordered on a romantic date. She wasn't sure she wanted to take that next step with such a dangerous man. It didn't matter that he'd never hinted at what he did; she knew he'd nearly died on several occasions and wasn't about to follow in her mother's footsteps. "Can I get back to you on that? I have to check my schedule."

She ended the call with the promise to let him know her decision within the hour. Dillon sounded disappointed she hadn't accepted immediately but she couldn't think about that now. While she'd managed to keep him at arm's length so far, an evening with him just might tip the scales and throw her into territory she wasn't prepared for.

"Take him up on it. He's got a streak for you, you know."

Replacing the handset on its cradle, Jordan turned to her cousin in surprise; she'd forgotten his presence. "What? Who are you talking about?"

"Your Mr. Gavin," Dan informed her with a grin in his voice. He'd obviously been listening in on her conversation. A cushion puffed as he sat down at the other end of the couch. "Who's all so hot for you."

Jordan suppressed a frisson of pleasure at his phrasing. *He's not your Mr. Gavin!* "That's impossible."

"Why?"

"He's—" *What?* She wasn't even sure what his job actually involved, besides danger and dying. "He's just visiting. He'll be gone soon enough." She tried to make her statement matter-of-factly, but suspected she hadn't quite succeeded. Certainly she hadn't convinced Timothy since he jumped to her lap to soothe her with a head butt.

"So?" Dan's quizzical tone said he didn't see any problem. "He seems tolerable. It isn't like he's out to use you. And it's been some time since you've had some fun."

Jordan wrapped her arms around her pet, running her hands through his thick fur. "He says he's a troubleshooter. But there's a lot more to it than that. There're guns and spells." *A lash of electric-blue power. Guns firing in her direction.* The flash of memory sent a shiver up her arms.

That gave her cousin pause. "Really?" He knew better than to question her sight and couldn't dismiss her statement out of hand. "Cool!"

His response staggered her. "*What?!*"

The couch rocked and creaked under her cousin. "Nothing wrong with guns and spells."

She blinked at the casual acceptance implicit in his easy statement. When had Dan, who preferred to make toys, decided that guns and spells went together?

"He could go away on a project and get himself killed doing his troubleshooting! You never saw what it was like for my mom whenever Dad responded to a fire. I still remember how she paced the floor, waiting for news." How she'd cried in fear for his safety, she who was a rock of strength at all other times. And had died in her sleep, heartbroken by his death.

"It's not like he wants to marry you. You're being too serious about this. It's supposed to be fun. Some bouncing around in bed, some grins and giggles. Enjoy yourself!"

Kneading her lap, Timothy seconded her cousin's claim with a chirp of concurrence.

"See? Tim agrees with me," Dan remarked, laughing.

Jordan smiled reluctantly. "You really think I'm making too much out of this?"

"I know so."

She chewed her lip, tempted despite her fears. She wished she hadn't learned Dillon slept in the nude. Watching him sleep had become a guilty pleasure, one she—unfortunately—couldn't seem to deny herself. She fought down a blush, not wanting to betray the tenor of her thoughts to her cousin.

If she didn't go into this expecting something long-term, then the danger of Dillon's job wouldn't matter. Right?

Maybe the concert wouldn't be so bad. Her heart raced on a surge of anticipation, her body tingling with heat. *Take a chance, Jordan.* She smiled to herself. Trying to ignore the uncharacteristic attraction wasn't working. Maybe giving in to it would get it out of her system.

There was something different about Jordan tonight. A subtle change that—for want of a better term—drew the eye. Dillon couldn't put his finger on what it was. It teased him, defying identification.

Not her clothes, though they were more formal than how she dressed for lunch. A cream peasant blouse in silk with a deep, laced-up neckline that afforded provocative glimpses of pale skin, and floral embroidery that obscured the tantalizing details of the bra visible through the sheer fabric. A black pencil skirt with a side slit that emphasized her slender legs. Over it all, she wore a plush velvet shawl in midnight blue with silver beadwork; it brought out the color of her eyes and glittered when it caught the light.

All throughout dinner his inability to pinpoint the difference nagged at him.

What had changed?

Whatever it was had the hairs on his arms prickling. An intimation of imminent breakthrough filled the air—heady and unsettling—like an electric charge before a lightning strike.

He took a deep breath to quell the restlessness fizzing through his veins. After nearly two weeks of temptation, even his practiced patience was getting strained. Fantasies weren't enough; he wanted her in his arms, returning his kisses and demanding his possession. Under him. Wild and willing. Running her hands all over his body.

Dillon inhaled again to bolster his restraint. "More wine?"

Jordan smiled, wider and rather more freely than usual. "Just don't get me drunk."

"Of course." Getting her drunk was the last thing he wanted. He refused to take undue advantage, even if he was on the edge with frustration. Two weeks was a damned long time to go without sex when he was on R&R, and it had been even longer since he'd last had a lover.

But instinct told him that was about to change. Because something was different.

Was it her manner?

Maybe.

There was an undercurrent of excitement in the way Jordan comported herself. She seemed more open: touching his hand to emphasize a point while they discussed the prudence of cosmetic healing, allowing him to feed her some of his curry without her usual deliberation, toying with her fork while eating dessert. The sensual image of her lips sucking on the tines had him adjusting the fit of his slacks to ease his discomfort.

Dillon tried not to get his hopes up, reminding himself that Jordan had hesitated over his invitation, but his cock twitched anyway. If he didn't get lucky tonight, it wouldn't be from lack of trying.

Dillon looked quite dashing, all in black, save for his dinner jacket, which was the red of rich, fine wine. Despite her blindness, he'd obviously made an extra effort for tonight. Somehow the contrast between all the lace of his poet shirt, the double ruffles at the shirt's cuffs and the simple lines of his linen jacket merely heightened his masculinity.

And while he seemed quite aware of their surroundings, his attention didn't wander, didn't scan the restaurant in search of admiration; Jordan's clairvoyance was so fixated on him, she'd have noticed if it were otherwise.

Her libido muttered that Dillon's clothes weren't important. It was what lay beneath that she craved—those smooth ripples and slabs of muscle, his sinewy strength, even his lethal potential. To have this man in her arms and inside her body, moving over her . . . surely any risk was worth that.

She fought down a shiver of anticipation as she sipped from her glass, breathing in sunlight and spice. The ice wine flowed over her tongue in a rich medley of fruity flavors: mango, pear, apricot, pineapple, lime, and lemon candy. *Not too much, now. You're already almost giddy.* She chased it with a bite of baklava to be on the safe side, relishing the taste of honey, pistachio, and cinnamon, enhanced by the tartness of the wine.

"So where did you first hear a gong orchestra?" Jordan asked, to divert her increasingly unruly thoughts.

"A market in Bali. I was there on business but extended my stay for a couple of days for vacation." Dillon's lips curved in reminiscent pleasure, his dark gaze softening at some gentle memory.

Business in Bali? The reminder of his dangerous work derailed her descent into complacency. *Silly twit. This isn't forever, remember?*

"It was a traditional gamelan that accompanied a pair of dancers." He fluttered his hands, his fingers spread and stiff, possibly illustrating some dance movement, then stopped suddenly, chagrin flashing across his face. "Very energetic," he added, making a quick recovery.

Dillon paused to sip water; she noticed he'd limited his wine consumption. "Diuata, on the other hand, has a more international repertoire, not limited to Balinese sounds."

"What do you like about it?" Jordan laid her hand on the broad back of his, unable to resist despite the possibility of triggering her psychometry.

Thankfully, nothing intruded on her vision.

He was warm to the touch, his palm rough as he turned his hand over, capturing her in a gentle grip. "There's something primal about gongs, almost—you could say—elemental." He laid his other hand over their entwined fingers. "It stirs the blood."

The concert was to be held at the Museum of Arts. Typical of such institutions, the complex was a warren of interconnected chambers with no direct route to the theater. Alcoves jutted out into hallways, framing sculptures and other artwork. Little curios were displayed in shadow boxes protruding at eye level. Larger pieces were planted in the middle of everything, in a seemingly deliberate effort to create bottlenecks. Just a few minutes in the building told Dillon the planners had succeeded.

A throng of gaily dressed people filled the halls with a deafening tumult of conversation. Dillon had worried Jordan would be dis-oriented in the crowd, not a serious problem with him to guide her, but it might have dampened the mood.

Since dinner, his gut had been telling him tonight was the night his fast would end. He was more than ready for it; after back-to-back missions, it had been months since he'd last had sex.

He intended to forestall anything that might change Jordan's mind. However, his concern seemed unnecessary.

"How do you do that?" Dillon wondered aloud as Jordan un-erringly sidestepped yet another statue in the middle of the corri-dor before he could guide her around it. The graceful movement parted her narrow skirt's high slit, drawing his eye up her shapely leg to the feminine curve of her hip.

He'd noticed her doing something similar at the exhibit, but had attributed it to familiarity with the Walsen Galleries' layout. But this being her first visit to the museum—she'd said so earlier at dinner—familiarity couldn't explain her adroit navigation of the maze of artwork and chattering masses. Now that he thought back on it, she'd been equally sure-footed at the restaurants where he'd taken her for lunch. The expected hesitation only surfaced when she reached for something.

"Do what?"

"Avoid obstacles," he explained automatically, keeping an eye out for the occasional heedless bulldozer barging through the crowd; he'd already shielded Jordan from a few.

Jordan paused, tilting her head side to side in a self-conscious listening posture, almost as though she were checking for eaves-droppers. "I'll explain later."

Curiosity aroused, Dillon took his time studying the press of strangers mingling around them like a hyperactive aurora. He had to admit the venue was a trifle public. It would probably take a bomb to evacuate the place. "I'll hold you to that."

The theater doors soon opened, precluding any chance of pri-vate conversation. By the time the lights dimmed, it looked like

he'd picked up Jordan's fervid excitement. That was the only reason he could think of to explain why he slung his arm over her
shoulders as the curtains rose. Somewhat to his surprise, she
didn't pull away. In fact, she actually seemed to snuggle closer. In
the darkness, he could make out the merest hint of a smile curving her lips. *Well, now. Definite progress.*

That sense of being poised on the brink of something new
and wondrous returned, even stronger than before. He took a
deep breath to shore up his tenuous control as the members of
the gong orchestra were introduced. For his trouble, he got a
whiff of cherry fragrance that had him salivating. He wanted to
bury his face in it.

But that would be too aggressive. Now wasn't the time to
pounce. Not yet. He had to bide his time, wait just a little longer.
Enough for her to grow comfortable with the way things were
going.

Oblivious to his struggle for control, Jordan curled against
him, seemingly spellbound by the fluid rush of exotic sounds.
Soon, she was swaying to the bronze gongs playing melodies from
tropical rain forests, her face glowing with enjoyment.

His heart leaping at her pleasure, Dillon smiled, glad he was
the one to introduce her to the music. A corner of his mind niggled at him, worried by the strength of his delight. He hadn't even
bedded her yet!

The car door shut with a discreet thump beside Jordan. With only
the trip home left, she closed off her clairvoyance, allowing the familiar darkness to blanket her sight.

The music had been as spellbinding as Dillon had promised,
the gongs and drums very different from what she'd expected.
The variety of sounds produced by such similar instruments had
surprised her . . . and stirred her. Set her pulse racing as she nestled against Dillon's solid warmth.

The sparkling tones ringing in her memory, Jordan sank into her seat, soft leather cradling her body as the car rumbled around her. When Dillon chuckled, a low, intimate sound that sent heat coiling in her belly, she realized she'd been trying to vocalize one of the brilliant runs playing through her head.

"Enjoyed yourself?" There was a smile in his voice as he stated the obvious.

Still, it was only polite to answer. "Oh, yesssss," she purred happily, reaching over to emphasize her gratitude. "Thank you for taking me." Her hand landed on his thigh, which tensed immediately. She snatched it back, mortified by her mistake, the heat flooding her cheeks totally different from the one that had filled her core. "Sorry."

"No, no. It's alright." He replaced her hand on his thigh, the muscles bunching beneath her curious fingers.

Jordan smiled in relief at that promising reception of her clumsy overture. But what if Dillon was being polite? Pulling her shawl tighter around her shoulders, she tried to shrug off her doubts. The night wasn't over yet. A frisson of excitement shot up her spine at the reminder. *That's right. Don't jump to conclusions.*

"So, which parts did you enjoy most?"

"I think—" She mimed using mallets to play, welcoming a reason to take her hand off his thigh without any awkwardness. "The rapid passages on the tuned gongs."

The conversation flowed easily, touching on music and other topics, the drive home passing in companionable discourse. She tried to remember another night she'd enjoyed more and couldn't. Hopefully, this would just be the first of many. After all her caution, she wished she'd accepted his invitations sooner.

The scent of honey greeted her through her window as the car crunched to a halt on the gravel drive. She opened herself to her sight and confirmed her assumption. Back home. The evening was over.

But she didn't want it to end just yet.

As Jordan pummeled her brain for some way to extend their time together, Dillon trailed a finger down her neck.

She shivered with delight. He'd been so attentive during the concert, taking extra care for her comfort, putting his arm around her after she rubbed her arms against the air-conditioned coolness of the theater. She'd reveled in his solicitude.

"You said you'd explain."

Explain? It took a moment before she understood. She bit her lip at his gentle reminder. Her clairvoyance. He'd asked about it back at the theater. In the wake of the wonderful music, she'd forgotten she'd promised him an explanation.

Now parked in front of her garage, without anyone who might overhear, there was no reason left to delay. She couldn't even hope Dan would interrupt them; her cousin was spending the weekend with a lover.

Unmoving, Dillon watched her in silence, her sight showing only patient curiosity on his face. He sat there waiting, as if they had all the time in the world for her confession.

Her stomach lurched at the prospect, shocked out of the pleasant anticipation of becoming intimate with Dillon. He had no idea what he was asking. It was an understandable question and only to be expected after her performance at the museum. What was surprising was that he hadn't asked sooner.

She couldn't refuse him, not and hope to keep his friendship—much less any chance of greater intimacy. And yet, if she told him, she might lose both anyway. The thought sent a pang through her heart; it hurt, more than she expected.

Drawing back into herself, Jordan blocked out her sight, not wanting to see the calculation that was the first step in her alienation. She wished Timothy were there; she was in dire need of his reassurance.

How to begin?

The figured nap of her skirt clung unpleasantly to her damp palms. She gripped her hands to give them something to do, her fingers weaving together convulsively while her mind spun in circles.

A hard, warm hand covered her hands, squeezed them gently. "It's okay. Whatever it is, it's okay."

Jordan welcomed his touch, grabbing it like a lifeline in turbulent waters. His heat seeped into her, comforting in its physicality. "I'm not used to talking about it."

"Take your time," he murmured, placing her hands on his knee. His thigh had very little give under her fingers, his strength evident in every muscle.

With gentle pressure on her chin, Dillon turned her head toward him. "Would it help if I promise not to take out an ad in the papers?"

She giggled reluctantly, appreciating his levity for what it was: an attempt to reduce her tension. "I'm serious. This isn't something I want bruited about."

"I'm not one to partake in senseless gossip." His voice was undemanding, his patience a tangible presence between them as he waited for her to unburden herself.

Jordan sighed, unable to put off the inevitable. If he couldn't accept her clairvoyance, wouldn't keep her confidence, saw it as something to exploit, it was probably best that she find out now, not when they were . . . more intimately involved.

"I'm not totally blind," she finally confessed, her hands clenching convulsively. "I mean, not exactly. I can't see anything through my eyes but—" She took a deep breath to steel herself, dreading his reaction. "I-I'm clairvoyant," she concluded in a feeble voice. She'd downplayed her ability for so long, it was habit not to speak of it.

Dillon was so silent beside her it was like she was alone. Jordan couldn't even hear him breathing. Only the warmth of his touch and the hard muscles under her fingers told her he was still there.

CHAPTER SIX

"So? You're not the only one. And it isn't like there aren't scrying spells that do the same thing." Only curiosity colored Dillon's even voice when he finally broke the humming silence. It had none of the voyeuristic avidity or exploitive greed Jordan remembered from growing up, the main reason her parents had home-schooled her. "Your secrecy seems rather extreme."

It probably was, from his perspective. Her parents had taught her to hide it to avoid unpleasantness. When she grew older, she'd continued to downplay it for her own purposes.

Jordan took a deep breath, then confessed her vanity: "I use it to hide my blindness."

"You do it quite well." Admiration warmed his voice. "How does it work—exactly?"

"My clairvoyance?" *Silly twit, what else could he be talking about?*

"Um-hmm." A low, heartening rumble, almost a purr.

His thumbs pressed into her hands, soothing the strain in the tendons. A gentle, reassuring massage. She couldn't help but respond.

"The same as others', I guess." From her readings, the few clairvoyants willing to face public curiosity described their common gift as operating in a similar manner. "I can see distant places I've never been to. Events happening right now. I just have to be interested or have some knowledge—usually an awareness of the people involved—to focus my sight."

"You use it to see around you." His voice remained neutral, as though merely clarifying matters for his own understanding.

"Usually when I'm in public places. It's very draining."

"So you've seen me?"

She nodded, heat spreading over her cheeks, a heavy drumbeat thundering in her ears. She'd seen all of him, in fact.

"Was that what you were afraid of? My reaction to your clairvoyance?" He was stroking her hand lightly, as though gentling a feral cat. "It's no problem." Soft lips caressed the back of her hand.

Jordan shivered at the heated desire his sensual gesture awoke. What would happen if she reciprocated?

Was she really contemplating such a risk?

She turned her wrist to trail her finger over Dillon's lips, tracing the sharp edges. She paused at the fullness and pressed inward, her heart racing as she teased him.

He hissed, his indrawn breath chilling her fingertip. Then he caught it between his teeth, holding it with delicate care, and drew it into his mouth. He sucked it, his welcome obvious even in her blindness. It was like he sucked something else, something lower, smaller, more intimate.

Jordan's nipples hardened, aching with desire. Her core clenched and throbbed, spreading heat throughout her limbs. She could feel her clitoris swelling with each pounding beat.

"Was that what you were afraid of?" Dillon repeated gently.

Jordan nodded, unable to trust her voice. It had been so long since she'd taken pleasure with a man, had been interested in one, she didn't care if it wasn't forever.

"It's alright." He pressed his lips to her wrist, right where her pulse fluttered, gave it a teasing lick and blew.

She caught her breath at the coolness, thrilled by his reception. Wanting to do some exploration of her own, she shifted to face him, wedging her hip against the backrest. She found his shoulder with her free hand. His linen jacket covered taut muscle that bunched under her fingers, hard and unyielding.

What would it feel like under her hand—skin to skin? What would he taste like? Jordan's lips throbbed at the thought of kissing him all over.

Dillon nibbled at the inside bend of her elbow. He dragged his somewhat bristly cheek along the thin skin of her upper arm, sending shivers of frothy delight up her spine.

She'd forgotten how much pleasure a highly motivated lover could bring. And all without kissing her lips, touching her breasts, or other more-intimate portions of her body!

Then he was nuzzling her collarbone, working his way up her neck with excruciating slowness. The scorching caress trailed wildfire in its wake, searing her nerves with pleasure.

Reckless desire burned through Jordan. He was taking too long. She wanted to taste him. Now. Without thought, she hooked her hand on his nape, pulled him up to where she wanted him.

Her aggression seemed to trigger something in Dillon, something wild. He took her mouth with desperate greed, his hand sweeping down her back, pulling her so close her breasts were hard against him.

She pulled back, startled by the hunger in his kiss. No man had ever kissed her so ravenously. Surely such response couldn't be because of her.

He licked her lobe and sucked the tender flesh.

Jordan gasped as desire swirled through her being. No man

had wanted her this much, had kindled such tempestuous need in her body.

"Kiss me back," he demanded against her lips, just before he returned to steal her breath. He claimed that and more, kissing her as if he needed her more than he needed air. It was better than she'd ever dreamed.

The very strength of his hunger was a seduction all on its own. The thought that this powerful man wanted her that much was heady knowledge, an aphrodisiac Jordan had no defense against.

Needing an anchor, she clutched his shoulders, spearing her fingers through his silky hair. Then casting her apprehensions to the wind, she gave herself up to his passion.

Dillon kissed her over and over, practically devouring her, barely giving her time to catch her breath. His heat surrounded her, filling her lungs with his musky male scent.

He had the hands of a man who did manual labor: hard and callused with rough ridges on his fingertips and the sides and bases of his palms; even his knuckles were rough. His hands stole under her blouse, rasping pleasantly on her bare skin.

The tight quarters of the car made movement difficult, but Jordan managed to get closer. She scaled the console with Dillon's eager assistance, and straddled his lap with her skirt bunched taut across the tops of her thighs and her rear perched on the steering wheel.

Pressed against her, Dillon's desire was unmistakable, his erection caressing her right where she craved it most.

She whimpered in approval.

Dillon groaned. "Not here." Despite his protest, his hips rose, grinding that hard ridge against her deliciously.

"What?" Wrapped in a blanket of passion, Jordan shook her head, confused by his objection. "Why?"

"We're too exposed."

She laughed at his answer. "Of course we're exposed," she retorted, rolling her pelvis against him to emphasize her point. "Ummm . . . and about to get more so," she added, fumbling for his belt. As wonderful as the friction was, she wanted bare skin with nothing between them.

Choking out a chuckle, he caught her hands. "Inside the house."

Door locks clicked open.

The darkness swung sideways as he pushed her head down. It spun around her, then steadied, leaving her draped over strong arms. A car door slammed shut, interrupting the night's insect chorus. Then she was bobbing in time to the muffled crunch of footsteps on gravel and then their whisper on the stone path.

Jordan looped her arms around Dillon's neck, pressing her breasts against his chest. "I can walk, you know," she informed him breathlessly, nuzzling his neck. His warm scent filled her nostrils, heady and addictive and all-male.

"Carrying you is faster," he explained before claiming her lips once more, letting her up for air only to unlock the door.

In his arms, Jordan lost track of where they were. Not that she cared, so long as he didn't stop kissing her. The way he took her mouth was probably illegal somewhere.

"Bedroom?" Dillon asked, between intoxicating kisses.

"Upstairs." She recaptured his wicked lips, craving their seductive expertise. "First door on the left."

While he navigated the steps, she attacked his buttons, baring his chest to her palms. The dusting of hair she discovered tickled, making her wish she could rub her face in it. "Hurry," she urged him, hoping he wouldn't change his mind.

He set her on the bed gently, then claimed her mouth once more, his tongue tantalizing her with its salacious mimicry of what they both wanted.

Jordan took immediate advantage of Dillon's free arms, pushing his jacket and shirt off his shoulders, leaving only a thin undershirt between her and thorough exploration of his chest. His musky scent was stronger now, an intoxicating drug that extirpated any lingering inhibitions.

They divested their clothes in a frenzied flurry of kisses and caresses. Dillon disposed of her bra with a deft twist of his fingers, freeing her breasts with minimal effort.

"Perfect," he growled, fondling her breasts and burying his face in her cleavage. His hands lit a bonfire of need in Jordan, a conflagration only he could quench. She was burning with need, so much so she could barely stand the torment.

"Uh-uh." She knew what she looked like and her modest bosom fell far short of voluptuous. Sliding her fingers over the broad slope of his shoulders, she kneaded his hard, muscled back, enjoying the feel of prime, virile male. "You're the one who's perfect."

He pushed her down on her back, then stopped. His harsh breathing gusted above her, the bed dipping under his weight all around her.

Reaching up, Jordan cupped Dillon's face. A muscle twitched in the corner of his jaw. "What's wrong?"

"I've dreamt of this so often, my control isn't what I'd like it to be." He swallowed audibly. "I'm trying not to fall all over you like a sex-starved maniac." Despite the strain in his voice, his cheek flexed, a dimple making itself known under her thumb. "Wouldn't want to scandalize the cat."

Surprise flickered at his confession, then was banished. He had to be teasing. While not nonexistent, her feminine assets surely couldn't compare to the women he'd known. Despite his arousal, he might remember that, might change his mind.

She had to push him past that point.

When Dillon finally leaned down, his arms shaking, setting the bed quaking with his restraint, Jordan stopped him. "Wait. I want to see you first."

—⊗⊗⊗—

She wanted to check out his body the way she had his face?

Violent frustration boiled through Dillon. After all this time wondering and fantasizing, he wanted her silken skin sliding against him, wanted her beneath him, sheathing his aching cock. "But you've *seen* me already. You said so." He winced at the fine tremor of desperation in his voice.

"That's different." Jordan frowned, clutching the fluffy duvet beneath her. "There's no sense of scale, of size or proportion."

He stilled, his blasted curiosity raising its head. "None at all?"

"It's not like touching you." She smoothed the bunched-up fabric under her hand. "I don't get any size context. Nothing that relates to me." She turned aside, the flush of desire tinting her pretty breasts starting to recede. "Nothing solid."

Damn. If he didn't give in, she might change her mind.

"I don't know if I can hold myself back that long."

Jordan reached up, cupping his jaw once more, her small hand satin-smooth against his cheek. "But will you try?"

How could he resist such a heartfelt request?

Dillon lowered himself beside her with a sigh, anticipating the torments of the wicked. Damned if he'd tell Lantis about this; it would bid fair to shatter his friend's vaunted control. He could do without Lantis's laughter burning his ears.

"Go ahead." His cock throbbed, protesting the delay.

She scrambled to her knees, eagerness in every line of her body, her high breasts bobbing impudently in his direct line of sight. "Hands to yourself, okay?"

He held back a groan, wondering if Jordan was using her clairvoyance and was watching his face at this very moment. "Right." He took a deep breath to settle his control, the honeyed fragrance of the wisteria outside the window filling his lungs, then gripped the curlicues of her headboard. The cool metal bit into his palms, an aid to curb his hunger. "Okay."

It was even worse than he anticipated.

That same butterfly touch she'd used to explore his face was even more arousing on his body, exceeding his wildest fantasies. She learned his body at her leisure, gliding over his chest and belly, around and around his nipples, the sensitive skin under his arms, leaving fire in her wake. She nuzzled him everywhere, breathing him in and tasting him with a pert tongue that flicked and teased but not where he wanted it most.

Sweat rolled down Dillon's neck as he fought down a moan. His back arched, nearly coming off the bed. His heart pounded like a war drum from her attentions, his hard-on swelling more than he'd have thought possible. "Satisfied?"

"Uh-uh." Jordan shook her head, then shifted to his feet. She explored his body, using hands and mouth, working her way up. Slowly. Nothing in his training had prepared him for such sensual torment.

Dillon's hips jerked as her shaggy locks brushed the hairs on his inner thighs, sending pleasure arcing through his nerves. And then she was bent over him, her breath warming his cock with phantom caresses.

Metal squealed above him.

His muscles clenched with anticipation and incandescent desire. He stared, breathless with hunger, as Jordan's lips hovered over his cock. Her hands rose—torturously slow—playing with his balls in their sac tucked up tight against his groin. His lungs seized when she finally touched him, traced his length with excruciating slowness, over and over, leaving no patch of skin untouched. It was like she was sculpting his body with her fingers, transforming every aching bit into rigid, unyielding stone. She circled his shaft and squeezed it lightly. Fire bombs went off in his cock, burning away his control.

"Ooooh." Jordan's fingers toyed with its head, grazing the sensitive crown. "You feel so good."

Dillon moaned. He wanted to demand she kiss him, take him into her mouth and suck him. Only the fear he'd scare her off kept the order unvoiced.

She bent lower, so low it looked like he needed only to roll his hips to feel her soft lips on him. Her breath was an ephemeral caress that taunted him with carnal possibilities.

Struggling for control, Dillon shut his eyes against the heart-stopping picture she made. He had to divert his mind, think of something else while Jordan fed her curiosity.

Scrying. His mind leapt on the topic gratefully. It should be simple enough, even with his body screaming for relief. It was one of his specialties as a mage, after all. He tried to name the various spells that fell within its scope. *Remote viewing. Tracing. Retro—*

Raw pleasure streaked up his spine and detonated in his brain. *Shit!* He wrenched at the headboard, wrought iron creaking as stars burst behind his eyelids. And still she lingered over his cock, stroking and petting him.

How much longer could he last?

Jordan's hands on his face made him open his eyes. "Thank you," she whispered against his lips.

"All done?" Dillon released the headboard slowly, his fingers nearly frozen around the metalwork, unable to believe she was finally satisfied with her exploration, conscious of how his body trembled like a callow youth's.

Placing his hands over hers, he pressed hungry kisses on her slender fingers, cherishing each graceful, unadorned length in turn, using the time to shore up his threadbare control.

Unadorned! The absence of jewelry registered in his mind.

"Do you have a bloodstone ring?" The piece was the most common form of contraception available to modern women.

"Oh." Jordan took a while to answer. He hoped that merely meant she'd been caught up in passion, not that she didn't have one. "In the nightstand. I haven't needed it in . . . in months."

Dillon's heart missed a beat at her answer. *Months?* The spell on the ring could have faded by now; it needed regular recharging. "You haven't been using it?"

"It snags on the psyprinter," she explained absently, tracing her fingers along his jaw.

So it probably hadn't been recharged. Still, perhaps enough power remained for the contraceptive spell to be functional. "Just hang on." He didn't know if he meant Jordan or himself.

As he opened the drawer, Jordan cuddled against his back, rubbing her face against his shoulders like an affectionate cat. Her naughty fingers fluttered up his ribs playfully, stealing his breath.

Luckily for his sanity, Dillon immediately found the dark green ring with its flecks of red. He closed his fingers around it, trying to clear his mind enough to probe the spell.

She undulated her body, her hard nipples searing his skin like hot pokers.

He swore under his breath, his cock throbbing, hard and heavy. When Jordan gave in to passion, she gave it everything she had. But he didn't dare ask her to pull back, to give him room to work magic lest she change her mind.

She planted stinging kisses along his nape, kisses that exploded in his balls.

Groaning, he bent his neck to give her more access, his fingers driving the ring into his palm. He had to— Had to—

He struggled for control, tried to free a small corner of his mind. Enough to sense . . . No magic.

Before he could assimilate the meaning of its absence, Jordan reached around him, her hand landing on his groin then swiftly moving inward. She found his cock and balls in quick succession. Her fingers danced over him, did something wickedly sensational.

Dillon nearly swallowed his tongue as it conjured a fireball of unadulterated pleasure. *Damn it, no!* He arched against Jordan, clenching his muscles, resisting the siren song of rapture. He couldn't spill now. He wanted the first time to be inside her. But not without protection. Without the contraceptive spell on the ring, he risked getting Jordan pregnant. He couldn't do that to her.

"You're so thick," Jordan growled smugly, nibbling on his ear. "I want you inside me. Now."

He shuddered as vehement need clawed at his belly, nearly howling with desperation. So did he.

Suddenly remembering his fallback plan, Dillon fumbled for his pants, yanking them from under a brooding Timothy. Ignoring the cat, he ransacked the pockets, rooting through the oddments he'd thought for some inexplicable reason to be necessary. He was only interested in one.

Where the hell is it? He'd brought a bloodstone ring, but it wasn't sized for Jordan. Still, it might work.

He panted as Jordan milked him, pre-come trickling down his shaft. She was shredding his control like so much cotton candy, melting it with the heat of her hands.

The ring finally rolled out of the mess into his palm. It was somewhat larger than Jordan's with a wider band. He'd thought to transfer the spell, but the way Jordan was squirming against him, stroking him with her hands and body, there was no way in hell he'd be able to concentrate.

Her finger pressed on a spot just below the crown of his cock, setting off another jolt of fiery pleasure.

He moaned, long and low. How the hell did she know what drove him out of his mind?

Dropping the smaller ring, Dillon caught her hand before she could mount another assault on his sanity. "Does this fit?"

It was too small for her ring finger yet too big for her pinkie, almost falling off when Jordan relaxed her hand. Her other hand was no better. That wouldn't work. The ring had to be in snug contact with her skin for its spell to take effect.

Desperately, he hooked her ankle, spilling her onto her back, spreading her thighs in a distracting display of the dark pink petals of her dewy sex.

"What—?"

Trapping her foot against his chest, he tried the ring on her little toe. A perfect fit. He tested its grip, just to be sure. It didn't slip at all.

"Yes!" He pressed his lips to her arch, inordinate relief flooding his soul. Payback could wait. He wanted, needed to be inside Jordan.

Grabbing her hips, he sheathed himself to the hilt in a single, smooth thrust.

Jordan arched beneath him with a mewl of wordless delight. She reached for him as he pulled out, drawing him back insistently, her fingers digging into his ass.

Dillon gasped at her slick, heated welcome, the snug caress surrounding his cock. His control snapped. All thoughts of care, of finesse, of gentleness for this first time, fled his mind as he surrendered to the primal beat thundering through his veins. With a harsh cry, he lunged at Jordan, pounding into her with short, hard strokes.

Panting softly, she tossed her head on the pillows. "More!" Her legs locked around his hips, holding him close.

The pressure in his balls mounted, demanding release, rising with each thrust. He wouldn't last much longer. Rapture beckoned. He hungered for it, craved it with every inch of his being. He'd go slowly next time, be gentle next time. Right now, he had to have relief.

Needing to ensure Jordan's pleasure, Dillon sought her clit. "Now. Come, now."

She moaned when he found her little shaft and stroked it. Her sheath convulsed around his cock, sparking his own orgasm.

He howled in carnal triumph. Rapture boiled up from his swollen, aching balls in a blinding explosion of pure pleasure. His cock jerked with each ballistic spasm, a red-hot delight long overdue.

CHAPTER SEVEN

A restless caress pulled Dillon from the depths of satiation, woke him enough to become aware of a weight on his chest. He slitted his eyes open to inky blackness. The weight merged with a deep rumble, like a powerful motor idling in readiness.

Nothing in the night triggered any of his alarms. The normal nocturnal sounds were interrupted only by a pair of mating owls singing a duet and the cackle of a gecko in the garden. Whispering leaves muffled the distant noise of vehicular traffic. Even the neighbors were quiet.

When no threat manifested, he gathered his will and focused it on his wand, lying buried among hastily discarded clothing. The ensuing light startled the heavy presence on top of him, earning him a warning prickle from four sets of sharp claws.

Timothy gave him a brooding stare, silhouetted against the floating ball of magelight. When Jordan grumbled, sliding her soft thigh up Dillon's hips, the cat glanced at her then resumed glowering at Dillon, silently communicating his disapproval of the current state of affairs.

Too bad. Dillon smirked back. *Get used to it.*

Then Jordan cried out, her arms tightening around Dillon, her nails digging into his side.

Timothy shifted quickly, crouching over Jordan to chirp in concern. He stretched a white paw out to pat her cheek, apparently trying to soothe her or to rouse her from sleep.

Jordan shook her head, her eyes screwed shut. She moaned, a terrified sound that had nothing to do with passion.

A nightmare?

Dillon added his efforts to Timothy's. Crooning wordlessly, he stroked her back, gliding his hand over skin made familiar by long, sensual hours of lovemaking.

Gradually, Jordan succumbed to their reassurances, the nameless horror releasing her dreaming mind. Between piteous whimpers, the tension in her body melted away until she slept deeply, her breathing regular and easy, snuggled against Dillon's chest.

With a weary sigh, Timothy returned to his previous posture on Dillon's chest, his eyes closing as though standing down from long duty.

"So you guard her sleep, do you?"

At Dillon's words, Timothy opened his eyes, his ears canted forward, then blinked slowly as if in answer.

Since that was the case, Dillon decided he wouldn't insist the cat change locations. "Now there's two of us." He ventured a rub of Timothy's ears.

The large cat stared at him in silence for a few moments, then purred, dropping his head on top of his paws.

Dillon hoped that meant acceptance, if not approval. "No claws," he warned, just to be on the safe side.

With typical feline hauteur, Timothy looked away, his plumy

tail flirting along Dillon's ribs. But he did fold his front legs, taking the pads off Dillon's chest.

Satisfied with that concession, Dillon tucked Jordan against his chest and went back to sleep. He needed to recoup his strength after the night's excesses.

Jordan woke slowly, a hard, warm pillow lifting her head with gentle regularity like waves on a sandy beach. Crisp hairs met her curious fingers, not the usual soft fur of her pet. For countless heartbeats, she lay baffled, confounded by Timothy's absence. Then the scent of sex and warm, delicious male prodded her memory, recalling to mind last night's strenuous activities.

Dillon.

Smiling, Jordan stretched cautiously, her body heavy with sensual lethargy, her muscles rejoicing in the unaccustomed aches. Her breath caught as her mound rubbed against a hard, muscular thigh, her clitoris rousing with a demanding throb.

Velvety flesh prodded her arm in a restrained demand for attention.

"Hmmm," she purred, reaching down to pet Dillon's importunate member. "G'morning."

It quivered, swelling upward against her palm as though begging for more. She'd wondered what he tasted like but refrained from checking earlier, for fear of revealing the true purpose of her exploration. Perhaps now she could satisfy her curiosity. She nearly squirmed as heat kindled in her belly, desire anointing her labia with cream.

"I guess you're awake." Jordan traced his thickness, marveling at his girth. If Dillon's erection was any indication, today promised to be just as energetic as last night. Heat swirled in her belly, her core clenching with hungry anticipation. "Or you soon will be."

Dillon chuckled, his chest quaking beneath her cheek and breast. "I don't think there could be any doubt." His arm flexed beneath her. A hot, rough hand caressed her back in one broad stroke, then squeezed one of her buttocks. "An exceptionally good morning to you, too."

She twisted around to wrap her fingers around him, her thumb coming to rest on a gentle dip in his broad head that felt as though it was formed especially for her. She smiled at the texture, like a firm peach, ripe for the eating. The image that brought to mind had heat pooling in her belly.

"What are you doing?" he asked, when she rolled her thumb.

Jordan giggled in lighthearted discovery. "It's like a joystick," she remarked, applying steady pressure on the velvety hollow.

He cursed under his breath, laughter leavening his plaint as his penis pulsed in her grip. "Glad you think so." His hand glided off her backside, questing lower.

She held her breath as he probed between her cheeks and discovered her wetness.

His fingers strummed her sex in a lazy rhythm, sending devilish tingles of delight skipping through her. "You going to play games with it?"

Grinning, Jordan squeezed him again. His penis filled her hand so perfectly she could hold him like this for hours. "I haven't made up my mind yet."

"It's the weekend. We could always—"

A synthesized female voice interrupted Dillon, announcing "Monday" and a time and date nearly a year past. He straightened suddenly in Jordan's arms, obviously startled. Then—

"I'm home, Loverboy! Call me." The unmistakably male baritone fairly dripped with sensuality, the speaker completely confident of recognition and his reception.

And why wouldn't he be? Even Jordan could identify John Atlantis just from those five words despite the unfamiliar intimacy in the delivery.

The artificial voice added: "End of saved messages."

Jordan stiffened at the blatant reminder of Dillon's dangerous job. Knowing what she knew about his troubleshooting, the coded message was unmistakable.

"Timothy," Dillon growled, "give me that." His body jerked, then he was leaning over her, reaching toward the nightstand. "It was just the cat playing with my cell phone."

"*Loverboy?*" Jordan repeated, drawing away even as her arms broke out in gooseflesh at the loss of his heat. Suddenly feeling awkward lying naked beneath his big body, she groped for the duvet to cover herself. "That was—"

"It was whimsy. Just a— A bit of nostalgia!" he explained, a rationale belied by a peculiar undercurrent in his voice. He pulled her into his hard embrace, his hands kneading her stiff shoulders. "Ignore it."

At least he didn't pretend she'd misheard. She noticed Dillon didn't say it was a joke, even though it would have been the obvious excuse.

However, try as she might, Jordan didn't think she could forget it, just like that. She needed time out of bed, without sex and passion fogging her brain, to regain her equilibrium.

Timothy landed on the bed beside her, mewing for attention as he stropped his large body against her arm. Her pet was probably hungry; she and Dillon had stayed up all hours making love and must have slept late.

Grateful for an excuse to escape the room, Jordan scooped Timothy up in her arms. "Whoops! Have to feed the cat." She stretched her lips in a parody of polite amusement as she escaped the confines of the duvet and Dillon's oh-so-tempting scent. "What do you want for breakfast?"

Her feet snagged on a slew of fabric on the floor, making her stagger. Her heel landed on something hard with an uneven surface that rolled away as she caught her balance.

Dillon said nothing for a long moment, long enough that she

feared he'd ignore her question and insist on discussing their situation—affaire or whatever it was—right then and there.

"Whatever you're having is fine."

She exhaled slowly in relief. "It should be ready in ten minutes." Dropping Timothy to the floor, she grabbed her robe and made her getaway before he changed his mind.

Dillon stared at the empty door long after Jordan had fled the room. He wanted to rush after her and convince her—somehow—that the message didn't mean what it sounded like. The very lack of control implicit in his urgency held him back: going off half-cocked was likely to get him killed in most situations. Not that "half-cocked" accurately described his current condition.

Sighing, he decided to shower and exorcise his demons.

And what would he have said? That he was bisexual? *That would make a great rumor!* And definitely something he didn't want getting back to Kiera. Not when it involved Lantis. Hopefully, it wouldn't even occur to Jordan. A joke? Why did he have it saved, kept it saved for nearly a year? Business?

Turning on the shower, he grunted in disgust at the sentimentality that made him save that message. Soaping himself with Jordan's cherry-scented shower gel only encouraged his hard-on, to his frustration.

His internal argument continued unabated in his head. *That answer would only have given rise to more questions.* What sort of business required such subterfuge? How was Lantis involved? What exactly was Dillon's job? And *that* was the one thing he couldn't tell her.

Stepping under the spray of cold water, he gritted his teeth, dissatisfied with his conclusion. He'd have to leave it at whimsy and hope she accepted that explanation. Belaboring the point would make her wonder what he was hiding.

Normally, he didn't sweat the details. What did it matter when

it was just a fling, a diversion until he returned to the serious business of black ops? It was just sex, after all.

But what he had with Jordan felt different, not merely sex. It
was more. Sometime in the past two weeks, she'd gotten through
his seasoned defenses and claimed a place for herself. One of
friendship, at the very least.

And just because he'd had her, had taken his release in her
body—several times—last night didn't mean he was done. Whatever drew him to her was still there, calling to him like a beckon-
ing flame. His desires were still focused on Jordan. He couldn't
leave her now, even if he wanted to.

Dillon found himself wondering if they could sustain their
relationship over the long term—past his current R&R. Even as
he scoffed at the possibility, he couldn't help but remember that
Rio seemed to have managed it with his Amazon lady. Perhaps the
odds weren't so bad.

Jordan filled Timothy's bowl, then got fruit from the refrigerator
for washing. Every action was automatic; she could have done
them in her sleep. Her attention was taken up by something—
rather, someone—altogether different.

*Dillon was soaping himself in brisk, efficient strokes, the wash-
cloth clinging to every inch of muscled glory like an amorous snake.*
Not that she blamed it; who wouldn't want a taste of such prime
male flesh? Such rampant male flesh. *His erection swayed like a
flagpole in high winds, bobbing in time to Dillon's movements.*

She could kick herself for turning her back on his offer. If she
hadn't gotten cold feet at the last second, she could have been tasting him at that very moment, instead of spying on him like a
voyeur.

*His arousal subsided only gradually, his sex remaining tantaliz-
ingly thick as it hung between his thighs.* Jordan's sigh was heavy
with regret. She couldn't forget how he'd felt in her hands, warm

and sleek, firm and perfect. Were her doubts worth losing that? Why make a fuss when he would soon leave?

"I'm blowing things out of proportion, aren't I, Tim?"

Her pet flicked his tail against her calf, but made no other response; gobbling sounds from his direction said the cat was focused on filling his belly.

Frowning at his ambiguous reply, Jordan concentrated on preparing breakfast. Perhaps if she ignored what happened, Dillon would, too?

She set the table, hoping for the best. It wasn't as if she could dictate his actions, after all. She'd just have to take things as they came.

"This cat seems to've developed a phone fixation."

Dillon's disgruntled conversational sally caught Jordan off guard as she groped for the carton of orange juice in the refrigerator. "What?" She opened herself to her clairvoyance, seeking clarification.

Bare-chested, his hair damp from his shower, Dillon stood at the doorway with Timothy under one arm, his other hand busy with his cell phone. Her pet must have returned to the bedroom while she was busy.

Dangling in the air, the cat stared at the phone as though it were a new toy, following its disappearance into Dillon's pocket with fascinated eyes. When Dillon dropped him to the floor, Timothy rose on his hind legs to bat at the hidden phone.

"Oh, no!" Jordan laughed, her tension evaporating, banished like a terminated spell. "Tim, stop that. Go finish eating."

"Milk, too?" Dillon relieved her of the orange juice.

"Ah, yes," she answered in bemusement, unaccustomed as she was to male company so early in the morning. Happily, he seemed willing to ignore their previous awkwardness.

He helped her get the rest of breakfast on the table and seated her before taking his place at her right, setting his phone beside his plate.

Jordan's stomach rumbled loudly as she poured milk over her whole-grain cereal. She blushed as she added cinnamon sugar to the flakes, hoping Dillon hadn't heard the sound.

"I guess Timothy wasn't the only one starving."

"Uh-huh." Jordan started eating to avoid having to make conversation. It was probably a good thing they'd been interrupted earlier. How embarrassing it would have been if her stomach had growled in the middle of lovemaking.

She bit into a pear, supremely conscious of Dillon watching her, his dark eyes hooded. She shivered, remembering the intensity he'd brought to her bed last night and the rapture he'd inflicted on her senses.

Her heightened awareness extended to the air she breathed. Perhaps it had been a mistake to set their places side by side at the table. Every inhalation brought her a whiff of his male scent mixed in with the cherry fragrance of her shower gel. It wasn't Dillon's usual citrus flavor, but the mixture with its subtext of intimacy did strange things to Jordan's insides.

"Are you using your clairvoyance right now?"

Jordan blinked as she set her glass down. "Yes, why?"

"I'm wondering what you were seeing." His gaze dropped. "You've turned an interesting shade of pink."

What could he—? Her vision revealed the lapels of her silk robe gaping open in an improper display of assets, one pouting nipple nearly exposed.

For a brazen split second, she sat unmoving, wondering if he found her breasts too small. Then she came back to her senses and twitched her robe to a semblance of decency. "Sorry," she muttered, retying her sash.

"Don't mind me. I'm not complaining." A smile hovering on his lips, Dillon continued to eye her while they ate, perhaps hoping for another peek. You'd think he hadn't seen all of her last night . . . and done much more!

A creeping wave of white beside Dillon's elbow distracted her before she could comment. Two large paws curved over the table's edge, groping blindly. Timothy was apparently on a stealthy quest for Dillon's cell phone.

Sneak attack at breakfast! Jordan pressed her fist to her mouth to contain a snicker at her pet's cunning approach.

Dillon evinced no reaction. He had to be pretending ignorance, considering her obvious amusement, but he carried on as if nothing unusual was happening. Only when Timothy looked to succeed did he act, and only to transfer his phone to the other side of his plate.

"You're deliberately teasing him."

"Speaking from experience?" There was a hint of a challenge in his voice.

Experience? Jordan frowned. "What do you mean?"

Dillon looked at her over his glass as he finished his juice, his gaze dipping, then returning to her face. "You're doing it again."

Her robe had drooped open once more. Jordan fingered the lapel, an electric frisson of breathless awareness darting up her spine. "Like what you see?"

"You know I do." He touched the back of her hand lightly, a fleeting caress more imagined than felt. He slid his chair toward her, then his arm stole around her, his hand coming to rest on her hip. "But is this what you want?" After last night, he still wanted her.

Reassured by the reminder of Dillon's desire, Jordan allowed herself to settle against him, to savor his male scent enfolding her. She couldn't deny her desire, even if they had only now. "Uh-huh," she answered, ignoring a heavy *thud*.

With a warble of triumph, Timothy pounced on the phone.

Dillon scooped it up at the last moment. "Find another one. This one's mine."

Then he pressed a kiss behind Jordan's ear. "Shall we?" he whispered, an invitation she couldn't refuse.

CHAPTER EIGHT

A whimper of fear and loathing woke Dillon just before a heavy load landed on his chest. "Oof!" He counterattacked reflexively, driving his fist at the mass on top of him. Only the realization of where he was made him pull his punch short and hurriedly cast a magelight.

The bright rays of his spell revealed his furry assailant crouched over Jordan. Timothy had his back to Dillon, either ignorant of his peril or supremely confident of his ability to defend himself, Dillon couldn't tell which.

Whimpering again, Jordan clutched at the sheets. She tossed her head, writhing and twisting until the beddings wrapped around her and Dillon like a bandage.

"Easy, now," Dillon crooned, wondering what could be tormenting her. He stroked her back, hoping she somehow sensed she was among friends.

Batting her cheek, Timothy whined, sounding like he was begging Jordan to wake up. His distress was unmistakable with his ears back, flat against his skull, and his fur puffed up, easily doubling his apparent size.

This time Dillon and Timothy couldn't banish her nightmare despite their best efforts. Jordan continued to moan like a lost soul, her voice filled with agony and dread. Timothy finally butted her chin, mewling loud enough that he woke her.

Panting heavily, Jordan wrapped her arms around the cat, unalloyed horror etched across her pale face. When Dillon drew her into his embrace, she startled. Only the sheets wound around them kept her from falling off the bed.

He murmured wordless nonsense as he rocked her, knowing that in the depths of her fright it was the tone of voice that mattered, the reminder that she wasn't alone.

It took a while before Jordan's shuddering breath evened out. Every so often she flinched, possibly from some lingering reminder of her bad dream. She buried her face in Timothy's fur as though trying to hide.

Dillon frowned. It didn't look like she was going back to sleep anytime soon, as wound up as she was. He had to do something to help. "You seem to be getting nightmares frequently," he observed, hoping she'd confide in him.

Two nights in a row suggested deep-seated worries. But banishing Jordan's nightmares might be as simple as having her share her fears, bringing them out into the light.

"How did you know?" The plaintive question told him more than anything that her disturbed sleep wasn't an unusual occurrence.

"You had one last night. Timothy seemed to know what to do." Dillon kept his voice low and even. Undemanding. Conducive to confidences. "Want to talk about it? Maybe if you tell me, it won't feel so scary."

Night sounds filled the silence hovering between them: a train chugging in the distance; a dog barking fitfully; wind rustled the trees, bringing a fresh whiff of honey. Even the cat knew to keep quiet, his purring becoming almost subliminal.

Then Jordan sighed, deep and heartfelt. "They've been coming more often lately. Ever since I found those gloves."

Dillon stared down at her tousled head, trying to make sense of her statement as she snuggled against him. He ignored Timothy crawling over his chest, and Jordan's soft breasts pressed to his side, while he wrestled with her logic. "What do gloves have to do with your nightmares?"

Grimacing, she drew random patterns on his pecs. Her lashes fluttered, possibly reflecting some internal debate.

Dillon held himself to patience, even though instinct argued that Jordan was hiding something from him. Something that might be more important than her sight.

She's a private woman. Stroking her back, he remembered how much difficulty she'd had in disclosing her clairvoyance. Insisting on an answer would only drive her into silence.

She dropped her head to his chest, nuzzling him as if drawing comfort from the contact. "I'm not just clairvoyant," she finally said, her words muffled. "I'm also psychometric."

He blinked. From his studies, he knew psychometry was similar to a retrospection, except it was an innate talent—one of perception, much like clairvoyance—not a spell. Now that he thought about it, he shouldn't have been surprised her gift involved different ways of seeing. Certainly his strength in scrying included all of its many forms. "And something about these gloves you found is giving you nightmares?"

She nodded, her arms tight around his waist, her hands restless. "When I touched them, there was so much *blood.*" She infused such horror in the last word the hairs on Dillon's nape prickled. "I think—" She exhaled softly, then continued in a whisper, "I think they were used in a murder."

"Blood," he echoed, keeping his voice neutral. He didn't have the customary response to the body fluid, having become inured to the sight of it in his line of work.

Jordan shifted in his arms. "Not real blood. I see blood. It's dark. And someone"—she gulped audibly—"someone's being stabbed. And blood spattering everywhere." Her hands jerked into fists against his ribs.

Dillon stroked her back. "That's enough to give anyone nightmares," he conceded. His mind immediately leapt to figuring out a way to bring the situation to official attention without exposing Jordan to unwanted publicity. He didn't doubt what she'd seen was real, not when she had such a strong reaction. "Any details we can give the cops?"

She shook her head, her shoulders rigid. "Not enough to make even a psyprint." She buried her face against his chest. "It's horrible. I can't stand it for long."

After her unnerving nightmare, Jordan didn't think she'd be able to go back to sleep but Dillon convinced her otherwise. His solid strength and tender caresses soothed her tension. Combined with Timothy's purrs, they were enough to relax her defenses. It also didn't hurt that her body was still tired from lovemaking. Sleep crept up on her before she realized it approached.

The dream began innocuously enough.

A specialty ice cream parlor, like one of the many places Dillon had brought her to over the past several days to gratify her senses with some new cuisine or a different taste.

He insisted she try all the flavors, one scoop of each. The sun warmed their shoulders as he tempted her with "just one more," brushing cold sweetness across her lips. It seemed so perfect, like nothing could go wrong. She laughed up at him, licking her lips.

Then it was dark. And the taste on her lips was blood.

A glint in the darkness. Moonlight on steel. A narrow knife—familiar from her recent visions—upraised behind her lover.

Jordan opened her mouth to shout, to warn him. Her throat seized. Her voice failed her. Try though she might, nothing would come out. Her body was stone, heavy and inert. She struggled but couldn't move her arms, not even a twitch. Couldn't breathe to scream.

Dillon grinned at her, all unwitting.

The blade descended with shocking swiftness.

Thud. Thud. Thud!

Hot blood splashed her face. Trickled into her mouth.

NOOOOOOOOOO—

"—Oh!" Jordan jackknifed awake, her heart pounding loud enough to wake the dead.

Timothy wailed softly as he slid off her chest, dragging the bedcovers down with him.

Strong arms engulfed her in living heat as she sat gasping for breath, cold and shaking, her teeth chattering like dry leaves in an autumn wind. Tears dripped off her chin. *No!*

"Shhh. It's alright. Whatever it is, is gone. Everything's fine," Dillon murmured, stroking slow circles on her back through her shudders.

Mewling in confusion, Timothy pressed in, licking her damp cheeks.

It couldn't come true. She'd never been precognitive. It was just a dream. Clutching at Dillon, at the proof of his strength, she repeated that to herself, chanting it in her mind like an invocation. *Just a dream. Just a dream.*

"Hey, come on," Dillon whispered in her ear, his warm breath cutting through the ice encasing her. "Easy, now. You're scaring the cat."

Swallowing tears, Jordan laughed brokenly at his attempt to make light of her fears.

"You had another nightmare." He brushed a quick kiss on her lobe, his firm lips a gentle reminder of life. "Same one?"

"I dreamed," she sobbed, pressing her fists against his back and holding him close. "The murderer. Stabbing—" *You.* She couldn't finish, couldn't say it. Words would give it power. Make it real. Her mind said her fears were baseless, but her heart screamed she couldn't take the risk.

Jordan shook her head wildly, burrowing into Dillon's embrace, filling her lungs with his hot male scent.

———— ∞∞∞ ————

"Shhh. It's all right," Dillon repeated softly, hoping his reassurance helped. He tightened his embrace, frowning at the clamminess of her skin. The nightmare must have been worse than the previous one.

"I'm s-s-so co-cold." Jordan's tremulous whisper was barely audible, uttered against his neck.

Dillon snatched Timothy up from between them, draping the startled cat over her back like a living fur coat.

Timothy squeaked in protest, but as much as the cat might want to comfort Jordan, he'd serve her better as a warmer.

"Stay there," Dillon ordered Jordan's pet, keeping a hand on him to keep him in place.

With his other hand, Dillon chafed every inch of bare skin he could reach. Her intense reaction worried him, especially since he probably wouldn't be with her in coming nights. "I don't like how often you're getting these nightmares."

She sighed, resting her forehead on his chest. "It's just stress."

"I know Timothy'll be here for you, but I'd feel better if you could call me."

The cat's ears swiveled forward, as though recognizing his name. He continued to glare at Dillon, his blue eyes narrowed to outraged slits in their black mask, his muscles quivering under Dillon's hand.

"You won't—?" Jordan's arms tightened around Dillon, her nails digging into his back.

He brushed his lips over her short locks. "I don't think you'd like Dan to find me in your bed."

"That would be too awkward for words," she agreed with a reluctant laugh. She seemed somewhat recovered; at least her hands were no longer so cold.

"How about if I program my cell phone into your speed-dial? That way I'm just two buttons away. How's that sound?"

"Better than nothing." She closed her eyes, the bruised skin beneath them sending a twinge of concern through Dillon.

He released Timothy, allowing the whining cat to lick Jordan's face and reassure himself of her well-being while throwing indignant looks at Dillon.

Though he grimaced at her response, Dillon had to agree. Having her call him after a nightmare was a stopgap measure, more than anything, and he didn't like it any more than Jordan did. But it gave him a feeling of control to be doing something, rather than just acknowledging the problem. "I'll do the same to the phones downstairs tomorrow," he promised, sitting up.

Moving Timothy to one side, Dillon suited action to words, entering his number into the nightstand phone's unused directory under the cat's suspicious gaze. "Next time you want to call me, just pick up the handset and press Memory, then One. It doesn't have to be a nightmare. Call me anytime."

Come morning he intended to see if they could learn more about these horror-ridden gloves. Something had to be done about her nightmares.

Lying on the ottoman, the gloves looked innocuous, their black leather a stark contrast to the cream brushed-velvet upholstery. Nothing about the gloves suggested a savage history that could inflict horrific nightmares: no obvious blood stains, no tears, no metal studs. Just simple opera gloves, probably made from lambskin. Fashionable, not just practical, with cuffs that would reach way past the elbow. Designed for women, but they could probably be worn by a man with narrow hands and thin arms.

Kneeling on the carpet, Dillon turned the gloves over, using a silk handkerchief he kept on hand for such magical emergencies to insulate the leather from his hand. "Where did you find them?"

"That's the strangest part: at the gallery. The bar stool I sat on? You know, when we had wine?" Seated on the couch, Jordan shrugged, her restless hands combing through Timothy's belly fur, clearly uncomfortable with having the gloves out in the open.

The purring cat was reveling in her attention, lying spread-eagled, as limp and boneless as a sweat-soaked towel. He hadn't been that way at first, when Jordan took out the gloves from her purse, glaring at them and hissing as if they were vicious rats threatening his territory. He'd calmed down only after it was made clear to him that Dillon, not Jordan, would be the one handling them. Even now, sprawled like a minor tussock of rumbling fluff on his mistress's lap, he kept a cautious watch on the black leather from the corner of a pleasure-slitted blue eye.

Ignoring the incongruous picture Timothy made, Dillon winced inwardly at the reference to the wine. What an unfortunate association! No wonder she'd seemed disconcerted when he'd presented her with the bottle.

He shook off that line of thought as irrelevant. What mattered was where she'd found the gloves. He'd noticed many at the exhibit wearing gloves, but none of such length. Opera gloves would have drawn his attention—provided their owner had worn them with short sleeves or less, as was proper—if only because current fashion would have made them an unusual sight.

"Who was at the exhibit? Do you remember anyone in particular?" Dillon asked, to distract Jordan while he continued his inspection.

The other sides of the gloves were nearly as flawless: soft, light leather with fine stitching, no signs of wear, no cracks, no grime and no hint of dried blood, not even in the seams and creases.

Well-made and well-maintained. Marred only by an arc of ragged puncture marks from Timothy's claws.

Dillon whistled silently at the sight of the latter. The cat had obviously meant business!

Jordan's hands stilled as amusement spilled across her face, easing the lines of tension between her brows. "You." She gave him a strained but bashful grin. "You kind of put everyone else in the shade."

"Really now?" He grinned back with raised brows; she'd hidden her reaction quite well. He dragged his mind back to business with the promise to explore that topic in depth at a later date. "Anyone else?"

"Shanna, of course. John Atlantis and his wife." Jordan resumed stroking Timothy after the cat cuffed her hand in complaint. "Oh! There was a persistent woman who wanted a portrait done. And that snotty art critic from the *Times*." She waved a hand in dismissal. "I'm not really good with names."

Shifting his weight to sit on his heels, Dillon rested his forearm on the ottoman and propped his chin on his wrist. Up close, he still didn't see anything suspicious.

Finally conceding the physical examination to be a dead end, he directed his gaze across the ottoman at Jordan. "What do you remember from your visions?"

Frowning, she bent her head, her eyes troubled. She transferred her attentions to an ash-gray cushion, worrying a tassel while she gave some thought to her answer. Timothy batted the dancing ornament as though it was a familiar game.

"A knife." Her lips quivered before she compressed them, their corners turning down and white. "Blood on the floor and walls. A—" She gulped audibly, her cheeks paling. "I think there was a face." Her fingers dug into corduroy.

Dillon skirted the ottoman to sit in front of her. "Shhh, it's okay," he murmured, patting her hands. At an imperious look from Timothy, he got her to release the cushion and resume belly rubbing duty since she clearly took comfort from it.

The furry hedonist simply sighed and accepted it as his due, blanketing Jordan's lap like a fluffy throw.

"We can find out more. If you're up to it."

Jordan hunched her shoulders. "What do you have in mind?"

"You have to distance yourself from the vision. Control your reaction to it."

"How?"

"You hyperventilate when you're scared. Control that, and you've taken the first step." Easy to say, but Dillon knew how difficult it could be, especially when adrenaline ran high. "I want you to try this exercise: take a deep breath and hold it for a count of three, and then slowly exhale in four counts."

"Three then four?" Her hands slowed in their strokes over Timothy's belly.

"Uh-huh. That's to keep your mind on the count." He studied her face, checking her receptiveness to the idea.

Despite her uncertainty, Jordan seemed intrigued. Her jaw wasn't clenched as much, the furrows of her brow had eased and her lips were rounded, rather than pursed.

"Okay?"

She bobbed her head.

"Breathe in and two and three, then breathe out and two and three and four. Again." He talked her through the exercise a few more times, until she achieved a meditative calm, before he proposed the next step. "Now that you've gotten it. How about trying to get more details from the gloves?" That was the purpose of the whole exercise after all.

Jordan's body stiffened, the muscles of her arms suddenly knife-taut under his hands. "Now?"

He kneaded her forearms, trying to get them to return to their earlier pliancy. "Why not? At least I'm here already."

"I guess," she agreed with manifest reluctance, her lips tight with dismay. Despite it, she transferred her pet to the couch with only a single lingering stroke and a deep breath before rising to confront the gloves.

When she knelt before the innocuous-seeming leather, Timothy sprang to furious life. Jordan's pet vaulted straight into the air from his supine position, long fur fluffed out and growling like an overworked buzz saw. He landed in a crouch, his round head framed by a bristling mane of white fur, large black ears flat on his skull, belly flush with the ottoman, long bushy tail lashing angrily— a wildcat in full hunting mode.

Dillon stared at the transformed cat. He'd known Timothy was protective of his mistress, but he hadn't thought Jordan's pet was capable of quite that much temper. "Uh . . . ?"

Pressing her hands to her mouth, Jordan laughed shakily. "He's been that way since I first tried to read the gloves."

Timothy turned his high-powered glare at her as if willing her to see sense, growling all the while. He took a slow, wary step toward his prey.

Jordan gestured at her cat. "Can you—" Do something about him, she probably meant.

Shrugging into his jacket, Dillon shot the heavy sleeves, making sure they covered his wrists, just in case Timothy lived up to his wildcat impression. While Jordan's pet was focused on her, Dillon caught him by the scruff.

With a startled yelp, Timothy went limp, his blue eyes snapping wide with shock. Thankfully, the cat didn't fight to get free though he did continue to remonstrate Jordan.

Dillon hated to upstage her pet when Timothy was only looking out for his mistress's interests, but Jordan needed to explore her visions to banish her nightmares. "Go on."

Bracing herself with a deep breath, she picked up the gloves, color leaching from her cheeks. Her hands tightened convulsively around the leather.

"What do you see?" Dillon prompted. "You said there's a

knife." He stroked the limp cat, needing to keep his hands occupied so he wouldn't reach for her.

Jordan nodded jerkily, her fingers digging into the gloves with white-knuckled strength. "A thin knife." Her breath hitched. "It catches the light before slashing down."

"Shhh. Easy. Breathe in."

Panting, she struggled to obey his instructions and regain a measure of control.

"Can you describe it some more?"

"There's blood on it," she whispered urgently.

"What else?" Dillon kept his voice even, hoping to cut through her burgeoning panic.

Jordan shook her head, her mouth half-forming words left unspoken. "So much blood." She pressed a fist to her pale lips, gulping for breath, her throat working visibly. Sweat gleamed on her cheeks.

"Slowly. Deep breaths," he reminded her, forcing calmness into his voice.

"It's on the walls, all over the floor!" Her voice shook with genuine horror.

Used to deception in his shadowy world, Dillon's instincts told him there was no pretense in her reaction. His gut churned as he tried to imagine what she was seeing.

Her hands jerked. "Stabbing. Sta—" Jordan crumpled, flinging away the gloves.

Unable to bear her torment, Dillon reached for her, releasing Timothy.

"I'm sorry. I couldn't—" Tears spilled down her cheeks. Her hands caught his jacket, clawing more material into her grip until the fabric bit into his skin. She shivered in his embrace, her cheek clammy against his neck.

Growling, the muscular cat cast glares of recrimination at Dillon as he tried to lick Jordan's wet face, obviously blaming him for her tears.

Dillon rubbed her back soothingly, his mind racing. When Jordan's tears subsided, he wrapped his silk handkerchief around the gloves, tucking the resulting bundle into his pocket. Something so fraught with evil residuals needed investigating.

"What's going on?"

Dillon looked over Jordan's head at the source of the uncertain, slightly hostile question.

Dan stood in the doorway to the hall, his pale blue eyes—so similar to his cousin's—narrowed with suspicion. His shirt, unlike Dillon's, was wrinkled from what looked like a couple of days spent strewn on a floor. The younger man apparently didn't keep a change of clothes in his car.

Jordan knuckled her eyes, rubbing the tear tracks off her face. "I'm okay." She pulled out of Dillon's arms with a quiet sniffle and hid her face in her cat's fur.

Dillon could feel her withdrawing and, with Dan around, he didn't have any chance of using sex to comfort her. *Damn.*

The nightmare unfolded exactly the same way. *She and Dillon at the ice cream parlor. Darkness. Blood. A glint of silver. The knife coming from out of the night, rising behind Dillon—*

"Oof!"

Something heavy had landed on Jordan's belly, jerking her out of nightmare into welcome darkness. Solid muscle filled her arms as Timothy whined at her.

Gasping with fright, her heart pounding fit to jump out of her chest, Jordan buried her face in the cat's soft fur. "Oh, Dillon!" It felt so real! The killer had almost gotten Dillon again. It was as if her consciousness was trying to tell her something through her recurring nightmare.

Timothy purred worriedly against her ear, his claws prickling as he kneaded her shoulder. Cradling her pet, she fled her bed, unwilling to suffer the blanket's stifling embrace and a return of her nightmare.

She paced in the familiar darkness, Timothy draped limply against her cold torso, his tail flicking against her thigh. She automatically extended her stride even though her cat wasn't weaving between her legs. Four long steps took her to the wall. The same number in the opposite direction brought her within kicking distance of her nightstand.

Back and forth and over again, trying to work off the adrenaline coursing through her body, her heart thundering the whole while. Flight or fight—except there was nothing she could fight. How could she fend off the maggoty products of her own mind?

"It can't be real. Precognition was never my gift."

Timothy chirped in agreement, licking the cold sweat trickling down her neck.

Jordan rubbed her cheek against his ruff. "Clairvoyance shows only the here and now," she reminded both of them.

He batted her ear gently as though trying to comfort her.

"But . . . what if it wasn't the future? What if it just happened?" She hissed at the possibility.

Flexing his paws, Timothy growled, objecting to her line of thinking. His claws bit lightly into her shoulder in warning.

"I know it felt like a nightmare, Tim," she argued, "a horrifyingly real nightmare—but what if it wasn't?" Might her vision have been a response to some unconscious desire to see Dillon?

Panic set Jordan's pulse rebounding, had her tightening her embrace until Timothy squeaked in protest. "Sorry." Forcing her arms to relax, she stroked his thick fur in apology as she gulped for breath.

Could it have happened? Could Dillon be lying in a pool of his own blood at this very moment, the victim of a savage murderer? She murmured her lover's name like a prayer, a mantra against the evil in her visions.

"Mew?"

"I need to call Dillon." The decision earned her an approving chirp from Timothy. It also calmed her somewhat, enough that she could get some air into her lungs.

Knowing she wouldn't rest until she was certain of his safety, Jordan stopped by the nightstand, set Timothy down and sat on her bed, torn between hope and fear. He had to be alright. *Please let him be alright!*

The bed dipped under Timothy's weight. The cat butted her arm, rubbing his chin against her bare breast, purring loudly as if in encouragement.

Breathing deeply, she fumbled for the phone, her hand shaking as she fingered the raised symbols on the buttons to find the speed-dial to call Dillon. She couldn't banish her nightmare until she heard his voice and knew that he truly was alright.

"Gavin." Her lover's light baritone was sharp, very much alert, almost as if he'd been expecting a call.

"Dillon?" Despite her efforts, Jordan's voice quavered shamefully as tears of relief filled her eyes.

"Another nightmare?" His tone gentled to a caress. "I could be there in—"

And have him travel through the night? "No!" Jordan cut short his suggestion. She wouldn't risk that. It was too similar to her nightmare. "I just need to hear your voice," she continued weakly, wilting against her headboard as vocal assurance of his well-being dissolved the caustic terror gnawing her belly.

"If I were there, I could kiss your fears away," Dillon countered in an intimate murmur.

"Yeah?" Perhaps if she kept him on the line, he'd give up the idea of coming to her side. He was fine now; she wouldn't tempt fate by calling him out into the night.

Clutching the phone in one hand and Timothy in the other, Jordan slid down to snuggle into her pillows, pulling the bedding over her legs. "How would you do that?"

"Maybe . . . soft kisses on your shoulders?"

"Hmm." She exhaled doubtfully, forcing lightness into her voice. "I don't think so." The attempt at playfulness was helping to distract her, slowing her frightened gasps.

"Guess not. It would have to be something drastic. Something dramatic enough to shock your fears away." Dillon's voice trailed off as though he was deep in thought.

"You've thought of something?" Jordan petted Timothy to assure him she was fine now, settling him on the bed beside her.

"Hot, wet kisses on your inner thighs. With a hint of tongue," he growled back.

She caught her breath at the suggestion. His firm lips trailing up toward her labia, teasing her with that most intimate of kisses? She groaned, raw desire stabbing her core with heat. "That would definitely distract me."

"Maybe even nibble a bit. Get some of your tender flesh between my teeth." Dillon's voice dropped to a whisper, as if he were imagining doing exactly what he'd said.

Jordan shivered with need. "Ooh! That would feel so good."

"And I could do *more*." He lavished carnal meaning in the final word, bringing to mind all sorts of lascivious acts.

"Yeah?" The images he evoked had her breathless, her heart starting to pound from something other than fear.

"If you want *more* . . ." His voice was heavy with promise.

"What *more*?" she asked, copying his erotic intonation.

"I could kiss you higher."

The thought made Jordan wet, had her labia plump and aching. She gulped, licking dry lips. "Where?"

"Your cunt." His whisper floated through the darkness, making his stark response almost romantic.

That flesh throbbed violently at his answer. She slipped her hand beneath the blanket to cup it, tracing a light finger over her labia. "You'd kiss me there?"

"Oh, yeah," Dillon growled. "I'd bet you're wet and pink and sweeter than anything." It was like he rolled his tongue over "sweeter," relishing the sound of the word.

Jordan squirmed. "Because I want you."

"First, I'll lick up your cream. Savor your taste. Ummm." His voice roughened. "So sweet. Can't get enough of it."

Her loins clenched at his words, her nipples tingling. Hot cream spurted on her fingers as she imagined him doing exactly that, his tongue probing her, cherishing her tender flesh.

"I'll spread your thighs so I can see you better, your pretty clit all thick and erect," he continued gruffly.

She moaned, her breathing turning ragged. She splayed her trembling legs, combed her fingers through her damp curls and parted her swollen folds. "Then you'd kiss me there?"

"*More*. I'll suck you like hard candy. Lick you over and over, in and out, until you melt against my tongue," he promised in a husky drawl that sent shivers of delight up her spine.

Whimpering, Jordan plunged her fingers into her slick vagina, stroking her needy flesh to the rhythm of his words. "Your tongue would be rough over my clitoris." Imagining Dillon licking her there, she circled that nubbin with her thumb, lighting gentle sparks of delight in her core. Her hips rose to join her fingers in their erotic dance. "I'd want more."

"But I wouldn't want to take advantage."

His words hung in the air for long seconds before she absorbed their meaning. "You wouldn't?" she echoed plaintively.

"I'd bring you to pleasure with my hands and mouth," he growled. "Sucking. Nibbling. Kissing. Licking. I'd thrust my tongue deep to get all your cream. In and out. Again and again."

"Yes," she groaned, touching herself to his dark encouragement. Her orgasm rose in a gentle inexorable wave as he crooned to her over the phone, drawing her to the crest.

"Then I'll caress your pleasure spot until you *come*."

At his words, his command, rapture broke over her, splintered through her body in a delicious spate of warmth that melted her bones. Jordan cried out in startled wonder as stars sparkled in her veins. "Dillon!"

A low groan filled her ear. "I guess you can sleep now?"

Jordan pulled the sheets up, a soporific lassitude overtaking her. "Ummmm . . ."

Chapter Nine

Dillon sat on the couch beside her, his clean male scent mingling with the perfume of spring flowers from the front yard and those of the orchids he'd given her. "It occurred to me that your nightmares might be a sign of anxiety: you feel things are out of control." His delivery was careful, his voice almost tentative.

Jordan opened her mouth to protest. That wasn't it at all! She shivered as a scene from last night's horror flashed before her mind's eye.

He squeezed her hands, speaking quickly. "I'm not saying your visions aren't true, but that their recurrence might be due to feeling helpless in the face of a physical threat."

Tucking her feet under her, Jordan pulled Timothy onto her lap while she considered Dillon's statement. *He might have a point.* Certainly her recent nightmares about Dillon's danger probably had their roots in fear. She pursed her mouth in doubt, but nodded to acknowledge the possibility. He was being so sweet and protective she couldn't tell him her main concern was not about herself, but for him.

Just like Mom feared for Dad?

She swallowed at the comparison. She wasn't going there!

Dillon's voice pulled her back from the brink of dismay. "It might help if you knew how to defend yourself. I'm not proposing a full course, but perhaps a few basic moves?"

It took Jordan a moment to grasp his meaning. "You mean, learn how to fight?" she asked, startled. Never had she imagined having such a conversation with anyone, much less her lover.

"More like, fight back. I don't expect you'll become a brawler," Dillon returned, laughter in his voice. "Doing something physical can give you a sense of control since you're acting, not just waiting for something to happen. At the very least, it would give you another outlet for your fear."

She couldn't resist his good humor. "Another outlet? What's the first?"

"Well, sex, of course." His light baritone deepened with husky meaning.

Jordan flushed, a gentle tingle washing through her body as she remembered the results of last night's panicked phone call. "What's wrong with that?" she retorted, pressing her thighs together against a trickle of heat.

Timothy chirped a complaint, pulling free of her embrace to jump to the floor.

"Nothing at all," Dillon averred, lifting her hand from her lap to hold between his own. "But it wouldn't hurt to have another outlet."

Eventually, she gave in—merely to indulge him, to give him the satisfaction of doing something to fix her problem—even though she didn't think it would work. But once he secured her agreement, Dillon wasted no time getting her to somewhere "suited to their needs."

"Where are we going?" Jordan asked as Dillon led her with a

hand under her elbow down another bland, nearly featureless corridor. They were in the basement level of an apartment building nearly half an hour's drive from her home. A bag bounced against her knee since Dillon had insisted she bring a change of clothes; fighting was apparently sweaty business.

"Lantis's old apartment," Dillon answered. "It's where I'm staying while I'm in town."

Jordan planted her feet. "His apartment?"

Dillon came to an immediate halt. "His *old* apartment from before he married Kiera. He's just using it for storage while their house is being built." He chivied her on.

The next door opened to something different. Past the threshold and a tingle of power that spoke of an active security spell, the antiseptic odors from the corridor suddenly disappeared, replaced by a faint scent of leather and something else that brought to mind virile males. *Testosterone?*

They were in a bachelor's quarters. Massive leather furniture, books, electronics with only a bunch of silk flowers here and a bronze there to hint at a woman's presence. It was an upscale version of her cousin's part of the house, though far less messy and dusty—hardly storage.

Dillon didn't give her time to explore. He led her quickly past a small kitchen, into a large chamber, its echoing emptiness underscoring its size.

At first, she thought it was an unused storeroom with only a lingering whiff of sweat to indicate otherwise. A closer inspection banished her misconception. Gym equipment stood near the door while a gray mat covered most of the floor beyond, which was empty save for lengths of chain suspended above it from the ceiling like an enormous, inverted tact board.

"Change here," Dillon told her with a flick of his hand toward a locker and laundry area she'd overlooked. "Then we can get started."

Jordan donned the short shorts and thin midriff T-shirt she'd brought in the hopes of tempting Dillon into dalliance. All of a sudden, it didn't feel like such a bright idea, especially when Dillon seemed intent on making a fighter out of her. His changing into a plain tank top and shorts only served to underscore his seriousness.

Due to the limitations of her clairvoyance, he taught her what he called "basic" moves—knee and elbow strikes, punching and kicking—rather than more-aggressive self-defense combinations. He had her perform them in slow motion, correcting her form and balance to his satisfaction, before continuing.

He touched her constantly with a dispassion that was all the more arousing for its lack of titillative intent, until Jordan's body ached with desire. Her sensual excitement swept from her mind the awkwardness of being taught to fight.

"It's better to practice the moves when you actually have something to hit," Dillon told her when he finally led her to the mat covering most of the floor. "The balance is different. There's also the impact, which you have to recover from."

Jordan stiffened. "I'm not going to knee you!" She stepped back, the thick mat cushioning her feet without much dipping.

Dillon chuckled. "Don't worry. I wouldn't let you."

"Speaking of kneeing . . ." He hung a large punching bag on one of the chains dangling from the ceiling. "Imagine the bottom of the bag is your attacker's crotch." He steadied the bag before shifting behind her, blanketing her with male heat.

"In many cases, your attacker would be holding you. Or you might be cornered. In either case, you can use the constraints to add power to your strike." He wrapped his strong, rough hands around her forearms. "Feel the difference in your balance?"

Jordan tested his hold, the friction sending a zing of need to tingle her tight nipples. "You mean I'm more stable."

"Somewhat." Dillon nodded easily; he looked quite unaffected in her vision. "Now try the knee strike."

She raised her knee quickly, aiming for the rounded bottom of the bag. It glanced off the edge to one side, barely making a dent. Her cheeks heated in irritation. One of the disadvantages of her clairvoyance was a flat perspective since it wasn't binocular vision. It didn't help that her arousal was playing havoc with her concentration.

"Straight up. You're tilting your leg." His murmured instruction tickled her ear, an ethereal caress she could have done without.

On her second attempt, Jordan hit the bag squarely, but it barely budged. The impact knocked her off balance. "Whoa!"

Dillon chuckled as he steadied her. "Feel the difference?"

"I see what you mean." She raised her knee, making her vision show her a top view and trying to memorize the feel of her muscles at the correct angle. Since Dillon was determined to teach her how to fight, cooperation seemed the only way to get it over with quickly.

"But what if the murderer isn't a man? The gloves are for a woman, after all." Balanced on one leg, she turned her head to direct her question over her shoulder.

Dillon's scent mixed with light sweat strengthened, conjuring memories of long sensual hours in her bed exploring him and being explored. "I'm told a blow to the crotch is also painful for women. But that isn't the only possible target for kneeing, you know. If your attacker's shorter, there's the belly. If he, or she, is bent down, there's the head—the nose and temple are both good targets—and the throat." He pressed the pads of his fingers to Jordan's neck, just below her chin, someplace that made her swallow with difficulty.

"Of course, for throat attacks, a fist or the edge of the hand or two fingertips would be better. Smaller surface area," he added in a conversational tone of voice, as though offering clarification.

"O-kay." Licking her dry lips, Jordan blinked in consternation.

The image of herself actually fighting someone refused to take on detail in her mind's eye; she just couldn't visualize it.

"Now hit the bag harder. I want to hear the chain jangling."

He had her practice all her strikes over and over, while using her clairvoyance and without it, until she gasped for breath, her muscles quivering from her exertions.

Dillon was right, Jordan decided as she bent over, propping herself up with her hands on her knees. There was something liberating about pummeling a blameless punching bag with everything you had, especially when your body burned with sexual frustration. But right now, more than anything, she wanted a cold drink—something tart and refreshing; she could almost taste it sliding down her throat.

"I think that's enough for one day," she panted, feeling blood suffuse her head.

"Come on," he coaxed, practically crooning his words, a rough palm rasping over her back. "Just one more set."

"If you tell me to be a good girl, I'll have to hit you," Jordan warned, waving an index finger at him. Her hair clung to her face in wet clumps as rivulets of sweat trickled down her hot neck. Her T-shirt and shorts stuck to her body like second skin.

"Never crossed my mind, I promise you," Dillon told her on a laugh. "But if it'll make you feel better, I'll let you hit me." He pressed her hand flat on the sculpted slopes of his chest. "Just one more set, then we can do something else." With his other hand, he stroked her wet back, weaving a coil of erotic heat through her body as his fingers traced the length of her spine all the way down to between her buttocks.

A sliver of carnal excitement pierced Jordan's tiredness. She pressed her thighs together against her automatic reaction as her arousal flared back to life, stronger than before. *Unfair!* How could she resist him when he did sensual things like that? He had to know no red-blooded woman could refuse such a tempting invitation.

"Just one set?" she repeated for confirmation, weighing the

promised reward against the necessary effort. Her core clenched, need adding cream to her already-sweat-soaked panty.

"Just one. Then I'm entirely at your mercy." Dillon brushed soft kisses along her collarbone, planted more across her shoulder, teasing her with tenderness.

All thoughts of rest melted away before that gentle assault. Upon further consideration, one set didn't sound like much. She could do that and more—so long as Dillon's lovemaking awaited her after.

"I'll hold you to that," she told him, inwardly shaking her head at her weakness. He certainly knew how to inspire a woman.

Drawing on her second wind, Jordan thumped the bag, setting it swinging, its chain clinking in primitive harmony. It might be bribery, but she wanted that reward. The promise of having Dillon at her mercy was just too intriguing.

All she had to do was one more set: ten solid blows for each "basic" move. Forty in all and then she'd have him. She licked her lips, her heart racing in anticipation.

Each strike rubbed the thin, wet cotton of her T-shirt across her sensitive nipples over and over, fanning the embers of need into a roaring bonfire. Making swift work of the set, she counted out the strikes with each *oomph* of the bag and ended with a punch that stung her knuckles.

"And done!" Jordan announced in breathless exultation. "Gimme!" She spun around to grab Dillon, plastering herself against him and pressing her tight nubs against his hard chest in search of relief. She liked the smell of her sweat on him; the resulting scent was such an intimate fragrance.

Wanting to get closer, she yanked his shirt out of his shorts and up. She buried her face in the hair dusting his chest, needing to immerse her senses in everything that was Dillon. Utterly delicious Dillon. Her Dillon.

He laughed even while he helped her strip him. "There's no rush."

"Says you," Jordan retorted. "I wanted this, two sets ago." She delved past his shorts and underwear to fill her hands with his hot, rampant sex. "Don't tell me you didn't, too."

"Okay, I won't." Dillon tugged on her wet T-shirt, peeling it off and forcing her to release her buried treasure. He pulled down her shorts and panty before she could say anything, leaving cool air caressing her heated skin.

"Hey, you're supposed to be at *my* mercy!" She tackled him at the waist, toppling him on the mat as she rendered him equally bare. "That's more like it."

Straddling Dillon as he lay chuckling under her, Jordan stopped to consider, glee bubbling up in frothy waves inside her. "Now, where to start."

She captured his shaft to toy with the frill at the base. His satiny flesh fascinated her, sheathing the way it did his steely hardness. And the body it adorned was nothing to complain about either.

She was strongly tempted to break her rule about portraits. A nude of Dillon as he was—sprawled beneath her, propped up on his elbows—would be breathtaking, she was sure.

Jordan tucked the thought away before it could distract her from more immediate matters. She also blocked her sight, not wanting to risk a stray vision.

Moisture bedewed her hand, rich with musk. Sliding down Dillon's body, she bent closer, taking the scent of aroused, virile male into herself with a deep breath. It drew her like kittens to catmint.

With a wondering finger, she followed it to its slitted source. Curiosity overwhelmed her. Unable to resist, she pressed her mouth to him, licking him the way she'd wanted to that first night.

Dillon groaned, his fists catching her hair. "Oh, yeah." His penis jerked against her lips, wet with more of that male essence.

She caught him between her hands to hold him securely in place and explored. "Ummm," she hummed around her thick mouthful, savoring the silky smooth feel of him along her tongue and against her lips. The heavy scent of his arousal made her head spin, fuel for her desire.

He arched off the mat, his thighs hard against her forearms, as she played with him, milking the length she couldn't accommodate. His fingers dug into her nape, pressing her closer, driving him deeper.

She nibbled him, delighting in his turgid thickness. Sucked him hard to get more of that salty sweetness. She wanted that and much more. Wanted to leave her mark on him, so he'd never forget her, even after he left.

"Jordan, I'm—" Dillon's voice was harsh with urgency. He grabbed her hair, his hips rising, his hard flesh pulsing.

"Not yet." She pressed her fingers under the flaring head of his penis, pulling gently on his sac with her other hand. "I'm not letting you off that easily." She wasn't done playing with him, not by a long shot.

Dillon swore with great fluency. "I'll get you for that," he threatened breathlessly. "Turnabout's fair play."

Jordan paused, wondering what he meant.

Large hands landed on her waist, lifting her easily, hauling her around until she was kneeling over Dillon's torso. "That's more like it."

The hands now on her hips urged her lower.

His tongue stabbed into her sex, trailing flame with a sharp, breath-stealing stroke that conjured hot cream from her shuddering core.

Jordan stiffened in shocked pleasure, held in place by his carnal magic. She moaned her delight, craving more of his sensual artistry.

Then a rough hand hooked around her neck, drawing her down until velvety flesh kissed her lips.

She took the hint, resuming her own game. She had difficulty keeping her mind on her lips though; his masterful tongue was a potent distraction.

Dillon's teasing rhythm woke a sense of perversity in her. Taking inspiration from his lovemaking, Jordan matched him stroke for stroke, copying his timing and lavish application.

Her lover groaned beneath her after a particularly fancy swirl of her tongue that focused just under the flare of his head. His body rocked her as he arched and twisted on the mat, a vigorous dance that spoke volumes of his pleasure.

Exhilarated by her success, she grinned, riding the sensual fury of Dillon's assault.

He caught her clitoris between his teeth and bestowed his carnal expertise on her swollen, aching flesh.

Lightning scorched her, flayed her with molten power. Its very force stole her breath, the strength from her knees. She screamed in abandon, needing to vent her excitement. She'd never dreamed so much raw pleasure was possible.

Seizing him between her lips, she took him deep, lashing him with her tongue, milking him with both hands as she drew his pulsing length out.

Creamy heat flooded her mouth, coating her tongue with Dillon's male essence. She gulped, making a face at a sudden tartness mingling with his salty flavor.

Dillon chose that moment to suck hard on her clitoris and Jordan forgot about the tang as rapture smashed through her, wind roaring in her ears as the orgasmic frenzy thundered through her veins. The storm set off fireworks throughout her body, bright stars flashing before her eyes, the heavens resplendent with color.

It was some time before Dillon recovered his breath. Jordan was draped on top of him, a soft armful and next to boneless in her languor. "So what do you want to do for the rest of the day?" he asked, his heart still pounding from his release. He licked the cream on his lips, relishing the sweet taste of her ecstasy.

Smooth fingers gripped his ass and squeezed as Jordan licked his cock to spine-tingling, flesh-hardening effect. His woman could probably get a rise out of a stone statue.

Dillon rubbed his cheek against a satiny thigh. "We've done that already." And so thoroughly he was amazed the mat—if not the building—hadn't gone up in flames.

She undulated her body against him suggestively, stropping the hard points of her nipples against his belly in unmistakable desire. Her accompanying growl was replete with satiation.

"We've done that as well."

Jordan pushed up, rising to all fours to smile at him, a flame of mischief burning in her blue eyes. "Doesn't mean we can't do it again. Besides"—she stroked his flank with quiver-inducing slowness—"more practice never hurts."

Eventually—after several false starts and a detour for a quickie in the shower—they made it to Lantis's enormous bed. Dillon heaved a sigh of repletion, content for the moment to lie under Jordan while her hands explored him. She seemed preoccupied with his scars, frowning with adorable fierceness as she glided her smooth palms over the ridges below his collarbone.

Her fascination was understandable. In this day and age of modern healing, scars were a thing of the past . . . unless you were injured a hundred miles and several weeks away from a competent healer. But he didn't want to think about that now.

"I hope he's dead," Jordan muttered suddenly.

Dillon blinked, thrown by the comment. "Who do you mean?"

She rolled her thumb over a round, puckered, old scar, the fortunate result of a timely bob on his part; the tango had been aiming a few inches lower. Despite his luck, it had still been a near thing; he'd almost died before they'd gotten to a healer. If it hadn't been for Lantis, he wouldn't have been extracted alive. "That man with the tattoo on his face." Something inside Dillon stilled when

Jordan traced a distinctive pattern on her left cheek—the same one the tango had sported just before it and half his skull had been blown away. "The one who did this."

"You don't have to worry about him," Dillon assured her automatically, trying to remember if he'd told her about it and compromised security. *How could she have known?*

Jordan kissed the scar. "Good."

The ferocious satisfaction that informed that one-word retort was oddly gratifying. He forced that surprising emotion to the back of his mind for later study. What mattered now was Jordan's inexplicable knowledge. Did he talk in his sleep?

"Did you blow up a warehouse in the desert?"

Ice coursed through Dillon's veins at her question. "Huh?" The ramification of her question was unavoidable: Jordan had penetrated black ops security—and she didn't know it. *But how?*

Save for a slight dip to her brow, Jordan's face told him nothing. She bent over his chest, her finger rubbing his scar. "I *saw* you hiding in the bush. And another time, you were in a railroad car with . . . some other men. You planted something among the cargo. Then you watched the train blow up while it was crossing a bridge over a valley with lots of trees."

Recognizing her description of a particular interception of illegal arms, Dillon shuddered in horrified realization. Somehow Jordan had witnessed something of his black ops missions. It had to be her psychometry. And it could only have been through her contact with him.

Which meant their very relationship constituted a security risk. No matter what he did, he couldn't control her sight. So long as they continued to see each other, Jordan was likely to pick up on things he couldn't discuss. For operational security, he'd have to break things off. His heart skipped a beat.

"I can't talk about it." The classified nature of his missions meant he was oathbound not to reveal any details.

"Can't talk about it?"

"You know that old saw, 'If I tell you, I'd have to kill you'? It's like that, and I don't want to kill you." He attempted a smile. "I could lie. But I'd rather not lie to you."

Jordan inhaled sharply. "But it's your job."

"Yes, it's my job." Dillon confirmed her supposition, since she'd guessed as much. "Don't ask me for details because I can't give them to you. Ever. But it's important and someone has to do it." He stroked her back, trying to ease the sudden tension that tightened her muscles.

Her pale blue eyes had widened at his last statement. The innocence implicit in her reaction touched him; this was what he and his fellow agents risked so much to protect. But would knowledge—never mind acceptance—of his work change the way she saw him? Turn her away from him?

Another realization struck him: any relationship with Jordan would endanger future missions and place her at risk. If an enemy learned what she could do with her psychometry, it and she might be used against him.

Oh, fuck.

Chapter Ten

Playing hooky revived Jordan's spirits better than anything else she could imagine. Even Timothy's exuberant welcome after being left to his own devices for most of the day raised only the slightest guilt in her.

Inspiration bubbled up: a woodland scene that just begged to be parsed, one unlike anything she'd done before. It didn't fit the theme Jordan had been considering for her next show but it might suffice for that original psyprint the Spatha Foundation wanted her to do.

Carrying Timothy, she danced down the hall to her studio, wanting to block out the image on the computer before the details blurred. She also needed to check her files to refresh her memory of the flowers she'd include in the psyprint.

It seemed like the gloom that darkened her mood lately had lifted. Maybe Dillon had been right: she'd needed the outlet the punching bag provided. Or perhaps it was the combination of that and explosive sex.

She laughed out loud, bouncing on her toes while she waited for the computer to start up. The prospect of days at the computer and then with the psyprinter didn't faze her.

Images and ideas flickered in her mind's eye. It was as if her muse was working overtime.

One thing at a time. She sat down as the computer chimed readiness. The Spatha image had first priority.

"You're up early." Dan stated the obvious with a smile in his muffled voice. Talking with his mouth full again. She'd bet he didn't do that around his lovers.

"I started on another piece yesterday and I can't wait to get back to it." Jordan grabbed the milk carton from the refrigerator and the cereal from the counter. Avoiding Timothy, who was weaving between her legs, she carried her load to the kitchen table, and then darted back for flatware and a bowl. When the phone rang, she picked it up as she headed for her chair.

She mumbled "Hello" as she spooned muesli into her bowl.

"Oh, good. I wanted to make sure I'd get you on the phone," Shanna's bell-like voice gushed. Her agent knew Jordan made a habit of ignoring all calls when the muse took her, to the point of not bringing a phone into her studio.

Jordan blinked at the flood of words. "Well, I'm here now."

"Are you sure about the psyprints on your list? They're rather rare and expensive. You should see the quotes for the ones already on the market; they're astronomical."

"Even better."

Shanna said nothing for a moment, as if waiting for Jordan to retract her statement. "Okay. Numbers: how many each?"

"Just one." Jordan inhaled slowly to give herself time to change her mind. The impulse didn't rise, so she took the plunge. "By the way, you can tell Spatha I'll do it."

"Do what? The original?" Shanna clarified.

"What else?" Jordan laughed, the enthusiasm from last night's frenzied drafting still bubbling through her veins. "I had this brainstorm yesterday and it's going really well."

"So I can tell Fab to expect the final image by the end of the week? He'll want it for the catalog."

"End of the week?" Jordan bit her lip, trepidation stirring at the prospect of unveiling something so different from her usual style so soon. She wasn't willing to do so with less than her usual preparation. "I can't promise that. Anyway, it might draw more interest if it's not included, don't you think?"

Shanna hummed thoughtfully. "Good point. I'll make sure Fab sees it that way. Talk to you next week." Barely waiting for agreement, her agent ended the call with her typical abruptness.

Jordan frowned as she returned the handset to its cradle, wondering if the shift in direction her art was taking was wise.

"Problem?" Dan's voice broke through her reverie.

Unused to questioning her muse, she threw off her atypical thoughts. "I'm doing a special piece for Spatha's auction, and they want it soon."

"The end of the week."

"That's just for the auction catalog." Jordan shrugged. "You heard what I told Shanna."

"But you'd prefer more time and you have Timothy's annual checkup this afternoon," Dan concluded.

"You know me so well." She shook her head. "That's the gist of it."

"I could bring Tim to the vet after work. You don't have to come hold his paw."

Jordan had to laugh at the thought of Timothy as a fraidy cat. "It wouldn't be too much of a bother?"

"Hah. If Tim's traumatized, I'll just stop for some takeout. Maybe sashimi."

She snorted at his nonsense. "You're the best. Thanks."

———∞∞∞———

"This is a surprise." Lantis put down the papers he was reading and pushed the pile to one side of his desk. "I didn't expect to see you until the weekend."

"Jordan's working on a psyprint, a limited edition for a charity auction." Grinning, Dillon settled into the visitor's chair across from his friend. "Apparently, it takes several hours just to get it on file. Then she still has to refine it to her satisfaction, so I'm keeping out from underfoot."

He didn't know why he was planning to do this. What the hell was he doing involved with a woman he couldn't keep secrets from? He should have dropped Jordan faster than a racing wicce train—one of those newer high-speed express lines. Yet here he was. He studied Lantis, wondering how his former partner would take it if he knew what Dillon was contemplating.

Who was he kidding? Despite the extensive list of reasons he'd compiled last night, despite the browbeating he'd given himself, despite Lantis's possible reaction, he knew he wasn't going anywhere. And knew why.

There was no way he'd give Jordan up just yet. His desires— that something in him that made him a relentless hunter and served him well in his black ops missions—were still focused on her. With even more reason now.

Jordan needed him. He had to help her somehow, had to banish her nightmares. Lantis called it his White Knight complex. Dillon called it a pain in the ass.

At least while he was on R&R, Jordan wouldn't pose much of a risk to OpSec. *Surely?*

"You're holding up pretty well."

Surprised by the comment, Dillon raised a brow in a *How so?* inquiry at his best friend.

"Third week of R&R and you're not squirming with impatience

to get back into the field," Lantis explained, his deep-blue eyes unreadable. "In fact, you're looking quite contented."

Dillon stared back in shock. Truth be told, the last thing he felt was contentment.

"Alright, maybe *contented* isn't the right word," the other man conceded. "Challenged." His lips quirked the slightest bit, which for him indicated a great deal of amusement. "But with you, it's much the same thing. It's no fun if it's easy."

True, and except for worrying about how Jordan's clairvoyance and psychometry affected operational security, he hadn't given his job much of a thought. Normally, he'd have contacted the Old Man by now, cadging a return to the field.

"I'm getting by." He waved his silk packet in explanation.

Not wanting to consider the implications of his tolerance of the current state of affairs, Dillon changed the subject. "Are you sure you're not too busy?" He didn't want to impose, not after the last favor he'd asked of his friend had nearly cost the other man his life.

Lantis's calm gaze sharpened at his question. "You said you needed to do a scry. Sounded simple enough." His blue eyes asked if anything had changed.

"Just wanted to make sure. Knowing you, you're putting a rush on your projects to free up paternity leave."

"Nothing that can't keep." His friend stood up, waving him into the adjoining workroom. There, a salt shaker, a small pitcher of water, and a twelve-inch-wide, clear bowl awaited him on the worktable, ready for use.

Most scrying spells required water. As a matter of practice, Dillon preferred to use salt water since salt improved the conduction of residual energies.

Standing at one end of the table, he poured water into the flat bowl until a finger's width covered the bottom. Tapping salt from the shaker on his upturned palm he focused briefly on the salt to activate its potential, then sprinkled it into the water, using a glass stirrer to disperse it evenly. The ringing of the bowl filled the room, a pure note to aid concentration.

"Perfect pitch," Dillon murmured appreciatively. "You've excellent stuff." This was the flip side to his black ops work, the hunt that was 90 percent of their missions as opposed to the 10 percent that was execution. While it didn't provide the same adrenaline rush, it had its moments, especially since the many forms of scrying were his forte.

He rested his thumbs and first two fingers lightly on either side of the bowl. Closing his eyes, he gave the spell his undivided attention, calling ambient magic to him until its electric prickle danced over his skin.

With a sigh, he opened his eyes. Violet energy pooled inside the bowl, swirling between his hands. When the power filled the container, the water glowed a bright blue. "Ready?"

Seated on the bench, Lantis had his PDA out, stylus poised to jot down their findings. "Ready."

Dillon spread the folds of silk, exposing the gloves and arranging them side by side on the table. He carefully held the luminescent bowl above the gloves. The blue light sparkled and glittered, forming evanescent patterns on the water's surface. Probing the psychic energies embedded in the worked leather, he translated the images into names.

Using the slow cadence he and Lantis had adopted years ago for accurate note-taking, he dictated his findings: "Jordan Kane. Timothy. Linda Danvers. Tatianna Jones. . . ."

Sliding the bowl around, he quartered the gloves, adding name after name to their list. When the images broke up, the psychic residuals too faint to be read, he exhaled sharply, grounding the magic with an abrupt slash of his hand. The water stopped glowing immediately.

"That's all I could get." Dillon leaned on the table, his head bent, the exertion of power leaving him tired.

Lantis tapped his PDA. "That's a lot of names. What's this about?"

While they put away the spell implements, Dillon explained the nightmares Jordan was suffering and how they had apparently been triggered by the gloves. "I don't doubt her vision. It's got her spooked." He drummed his fingers on the scarred tabletop. "I really think there's a murder involved."

The other man huffed, his lips curling infinitesimally. The sound was a breach of his renowned self-control, the equivalent of a hoot of hilarity in another man. "Only you would stumble upon a possible murder during a course of R&R." His friend's blue eyes twinkled. "Hell knows, it takes a lot to keep you diverted. Why not a murder?"

Dillon made a face at him as they returned to the office. "I'm not that bad!" He stole a glance at his watch to check how much longer before he could reasonably drop by to visit Jordan.

"Tell that to someone who doesn't— *KIERA!*"

Startled by the pained exclamation, Dillon turned to his friend. The stricken expression on Lantis's paling face unnerved him. "What is it?"

"Something's happened to Kiera."

CHAPTER ELEVEN

Applying everything he'd learned of offensive driving, Dillon cut through the late-afternoon traffic, heading for kidTek. With office hours just ending, that was where Kiera was likely to be.

Beside him, Lantis stabbed at his cell phone, a display of barely leashed violence that turned Dillon's blood to ice. His former partner was one of the most controlled people he knew—cool under fire, literally. For him to reveal that much strain meant things were bad. What could have happened to Kiera?

What Dillon heard of Lantis's staccato interrogation of Claudette Perkins, Kiera's personal assistant and her father's before her, was more frightening. An explosion of some sort. She hadn't even known Kiera was among the injured.

"They're calling the police and medics," Lantis gritted out, glaring at the cars ahead of them.

"Kiera?"

"They don't know anything yet." His friend's control snapped back in place, his fear vanishing behind a mask of frost as his shoulders squared. "It was in the parking building." Meaning it wasn't an accident in the factory or the labs. "They still have to search the rubble for survivors."

Dillon clenched his fists around the wheel, wanting to hit something, preferably the idiot ahead dawdling in the passing lane. "How can I help?"

One hand around the grab bar beside his head, Lantis stared at him, his eyes narrowed, jaw tight. "Can you find out what happened? *How* it happened? I know you want to check Kiera, but—"

Reining in his fear for his childhood friend, Dillon nodded crisply. "No problem." If the explosion had been caused by a bomb, kidTek was where he could do the most good. "Just focus on Kiera. I'll nail this bastard." Spotting a break in the traffic, he overtook the slug in front of him and punched the gas.

They saw the effects of the explosion long before they reached kidTek. The highway was an excruciating crawl of impatient horns and creeping progress that ate at Dillon's self-control. Traffic backed up for miles as drivers gawked at the black smoke billowing from kidTek's parking building.

Dillon pulled every trick in the book and made up some new ones to make headway, stopping short of bulldozing his way through simply because his rental couldn't shift all the vehicles in front of him.

"Move your ass, wise guy," he muttered at the driver of a semi idling in front of him. He was tempted to cast a move-along spell despite federal regulations against magical influence on highway traffic. Only the black ops custom of maintaining a low profile held him back.

Lantis was less restrained. His former partner slid his wand the slightest inch out of his sleeve and shaped ambient magic in a hair-ruffling wave of power.

The semi lurched forward, giving Dillon room to maneuver. Slapping his horn to warn off a motorcycle trying to outflank him, he swerved his rental onto the median strip and sped away. Nothing was going to keep them from getting to kidTek.

Closer in and off the highway, access was gridlocked by a mess of emergency vehicles: medical, fire, police. They abandoned his car at a strip mall several blocks away, nearly forgetting to activate its antitheft geas, and ran the rest of the way, the sinuous column of smoke rising in the distance a sinister landmark.

Raucous chaos assaulted Dillon's senses as cops struggled to secure the building, while firefighters battled multiple blazes and medics bent over moaning, screaming people. The thunderous approach of two evac helos added to the cacophony.

"That way!" Lantis pointed at the probable landing zone.

They sprinted into hell. Beyond the crowd of onlookers, several bodies lay on rough asphalt, ominous in their stillness despite the medics in attendance. Some of the injuries were obvious: massive trauma, probably from airborne debris; an arm blown off, needing reattachment.

In the clearing, a cop waved down the first helo. Downdraft from the whirling blades sent dust and litter flying. A medic shifted to shield a patient, grabbing a flapping sheet.

Kiera.

As Lantis lunged forward, Dillon stopped in his tracks, his stomach dropping to his heels.

Blood covered her face. Even from a distance, he could tell her cheekbone was broken. The arm and leg he could see had compound fractures. Blood stained her dress at the hip. Even then, she had a protective hand draped over her distended belly.

Oh, no. The baby. His godchild.

A medic tried to intercept Lantis. His friend sidestepped the man, his focus entirely on getting to his wife.

Kneeling at her side, Lantis touched her wrist.

Kiera's eyes fluttered open, her hand turning over to grip her husband's. She seemed to gain strength from the contact.

She's alive. Dillon's vision blurred. *It's not over yet. Lantis won't let either of them go without a fight.* Clenching his fists, he breathed deeply, using cold fury to wall off potential anguish. *Damn it, this isn't supposed to happen here.*

Wanting to smash something—preferably whoever planted the bomb—he watched with stinging eyes as the medics loaded Kiera into the first helo with Lantis scrambling in after. He couldn't take the time to assure himself his heart sister would survive— not when he'd agreed to Lantis's request—but while she was here he couldn't take his gaze off her, for fear it would be the last he'd see of her.

Hang on, Kiera! I'll get the bastard for you.

Only when the helo had taken off and was out of sight could he force himself back to the charnel house behind him.

His second look was still a shock.

The cream parking building was a wreck, like something that belonged in a war zone, an intrusion of his other life. The blast had taken out a supporting pillar and broken two others, had blown holes in the floors of the third, fourth, and fifth levels. Cars lay crumpled like rubbish from a giant's tantrum with bodies slung over several in haphazard disarray.

Deep stress cracks scarred the damaged floors, shimmering in the heat and something else. Dillon narrowed his eyes at the almost invisible glitter. Reaching out with a mental hand, he sensed ambient magic pooling into the edifice, a tingling current washing over his skin, drawn by a powerful spell. Possibly only the building's structural-magic reinforcement prevented its collapse.

Several fires continued to rage. He grimaced at the all-too-familiar miasma of blood, roasting meat, and burning gasoline. The explosion must have ruptured the fuel tanks of some of the vehicles.

On cursory examination, he couldn't see any indication of magical accelerants. Even the fire mages were focused on maintaining protective shields, not fighting incendiary spells.

The chill that hadn't left him since Lantis's horrified exclamation deepened. To think Kiera had been caught up in that! How had she survived? Was she the target? KidTek? How the hell had a bomb gotten past security?

Clenching his jaw, he reined in his useless speculation and the fear for his heart sister that threatened to leave him trembling. *No time for that.* Drawing on his training, he shoved his unprofessional reactions to the back of his brain. They'd be useless to Kiera and would only hamper his investigation.

With a clearer mind, he surveyed his surroundings, noting the positions of external security cameras. *Good.* He'd have records to work with.

Onlookers, probably mostly kidTek employees, crowded the police line glowing in amber warning. No one seemed to take an unusual interest in the blaze, although he still intended to check the security video. Of course, one didn't have to be on site to rubberneck. Sure enough, on the heels of that thought, the first of a swarm of media trucks appeared around a corner.

Damn vultures. Not wanting his face flashed across millions of screens, Dillon turned his back on the concrete rubble and charred car parts, the crying survivors, all strewn across the street. He strode into kidTek, forcing himself to maintain a deliberate, dispassionate pace. The last thing he needed was to get shot by a guard with a twitchy trigger finger. Though if one tried to stop him, he'd feed him his gun.

Records first. There was nothing he could do on site until the fires were out and the cops got everything they needed. As much as he wanted to wade in and examine the blast zone himself— demolition was one of his specialties—the best thing he could do right now was to let the cops do their job. Finding out what they had was a problem for later.

Luckily for security, Claudette—who'd known him since childhood from visits with Kiera to her father at work—cleared his way. Normally a bastion of efficiency, the older woman fell weeping into his arms as soon as he crossed the threshold of Kiera's outer office.

Dillon held her while she gave vent to the fear bottled up inside her. He let her cry for both of them, holding in his own anger and frustration for when he could vent them on Lantis's punching bags. Stroking Claudette's back, he could find no words of comfort for her, not after seeing Kiera's injuries.

"Let's get to work," he suggested when her tears finally slowed to an occasional hiccup. Lantis had told Claudette to expect Dillon. Hopefully, the investigation would distract them both from the day's horrors.

Once he was confident she'd recovered her composure, Dillon left her in Kiera's office to hold the fort. His own duty required him elsewhere. From long practice, he ignored the shakiness in his belly as his adrenaline rush faded, stalking through kidTek's halls to the Security department.

With Claudette to champion him, no one at Security gainsaid Dillon's access to the records. In very little time, he was bent over the layout of the parking building and assigned employee slots while Warham, the head of Security, directed the reconstruction of events. A list of victims and unaccounted persons who were in the blast zone immediately prior to the explosion would help rescue efforts. However, Dillon was more interested in where and how the bomb had been planted—that information would help him identify the bastard responsible.

An uneasy silence prevailed in the monitor room, punctuated by sobs and gasps of shock, as horror-stricken staffers reviewed the parking building's records. To Dillon, the victims were mostly faceless individuals, but to the people around him they were friends and coworkers, someone they might have sat beside at lunch or traveled with on vacation. Their task was made more difficult by the timing: the end of the workday had resulted in a mass exodus.

"My fault this could happen. Should have stood pat on my

resignation last year," Warham muttered bitterly, crow's feet crinkling beside his pale green eyes as he scanned the banks of monitors replaying those last deadly minutes. He'd offered to step down when an investigation revealed his nephew's involvement in industrial espionage targeting kidTek. "No longer at the top of my game."

Damn right, you're not. Forcing himself not to respond to the older man's self-recrimination, Dillon plotted the locus of the explosion. He isolated it to the fourth floor based on external records of the fireball. A familiar name among the parking assignments for that area sent a spike of fear up his spine. *Damn it. Please, no!*

"I need the video for"—Dillon checked the sector—"level four, B-five." His delivery was clipped. Trepidation had his pulse racing as he waited for the record to play on the closest monitor, childhood prayers suddenly running through his head.

He'd thought he was prepared for what he would see, but the first screen still hit him like a roundhouse kick to the gut. Kiera exited the skywalk in animated conversation with a thin man who stood nearly a head shorter. She accompanied him to a red sports coupe, then took her leave with a wave.

As Kiera waddled through the departing crowd back to the skywalk, her companion turned to watch her passage, finally showing his face to the camera.

Damn. Dillon's heart stopped. It *was* Jordan Kane—his lover's cousin and namesake.

With an exultant grin, Dan slid into his car. A few seconds later, it exploded.

Chapter Twelve

Warham set down the phone, oblivious to Dillon's inner turmoil. "That was Claudette. The police is requesting copies of the parking building's records—access and egress, both vehicle and personnel."

Dillon's brows rose in surprise. *That was quick.* The police were giving the situation top priority. Such a cold, impersonal term: *situation.* But that was how he had to think of it; he wouldn't be able to function otherwise.

Throttling back his rage behind a mask of control, he threw a glance at the monitors displaying real-time exterior video. The firefighters had extinguished the various blazes, leaving the parking building a charred hulk. Most of the victims were gone, only bystanders remained—easy prey for the media vultures jockeying for position along the police line.

A few reporters were trying to gain access to the main complex. So far, it looked like kidTek's reinforced frontline security detail was enough to keep them out.

Following his gaze, Warham added: "Some of my people have also gotten hints from reporters that they're willing to pay well for footage of the blast."

Damned bloodsuckers. Dillon scowled. "Can you code it for access lock?" That would limit access to authorized personnel and allow them to trace the source of any video. It wouldn't help Lantis to have a constant reminder of the magnitude of Kiera's injuries splashed in the news.

The older man nodded. "Yes, we can also put in a watermark to degrade broadcast images."

The suggestion gave Dillon pause. "Tempting. Will it affect the actual video?"

Warham shook his blond head. "It's more on the level of encryption. It's not foolproof, but it's better than nothing."

"Do it, on my authority." Kiera wouldn't object. The records wouldn't compromise the security of kidTek's projects, and Dillon intended to take copies of the same records for later study. "And let me know before you give the files." He had to inform Jordan of Dan's death before she found out from someone else, someone who might not care. But he couldn't leave until things were under control at kidTek, not when Kiera and Lantis were depending on him.

Which reminded Dillon he had yet to get an update on his heart sister's condition. *Best get it over with quickly.* He braced for bad news. "Any word on Kiera?" The first few hours were critical for survival, as he well knew. If she lasted that long, she had a good chance of making it.

The room fell silent as the staffers strained to hear their chief's answer.

"She's still in surgery," Warham replied, his narrow face crumpling in anguish.

Giving the older man a tight smile, Dillon nodded acknowledgment, conscious of their audience. "She's a fighter. You have to believe that." And Lantis was at her side. He'd keep her alive. *And the baby?*

Relief and anger clashed in his heart and gut. He forced it all down and under control. He had to do something: beat on a wall, break some heads, anything but wait for updates. Standing around, overseeing video reviews, made him feel trapped, like treading water waiting for a shark to bite. To vent his restless energy before he unnerved the staffers, he left the monitor room with a cursory "Have Claudette call me, if anything comes up."

Sheer fury bore him down the corridor, a thundercloud that urged him to lash out, smash, kill. Shooting would be too good for the bomber. A neuro spell would be too fast—probably satisfying while the screams lasted—but too fast. When he got his hands on the perp, he'd string him up by the balls then get his fists bloody. But to do that, he had to find him first.

To give his roaming purpose, Dillon headed for the blast zone. He found a row of windows on the fourth floor facing the gaping hole in the parking building. The thick safety glass was a wall of shattered prisms glittering in the late-afternoon sun, bearing witness to the ferocity of the blast. He reported the damage to Claudette as he searched for somewhere with a good view of the destruction.

As he got closer, a panel gave way, falling in a tinkling cascade of a thousand shards. Its advent was greeted by a chorus of weary curses on the ground.

"Just lost one," Dillon added into his cell phone. "Better have the area below roped off, and up here, too. The others may go anytime."

Claudette acknowledged his instruction with a soft sigh before breaking the connection. She was another one who'd put in long hours, finding out who of the injured had been sent to which hospitals and contacting their next of kin with the information—in addition to everything else.

Leaning against the inner wall, Dillon studied the parking building beyond, which was framed by jagged glass fringes, then closed his eyes against a wave of horror. If Dan hadn't waited, Dillon would have lost Kiera just like that—and in all probability Lantis soon after, given that intimate, ineffable bond between wife and husband he'd witnessed. He drew in a shuddering breath, murmuring a prayer of gratitude. It was a miracle Kiera had survived, considering just how close she'd been to the blast.

The last media van rolled out of sight, taking with it most of the risk of immediate notoriety. Welcoming that dubious safety, Dillon stepped out of the building, onto the rubble-covered street, his muscles stiff from several hours seated in front of a monitor.

Magelights hung in midair. The miniature suns turned the early spring night into more than daylight, dispelling the shadows around the wrecked building. The firefighters and ambulances had long since abandoned the site, leaving the police to pick up the pieces. The bystanders had also gone home to gossip, to celebrate their survival, to mourn.

He wished he could do the same.

To think just this morning the most serious thing on his mind had been plotting how to bribe Timothy to his side. He'd have welcomed an evening of wooing Jordan and circumventing the cat's interference. Instead he was faced with this.

Dillon checked the time. Warham had managed to keep the casualty list under wraps, but Dillon didn't expect that to last much longer, not once the cops got hold of it.

And Jordan still had to be informed of Dan's death.

He rolled his neck to banish the tightness that threatened to take up permanent residence in his muscles. He couldn't let Jordan face that alone. It might be selfish of him but he needed to be there, to provide emotional support when she was told.

Luckily, Jordan was quite single-minded about her art and would probably be busy working on the psyprint for the charity auction for a while longer. That should give him enough time to talk to the cops and handle what was left that could be handled of kidTek's situation. Then he could go to Jordan without letting Kiera and Lantis down.

Straightening his shoulders, Dillon strode to the police line for a closer view. No matter how many times and from how many angles he'd watched the explosion, he still needed to walk the actual site.

The amber ward floating at chest height flared in warning at his approach, calling the attention of a distant cop monitoring the police line.

A cool breeze stirred the lock on Dillon's forehead, bringing with it the acrid smell of burnt fuel, melted rubber, and concrete dust. And beneath it all was the stench of blood and charred meat— a jarring reminder of his other life. It made his stomach growl.

Crime scene techs prowled around, taking pictures and gathering debris. Radios crackled, cameras clicked, hushed voices rose and fell. Traffic along the distant highway barely impinged on the heavy silence.

Moving away from the cop, he paced along the police line, looking for anything red. He didn't hold out much hope of finding scraps of Dan's car—the bomber must have used the equivalent of a few blocks of plastic explosive—but stranger things could happen.

Large masses of concrete cratered the pavement, remnants of the blown-out supporting pillar Dan's car had been parked behind. Any scraps would likely be beyond them. Had the cops found anything?

Tucking his hands into his pockets, Dillon stared up at the gaping hole, wondering how soon the cops would release the site. With an accurate starting point and sufficient psychic residuals, chances of a successful retrospection that showed what exactly had occurred were good. But casting the spell couldn't be delayed for long. As time passed, the risk of missing something increased, as the residuals dispersed and the vicinity changed.

A chill ran up his spine at the thought of seeing Dan's final moments up close. It could just as easily have been Kiera.

Wrenching his thoughts back to business, Dillon reviewed the sequence of events in his mind. Dan had gotten into his car, closed the door, and then a few seconds later, it blew up.

That ruled out temperature and acceleration switches, probably even tilt switches. Still, the bomber could have used remote control, the ignition, a timer, a psyche switch, even a pressure switch—although the latter was unlikely, given the delay in detonation.

The only locations with a good vantage point of Dan's assigned parking slot were all in the sprawling kidTek complex. Which meant a remote-controlled detonation required an insider: someone with a grudge against Dan and the company. He'd have Warham's team investigate that possibility, although the cops would probably look into it as well.

A timer was chancy unless Dan made a habit of leaving work exactly on time. Pulling out his PDA, Dillon made a note to check that.

Knowing the method would help narrow the pool of potential bombers. Wiring a bomb to a car's ignition was fairly basic, but usually meant detonation at the victim's place of residence.

Dillon's stomach roiled at the thought. It could have killed Jordan.

A psyche switch, on the other hand, was more sophisticated, requiring an elaborate spell to activate the detonator—and therefore a mage to set it. Depending on the parameters of the spell, it might mean kidTek was the target and—possibly—easy access to Dan's car presented an opportunity.

"See anything interesting?" a hostile voice rapped out in challenge, close by his shoulder.

A burly man, his balding brown hair and close-cut beard running to gray, stood on the other side of the police line, eyeing him with extreme suspicion. A gold shield clipped to his jacket lapel identified him as a cop. He wasn't one of Dillon's police acquaintances though, certainly not the commander of the tactical response team he'd worked with last year.

"Not yet." Sheathing his stylus, Dillon pocketed his PDA. "Any idea when you'll release access?" Kiera would want to know. He clung to that belief. As soon as she was better, she'd want to know. That, the identities of the casualties, the status of the investigation—everything. He meant to have it for her.

"You're in a damn hurry," the cop observed, his voice harsh with the hoarseness of a longtime smoker.

"The building's structural magic needs to be checked, maybe even reinforced. Our people need their cars."

"Is that right?" The other man's heavy brows beetled, his brown eyes flat and cold. "Well, I need to solve a multiple homicide. That takes precedence."

Dillon flexed his wrist, his wand a reassuring presence strapped to his forearm under his sleeve. "No argument there. But that'll be much more difficult if the floors collapse." He met the older man's gaze, refusing to look away.

A scuff broke the visual deadlock. His opponent turned his head to check out the new arrival.

"L-T. Dillon." An athletic woman with a striking white lock streaking through wavy, black hair nodded in greeting on the other side of the police line. Dillon recognized her: Sergeant Cynarra Malva of the tactical response team. Rio's lover. "Something up?"

"You know him?" Another brusque question. Obviously, Dillon's reception wasn't special treatment.

"He's Dillon Gavin. With kidTek," Malva replied, an arched brow rising.

With a cryptic grunt, the thickset cop raised his badge to the amber ward—which flashed green along a short section near the badge—then walked through. "Lieutenant Thomas Derwent. Homicide," he introduced himself, his delivery only slightly less aggressive.

Malva quickly duplicated Derwent's action and joined them on the same side of the police line. "What's up?"

Focusing his will through his wand, Dillon cast a privacy spell around the three of them. While everyone in sight appeared to be on police business, there was no telling who might be hiding in the shadows.

Malva's gray eyes narrowed; evidently, she'd sensed the power he'd raised, but she didn't comment on it.

Turning his back to the magelights, Dillon tilted his head, placing his mouth in shadow—a defense against lipreading. "I'm hoping to do a retrospection. The sooner, the better."

"That's our job," Derwent growled.

"We need to know what to protect against, what got through security. We can't resume operations until then," Dillon countered. "The longer we wait, the more changes there'll be. That could kill our chances for a successful retrospection."

"You'd need a very specific target for the spell," Malva remarked. "That's more important."

Dillon nodded, acknowledging her point. "The bomb was in a red, late-model Sirocco parked on the fourth level. It was right behind that pillar." He jerked his chin toward the massive concrete blocks lying some feet away.

"How'd you know that?" the older man demanded, a glint of suspicion in his eyes.

"We've been going through the records to identify the casualties. Making sure everyone's accounted for." Dillon clenched his jaw against a surge of outrage, his teeth aching from the tension. "The blast nearly killed kidTek's president. And there's no guarantee it still won't."

The lieutenant's face went blank, then was filled by a darker scowl. Malva's eyes widened, their ash gray lightening to silver. It seemed that little bit of news had yet to leak out.

"She was the target?" Malva pulled out a PDA and scribbled on it.

Dillon shrugged, keeping his face still with an effort. "It wasn't her car. The driver was killed."

Derwent's bushy brows lowered, his thick shoulders bunching in his wrinkled suit. "I want to see what you have and copies of everything." The homicide lieutenant clearly felt his territory was under threat.

Tough. Dillon wanted his hands around that murdering bomber bastard's neck soonest. He'd do whatever if took to get it done. If that meant stomping all over the cop's feet, too bad. The older man would just have to live with it.

Of course, if cooperation would get the retrospection done sooner, he was willing. He didn't have the manpower to duplicate the official investigation.

"Come with me." Dillon turned back to kidTek's office building, steeling himself for another session of seeing how close he had come to losing Kiera and Lantis.

Derwent stared at the blank screen long after the video ended, his eyes bleak. The lines on his face were etched deep, as though he'd aged decades in the viewing.

Malva had her arms crossed over her belly, ice-cold fury stamped on her aristocratic features. An outraged Amazon queen bent on extracting vengeance.

Dillon turned away, his gut churning once more from the reminder of Dan's death and the certain knowledge of Jordan's grief still ahead. Through the open conference door, he could see Warham's staff at their stations, picking at their food, working to identify the last of the casualties. The conversation that reached him was dispirited, the horrific present and uncertain future hanging over the room like a dismal shroud.

A tired huff pulled his attention back to his companions.

"Can you do it? This retrospection. Personally?" Derwent's

brown gaze drilled into him, hard as polished granite, clearly skeptical of Dillon's claim.

"Alone?" Anticipation stirred in Dillon, the sense of a hunt in progress. His gut settled at the prospect of action. "Maybe. Depends on the site."

"What about the site?"

"Its stability. That would dictate the size of the perimeter." From what Dillon had seen, the spell would have to enclose an area of at least twenty feet in diameter, or even larger, if the floor around the blast zone was weak.

Derwent shot a silent query at Malva, who shook her head. "Carmichael couldn't, even if he were here. Not a site as large as that crater."

A look of bitter revulsion flashed across the homicide lieutenant's bearded face, as though he'd been served a meal of monkey brain. "Our scrying specialist is out of town for training." He had to mean Carmichael. "He won't be back until next week."

Dillon suppressed a protest. They couldn't wait that long; with retrospections, time was of the essence. But it wouldn't do to bull his way through either, even though he could go over the cop's head and jump the chain of command. He couldn't afford to be on the wrong side of Derwent right now, not when he might need police assistance.

"How soon can you do it?" The burly, older man glowered up at him as though Carmichael's absence were Dillon's fault.

A surge of relief made Dillon's breath catch. He cleared his throat. "When can I get access to the site?"

"Not for a couple of days. Fire chief needs to sign off on structural integrity. Right now, no more than two men are allowed in the affected areas at any time." The scowl on Derwent's face suggested that the limitation was casting a hex on the investigation.

"Besides," Malva added, "we'll need time to arrange for a doc crew and at least three cameras, preferably four."

Dillon nodded, forcing back impatience. As much as he wanted to get the retrospection over and done with, it wasn't possible. "I can plan the spell from the records on hand." And use the time to get the materials he'd need.

"Good." Derwent nodded once, sharp and almost surly. Dillon supposed the other man was unhappy about the delay—or perhaps the need to involve a "civilian."

"Cyn'll let you know when we have clearance." The homicide lieutenant looked at Malva, who bobbed her head in affirmation.

One down. Dillon couldn't let himself relax, despite getting the green light for the retrospection. Jordan still needed to be notified of Dan's death.

Leaving the input plate, Jordan ran her hands over the psyprinter's tact board to check the image one last time. Under her palms, the protruding sharp-tipped pins depicted a dark-haired male lying in shadow, naked and facedown on a bed of moss, and surrounded by wildflowers. She trailed her fingers over a muscular, bare shoulder, wishing it were the real thing.

The image seemed anonymous enough; only those who knew him well might recognize Dillon as the model from the lines of his back. *I wonder how he'll take it?*

She stretched slowly, arms wide, arching her back with a sigh of satisfaction. She was lucky Dan had offered to take Timothy to the vet for his routine checkup. Her feet ached from standing and her palms were itchy from the sharp pins, but in the meantime, she'd managed several hours' work on the psyprint for Spatha's charity auction without any distractions.

She stepped back to confirm the psyprinter's tray was full of standard-size Kirlian paper, then had her faithful machine save and print the image. It was just the initial version. She'd tweak the color and composition several times more before she was done and the final outsized image was printed.

A soft mewl of hunger interrupted the quiet buzz of the psyprinter. Timothy followed up with another slightly more insistent cry, informing her that he'd been politely patient, but he wanted his dinner.

"Don't tell me Dan didn't feed you after the vet," Jordan chided the cat in amusement. Even if he'd been in a hurry to go someplace, her cousin wouldn't have overlooked that, not when it gave him the chance to sneak Timothy some fresh salmon.

Her pet whined piteously, planting a furry paw on her foot.

"Oh, alright." Jordan gave in as she always did since her pet was usually good about not begging. Because he hadn't interrupted her while she worked, she decided he deserved a reward. She accompanied Timothy to the kitchen, wondering where Dan had gone off to tonight.

Her pet dug into his meal with a vengeance, not waiting for her to finish dishing out his food. He scoffed down his cat food with low growls of relish, as though he hadn't been fed in days. The sounds awakened hunger pangs in Jordan's stomach, reminding her it had been some time since the sandwich she barely had for lunch, eager as she had been to get back to the psyprinter.

With the urge to create no longer driving her so insistently, her stiff muscles were making themselves known—particularly those that had gotten a workout yesterday. Not that she regretted any of it—just the memory sent a shiver of raw need through her and a trickle of heat between her thighs.

"Prrp?"

"It's nothing, Tim." Blushing, she dealt with the dirty dishes. As she dried her plate, the doorbell rang, filling the kitchen with its low robust tones.

Who could be dropping by this late? Caution compelled Jordan to open herself to her clairvoyance as she went to the door. *Dillon stood on the porch, a thickset older man at his side. Despite his customary watchfulness, her lover seemed preoccupied. Tired. And so very grave.* Why was he here?

"Jordan? It's me." The tension weighing on Dillon's normally light baritone matched the tightness of his jaw. It triggered a chill wave of unease that raised the hairs of her arms. The wrinkle between his brows made her uneasy as did the meaningful look he exchanged with his companion.

She picked up Timothy, wanting the softness of her pet's fur in her hands, then opened the door. "I wasn't expecting you. What are you doing here so late?"

Dillon's hesitation was quite unlike him. He opened and closed his mouth as though at a loss for words. Finally, he gestured toward his companion. "This is—"

"Lieutenant Thomas Derwent, Aurora PD, ma'am," the shorter man introduced himself with a curt bob of his balding head. Sporting graying brown hair, white at the temples, and a full grizzled beard, he presented an image of competent authority. "Ms. Kane? Do you mind if we come in?"

"Oh, of course." Still wondering about their purpose, she led them to the living room. She took refuge in the corner of the sofa, tucking her feet under her and settling Timothy on her lap. Dillon sat beside her, his leg touching hers, his heat and scent stirring memories of breathless, sensual pleasures—something she didn't need in the presence of the police officer.

Lieutenant Derwent chose to sit on the ottoman. "I'm afraid we have some bad news. Your cousin, Jordan Kane, was killed in an explosion this afternoon."

A chill shot through Jordan. "What?" She pulled Timothy to her chest, taking comfort from his rumbling purr.

"Dan's dead," Dillon said gently.

"That's preposterous. He's in perfect health." Jordan clutched at Dillon's hand. *How could they make such a tasteless joke?*

Dillon exhaled sharply, as if bracing himself. "There was a bomb at kidTek. Dan was killed."

Concrete rubble made a maze of the street. People lay on the

*sidewalk, dirty, bloodied and dazed, like castoff rubbish after a gory
parade. A strangely flat image of the back of her cousin, half-hidden
as he walked beside Kiera Atlantis. A video on a monitor, she realized. They stopped by Dan's babe car, his largest expense that he lavished so much care on. Her cousin's beaming face just before he
opened the door. He sat in the driver's seat looking out his window,
then a flash of light—so fast the reds and yellows barely registered—
and a wave of destruction. The screen went black.*

Flinching, she hugged Timothy close, slammed her shields
down on her sight. It couldn't be true. For once, her psychometry
had to be wrong!

"Jordan?" The touch of a rough, hot hand on her arm jerked
her out of her daze.

She shook her head weakly. "That's impossible. He brought
Timothy to the vet this afternoon. He's just—" She waved a hand,
unable to find words. "Out. You must be mistaken." She couldn't
think, couldn't speak. Couldn't breathe.

Timothy butted her chin, chirping a question, but as frozen as
she felt, she couldn't answer him.

"I'm sorry, Jordan." Dillon's voice was tight, husky with fa-
tigue and— Jordan's mind shied away from the thought. "I saw
the video myself." *A flash of light, reds and yellows.* He inhaled un-
steadily, his grip tight. "It was Dan."

Dan's dead? A bomb?

Something shuddered inside her.

She wouldn't talk to him ever again. Wouldn't tease him
about his work. Wouldn't laugh at his pampering Timothy behind her back. Wouldn't hear him joke about his love life or—

Jordan's control shattered, tears spilling as she shook her head
in wordless denial, as much a wreckage of the explosion in the
video as the rubble in the street. She buried her face in Timothy's
fur as she continued to shake her head. *It can't be true! Dan—* Her
image of her cousin disintegrated in a flash of reds and yellows.

Dillon's arms enveloped her in warmth; she knew they did but couldn't feel it. His heat didn't penetrate the thick ice around her. Even Timothy's purring felt distant.

The memory of other explosions involving Dillon intruded, touching her heart with frost. Shoving them out of her mind, Jordan turned to her lover, sobbing as she pressed her face against his chest. She'd already lost Dan, she couldn't face losing Dillon as well. Not yet.

Chapter Thirteen

Jordan's hot, hard pillow rose against her cheek. She didn't stir, feeling emptied, enervated. Grief did that, she remembered. Before, it was because of her father, killed in an arson fire, followed shortly by her mother. This time, it was Dan, her younger, easygoing cousin who'd moved in with them to attend college, then never left.

Now, he was gone.

As her eyes watered, her pillow shifted. A heavy, furry weight slid across her back with an indignant yelp, then her pillow gathered her close.

"Are you going to be alright?" Dillon whispered, his lips brushing her ear. "I have to check on Lantis." His comrade, whose wife—Dillon's childhood friend—was seriously injured; of course, Dillon would want to talk to him.

Tightening her arms, Jordan buried her face against his chest in self-indulgent refusal to face the morning, breathing in his musk and heat, wishing they could stay like this forever.

Except they couldn't.

Dan was dead, but life went on. She remembered that from last time as well. "Yeah," she sighed.

Dillon's hands started exploring, his rough palms waking sensual responses she'd thought shocked to quiescence; she didn't remember *them* from last time. Lambent flames gathered under her skin, fanned to life by his caresses. "You sure?"

Need responded sluggishly, a slow melting in her core that welcomed his attentions. He might have meant to be comforting, but Jordan's body had other ideas, heating and preparing for greater intimacy. He hadn't made love to her last night, merely held her in his arms while she grieved. Now, she wanted more.

Here, now. She wanted to forget about death and loss. Dan had been killed by random violence, but Dillon sought it out, deliberately put himself in danger with his job. When his vacation ended, she might never see him again.

Needing stronger contact, Jordan pressed her mound against him, wanting to imprint his touch on her body. It wasn't enough. She tangled her legs with his, straddled a hairy thigh and rolled her hips, grinding her pelvis on hard muscle. Sweet delight eddied through her, rewarding her efforts.

Against her belly, his penis twitched and thickened. "Jordan?"

She took him in her hand, stroking his silken length with carnal intent. "I will be." It wasn't as if grief was new to her, after all. Sex would be just another way of coping.

Dillon hissed when she rubbed the flare of his head, his shaft swelling prodigiously in her grip. "Are you shh—"

Jordan set him at her vulva and drew him in. Penetration was awkward and uncomfortable; she was tight and barely wet but she wanted him inside her right now. No waiting until she was ready for him.

"Take it easy."

Still trying to take more of him, she panted. "No, now!"

"You're a stubborn one," he murmured into her ear, his lips

gliding down the sensitive edge. Then he nipped her, right where her neck met her shoulder.

Pure lightning struck her core, searing her with raw pleasure. Jordan squealed as cream gushed between her thighs and Dillon sank into her, all the way in. "Ooooh!"

He groaned in answer, his hard sex pulsing against her tender folds. His hands on her buttocks holding her securely in place, he kissed her with exceeding sweetness, tempting her to take her time, unswerving in his seduction of her senses. He rocked her gently, more of a sway than a thrust, yet putting just enough pressure on her clit.

She let him, content with his pace now that she had him where she wanted him. In her arms, between her thighs, so deep inside her he nudged her core. Surrounded by his body like this, she could pretend nothing bad would ever happen again.

Her orgasm gathered slowly, rising as inevitably as the tide. It broke over her in a wash of glory, restrained in its power. Leaving her breathless.

Dillon growled as he took his release, his penis pulsing against her inner membranes as he bathed her with heat. His fingers dug into her buttocks, a tactile reminder of his lethal expertise and the perils he faced. At least while on vacation, he wasn't in any danger.

Jordan hummed, her mood lifting with the aftermath of pleasure. "Now, I'm alright." She kissed his shoulder in thanks.

"I'll be back tonight." Dillon's lips brushed her temple. "Lantis will want to stay with Kiera. I have to help him out with his projects. It'll be one less thing for him to worry about." He sounded truly apologetic, as if he wanted to stay with her despite everything he'd said.

Don't read too much into it, Jordan.

"Of course you have to help him."

∞

Needing noise to drown out her doleful thoughts, Jordan switched on the radio. "—terday. Nineteen people were killed and forty-eight injured by the blast," a man announced in a pompously grave tone. Appalled, she stood unmoving as the reporter continued his litany of tragedy. "Four of the victims later succumbed to their injuries. Police—" *Click.*

She switched to another station, hoping to hear music.

"—no one has claimed responsibility—" *Click.*

"—was driving down the highway. There was a loud—" *Click.*

"—people were scre—" *Click.*

Biting her lip, Jordan shut off the radio, unable to listen to more. The abrupt silence was a balm to her nerves. She shuddered. *Four more senseless deaths!*

"Mew?" Timothy planted his paws on her waist, his claws prickling through the thin cotton of her blouse. The pointed threat pulled her out of the downward spiral of her reverie.

"Right." She nodded acknowledgment of his warning against excessive melancholy, laughing shakily. "Thanks, Tim."

The import of the news suddenly dawned on her. *Oh, no. Dillon!* She could only hope John Atlantis's wife wasn't one of the four mentioned.

The doorbell rang before she could seek the refuge of her studio and the work that awaited her. That couldn't be Dillon; he wouldn't have forgotten anything important enough to deflect him from checking up on his childhood friend.

Opening herself to her clairvoyance, Jordan directed her vision to the porch. *Shanna stood there, fairly jittering with tension, her short hair a pretty blue Jordan had never seen on anyone else. She wore a smart greenish blue suit that complemented her hair, obviously dressed for work.*

Walking quickly down the hall, Jordan reviewed her schedule for the day. Had she forgotten a meeting?

"Dillon just told me about Dan. How horrible!" the other woman exclaimed as soon as Jordan stepped out.

Jordan stood there, dumbfounded. While Shanna had been to her home before, it had rarely been for social purposes. *Dillon called her?*

Tears welled up in the other woman's brown eyes as she pulled Jordan into a tight hug. "I'm so sorry."

Oh, no! Jordan froze with her arms out, her hands fisting in self-protection. Her agent knew Dan, had been one of his many lovers years ago. She didn't feel up to seeing a memory of her cousin and knowing he was—

Luckily, Shanna burst into speech, interrupting the flow of Jordan's thoughts. "Don't worry about Spatha. I'll—"

"No, no," Jordan protested hurriedly. "I can do it." In fact, she needed to do it, needed it to occupy her mind. If she obsessed over Dan's loss, she'd dissolve into impotent tears.

"Are you sure?" Shanna loosened her embrace, her arms quivering with restraint, her brows lowered in concern.

"Yes."

"If you can't, I'll make sure Fab understands the situation."

The door creaked as Timothy managed to curve his paws around its edge and pull it open. "Mew?"

Her agent bent down to pet the cat. "Dillon asked me to come stay with you today. You shouldn't be alone at a time like this." Her hazel eyes darted to Jordan, obviously wondering about her connection to Dillon.

Jordan reluctantly invited the other woman inside. As much as she craved solitude, wanting only to be left alone to lick her wounds, it looked like she wasn't going to get it.

Shanna hovered protectively as a relentless stream of friends and acquaintances, neighbors more known to Dan, dropped by with food and condolences, sympathy and morbid curiosity shining in their avid eyes. She managed to roust out most of the gossips, leaving Jordan to take comfort from the rest.

Despite her agent running interference, it took all that Jordan had to feign ignorance of the specifics of the bombing in the face of prying questions. It was enough to know that Dan was dead; she didn't want to relive the visions of his murder she'd picked up from Dillon. Then news reporters descended on the house.

Turning on Lantis's equipment, Dillon set one screen to monitoring current news. Though Claudette was holding the line at kidTek, it wouldn't do to get caught flat-footed by sudden developments. Forewarned did mean forearmed.

Most of the local channels continued to devote airtime to the incident: factual reports, opinions, reactions, firsthand accounts, rumors, grandstanding. He settled on a channel whose news reporting was less hysterical than most.

The screen showed only an aerial shot of kidTek's parking building from a distance. It looked like the police had managed to keep the video under wraps so far. Dillon stared at the black smoke billowing up in the afternoon sky, remembering the chaos that had met him yesterday. At least Kiera was in the hands of the best healers available; Lantis wouldn't have it otherwise.

Discreet chimes recalled him to the present and the task that awaited him. With raised brows, he activated the screen for the external cameras, which Lantis always kept running. His former partner didn't have an appointment scheduled for today, so who was at the door?

The security monitor showed Rio Rafael—Riordan to his enemies—casually dressed in a red muscle shirt, black jeans, and hiking boots, leaning against the far wall, his thumbs hooked in his front pockets. A quick cycle of the other cameras on the floor showed that his fellow black ops agent was alone.

Dillon unlocked the steel door to stare at the lounging Latino. "What's up?"

"Besides gas prices?" The younger man pushed off the wall. "Heard about the bomb at kidTek. Cyn suspects you're looking into it."

Cyn? *Ah, Detective Sergeant Malva.*

"So?"

"Need help?"

In one simple gesture, the detective acknowledged she couldn't stop him from investigating the bombing, inserted a sympathizer into his ranks, aided his efforts, and opened another line of communication with him. *Efficient woman.*

"Wouldn't turn it away." Pivoting on his heel, Dillon jerked his head toward Lantis's office.

As Dillon closed the door, Rio stopped beside him and laid a hand on his shoulder. "I also heard Kiera was injured. How's Lantis taking it?"

"He's hanging in there." When Dillon had stopped by the hospital earlier, Lantis had been outside Kiera's room, keeping vigil, while healers worked over her. He'd practically been in a trance, so focused on Kiera he hadn't noticed Dillon's approach. From the lines on his face, his former partner hadn't slept yet.

Dillon briefed Rio on the status of the investigation, then put him to work double-checking the faces on record as entering or leaving the parking building against their official pictures. The media were bruiting about terrorist conspiracies. Dillon had his doubts, if only because of the unlikeliness of the target, but if they were right, Rio with his artist's eye for detail had a better chance of identifying the perp.

At the same time, Dillon could devote his time to planning the retrospection. At its core, the spell wasn't a complicated working. It tapped on-site psychic residuals and projected them through prisms to create a holovid that could be seen and recorded. What made it difficult was the need for a specific time to target and the size of the area the spell would cover.

Dillon opened the security files Warham had provided him, looking for good angles of the blast site. He eyed the time stamp on the records. Luckily, as he'd told Rio's Cyn, he had a target and could pinpoint the time to within a few seconds of the blast.

Which, spell planning–wise, left the problem of coverage.

He called up a blueprint of the parking building and zoomed in on the affected fourth floor section. While news reports chattered in the background, he superimposed the blast site on it, took measurements and made a working image.

The crater alone was over twenty feet in diameter. Adding a few feet of safety margin all around—since the explosion would have weakened the concrete along the edges—and the resulting area described was nearly thirty feet in diameter.

He took a deep breath to settle his stomach.

That was much larger than optimal. It would be a strain to cast a spell over that much area—if he could even handle it. The largest he'd ever done was twenty-five feet with sixteen prisms; even with Lantis's support, it had been a bitch to cast.

Dillon chewed his lip in thought. Lantis probably had enough prisms, but balancing that many with the amount of power he'd have to use to cast the spell would be . . . a challenge.

Normally, for black ops purposes—usually simple information gathering—he didn't need to sweat the details. But this retrospection would be documented and might be used in court, which meant it needed to be a sharp rendition to stand up to close examination.

A retrospection could be cast with only two prisms but most mages worked with a minimum of three in an equidistant, triangular arrangement that provided two light sources for most points within the spell area. More detail as well as larger areas automatically required more prisms—resulting in a more difficult balancing act.

The location of the site also complicated matters. Dillon immediately disregarded the thought of adding scaffolding to span the empty space where the supporting pillar used to be. Three days weren't enough to make scaffolds that wouldn't interfere with the spell. He had to work with what he had, even though that meant it wouldn't be a complete circle. But the need for detail meant the pattern couldn't be just a semicircle: the arc had to exceed 180 degrees—requiring an even larger diameter, one over thirty feet.

Gritting his teeth, he studied his working image and added a blue circle to the diagram, adjusting its size and placement until it was concentric to the crater and matched his specifications. When he divided the circle into eight equal arcs, only one of the marks was on thin air.

He snapped out a measurement: thirty-two feet. But only seven prisms. He took a deep breath, his stomach rolling over uneasily. *Best-case scenario.*

Now, he had to take interference into consideration.

If he wasn't careful about where he drew that power from, he could inadvertently weaken the building's spell supports. Normally, that wasn't much of a problem. In the case of kidTek's parking building, however, structural magic was probably all that was keeping up the floor around the crater. Only a civil thaumaturgist would be able to tell what other damage the edifice had suffered. If its spell supports were weakened—even inadvertently—the whole thing could come tumbling down.

Dillon opened another file, the one with the status of the building's structural magic just before he'd left last night. The green and yellow lines of the spell modules for the fourth floor filled his screen. Thanking Kiera's father for his foresight in connecting that system to the sensor network, he propped his chin on his hand and slowly started deciphering the shorthand used by civil thaumaturgists to find the information he needed.

". . . local artist Jordan Kane." The rapid-fire words cut through the thick buzz of Dillon's concentration.

As he looked up, Jordan's image appeared, ringed by sound pickups, on the screen he'd set to monitoring news; obviously the media had finally discovered her connection to Dan. Lines of stress bracketed her lips, her eyes red from tears.

His gut tightening at the sign of her distress, Dillon turned up the volume. A gabble of voices ensued: shouted questions, speculation about terrorists, badgering.

Jordan shook her head in bewilderment, the camera angle shifting to reveal Timothy cradled defensively across her chest. "He designed toys."

"Do the police have any suspects?" someone shouted.

Hefting the cat higher, Jordan stepped away from the camera, her back against the door. "Why would they tell me if they did?" Her eyes were so wide Dillon could see red-streaked white all around her irises.

Anger stirred at the reporters' treatment of Jordan. *The bloody vultures don't care she's lost a loved one.* He dearly wanted to go over and break some faces.

"Ms. Kane doesn't have any further comments," interjected an aquamarine-haired Shanna, pushing her way to Jordan's side.

Timothy twisted in his mistress's arms to stare into the camera, his muzzle looming closer until his round blue eyes filled the screen. "Mew?"

Dillon snickered reluctantly, his concern easing at the cat's antics. At least his lover wasn't facing the assault alone. He forced himself back into the complexities of structural magic. He couldn't be with Jordan, but he could help discover who'd murdered Dan and injured Kiera.

It was a while before he managed to extract the information he needed. Lunch had come and gone before he was satisfied he hadn't overlooked any important detail. He took the grid that represented the spell modules, superimposed them on his working image and hissed in disgust.

"What's wrong?" Rio eyed him over the laptop he was using.

Drumming his fingers on the desk, Dillon scowled at his own screen. "What's not wrong?" He exhaled sharply, studying the telltale lines. "Half of the prisms will be sitting on support grid nexuses."

The Latino took his answer as an invitation for discussion,

standing up to join him behind Lantis's desk. Dillon couldn't complain; the records his friend was handling couldn't be all that exciting.

"You mean these?" Rio tapped the points on the screen where the marks on the blue circle coincided with intersections of yellow lines that signified weakened spell modules.

"Exactly."

"What if you rotate this slightly?" the Latino suggested, indicating the circle.

Rather than waste time arguing, Dillon showed him. There was no angle where fewer than three marks were on nexuses: moving a mark off a yellow cross shifted another one on. Given the proximity of the spells, if Dillon used ambient magic to cast the retrospection, it was guaranteed he'd draw on the building's structural magic.

Rio shook his head slowly. "You are soooo fucked." With a commiserative thump on Dillon's shoulder, he returned to his records.

Agreeing with his friend's assessment, Dillon stared at the daedal mess on the screen. No matter what he tried, the outcome remained the same. But that didn't change the bottom line: he had to cast the retrospection. At the same time, he couldn't risk interfering with the spell supports.

He scrubbed his face, forcing his tired brain to work. There had to be a way to solve this mess. If he couldn't go through it, couldn't go under or over or around, what did that leave him?

Redefine the problem. Change the board. Alter the playing field. Previous advice from Lantis drifted through Dillon's memory. Just because they'd been on one mission or another at the time didn't diminish the merit of his friend's counsel.

Get out of the box. Right. He needed sufficient power to cast the spell and couldn't depend on ambient magic. *Which leaves . . . ?*

The solution unfolded in his head with absurd, almost suicidal simplicity. It was so obvious he could have kicked himself for not thinking of it sooner. Of course, if Lantis knew what he was considering, his former partner would probably kick him for even thinking of it. This was crazier than his other mad ideas.

Dillon thought on it a bit longer, just so he could say—with all honesty—that he'd weighed the odds, then returned to his conclusion.

He'd have to work directly with the source.

A frisson of excitement flashed through Dillon at the prospect. Wicce lines—those channels of pure magic that sprung from the Earth's core and crisscrossed its surface—were notorious for unpredictable surges in power. Tapping a major one directly was ill-conceived, even in the direst situations, like hooking electronics to a lightning bolt when you needed a generator. A mage had a good chance of getting burned to a crisp if he tried.

But as he saw it, he didn't have a choice, not if he wanted to cast that retrospection. He acknowledged the risk, then shrugged it away, determination hardening his jaw. At least he had a fighting chance.

But is *there a major wicce line around kidTek?* One thing Dillon was certain of: if there was one, it wouldn't be nearby. Kiera's father had made a point to minimize the use of magic in kidTek's complex because of Kiera's sensitivity to it; that consideration would also have influenced his site selection.

He accessed Lantis's files, searching for a map of wicce lines in kidTek's locality. Knowing his former partner, there was one on file somewhere, if only left over from last year. He found one that showed a major wicce line near kidTek within his range. That solved the immediate question about power; whether he could wield it was a different problem altogether.

Since the point was moot, he didn't waste time contemplating his chances of failure. He still had to plan for worse: an even-larger circle.

But before he could do that, he had to inspect Lantis's supplies. For documentation purposes, the image had to appear as solid as possible—it wouldn't do to introduce more uncertainty into the investigation because of vague details. At the very least, his professional reputation was at stake.

That meant he had to get his hands on achromatic glass. No matter how well he planned, if he didn't have any or couldn't get enough, his plans would be worth less than the paper they weren't written on.

"I need to check something."

Rio waved at him absently, his other hand flowing over the keyboard in a stutter of keystrokes nearly drowned out by the murmur of voices from the news channel.

Lantis's secure storeroom was a mage's treasure trove, complete with a triple-locked rack of *materiae magicae*. Since Dillon didn't need anything there, he barely glanced at it, except to confirm that the rack's telltales were all green.

He paused at a china cabinet filled with enough glassware to satisfy an alchemist. The number of flat-bottomed bowls on display was more than he'd ever require for the retrospection, so he quickly moved on to a hardwood chest.

The first drawer he opened held semiprecious stones already shaped and polished for spellwork. The rest of the drawers contained more of the same: bloodstones, cairngorms, moonstones, tigerseye, and the like.

Going sunwise around the windowless chamber, he quickly opened doors and pulled drawers until he found prisms. There, his progress slowed since he had to inspect the transparent polyhedrons, working his way through diagnostic, chemical detection and other special-use prisms to no avail. None of them was suitable for a retrospection.

Luckily, he hit pay dirt in his next attempt. The drawer hung heavy on its slides, its weight resisting his pull. It contained thirty-six high-temperature-treated, fully coated achromatic glass prisms, still in their boxes.

Dillon blinked at the sizable investment they represented. *Damn, where does Lantis expect to use all that?*

He took the boxes out, piling them on the table in the middle of the room. Despite a sudden foreboding, they all contained exactly what the markings said.

With a sigh of mixed feelings, he returned the prisms to the drawer, storing them as he'd found them. The possibility of balancing thirty-six prisms didn't agree with his lunch. He realized he'd been nursing a vague hope in the back of his mind that Lantis wouldn't have enough prisms, that the decision would be taken from him by default.

Dillon shook his head. *You're an idiot, Gavin.*

A phone rang in the next room, an unfamiliar two-tone warble that barely drew attention.

He ignored the demure sound. Since he was in the storeroom anyway, he might as well see where he could find a box of colored chalk.

Rio answered the phone's summons. The intimate tone he used from the onset of the conversation identified his caller to Dillon as female. Perhaps a certain police detective?

Dillon completed his inspection of the storeroom without further luck. Scratching his jaw in thought, he turned on his heel to take in the whole chamber, lined from floor to ceiling in plain, uncommunicative ironwood.

Except for the glassware on display, it might have been mistaken for a walk-in closet. Even the rack of *materiae magicae*, conspicuous for its heavy spell protections, could have passed for an elaborate safe-deposit box for expensive jewelry.

But knowing Lantis, there had to be chalk on hand somewhere and it would be kept with the other spell materials. A shadow under the central table caught his eye, which proved to be a footlocker for more mundane supplies, including chalk.

He opened the box with a sense of validation. Despite his former partner's marriage, he still knew him well enough to follow the other man's thoughts.

Humming under his breath, Dillon considered the palette available to him. Any color would have worked just as well, but indigo was the closest to the violet he associated with his magic, so he decided that was what he'd use when the time came to cast the retrospection.

All he needed now was the green light from Derwent.

"It's Cyn." Cell phone still pressed to his ear, Rio swiveled his chair to face Dillon as he stepped back into Lantis's office. "Looks like her lieutenant's got a hammerlock on the fire chief."

Dillon grinned at the image.

"She wants to know if you can do the retrospection tomorrow at three in the afternoon." A dark brow quirked in question.

At the tighter deadline, Dillon's grin widened in predatory anticipation. Despite his foreboding, his heart gave a leap of eagerness. "No problem."

"He's good." Rio tilted his head in a listening stance. "Okay, I'll tell him. See you later." His voice dropped to a more intimate tone for the farewell as a smile crossed his face.

Sliding his cell phone into his jacket, the Latino turned to Dillon. "They'll meet you at the parking building at three."

Dillon nodded acknowledgment. That would give him time tomorrow to check Dan's lodgings and pull together the supplies he needed for the spell.

Chapter Fourteen

Dan's apartment lay on the second floor, just past the library with the busts of Jordan's parents. The room appeared untouched, as if awaiting the return of its occupant. If Jordan's cousin had hidden something, there was no sign anyone had come here looking for it before Dillon.

He wouldn't have been surprised if someone had. Searching it wouldn't have been that difficult even with Jordan around most of the time. Dan's apartment was almost separate from the main house, located as it was over the garage; it even had private access in the form of stairs from the garage.

Jordan's security spells wouldn't keep out a determined intruder. They were standard homeowner security, meant to repel ordinary housebreakers. It would take him less than five minutes to get through them; if he were Lantis, they wouldn't slow him for even a minute. And that was if he were going for stealth.

He glanced over his shoulder to check the short corridor behind him. He couldn't see much since the hall had an ell that ended at Dan's door, but it was empty and he didn't hear anyone behind him. *Good enough.*

Jordan would be busy for the next hour or so, working on the psyprint. He should have enough time to finish checking.

Although it looked like no one had searched Dan's room, there was only one way to be sure. He couldn't search it himself since this was a police investigation—leaving his own psychic residuals in Dan's quarters would only muddy the waters—but he didn't have to. A simple scan of the room would tell the tale, no need for a full retrospection.

Bending down, Dillon got a flat bowl he'd borrowed from Lantis's office out of his duffel bag. The bathroom in the hall provided him with water, which he sprinkled with salt.

He knelt in the hall and fished in the bag for the pouch with the prism.

Fur brushed his leg, nearly making Dillon jump. "Prrp?"

"Damn it, cat, don't startle me like that!"

Sitting back and wrapping his tail around his forepaws, Timothy stared up at him with a wide-eyed innocence that didn't fool Dillon. The cat was probably snickering to himself about catching him off guard.

Just then, Dillon's hand brushed the unmistakable pyramidal shape of the glass. He spilled the prism out of its pouch onto his palm, under the curious scrutiny of Jordan's pet, and placed it in the water-filled bowl, which he set at his feet.

To be on the safe side, he picked up the cat to make sure Timothy didn't do anything that might influence the spell. Luckily, Jordan's pet was content with his position and remained placid and silent in Dillon's arms even when he started to gather power.

He stroked Timothy, hoping the cat would be on his best behavior. He'd rather not attempt spellcasting while wrestling with a frisky pet.

Violet energy manifested over the bowl as ambient magic answered his summons. His skin tingled from the electric intensity, a common neural response to magic but one he'd yet to grow tired of feeling.

Claws prickled on Dillon's forearms as Timothy flexed his paws, his plumy tail flicking restively against Dillon's thigh. Jordan's pet probably felt the power, too, unless he was reacting to the growing brightness.

Mouthing the syllables of the spell to focus his intent, Dillon freed an arm from under the cat for the next stage. He tensed, wondering if Timothy would make a break for it. Now—while he drew in ambient magic—would be a likely time, but it looked like the cat had decided to stay put.

He scratched behind Timothy's ears in gratitude. The cat's long fur was standing on end and clung to his arm like iron filings to a magnet.

When he judged the power level to be sufficient for his needs, Dillon gathered his magic under his palm and forced it down, into the submerged prism. The spell sprang into being with a flash of white light and a hum of power he felt in his bones— along with the pointed bite of several claws.

He opened his eyes to a ghostly apparition.

Jordan stepped away from the tact board, knowing she had to be satisfied with what little progress she'd achieved. If she pushed at this point, as tired and depressed as she was, she'd only have to undo the damage to the psyprint later.

Now would be a good time to take a break and force herself to eat something. She was tempted to call Dillon, but he was busy in an office somewhere and probably couldn't take the time to come hold her hand. Luckily, her clairvoyance hadn't shown him doing anything intimate this time.

She headed to the pantry and the hatch for the groceries. Her order should have arrived by now and she hoped the prospect of ripe, juicy strawberries would wake her appetite. All the food gifts in the refrigerator and the media attention of the past days had only served to underscore Dan's death. Dillon's efforts to tempt her to eat had been in vain.

"Prrp!" Timothy ran ahead, ever hopeful of a handout.

Jordan laughed rustily. Her pet wouldn't be so eager once he saw the fruit. While he had a penchant for cantaloupe and honeydew melon, Timothy turned up his nose at other fruits, deeming them beneath his notice.

The hatch proved to contain her order, the strawberries still cold and fresh.

Timothy whined at her as soon as she pulled the container out of the bag, batting her ankles in reproach.

She washed the succulent fruit and set them to drain, ignoring her pet stropping her calves. Deciding she needed cream, she opened the refrigerator and reached inside. Soft fur brushed her hand as her pet stuck his head into the compartment, then a large paw pushed her grasping hand against the cold bottle she was looking for.

"Thanks, Tim."

"Mew?" he urged, clearly expecting a reward. He propped a forepaw on her hip, then claws clicked on the bottle in gentle demand.

Acquiescing gracefully, she placed a dollop of cream in his dish, then sat down to have her snack in peace.

Her hand faltered as she picked up a strawberry, the silence in the kitchen suddenly overwhelming. She almost expected Dan to come bounding in, to tease her about keeping Timothy on a healthy diet. He'd never do that now.

Tears welling up in her eyes, Jordan forced herself to dip the fruit into the cream and take a bite. It tasted too sweet but she made herself eat more, all the while crying in silence.

Starving herself until she fell ill wouldn't bring Dan back; she'd learned that bitter lesson when her father died. Maybe when Dillon got back, she could relieve his worry by eating a full meal.

Derwent's documentation crew was hard at work, lugging equipment to the fourth floor of the empty parking building, when Dillon drove up. To his surprise, both the homicide lieutenant and Malva were on hand, keeping a watchful eye on the proceedings.

As he got out of his rental, a van sporting the crossed-staves-and-flame seal of the fire marshal's office turned into the street to park behind him.

After exchanging nods of greeting with Derwent, Dillon turned to the tall Amazon. "I didn't expect to see you here." Not when her lieutenant was already present.

Malva arched a regal brow. "Are you kidding? Miss a retrospection of this size? I pulled rank to be here." Crossing her arms, she gave him a smug smile. "Carmichael will cry when he hears he missed this."

"She'll make sure he hears about it, too," Derwent grunted, a sparkle of amusement in his brown eyes. "If I hadn't put my foot down, you'd've had a gaggle of homicide cops here rubbernecking." He greeted the firefighter who joined them, made introductions, then led the way up the stairs to the fourth-floor site.

Dillon followed, silently giving thanks for small favors. The last thing he wanted was more witnesses. The specter of a massive failure floated through the back of his mind before he shackled it into submission.

"So, where's Rio?" Malva casually tossed the question over her shoulder as she reached the landing after the third-floor exit, and Derwent and the firefighter left the stairwell.

Dillon grinned as he climbed the stairs behind her, the duffel bag containing his precious supplies bumping against his hip. "In the office, slogging through the records."

She made a face, probably wishing Rio were here or in sympathy over the mind-numbing tedium of the Latino's task.

Outside the stairwell, the fourth floor stretched out in all directions, populated by silent cars. Voices echoed eerily in the emptiness, a muffled curse sounding as loud as a shout. Derwent was headed toward a narrow yellow ward glowing halfway down the row to their left.

"You really think you can do this?" Malva frowned at him, the low heels of her boots allowing her to look him in the eye without tilting her head. She flexed her broad shoulders, the movement emphasized by the black leather jacket she wore that swallowed light. "The largest Carmichael'd be willing to handle is ten feet."

"It's got to be done." He left it at that, unwilling to entertain the possibility of failure. If he couldn't do this, it would make catching the bomber more difficult. Jordan, Kiera, and Lantis were banking on his success.

Her concern aired, Malva didn't push the issue. Not that he expected her to; her relationship with Rio wouldn't have lasted this long if she were the type to pry. She left him to talk to some people clustered around an enormous pile of equipment.

Derwent approached him as Dillon carefully set down his duffel bag near what he judged to be the center of the crater's arch. "Still think you can do this?" The older man crouched down to scowl at the gaping hole ringed by a floating band of yellow protective magic. "There's no shame if you back out."

"If I don't, who will?"

The homicide lieutenant ran a hand over his grizzled beard. The glum look on his face said the police didn't have anybody else to throw at the problem besides the absent Carmichael.

Considering the matter closed, Dillon paced along the amber ward that defined the edge of the safe zone, according to the fire marshal's office. The size of it chilled him, had his heart pounding at the challenge. The area it described was nearly forty feet in diameter—much larger than he'd expected—and would take more power to cover.

He'd have to use more prisms. *Time for Plan B.*

His stomach churned at the thought of wielding that much

energy. If he couldn't control it, the least that might happen was he'd burn out his gift. The worst: he could interfere with the building's structural magic, and the entire edifice—all six stories of it—would collapse on them.

Not only would that put paid to any attempt at a retrospection, but falling almost thirty feet to a hard concrete pavement would be no fun, especially without any magic for protection from the drop and the rubble that would batter them. Explaining to Lantis how he managed to botch the spell would be even more painful.

That's the spirit. You don't want to fail.

He bent down to mark the spots for the prisms with indigo chalk, focusing on keeping his respiration even. Concentrating on the little details helped stave off the jitters.

Behind him, the police documentation crew had finished unpacking their equipment and was setting up cameras. Derwent had apparently instructed them to pull out the stops. They'd chosen six locations around the crater with cameras at three levels: overhead, eye level, and knee height.

Here's hoping they'd have something to record.

Ignoring their preparations, he pulled out flat bowls from a nest of eiderdown in his duffel bag—four more than he'd originally planned—and filled them from bottles in the bag. The mere act of pouring salt water into them had the thin glassware humming, almost as if by magic. The pure note helped soothe his nerves and center his thoughts.

A low whistle caught his attention. "Eleven? You can handle that many for an area this large?" Malva asked, crouching beside him with a frown knitting her brows. Seeing the size of the crater up close must have shaken her confidence.

He didn't blame her.

"Only one way to find out." Dillon opened the pouch of prisms in the bag and placed one in a waiting bowl.

"Damn, those are big." Malva picked up a prism by the corners and blinked. "Heavy, too." She raised it, turning the pyramid from side to side so that it caught the afternoon light and refracted it in bright flashes. "We don't have anything this good in the department." She squinted at the prism, then hefted it appraisingly. "This isn't just clear quartz, is it?"

Welcoming a distraction from the second thoughts clamoring for attention, Dillon grinned at the suspicion narrowing her gray eyes. "Fully coated achromatic glass. It's used for telescope and microscope lenses."

Her eyes widened. "Must be expensive."

"For high resolution, they're worth it." He placed the last prism in the pouch in a salt water–filled bowl, then zipped up the duffel bag. "Besides, private practice pays better."

She nodded in reluctant agreement. "Can I help?"

Dillon plucked the remaining prism from her grasp and submerged it in the last bowl. "Put these centered on the chalk marks. You take that side; I'll do this side."

It didn't take long to place the eleven bowls on the marks around the crater but Dillon took his time, moving in a measured pace that helped him rein in his surging impatience. Malva seemed to understand, matching her speed to his.

Returning to his chosen spot in the middle, he checked the five bowls on either side of him with a quick glance. They described an area around forty feet in diameter—more than half again the size of the largest retrospection he'd ever cast. His stomach fluttered with uncertainty and excitement, adrenaline flooding his veins with every beat of his heart, much like the first time he'd jumped out of a perfectly good airplane with only a parachute and an emergency angel spell on his back. *This is it!*

He checked his watch. *Almost time.* His pulse sped up.

Taking a deep breath to center himself and lock down the gibbering doubts that threatened to undermine his resolve, Dillon nodded readiness to Derwent. At his signal, the homicide lieu-tenant turned to the doc crew, who also signaled an all clear, then gestured to the waiting firefighter to deactivate the safety ward.

The amber glow shifted to red then vanished, leaving only a small bowl between him and the edge of the crater. Beyond them were empty space and a twenty-foot drop to the second floor. High enough to break a leg—if you weren't careful or lucky. It would have been nice to leave the ward on, but it would have in-terfered with the retrospection.

As chill wind blew in his face, Dillon twitched his wrist, re-leasing his short wand from its sheath and catching it in his hand. With the magnitude of power he had to summon, he'd need its buffer to succeed.

Closing his eyes, he stretched his arms out in front of him, the familiar staff cradled in the palms of both hands. At the very edge of his range, he sensed a major wicce line running strong from east to west, parallel to the highway, exactly where Lantis's map said it would be. He reached out to it warily; a sudden influx of power would be just as devastating to the building's structural spells as draining them of power.

Someone muttered impatiently behind him but was quickly shushed, leaving only wind to fill the silence.

Dillon ignored the exchange as he tapped the wicce line, opening himself to its treacherous potency. Firming his grip on his wand, he called pure magic to his location.

Power crashed through him like a bolt of lightning, searing his nerves with the energy of creation. His muscles locked under its onslaught, his heart stuttering, his lungs seizing in shock. His balls tried to climb into his belly.

Loud gasps sounded from all around him.

Oh, hell.

The elemental power threatened to overcome his autonomic system.

Breathe, damn it. Breathe!

It bore hard upon his defenses, raging for an outlet. Surge after scouring surge of burning energy battered his frozen body.

Damn it, they're depending on you! He fought the wild magic, forced it back an impossibly minute distance. Clawed at its bindings. Willed his paralyzed body to *MOVE!*

He gasped, cold, sweet air filling his lungs. With that breath, he gathered his resolve and wove it into a threadbare vestige of control, harnessing pure magic.

Panting, Dillon opened his eyes to slits. If his muscles weren't still mostly locked, he might have staggered.

His wand shone a brilliant purple, barely insulating him from the sheer power that had answered his summons.

Yes! Raw exultation flooded his veins at the sight, his heart leaping in triumph.

Gritting his teeth, he channeled magic to the line of waiting bowls arching away from him. He had to relax his restraints to reach the furthest pairs. As if sensing weakness, the power strained against his control, surging forward like a spring tide driven by high winds. The carved edges of his wand bit into his hands, his fingers cramping from the tightness of his grip. He hung on defiantly, trying to keep the flow of searing energy to manageable proportions.

An instant later, violet pools of power swirled over the glass, splashing against the rims with near-sentient delight. Eddies of magic flared up from the bowls like dust devils challenging his mastery.

The electric prickle strengthened, searing his nerves and wreathing his forearms with crackling violet sparks.

Dillon found himself baring his teeth in a savage grin as he gritted them against the burning intensity. The challenge sent blood singing through him, heady with vitality.

Forcing his knees to unlock, he knelt down and closed his

eyes as he mustered his will, whispering the spell to direct his intent. He steeled his resolve, commanding the wild magic to find the psychic residuals for those fatal minutes almost exactly forty-seven hours past.

Roaring power smashed against his control. He struggled to hold it swirling above the bowls as energy swept up his arms in sizzling arcs. His heart pounded at the danger, his pulse a drumfire in his ears. His breathing deepened, lungs pumping like the bellows of a forge. A dull throb in his head, his magic sense rebelling against his demands, was a minor annoyance.

His muscles quivering at the effort, Dillon extended his clenched hands over the bowl before him and shoved the seething energies down into the prisms. Red flared across his lids as the retrospection spell snapped into place with a near-audible crack of power. *YES!*

Yells of surprise erupted around him. Then someone whistled, long and low, as his audience recovered.

He kept his eyes shut for a moment longer, opening them slowly to give them time to adjust.

Eleven prisms blazed, filling the open space with beams of white light, recreating a days-old event in full color with seeming solidity. The hole in the floor was gone, replaced by concrete and an orderly row of vehicles. Only sound was missing as dead people chatted and made plans, waving farewell to each other as they walked to their cars, never expecting they wouldn't live to see the sun set.

He'd done it! Despite knowing what would follow, Dillon grinned, buoyed by a towering wave of elation, wishing his former partner were around to see his triumph. If he'd been alone, he'd have laughed or crowed in delight. *Yes!*

Now he had to keep it up until the scene was recorded.

Flexing his hands on his wand, he braced himself against another wild surge of power.

Walking down the corridor to Lantis's office felt almost anticlimactic after his tremendous expenditure of power. Despite the jolt of shock he'd felt at once again seeing Dan's death and Kiera's close call, Dillon had been able to hold the spell, if only by the barest tips of his fingers. It had been a near thing, but he'd held it together.

The exultation that had coursed through him earlier had faded with time, leaving him tired with a throbbing headache at the base of his skull from overexerting his magic sense. The duffel bag on his shoulder must have gained a full ton since he got it out of the car in the basement.

Dillon kneaded his nape, digging jerky fingers into steel-hard tendons. Good thing he didn't have anything major planned for the rest of the day. Coming down from the adrenaline rush had his muscles twitching.

But, damn, wielding that much power was a rush!

He grinned at the steel door guarding access to the Depth Security office, the memory of the pure energy that had nearly singed his nerves making his heart skip a beat. Hard to believe this was R&R.

With the retrospection done, the police had released access to the parking building. He'd informed Claudette before leaving kidTek; she'd make sure repairs would be effected immediately and that Warham implemented security upgrades before kidTek resumed normal operations.

Drawing ambient magic around his body, Dillon wound it in the pattern Lantis had taught him, then held his hand above the hidden security panel on the wall and triggered the access spell. Power filled the corridor and played over him, probing the energies surrounding him. He held his breath, hoping he'd cast it properly. Knowing his former partner, if he hadn't, there would be a painful, possibly debilitating, price to pay.

Although with Lantis, it wasn't really the pain Dillon was afraid of but the potential embarrassment of admitting failure. He'd never be able to live down flubbing something so basic; it would haunt him forever.

The steel door slid aside with alacrity . . . and a definite lack of drama. Given the level of security Lantis maintained, one would expect a slow, ominous opening of the hatch, maybe with some steam creeping out and the hiss of venting pneumatics. *Complete with a creepy bass drumroll, yeah?*

With a grin for his whimsy, he stepped through the threshold and waited for the door to seal shut before dismissing the power he'd summoned. Most people would have done so as soon as the door opened. That would have been a mistake.

Rio looked up from his laptop as soon as Dillon reached the inner office. "How'd it go?" The Latino's eyes were narrowed and bloodshot.

"Got what we needed. Derwent's playing things close to the vest, but the bomb was definitely in the car, not under it, and it went off when Dan started the engine."

Dillon lowered the heavy duffel bag to Lantis's desk gratefully and eased onto a visitor chair. "How're you doing?"

Rio leaned back and rolled his neck, working out the cricks that had come from eyeballing several hours of video for the past two days. "Everyone checked out fine—all on the up-and-up. All kidTek employees, no unknown individuals, no visitors. No suspicious behavior."

Dillon repeated his question, changing his emphasis for greater clarity. "How're *you* doing?"

The Latino knuckled his eyes briefly and shrugged, dismissing his discomfort as unimportant. He set his elbow on the table beside him, rested his cheek on his fist and turned to Dillon. The laptop screen cast a sober light on his face. "No one spent excessive time near Kane's car. And so far, there aren't any jumps in the records for the day, no glitches that I—or the equipment for that matter—noticed. I don't think the bomb was planted at the building."

Running a hand through his hair, Dillon nodded. "I agree. That means it didn't have a simple detonator. I've already ruled out a timer. Dan didn't keep to a strict schedule when leaving work."

"But it looks like he—specifically—was the target." Rio stared at him, his brown gaze unwavering. "There's something else I noticed."

Concern woke at the other man's gravity. "Go."

"The bomb was emplaced under the driver's seat."

Dillon blinked in surprise. He didn't question the Latino's conclusion; his fellow black ops agent wouldn't have phrased it that way if he had any doubt. "How'd you find out?"

Straightening, Rio opened some files on the laptop and waved him over.

With a light kick off the floor to get under way, Dillon rolled his chair sidewise to prop a forearm on the back of the other man's seat and look over his shoulder.

"This is from the third level, just before the explosion. Watch this." Rio moved the cursor to indicate a section of the ceiling. "It'll run at a tenth of normal speed." He started the video clip.

Even in slow motion, the cracks that appeared on the ceiling spread rapidly, giving way to a downward blast of explosive force as smooth concrete turned to rubble mere seconds after the bomb's detonation. The image froze with the dust just about to spread.

Dillon leaned closer to study the screen, then tilted his head toward his friend. "Okay, it wasn't a shaped charge. We knew that, so what else did you see?"

Rio switched to another window that showed a frame from the clip where cracks were just starting to appear on the ceiling. A small red cross marked the center of the fissures; a white line led from it to a nearby pillar. He tapped the line. "Based on this . . ."

The next window that appeared on the screen was of the fourth floor, with Dan's red Sirocco in the foreground. An identical white line ran from the pillar and ended precisely under the driver's seat.

"Huh." Dillon stared at the line blindly, his mind racing with calculations. "That makes it highly unlikely the bomb was slipped in on site. This changes things."

The Latino sighed. "Wish I'd thought of it earlier. It'd have been more efficient."

Dillon patted his friend's shoulder. "Still, good job. I'll have to inform Derwent." He reached into one of the duffel bag's pockets for his cell phone, where he'd stashed it on silent mode so it wouldn't distract him while he cast the retrospection. The device vibrated just as he touched it. A quick glance at the small display told him the call was from Jordan.

He accepted the call, a surge of delight washing through him at the thought of hearing her voice. Just the memory of that hot bout of phone sex still made him hard.

You're pathetic, man. Despite the gibing thought, Dillon eyed his companion speculatively. Maybe he should take the call in privacy. He was sure the Latino would understand.

"I can do that," Rio offered, giving him a sidelong glance with an eager smile. "Cyn should find it very interesting—"

An urgent meowing reached Dillon even before he brought the phone to his ear. Flicking a hand up to silence the other man, he frowned in disconcertment. *What on earth?*

"Mrroow!"

"*Timothy?*"

The cat's plaintive cries redoubled into near-yowls that sent ice shards spearing through Dillon's veins. His gut jerked taut, dread a heavy lump in his belly.

Jordan was in trouble.

CHAPTER FIFTEEN

"What the fuck is going on?" Rio shot the question at him with one hand tight around the grab bar. The Latino braced his legs as Dillon took the next turn almost on two wheels.

"Something's wrong at Jordan's." Dillon muscled the rental into a cloverleaf exit, keeping an eye out for traffic.

"You can tell that from *that*?" Rio stared at the loud cell phone, which continued to project Timothy's urgent meowing.

"Yes."

His fellow black ops agent shot him a searching glance but said nothing more, leaving Dillon to his worried thoughts.

The drive to Jordan's cottage took forever—even at twice his usual speed. He could only hope it was Timothy who was in trouble and Jordan would bawl him out for what he intended to do; he'd even let her pound on him if she wanted. However, he couldn't imagine the cat raising a fuss for anything less than danger to Jordan. And he couldn't dismiss Timothy's incessant cries as a prank.

Running up the path with Rio at his heels, Dillon got the full effect in stereo as he reached the front door. He rapped on the hardwood panel, hoping against hope he was wrong. "Jordan!"

The yowls broke off, his cell phone falling silent. Steady thumps approached, then Timothy whined from close by—probably just behind the door.

Dillon's gut clenched at the cat's apparent good health. *Jordan!*

He bent over the lock, then kicked himself mentally for his stupidity. There was no time for such niceties; he didn't have five minutes to spare. "Timothy, move back," he ordered, wondering at himself for addressing the cat as if Jordan's pet could understand him.

Rio caught his shoulder before he could charge the door. "Wards?"

Dillon swore at himself for the near-blunder. What was he thinking? Had he abandoned his training along the way? It wasn't like him to make such a rookie mistake.

With a flick of his wrist, he released his wand from its sheath around his forearm, catching it as it fell free. Focusing his will on its short length, he gathered ambient magic, flooding his wand with power, and wielded it in a concentrated thrust, targeting a single point in the security net.

It was brute force but he didn't have time to waste. Every second could count with Timothy's mysterious emergency. The door wards collapsed in a shower of red sparks, setting off an alarm.

Ignoring the wailing siren, he snapped a quick spell at the lock, then rammed the door, his shoulder going numb at the impact. The panel held against his assault—the deadbolt shattered with a brittle snap, wood splintering as torn metal scraped the edge and the door swung free.

Timothy was on him almost before he was inside, crying piteously, his front paws scrabbling on Dillon's belt.

"Where's Jordan?"

The cat darted off as soon as the words were out Dillon's

mouth, sprinting for the kitchen. At the door, he paused to whine entreaty at him then disappeared around the corner.

Dillon followed Timothy at a more measured pace, not wanting another reminder from Rio to keep his guard up, but the other rooms were empty.

At first glance, after he activated the light spell, the kitchen seemed just as vacant. Then he saw Jordan sprawled by the counter, the cat crouched beside her.

"Call for medics," Dillon ordered Rio, pointing out the kitchen phone with its overturned handset.

As he rushed to his lover, she convulsed, moaning and shivering. From the state of the tile floor, she'd thrown up several times. Flailing wildly, she gabbled something incomprehensible, the terror in her voice clawing his gut.

"Jordan?" Throttling his fears into silence, he picked Timothy up before he got into the vomitus, cradling the whining cat while he tried to assess her condition.

She went still, unresponsive to his calls. Her pulse fluttered visibly in her throat, abnormally fast, her skin clammy to his trembling touch. Then her neck muscles suddenly went rigid under his hand. He jerked clear just before her arms lashed out, almost hitting Timothy.

The cat squeaked in surprise.

Dillon's heart sank as he noted her symptoms: vomiting, chills, convulsions, delirium, abdominal pain, possibly stomach cramps. He studied the red bits of vomitus conspicuous against the cream tiles. Food poisoning?

"They're on their way," Rio reported. "I'll man the door."

"Take Timothy with you. I'll need my hands free." In case he had to administer CPR. Dillon passed the whining cat to him, nodding his thanks, then returned to Jordan's side, cursing his helplessness. Killing was easy. This? She was beyond his basic medical training. He could only stop her from hurting herself while he waited for professionals to arrive.

He stroked her shoulder, hoping his touch would comfort her at some level. But as he knelt there, his professional paranoia couldn't help suspecting something more deliberate.

Dillon turned his rental into Jordan's driveway and parked short of the garage. He pulled his weary body out of the car, feeling like several boulders had rolled over him. On missions, he could go for days without sleep with no problem, but one night at the hospital, hovering at Jordan's bedside, had taken it out of him. How did Lantis do it? He'd be glad to have Jordan home where he could cradle her in his arms without a medic sticking his head into the room to scold him.

Shouldering his carryall, he detoured around the house to the front porch. There, he found Rio at work on the door with Timothy prancing at his feet.

"Moving in?" Rio asked, looking up from where he knelt to eye Dillon's bag.

"If it'll let me be on hand." Since Dan's death, Dillon had been spending the nights in Jordan's bed, but he'd kept his things at Lantis's old apartment. With Jordan needing care, he couldn't afford to waste time shuttling back and forth.

"Very convincing."

"You're not the one who has to agree," Dillon pointed out. "Thanks for handling that."

"No problem." Rio pitched Timothy's toy mouse down the hall, a fast shot that sent the cat streaking away in pursuit. "How is she?"

"Okay, now. They're releasing her this afternoon." Guilt reared its head as he remembered how he'd left his friend to handle the cops who'd responded to their break-in while he accompanied Jordan to the hospital. "The healers think it was food poisoning," he offered by way of reparation.

His face carefully blank, Rio aimed the screwdriver and triggered it, the short burst sinking another screw of the replacement door lock. "The cops believe it was deliberate."

"They do?" Dillon lifted a brow.

The other man shrugged. "I had to call Cyn, tell her why I couldn't make it." Gone unsaid was that the Latino also had his suspicions about Jordan's ailment. He must have convinced Malva of the same to have gotten such quick results.

Timothy came bounding back with toy in mouth, making a beeline for the other man. Catching the cat before he jogged Rio's arm, Dillon frowned at his fellow agent. "And?"

Jordan's pet twisted in his hold, his pink nose twitching. He sniffed Dillon's chest where his mistress's head had rested for most of the night, then stared at him with an interrogative blue gaze. "Prrp?"

"She's fine. Don't worry." Dillon stroked the cat down the spine, noting the fine tension in his muscular body. "She'll be home soon," he added soothingly, scratching the sensitive spots behind the large ears.

Closing his eyes, Timothy sighed, then butted his shoulder.

Rio continued to the next screw as he explained. "According to Cyn's sources, a half-empty package of strawberries tested positive for praxialle with unusually high concentrations on both fruit and container." Praxialle was a popular pesticide and a favored poison in certain circles since it was odorless and next to tasteless. Applied as an aerosol, it dried into a clear film that was difficult to wash off. "They think someone sprayed the entire package. If your woman hadn't eaten the strawberries with cream, she wouldn't have survived." He paused in his work to stroke Timothy who was craning his neck over Dillon's arm. "So, who wants her dead?"

Good question. Dillon stared down the hall, lost in thought, the sight of Jordan as they'd found her last night filling his mind's eye. He couldn't imagine anyone holding a grudge against Jordan. "I don't know."

The sight of the stocky, brown-haired man sitting on the bench outside Kiera's hospital room, half-hidden behind an open book of crossword puzzles, drove Dillon's confusion from his mind.

Brian Curtis was another of his friends from his other life. From his relaxed slouch, the other man was standing guard.

"When were you called in?" Dillon asked in an undertone, leaning against the opposite wall to leave the other man with a clear field of view.

Sharp gray eyes met his over the top of the book. The other man shook his head once in brusque negation. "Flew in to interview. Found this."

Dillon blinked, though not at the laconic response; Brian never used three words when one would do and preferred gestures to talk. It was the implication that his fellow agent was leaving black ops that threw him. "Here? What for?"

"KidTek. Head of Security." Those gray eyes watched him, unblinking, as he digested the information. So Kiera had been planning to replace Warham?

Dillon briefly considered handing off the security aspects to Brian, then dismissed the temptation. For one, Lantis probably approved of the security detail, if not specifically assigned it to their mutual friend. That had priority. For another, Kiera had yet to interview the man, although his former partner had obviously recommended him. Besides, Brian was a complete unknown to Claudette; even if he hit the ground running, she'd be less forthcoming with support. No, it was best if Dillon continued to handle things himself.

Then he remembered his confusion. "How are they?" He hadn't been by since that first day; what with everything he had to stay on top of, he'd had to settle for phone check-ins to touch base with Lantis.

Brian's shrug disavowed knowledge, but at least it didn't convey grief. Dillon took heart from it as he entered Kiera's hospital room. *So why—?*

He froze in the doorway, shocked by Lantis's condition. He'd never seen his friend look so haggard. Several days' growth of beard darkened his normally clean-shaven face but failed to disguise the lines of pain and worry bracketing his mouth. Dark pouches sagged beneath his eyes. His former partner looked like he hadn't had any sleep since Kiera was admitted.

Had something gone wrong? He'd thought the curator at the front desk mistaken when she'd directed him to Intensive Care. Surely there'd been enough time for the healers to have done their job.

Kiera lay pale and unmoving on the bed, looking as though she were merely resting. The blood on her face was long gone, the vivid pink scars on her cheek the only visible reminder of her earlier injuries. But even those were wrong. They should have cleared up by now.

He had to force himself to enter the room.

Lantis looked up as the door shut, his shoulders rounded with weariness.

"How is she?" Dillon's gut clenched at the torment in the other man's eyes. *How are you?*

"She's still hanging in there." Lantis lowered his head to press his cheek against Kiera's hand clasped between his own.

Skirting the foot of the bed, Dillon touched his friend's shoulder. "What's wrong? Shouldn't she be in recovery by now?"

"She's mostly fine, now." Lantis took a shuddering breath, reaching up to stroke his wife's scarred cheek. "It's the babies."

Babies? Dillon's heart stuttered. *Babies!?*

"They were also injured. Since they aren't fully developed yet, the healers are being very cautious about how much they do," Lantis continued in a soft monotone, probably to avoid disturbing Kiera's rest. "And they can't draw on the babies' energies for the healing. So they're tapping Kiera's and doing it in stages to give her time to recover."

Dillon's blood chilled at the explanation. After all this, they could still lose— The thought was like a knife in the belly. He couldn't complete it, refused to consider the possibility. The feeling of helplessness it engendered infuriated him. Whoever had planned the bombing would pay. He'd make sure of it.

"You should go home. Get some rest," Dillon suggested, despite his gut cramping at the thought of being separated from Jordan. It shook him to see his friend looking like he was at the end of his endurance. "Let me stay with her for a while."

The other man rejected his advice with a quick shake of his head. "I have to be here. Have to anchor her here. If I don't, she might—" Lantis' lips compressed, white showing at the edges.

Understanding flooded Dillon. *Their link!*

Lantis and Kiera's spirits were entangled, an unintended side effect of a spell Lantis had cast. Kiera had used it once to keep Lantis alive. Dillon hadn't known Lantis could use it in the same way. The other man had to be feeding Kiera some of his own energy, if only to speed the healing of the babies.

His request died unspoken. He'd wanted a talisman to protect Jordan, but he couldn't ask Lantis to leave Kiera. Even mentioning his need would only add to his friend's torment. Lantis would blame himself for not being able to help.

"I can dress myself," Jordan insisted with a worrying shortness of breath. "You don't need to hover."

With grave misgivings, Dillon handed her the clothes he'd picked up from her house, then followed the healer out the room. He raised a finger to ask the healer to wait while he made sure the door was closed and they were safely out of Jordan's hearing. "Is there anything special I should keep watch for?" He ignored the sudden silent ictus of his cell phone. Whoever was calling could wait.

The healer shook her head, giving him a tired smile. "We've fixed the damage. You just have to make sure she rests and doesn't do too much for the next few days." She pushed back a brown tendril of hair that escaped her braid. "We had to purge the poison from her system. While she's fine now, Ms. Kane will feel like she's been beaten up. If you know how to give a massage, I'm sure she'll appreciate it."

He nodded his thanks and allowed her to rush off to wherever she was needed. Leaving the building, he took out his now-quiescent cell phone and halted in midstride to stare at the number on the display.

The Old Man had tried to contact him. His commander wasn't one for small talk—which meant he was being recalled early for a mission. He pocketed the phone to look back at the sprawling hospital complex, uncertain how he felt at the chance to return to the field.

The usual, almost reflexive rush of adrenaline was there. Chomping at the bit to get at the tangos, yes, that was there, too. But to leave Jordan now, when she needed him most? Just the thought made his gut churn, never mind the risk she posed to operational security. He couldn't fool himself that she wouldn't wonder where he'd disappeared to.

And then there were Kiera and Lantis. He turned to the wing where Kiera lay, his eyes scanning the windows of the Intensive Care ward. How could he even think of leaving them at this time?

There was only one answer: he couldn't. The Old Man would just have to shift him to reserve status until further notice. He stifled a pang of concern at the thought. His decision shouldn't scuttle his chances at another mission. The reserve list was intended precisely for emergencies such as this. But it would be the first time he'd be on it; he hadn't had to go on reserve status when Kiera's father died.

Yet if the Old Man was recalling him early, that meant something bad was going down. His gut cramped at the thought.

Chapter Sixteen

Jordan leaned against Dillon, accepting his support gratefully. Despite her bravado in the hospital, the short walk to the porch left her tense and shaky, jumping when a sudden gust of wind rattled a tangle of dry twigs somewhere nearby. It didn't help that her head throbbed with every step she took.

Reaching for the lock panel automatically, she imaged her pass pattern as she pressed on the warm metal.

A beautiful, muscular man knelt before the door, one hand on the panel, his powerful shoulders bunching as he did something to the lock, grim concentration knitting his dark brows. She shoved the vision away, grinding her teeth at the proof of her fraying control.

Jordan frowned when the wards remained active, the panel still warm under her palm. She'd never fumbled with the lock panel before—not when the technology for the panel was nearly identical to that of input plates in psyprinters.

"Sorry." Dillon brushed his hand over the panel. "I broke through your door to get to you. Burnt your system. We had to replace it," he explained, turning the knob to let her in. "We'll key it to you later. After you've rested."

Jordan nodded jerkily, her neck drooping like a limp rag. As soon as the familiar environs of the entry hall surrounded her, she blocked her sight, sighing with relief as the barrage of images ceased.

"Prrp?" Timothy's concerned chirp barely roused her from her daze.

"Shhh," Dillon crooned. "Not now. She's all done in."

A furry paw brushed her cheek, followed by a cold nose. Dillon must have picked up Timothy. Her pet's deep purr merged with the silence, a throbbing, reassuring beat. He sounded fine and a fist inside her loosened its grip. She'd worried the cat might have gotten into whatever had poisoned her. *So silly to think that. Dillon wouldn't have permitted it.*

She allowed her lover to lead her through the darkness, lengthening her stride as she normally would to avoid stepping on her pet and automatically counting her steps. Four meant they'd reached the staircase. Sure enough, Dillon turned her to the right, murmuring, "Stairs."

They ascended to her bedroom in weary silence.

Jordan resisted the siren song of her bed, needing to wash off the noisome haze of sickness clinging to her skin.

Dillon seemed to understand instinctively what she needed. "I'll draw your bath." He urged her to sit, placing Timothy on her lap before she could even consider protesting.

Jordan buried her face in her pet's fur, the familiar texture and his comforting purr another welcome step toward normalcy. Ever since she found those gloves, her life had spun off into nightmare. It seemed unreal that Dan was dead by a car bomb. Such things only happened to other people, in other countries. Now, deliberate poisoning!

She didn't know how long she sat there before an incredible fragrance insinuated itself into her consciousness, teasing her with hints of tranquility and exotic pleasure. Jordan raised her head to better appreciate the beguiling perfume. A blend of citrus, woody and floral notes, it wasn't familiar, certainly not one of her bath crystals or bath oils.

"Your bath's ready." Dillon took Timothy away, murmuring something she didn't quite catch. He undressed her, saying little and allowing her to do even less.

"What are you doing?" she asked when he stopped her from fumbling with her pants.

"All the work. I figure you're due for some pampering." His answer was accompanied by a gentle caress on her cheek. "Just relax. Leave everything to me."

Jordan's eyes watered, her heart stumbling at his words. He was being so sweet!

The bathroom was steamy, the air redolent with sensuality. The narrow lip of the tub was warm, not the usual cold assault on the buttocks. The first dip of her fingers into the water was pure bliss: hot—but not too hot—silky with oil, frothing with foam. With a sigh, she slid in until she was neck-deep, thousands of bubbles caressing her all over. Even the neck rest was already warm.

Floating in liquid, perfumed heat, the fizz and gurgle of water like music to her ears, Jordan felt the tight knots in her shoulders start to unravel. She soaked it all in, the pounding in her temples gradually dissolving with each balmy breath. She could easily imagine herself in some tropical pool, surrounded by lush foliage and riotous blooms.

The touch of the washcloth, when it came, was just another part of her fantasy. It glided over her shoulder, soft terry cloth wielded by a gentle hand. Jordan smiled, content for the moment to accept his ministrations.

Dillon raised her arms, one at a time, kneading her flesh with undemanding pressure before running soapy, scented fabric over her weighted limbs. From the angle of his hands, he was probably kneeling beside the tub.

hand, finding and stroking his bare shoulder with its dips and ridges of hard muscle. "Make love to me?"

He brushed firm lips over her fingertips. "Of course." He urged her back into the hot water. "Just relax while I set things up. Remember: I'll do all the work."

Breathing in the perfumed steam, she wondered idly what he had in mind. Just this moment out of time was in itself already an extraordinary gift. *There's more?* She smiled at the prospect.

After a while Dillon had her stand up, then rinsed her, playing warm water over her tingling body. He helped her out of the tub, enfolded her in fluffy towels and patted her skin dry with light, lingering strokes.

"Here," Dillon said, guiding her forward and to the left, his rough hands on her shoulders, until her feet touched cloth.

Hmm? She didn't have rugs in her bathroom because of the risk of her tripping or slipping on them. She nudged the cloth with her toes experimentally. This felt thicker, more substantial than an ordinary rug.

"Kneel down, then lie on your front."

Surprise had Jordan obeying before she'd processed his instruction. Her knees landed on wet fabric. Her hands told her it was squishy with oil. Her nose told her it smelled wonderful, adding a cinnamon note to the exotic scents filling the room. But when she was prone, her cheek nestled on dry, fluffy cloth.

She settled down, laying her arms beside her head. The tingling in her nipples when her breasts, then her thighs and belly, skated over slippery cotton startled her. Oil coated her front from above her breasts to her insteps, turning the gentle friction of the sodden terry cloth into something erotic. *Trust Dillon to elevate pampering to an art form.*

He poured warm oil along her back, the cinnamon scent growing stronger. The oil turned his hard palms into a delicious roughness as he spread it over her skin in slow, sweeping strokes that hinted at boundless patience, as though they had all the time in the world.

Dillon started by kneading her nape, until her neck muscles felt buttery-soft, all tension banished. After running his hands over her back, he replaced them with his chest: a full-body stroke that scraped his chest hair against her skin, pressed the hard slabs of his pectorals and abdomen against her back and buttocks, and her slick body into the oil-soaked towel.

Jordan moaned at the friction as heat kindled in her core, slow and inexorable, lapping at her nerve endings like a playful cat determined to lure her into a game.

When she pushed back, he stopped, his body holding her down, keeping her motionless. "No, don't move. I'm doing all the work, remember? Just tell me what you want."

"Then push harder," Jordan grumbled halfheartedly. "It's too light."

Dillon chuckled at her complaint, but he definitely let her bear more of his weight when he resumed his strokes. He ground her into the towel, mashing her mound against the terry cloth.

Jordan groaned at the burst of sweet delight, relishing the hard ripples of Dillon's belly skating over her bottom.

He used his body to caress her back and buttocks, slowly moving from side to side, up and down, diagonally, rocking his weight to vary his pressure. His movements rubbed her front against the towel. The oiled cloth was like extra hands, teasing her nipples to tight peaks, warming her flesh to readiness. Her core clenched restively, dew trickling from her vulva.

When Dillon pushed up, Jordan nearly sighed with disappointment. Her lover set his hands to kneading her back. Remembering that he wanted to pamper her, she stifled her objection. As much as she wanted him inside her, she didn't mention it. Dillon seemed to have a need to take care of her, maybe because he hadn't been able to do much at the hospital. If this massage eased his conscience, she'd suffer it in silence. *Not that it's any hardship.*

He straddled her legs, sweeping his palms up her back, his hair-roughened calves tickling her thighs. On the downstroke, he sat back, his swollen erection a hot brand trailing between her buttocks.

She hummed in approval. *That's more like it!*

Continuing his massage, he rocked over her. Each upstroke rubbed her breasts against the slick towel, and his penis and scrotum gliding over her buttocks. Each downstroke pressed her belly and her mound into the terry cloth, and his rampant sex against her thighs. He kept rocking as he massaged her back, teasing them both with the promise of completion.

Jordan found her attention narrowing to that scorching contact, sighing whenever she lost it and purring at its return. Then it slipped lower, tickling the lower curve of her buttocks.

She caught her breath.

On the next slow upstroke, the broad head of his penis nudged her labia. *Oh, yes. Infinitely better.*

She lost that blunt touch on the downstroke, but she knew she'd have it back soon. She quivered with anticipation.

Dillon's hands swept to her shoulders, a smooth measured flow of hard pressure that drove her breasts and throbbing nipples into slick friction with terry cloth. Even better, the motion had his penis kissing her labia, bobbing against her as he shifted his weight to adjust his grip, his thumbs gliding over her shoulder blades.

Over and over, he tantalized her, each upstroke bringing his penis the slightest bit deeper into her vagina. He varied his rhythm, sometimes staying longer while his fingers circled and kneaded, his sculpted abdomen rubbing over her buttocks.

Even when Dillon was finally completely sheathed inside her, he continued his sensual massage, pouring more oil over her back, evidently intent on doing a thorough job of pampering her. The scent of cinnamon strengthened in the steamy air.

Each new stroke brought warm, gentle pleasure in its trail,

lighting a fire under her skin until Jordan was weightless, soaring from the sensual heat, sheer delight wafting her higher.

Then he peppered his strokes with little variations: brushing his lips across her shoulders, licking along her spine, sprinkling teasing little nibbles. The contrast had her shivering on a delicious precipice, but he didn't take it further.

"Damn, you taste wonderful," he crooned after a long, slow lick. "Enjoying yourself?"

"Oh, yes," she sighed into the towel, giving a low moan when his penis nudged a particularly sensitive spot inside her.

"Good." He pressed a kiss on her nape. "Turn over." He withdrew his penis slowly, but had slipped out before she realized what he intended.

"Turn over?" she asked rather plaintively, missing his thick erection inside her. She'd been so close!

"Let me do your front." With insistent hands on the ball of her shoulder and the curve of her hip, Dillon shifted Jordan until she lay supine, her arms bent beside her head.

The loss of his possession leaving her feeling empty and strangely enervated, she lay on the towel passively awaiting his next move.

He began all over again.

Oil dribbled on Jordan's front, spattering her tight nipples, flowing down her breasts, over her belly, pooling in her navel and trickling between her labia. Disappointment fading, she smiled as a quiver of anticipation shook her body, now knowing what pleasures lay ahead.

He spread the oil over her breasts, pausing to twirl his fingers around their hard peaks, along her ribcage, to her hips, her inner thighs and down to the thin skin behind her knees. Warmth followed his hands, tingling bliss, amplifying her intense arousal yet leaving her body languid.

The first touch of Dillon's chest on her breasts set tiny prickles of delight washing over her body. Jordan took a deep breath, relaxing into his care, drifting in overwhelmingly sweet pleasure. She moaned as another whiff of cinnamon sent her senses spinning.

He used his chest and abdomen to stroke her—from her shoulders, to her belly, her hips, even her thighs weren't ignored. Over and over, she caught tantalizing hints of his desire, his turgid penis and furry scrotum glanced off her hip, rubbed against her thigh. Once or twice, she thought she felt the velvety head caress her breast.

Then he straddled her again, plying his hands in the same sweeping strokes that had whetted her desire.

Breathless with expectation, she waited, wanting that hot brand inside her.

He teased her mercilessly as he massaged her body to a boneless pool of hungry need. A touch here, his crisp pubic hair ruffling her delta. A graze there, his silken shaft skating against her inner thigh.

"Dillon," Jordan moaned, wanting so much more. Her back arched in reflex when his upstroke brought his hands to her breasts.

Stopping, he held her down. "No. Don't move. Just take it easy and relax."

"More," she demanded.

"Patience," he murmured. "I'll give you more."

He resumed his sensual attentions, finally allowing that hot brand to nestle between her thighs. When he pressed his lips on the lower curve of her breast, the blunt head of his penis kissed her creaming vulva, nuzzled her swollen labia.

When he started the slow rocking that had raised her to the heights, Jordan murmured wordless encouragement, controlling her impatience. Dillon was taking his time, but she knew eventually he'd be inside her once more.

Slowly, tenderly, using his entire body, he cherished her. That was the best word she could think of to describe his lovemaking. He made her feel cherished.

As each upstroke took him deeper, her pleasure grew, golden sparkles wafting through her languid body. His expert touch and tantalizing penetration drove her higher, sent her floating with delight, soaring through the heavens. Need coiled restively in her core. She could feel her peak approaching, one even higher than before.

Then came the downstroke that took him from her. His penis nudged her labia but moved no deeper. He lifted her knees, pushed them up and back until they were pressed against the sides of her breasts, hooked her heels over his shoulders.

Only then did he return to her. With a rumbling purr, he delved into her, reaching deeper than ever before, his hips caressing her buttocks.

Jordan gasped at the overwhelming fullness of his possession. His erection flexed inside her gently, stroking her intimate flesh, tipping her over the precipice.

Rapture burst through her veins from deep within, flooded her being with ineffable sweetness. Wave upon wave of ecstasy sent her flying through the heavens, borne by warm gusts of pleasure. Her lover groaned above her, crooning encouragement even as his penis jerked and spurted inside her, adding fire to the depthless, blistering orgasm scorching her.

Dillon rocked them both, showering her senses with delight, fueling Jordan's climax to greater heights. Colorful stars burst behind her blind eyes, their light dazzling in the extreme. She moaned in breathless release, all tension fleeing her body.

In the aftermath of her orgasm, Dillon gathered her in his arms, stretching out the lingering quakes of rapture. Boneless in her repletion, Jordan sighed, content to remain there, surrounded by hard male and the heady scent of sex, cinnamon, and tropical delights.

Dillon trailed his fingers along Jordan's back, savoring her lax state and general good health. It would be a long time, if ever, before the sight of her sprawled on the floor, delirious and surrounded by vomitus, faded from his memory. It chilled him that she could have died, were it not for her pet.

At the sound of Timothy pawing at the door, she stirred, rubbing her cheek against his chest. "You need to let him in."

Satiation had left Dillon's limbs heavy. He frowned at the door, wishing the friendly cat's patience had lasted a little longer. He'd have enjoyed a few more minutes of having Jordan all to himself. Untangling his limbs from his lover's, he got up and unlocked the door, leaving it to gape just the slightest bit, then returned to Jordan.

The towel squelched, not unpleasantly, as he lay back down beside his lover and drew her into his arms, hooking a leg over her hip. He gave it no mind, having lain on far less appealing surfaces in the field.

He was drowsing off when something rasped against the back of his thigh, rousing him to combat alertness. Only long training and experience kept his muscles loose, not to betray his readiness to the intruder.

The furtive rasp—like a fingernail scratching or digging—moved downward, transferred to his inner thigh, moved toward his exposed balls. *What in hell?*

"Mew?" A large paw pressed down on his thigh tentatively.

Dillon's head shot up. "Timothy," he growled, glaring over his shoulder.

Jordan's pet gave him a look of innocence from black-masked blue eyes, a look heightened by the thick ruff of white fur that framed his round head. "Prrp?" Wide ears bent toward Dillon attentively as a pink tongue flicked out to lick a white muzzle, slick with oil.

"I'm not sure that's good for you," Dillon finished weakly, feeling foolish at addressing the cat in such a conversational manner, now that he didn't have worry to distract him.

"What's not good for him?" Jordan muttered, snuggling deeper into his arms.

"The massage oil."

"Weren't you licking me earlier?"

"Well, yes. It *is* edible. But I'm not sure it's safe for cats." Dillon grunted as Timothy gingerly picked his way up Dillon's hip—thankfully avoiding his balls—to settle his muscular bulk on Dillon's ribs. At least the cat kept his claws sheathed.

"Cinnamon should be no harm."

Then Timothy bent down to lap at Jordan's plump pink nipple and a territorial instinct Dillon hadn't realized he possessed reared its head. "Nope, that's mine," he chided, fending the cat off. *Mine? Hell, where did that come from?*

"Hmmm?" Jordan shifted, her breasts sliding against his chest, distracting him from pursuit of that peculiar thought.

"I think we'd better wash off the oil." He gave the cat a hard stare. Ignoring him, Timothy dipped his head to run his rough tongue along Dillon's belly.

Collecting Jordan's pet to keep him from taking additional liberties, he rinsed the tub with Timothy slung across his shoulders like a heavy living shawl, the cat's fluffy tail twitching idly along his right bicep.

Leaving the water to rise, he gathered Jordan, his muscles flexing easily as he stood up, loose from all that fantastic sex. She filled his arms sweetly, turning to rest her cheek on his chest with complete and open trust.

His heart leaped, racing with lust and unexpected affection. He wanted to keep her there forever. Wanted to protect her from everything and everyone who would hurt her. Impractical, he knew, but there it was.

"Mew." Timothy's batting on a ragged, honey-brown lock broke Dillon's trance. Where the hell were these alien thoughts coming from? Hold her forever? What was he thinking? Sure, he'd had the Old Man put him on the reserve list, but his place was in the field. Wasn't it?

Shaking his head at the uncharacteristic sentiments, Dillon

slid Jordan into warm water, then turned to bundle all the oil-soaked towels into a laundry bag, safe from Timothy's mischief.

After checking to make sure the bottle of massage oil was securely capped, he set the cat on the floor. With a bit of judicious footwork, he managed to settle behind Jordan in the narrow tub, pulling her between his legs.

She gave a murmur of approval, using his chest as a backrest.

Feeling unusually lighthearted and unwilling to encourage his introspection, Dillon slathered bath gel on the washcloth and proceeded to wash off the oil from their bodies. He took as much care this time as he had earlier, taking satisfaction from the mere feel of Jordan's skin gliding under his hands.

Her breasts were a perfect handful, not as voluptuous as some of his previous lovers. Topped by large pink nipples that puckered quickly at his touch, they somehow were just right. Her gentle belly and shapely thighs didn't display the musculature of some of the female agents he'd worked with, but the contrast simply underlined the reality that she wasn't part of that world and he liked that just fine. In fact, that innocence was one of her attractions.

The way she welcomed him without calculation was another draw. Even outside the black ops world, most women of his acquaintance seemed to have some sliding scale they used to judge if his companionship had merit: good-looking escort, social acceptability, old money. Not with Jordan.

He cupped her mound, combing through her brown curls to lave her veiled flesh. He probed her sheath gently, inordinately delighted when she clenched around his finger.

Jordan seemed to enjoy it just as much as he did, purring and undulating against him, her breath hitching in a most complimentary way.

He looked up to check Timothy's position and found the cat crouching on the ledge at the foot of the tub. *Uh-huh.* That purr was coming from Jordan, alright.

With his arms full of wet, willing woman, Dillon had the inevitable reaction, his cock hardening against her rounded back-side. He savored the ache, knowing he could slake his hunger at any time.

He alternated between scrubbing her back and his chest, teasing both of them with possibilities.

Mewling softly, Jordan braced her hands on his knees and arched her back, bringing the crease of her backside in provocative contact with his hard-on and sending a flare of need rocketing up from his balls. He could feel his cock thickening further at her encouragement.

"You sure you're up to this?" he whispered, rinsing the last of the foam from the bath gel from their bodies.

"Um-hmm. I want you again," Jordan confessed in an undertone of surprise.

Dillon lifted her up, his hands on her thighs, then brought her down on his cock carefully, giving her delicate membranes, still swollen and sensitive from their earlier lovemaking, time to adjust, until she was settled firmly on his lap, sheathing him to the hilt. He sighed at the feeling of completeness. Her breathless coo of pleasure amplified his sense of rightness. Nothing could go wrong in the world, not while they had this.

She rolled her hips, her slick channel stroking his cock and sending flames blazing through his erect flesh. Arching her back, she pressed a hard-tipped breast into his palm, her head falling back against his shoulder.

Jordan pushed off, forcing his cock from its warm haven, dragging her tight sheath over his sensitive head. Dillon ground his teeth to hold back a groan, then lost it anyway when she took him back in.

"Harder," she urged.

"Jordan . . ." He wasn't sure anything more strenuous was wise, so soon after her release from the hospital. Hell, none of the healers' instructions covered post-hospital coital guidelines.

"Please? I'm not made of glass." A tremor in her voice, more sensed than heard, conveyed doubt, a need for confirmation, for reassurance that she was truly recovered.

He couldn't refuse her.

Lifting her with stealthy caution, making certain he wasn't supporting Jordan by her belly, he thrust home, giving her the harder possession she wanted.

"Oh, yes," she moaned, her flesh grasping at his cock, milking him, lighting a bonfire in his balls.

Pumping solidly into her welcoming sheath, Dillon reached between her thighs to circle her clit. Gasping, she quivered around him, communicating his success.

"Hell, yeah," he gritted as the fluttering around his cock detonated fireworks right up his spine.

"Harder. Deeper!"

Dillon pistoned his hips urgently, driving his shaft in hard thrusts. Over and again, he took her, huffing as though at the far end of a sixty-mile forced march with a full pack. Water splashed in counterpoint to her cries of gratification.

He relished the sounds of her pleasure, her unfettered enjoyment of their passion, but didn't allow himself to be distracted. He couldn't draw out the forceful lovemaking, not when his concerns about Jordan's recovery remained. It was a fine balance between reassuring her and himself.

Seeking her pleasure spot, he shifted the angle of his thrusts. He could tell when he found it: she jerked against him, gasping with delight, the growing contractions of her sheath fanning the blaze in his cock.

Now, damn it. Now! Tweaking her clit, he clung to his control desperately, needing to ensure her satisfaction.

"Oh!" Jordan gasped in surprise, her rigid back arching over him as her orgasm broke. Her sheath spasmed around him, her thready moan leaving no doubt as to her release.

His fraying control snapped.

Pleasure boiled up from Dillon's balls, his own release thundering through his cock. Roaring in ecstasy, he gave himself up to utter, radiant relief. Powerful waves crashed through him, leaving his body shaking and sweetly drained.

Whoa. He couldn't remember reaching such heights before. In fact, he might need a vacation to recover from this vacation. He grinned. In the short term, they'd probably be as wrinkled as prunes by the time they got out of the tub.

CHAPTER SEVENTEEN

The psyprinter finally ejected the outsized sheet of Kirlian paper into the out tray, presenting Jordan with the definitive version of her latest piece. Transferring it to the table, she inspected the image with her clairvoyance. It looked good—better than good, in fact. It was probably her best work to date, she decided, admiring the way sunlight dappled the flowers while leaving her subject in shadowed mystery.

Working on the psyprint had saved her sanity after Dan's death and her poisoning. It was the one thing she'd had control over and she'd driven herself to finish it to prove—to herself, if no one else—she still controlled her life.

"Prrp?" Standing on the table next to her elbow, Timothy crouched down to sniff at the paper, by now knowing better than to place his paws on the psyprint.

"Um-hmm. It's done," she answered her pet with a sigh of artistic satisfaction. "Looks good, doesn't it?"

His ears pricking as something else caught his attention,

Timothy didn't answer. The cat straightened, hard muscles quivering with anticipation, his round head cocked to one side in a listening posture. Then, blue eyes rounding in recognition, her pet abandoned the table with a glad cry, loping to the hall in fluid motion.

The soft click of the front door reached her, followed soon after by Timothy's welcoming chirp. The new arrival had to be Dillon returning from John Atlantis's office to bring her to the Walsen Galleries.

With guilty haste, Jordan grabbed one of the heavy-duty cardboard tubes she used for storing and transporting psyprints. She had the sheet rolled up and hidden by the time her lover joined her in the studio carrying her purring pet. Uncertain how he'd take his new role, she didn't want him seeing it just yet. While she'd been unwell, he'd moved in quietly, doing what he believed was necessary without any discussion. When she surfaced and realized what he'd done, she hadn't found the desire to object. Or the nerve to ask how long he intended to stay.

"Ready to go?" Dressed in brown trousers and a plain, soft-looking, white tunic that clung to his chest and sported a few long, black cat hairs, Dillon looked more like a model than someone who dealt in violence. He gave Timothy's ears a final rub, then set him on the floor.

She patted her pocket to confirm she had the memory strip from the psyprinter. "Uh-huh."

"Is this it?" Dillon picked up the tube, one hand rasping down its length as he hefted it curiously. In his hands, the tube looked small, not the bulky cylinder it was when she carried it.

It gave her a strange feeling knowing that only a thin layer of cardboard separated Dillon from a nude of himself. *Perhaps this wasn't such a great idea?* She rejected the thought immediately, remembering the beauty of the piece and how much time and effort had gone into it. So long as Shanna agreed with her judgment, it deserved to be displayed.

Besides, it wasn't like it depicted anything distinctive: just a sleeping man lying facedown at the edge of a sunlit glade, albeit in his naked glory. Nothing about the figure's dark hair, bare back or muscular legs was identifiable as Dillon's. There were no distinctive scars, just one long delicious display of male flesh. Her cheeks heated at the memory of the sensual delight she'd taken in making the psyprint.

Anyway, she'd promised Spatha an original for the auction and she couldn't conjure another one out of thin air.

"May I look?" Dillon's soft-voiced query shattered her reverie like footsteps in a silent night.

No! Jordan strangled on her instinctive answer, her lungs seizing, sudden apprehension raising gooseflesh on her arms. "Shanna hasn't seen it yet," she squeaked, wondering if she was fooling herself about her model's anonymity. Only the risk of rousing his interest to the point he insisted on seeing the psyprint kept her from snatching the tube from his hands.

She plucked the cat hairs off his chest to buy time to think and recover her composure. "You'll have to wait for the auction like everyone else," she finally managed in what she hoped was a casual tone.

"Being your lover doesn't even get me a preview?" Dillon made a face of exaggerated disappointment, fluttering absurdly thick lashes and pouting his kissable lips.

She grinned at his expression, bracing for more cajolery. "Nope. Shanna gets to see it first because she's my agent."

"How about if I promise to let you have your wicked way with me later?" He caught her hand against the hard slopes of his chest as his light baritone dropped an octave, hinting at scandalous intimacies. "Will you let me take a look, then?"

Biting her lip against a hysterical giggle, Jordan shook her head emphatically, praying he'd leave it at that.

"Hard woman. Oh, well. If you insist." Now his voice sounded like he was in the depths of despair.

Laughing in relief, Jordan swatted his arm. "I insist."

—◦◦◦—

Theodore Walsen, the founder and owner of Walsen Galleries, walked up to Jordan as soon as the street noise disappeared behind the gallery's front doors. The first to recognize her talent and offer to represent her, he was semiretired, having passed on much of the responsibility for day-to-day operations to Shanna, so his presence was a surprise.

"My dear, I just heard about your cousin. You have my utmost sympathy for your loss. Such a tragedy." The elderly gentleman patted her wrist, his dry skin thin and papery to the touch. "I hope the police find the bastard who did it quickly and string him up by the balls."

Jordan bit back a smile, tears threatening to spill down her cheeks. While she agreed with the sentiment, it startled her to hear it from such a dignified man. "Thank you." She inhaled sharply, fighting for composure. "I'm here to see Shanna."

"She's in her office, I believe, grappling with a late delivery. Allow me to guide you to her." Theodore freed one of her hands from the cardboard tube she carried and hooked it on the crook of his elbow before she could stop him; thankfully, the tight weave of his coat didn't trigger her psychometry. "Is that a new piece?"

"Y-yes," Jordan stammered, suddenly remembering the psyprint. "It's for the Spatha auction."

"Ah, yes. It's that time of year again, isn't it?" he murmured knowledgeably; she'd taken part in the first auction at his advice.

"Well, now. Here's Shanna," Theodore said as they turned a corner. He hailed the other woman with a "My dear, you have a visitor." Giving Jordan's hand a final consolatory pat, he took his leave.

Jordan smiled at Theodore's kindness, warmed by his grandfatherly manner.

"How're you doing?" Shanna left the display of bronzes she was supervising to hug Jordan. "Is that the one for Spatha's auction? Your latest work?" Today, her hair was violet with matching eyebrows and lashes.

Smiling, Jordan answered the rapid questions in the order they were asked, "I'm fine. Yes. Yes," concluding with "I have the file right here, including printing instructions." She plucked the memory strip from her pocket with her free hand and flourished it.

"Here's the color guide." She set down the bulky tube, glad she'd managed to talk Dillon out of accompanying her to this meeting.

"Oooh! Let me see!" Shanna exclaimed, swiping the tube from Jordan's grasp. Her lively enthusiasm was always heartening, no matter how often she expressed it.

While her agent burbled on about wrangling with Spatha about the auction catalog not needing an image of Jordan's new work, they walked the short distance to the back rooms where the business of the gallery was handled. Once they slipped through a discreet door, the sleek—almost severe—space of the showroom floor gave way to a jumble of boxes, stacks of paintings propped against walls, several thick sheets of display glass, and at one point a small pile of lumber surrounded by sawdust. The myriad scents permeating the corridor were equally varied: pine and paint thinner, wax and perfume, peanuts and cleaning fluids.

Shanna's windowless office was so cluttered with catalogs, posters, artwork and various supplies, including several cardboard tubes, it was a wonder she got any work done.

"It's good you were able to get it done despite everything that's happened," her agent commented as she cleared a drafting table covered with gallery brochures.

"You do what you need to do." Jordan shrugged, uneasy with the praise and wanting to forestall further discussion along those lines. "I was surprised to see Theodore around."

"Believe me, so was I," Shanna answered absently, working one of the plastic end caps off the tube. "I got the impression the old codger's here to see you, just drove up to make sure you're holding up alright. He's been hovering by the doors all morning. You were always one of his favorites." She tacked on a teasing grin thrown over her shoulder to her last statement.

Jordan was the youngest of Walsen Galleries' discoveries. Theodore had never made a secret of his partiality and she would forever be grateful for it. The thought he'd made a special trip to the city just to condole with her eased Jordan's pain somewhat, as did the image of that dignified, old man haunting the gallery's entrance.

Finally succeeding with the cap, the other woman eased the psyprint out of the tube and unrolled it on the table, weighing down the corners with a cube of notepaper, a ceramic cup filled with long sticks of cinnamon bark, a calculator, and a box of elaborate paper clips. At her first good look at the image, she gaped, for once struck speechless.

Jordan held her breath while Shanna studied the piece silently. It was such a departure for her; she wasn't sure how her agent would take the change.

"It's so different from your usual style. It's . . ." Her greenish brown eyes wide, Shanna shook her violet head in a slow, wondering gesture, clearly at a loss for words. "My goodness, this will boost your prices. Fab is going to love this. Spatha'll make a killing at the auction."

Jordan bit back a shout of triumph as a tidal wave of relief slammed through her at her agent's endorsement. The ferocious emotion shocked her with its intensity. After Dan's death, she'd been so swamped with grief all of the past week that only sheer stubbornness and self-preservation enabled her to finish the piece she'd started on that horrible day. She'd poured so much determination into parsing the psyprint that she'd begun to doubt her own judgment.

"I want a copy for myself," Shanna informed her in a definite, no-nonsense tone.

"What?" While the other woman ran the gallery, it was rare for her to buy a piece for her own collection.

"I think it'd look great over my fireplace."

Reassured by her words, Jordan smirked. "I want it on canvas—just one print. Any later print runs to be on paper, and I don't have any plans just yet for those."

"What?" Shanna echoed, taking a step back, her voice lilting with surprise. "Just one?" she parroted indignantly, her hands coming to rest on her hips.

"Well, it's a different style." Jordan smiled broadly, leaning on her hands to rest her weight on a flat piece of furniture behind her. "I want to test the demand first. Besides, don't you think the uniqueness will drive up the bids?"

"That goes without question, and on canvas, too. But that would put it out of my price range," the other woman finished mournfully.

"It's for a good cause." Jordan didn't mind the loss of income; knowing she'd helped ease the burden of public service for some military and police personnel more than made up for it. The exposure she got from her participation didn't hurt, either.

"You're getting canny in your old age." Shanna scowled, her lower lip jutting out momentarily, then her expression cleared as she switched mental tracks. "Tell me, is this a new direction you're taking or are you just experimenting?" She looked around her office as though checking angles. "If it's typical of the stuff for your next show, I might be able to put together something really special around it."

Perched on the edge of Shanna's desk, Jordan held herself motionless while she considered doing more in the vein of Dillon's nude. Was it something she really wanted to explore in greater depth? She'd never focused on human figures before, choosing to concentrate on scenery and still life.

One thing she was certain of: she wasn't ready to resume her usual style; it had too many associations with Dan. Perhaps changing directions was the way to go.

At least she could be reasonably sure the market wouldn't reject her work. When it came to business, Shanna had never steered her wrong before.

Presented with a fresh challenge, an eddy of eagerness swirled inside her, urging her to return to her psyprinter.

Jordan smiled. She just hoped Dillon wouldn't mind the new direction her art was taking her. If she spent even more time in his company, she had a feeling he'd have a prominent place in future works—whether he wanted it or not.

Dillon folded the newspaper he was using for camouflage, while he kept watch for possible hostiles. Most people might scoff at his caution, but after Jordan was poisoned and nothing suspicious had turned up in the bombing investigation, he was beginning to suspect Jordan—not her cousin Dan—had been the target of the bomber.

So he maintained a protective surveillance while Jordan conducted her business at the Walsen Galleries. It wasn't much of a hardship.

The SoJu district—the area south of Jupiter Street paralleling the gentrified waterfront—was lined cheek to jowl with art galleries and boutiques with a few chichi cafés in between and a bookstore that catered to the poetry-reading crowd. The only way another shop could be fitted in would be with explosives.

Artsy benches lined the sidewalk on his side of the avenue between colorful flower beds and tall trees bright green with young leaves, an invitation for shoppers to sit down and get the load off their feet. Store clerks shared the benches beside him, taking a short break from work to enjoy the clear skies, warm spring sun, and fresh air.

Behind them, a rowdy group of teenagers on rollerboards

swept by, jeering at a plank-toting contemporary on foot. Heads turned when the young bravo—not to be outdone—lowered his burden and took wobbly flight after them, executing a few flourishes in midair in the process.

Dillon grinned as shouts of surprise and a smattering of spontaneous applause trailed the boy down the street toward the esplanade along the waterfront.

The short, plastic plank the boy had been carrying was a Leviboard, kidTek's latest bestseller that had taken the holiday buying season by storm last year. Its undemanding levitation spell and nearly frictionless, muscle-driven propulsion had proved popular with the more active crowd as well as other markets. In a matter of months—a year on the outside, Dillon estimated—black ops might be field-testing one.

The teenagers were followed by bicyclists headed in the same direction, then a playschool group led by a handful of watchful adults in singing one of those lilting nonsense rhymes used to teach the basic spells that everyone learned.

Everything added up to a genteel ambience far removed from his usual haunts when on a mission. No hiding in dry brush being devoured by insects while hostiles hunted his team. No lugging ammo, various supplies and equipment for miles from the LZ into unfriendly territory.

He tracked his observation to its logical conclusion. Not much chance of a firefight. No adrenaline rush from a situation gone hot. Nothing going boom. *Well, you can't have everything.*

All in all, it was light duty.

It didn't hurt that traffic flowing through the district was sparse with no horns or sirens to disturb the tranquil morning. The few vehicles on the street—sedans and compacts for the most part, with a delivery van or panel truck trundling by every so often—sent only the occasional whiff of exhaust fumes to trouble civilian noses.

At this time of the day, most of the vehicles parked along the sidewalks were mercantile in nature, not the cars of customers. Unlike later in the evening when it would take a miracle to secure parking, there were actually several empty slots, including the area in front of Walsen Galleries—luckily for Dillon, since it afforded him a clear view of the gallery's entrance and black marble façade across the avenue.

Just then, Jordan, still deep in animated conversation with a lavender-haired Shanna, stepped up to the tinted double doors. Her arms were empty, so she must have left the tube she'd been toting with her agent. *Too bad.*

Despite her surprising insecurity about her work—her unexpected refusal to show him her latest psyprint being a case in point—everything looked okay. Jordan was smiling happily and Shanna was waving her arms in large enthusiastic gestures.

With a nod for the meter mage ensuring no one had tampered with the parking spells, Dillon dropped off the newspaper in his car and crossed the all but empty street to join Jordan.

While he wasn't certain she was the target of the bomb that had killed Dan, the lack of motive for the murder had his brain circling back to their sharing the same name. If the bomber didn't know Jordan was blind, he might have assumed she owned Dan's Sirocco and planted the explosives in it to kill her.

But for what reason? The gloves? Or something else? Jordan's discovery of gloves used in a murder and the subsequent attempts on her life could be a coincidence. But what else was there? And if he worked on the premise that the murder and the bombing were connected, how to investigate it?

Pondering the problem, he kept a watchful eye on the nearby pedestrians strolling down the broad sidewalk. Foot traffic was on the rise as lunchtime approached, congregating around the cafés and the alfresco tables just outside their doorsteps.

Cooking smells made Dillon's mouth water, distracting him momentarily. Perhaps they ought to have lunch out before returning home.

Shanna had trailed Jordan to the curb, still holding forth with great excitement that had his lover shaking her head in apparent disbelief although she continued to smile. If only for that, he could've hugged the doll-like woman, his heart made lighter by Jordan's pleasure.

The delivery van seemed to come from nowhere. Nameless. Anonymous. Just one of several serving the businesses in the area, of the few hundred in the city. Only instinct called it to Dillon's attention.

It drove up the street behind Jordan, gaining velocity with reckless disregard for safety, almost as if it were out of control.

Dillon picked up his pace, an uncanny dread clamping around his gut as the van hurtled closer. Then it swerved toward the side-walk, rolled over the curb, barreling forward.

Headed straight for his lover!

Shouting Jordan's name in warning, Dillon clawed the air as he raced toward her, throwing everything he had into an effort to move faster. He had to get her to safety, had to protect her, had to get to her in time.

Giving a savage roar of acceleration, the van mowed through a cheery flower bed, beheading blossom-laden stems and leaving an explosion of red, orange, and yellow petals flittering in its wake like so much thrown confetti in a vernal equinox parade.

People's heads turned in puzzlement, jaws dropping, all motion at a snail's pace, like animals caught in tar.

Picking up steam, the van howled onward, a torn leaf flapping incongruously from its grille. It rammed a wrought-iron trash receptacle, sending it flying with a loud clang without wavering in its berserk charge toward Jordan.

Grabbing more power from somewhere, Dillon felt a surge of adrenaline in answer and put on a burst of speed. He snatched Jordan off her feet and twisted his body, lunging desperately away from the oncoming vehicle.

Too late.

Dillon knew it even before he could complete the motion, but he had to try. Dire wind chilled his nape as he thrust Jordan before him.

THUMP!

The impact drove the breath from his body, made lights flash before his eyes. Then they were airborne, Jordan still safe in his arms.

At the edge of his vision, the van roared away, blood beading off a side panel. *Shit, that's bad.* It disappeared from sight, attended by loud crashes and screams.

The ground rushed up at them.

With a grunt, Dillon forced his torso around, spinning in the air to place himself between Jordan and solid concrete. His muscles screamed at the effort; the hit he'd taken must have done more damage than he thought.

This is going to hurt.

He tried to prepare himself as best as he could, but with his arms wrapped around Jordan, he struck the sidewalk heavily, unable to break his fall with the usual moves. They bounced once, still turning from his attempt to protect Jordan, and landed on his other side.

Inertia kept them tumbling wildly on the rough pavement. Pain clawed at his shoulder with broad, frenzied strokes each time he struck concrete.

Clutching his lover close, Dillon braced his legs to stop their rotation before they ran out of sidewalk. They slid on his back, the friction sparking a fresh blaze of pain up his spine.

Damn, should have worn leathers.

His head slammed into something hard. The world flashed white, then turned to gray as they came to a stop.

Driving back the blurring of his sight by dint of sheer hardheaded cussedness—not that his head felt all that hard at the moment—Dillon forced his eyes to focus. *On what?* He couldn't remember the answer, only that it was important.

A marble wall stood beside him, stretching up to the clear, blue sky. A dark, man-made blade challenging the heavens. Interesting. He could almost picture it framed in a gallery.

Sound returned slowly in pulsating, nauseating waves. Crying. Somewhere close by, a woman was screaming. . . .

A cold rush of fear swept through him, bringing pain with the sudden, reflexive tightening of his muscles.

Jordan!

That was the answer. How could he have forgotten?

Groaning, Dillon tried to turn his pounding head to check his lover. His back seized up in a white-hot flare of agony.

Everything faded to black.

What happened? Stunned by the sudden violence, Jordan lay still, her head spinning, her stomach swooping to her throat in a wave of sourness. Dillon's unexpected shout had surprised her, his urgency frightening in its intensity. After that—

She shook convulsively, her heart thundering in her ears, bounding in her chest as if it would leap out at any time. It was all a dizzying whirl of motion. Dillon had—

She gasped for breath, unable to get enough air to fill her lungs. He'd grabbed her; she knew that from her vision. Then something had happened and they'd rolled. Over and over, it seemed. She'd had to block her clairvoyance in self-defense as vertigo threatened to empty her stomach.

"Jordan! Are you alright?" Shanna's breathless voice from somewhere above her startled Jordan out of her daze.

Alright?

Her body ached, patches of raw skin and bruises making themselves known. Her knees felt swollen, pressed against a hard, rough surface. She flexed a foot and realized she was missing a shoe.

Jordan tried to raise her head. Her neck and limbs felt leaden, resisting all movement. Pain darted up her back at the attempt. She didn't think anyone in her right mind would classify her condition as "alright."

"Is he—" An indrawn hiss somewhat closer to Jordan's ear. "Ohmygoodness! Dillon!"

Dillon?

A familiar male scent filled her nostrils, mingled with those of blood and warm concrete. Heavy hands pressed down against her back and cradled her head. She was in Dillon's arms! He must have protected her from—

"What happened?" Jordan rasped out through a tight, dry throat. The world had spun around her in uneven, stomach-roiling spurts. She shivered fitfully.

Dillon wasn't moving beneath her, wasn't saying anything. Only the rapid beat of his heart under her ear and the fluttering of his ribs said her lover was alive. Her own heartbeat sped up, roaring in her ears. What had happened?

A clatter of heels and scuffing of leather. A cool breeze chilled her body as someone blocked the sun. A babble of voices drowned out Shanna's answer.

"Are they alright?"

"The driver didn't even stop! He must have been nuts or something."

"Where's the blood coming from?"

Blood? Jordan tried to ask, but her voice wouldn't work.

Strange hands touched her back, moved over her legs with horrifying intimacy.

"Just lie still," Shanna ordered. "I'm calling for an ambulance."

An ambulance?

Pained groans and shocked tones reached Jordan beneath the strident voices rising above her. Hysterics and muffled crying.

"He's unconscious."

"We have to do something."

"Must have hit his head."

Indignation and frenzied excitement. The harsh crunch of broken glass underfoot.

"What happened?!" Shock and morbid, prurient curiosity.

"Don't just stand there! Get her off him. He can't breathe."

The perfume of spring flowers from earlier merged unevenly with the astringent scent of cut grass and flowing sap. Under it all was the rich, nauseating smell of fresh blood. It filled her mouth with coppery sweetness. Made her stomach lurch.

"You shouldn't move them. What if they've broken something?"

"Man has to breathe."

Urgent hands scratched her aching back. Hard fingers dug into her waist. Long nails bit into her thighs.

No. Don't!

Darkness whirled. Her stomach rebelled, sourness filling her throat. Jordan gagged.

"Watch it! She—"

The world plunged. Hard flesh hit her belly.

She landed with a grunt and lost the battle with a violent heave. She retched out acid. Gasped in bloody air. Over and over. Her stomach continued to lurch even after it was empty.

"We can't leave her like that."

"Yeah, we can't."

Large, hot hands clamped around her head and neck. Others pressed on her body. The darkness moved and shifted, more slowly this time.

"Careful. Careful."

Hard roughness under her back. A pebble dug into her shoulder blade. Her swollen knees throbbed with pain. Someone whimpered.

"You shouldn't have moved her!" A thin tenor remonstrated in thunderous tones. "She could have hurt her back."

Jordan shivered in misery, her belly cramping.

Theodore? It sounded like her elderly mentor but he'd never spoken so in her presence. He compelled the strangers into order, stationed two people by her side.

"Don't move Jordan, unless she's vomiting again. If she is, roll her head, neck and body as one unit to the side so she doesn't choke. Support her head and neck. Don't twist her spine," Theodore ordered crisply.

People around her mumbled assent.

"He's bleeding badly."

"I think he broke his skull."

Dillon?

"We have to stop the bleeding." A matter-of-factly alto. "Kneel there and immobilize his head."

"What?" A younger squeak.

"He might have a spinal injury. Place your hands on both sides of his head and keep it aligned with his spine. Now, young lady."

"Mom, my pants!"

"Oh, hush and make yourself useful."

Dillon!

Terror mounting with every word she heard, Jordan fisted her hands and opened herself to her clairvoyance.

Surrounded by strangers, Dillon lay pale and unconscious. Blood pooled around his head. He must have hit it on the decorative pilaster jutting out of the black marble wall. What she could see of his shoulder and back was raw and gritty from the pavement. His dashing, white tunic was torn, the sleeves ragged and bloodstained.

"Jordan? How do you feel?" A light touch on her forehead.

The smell of vomit mixed with cloying perfume and rich, sweet blood.

A grimacing teenager crouched by Dillon's head, trying to keep her fashionable slacks from getting dirty. She held his head gingerly, her eyes wide with revulsion.

Beside her, an older woman in a smart pantsuit dug through

a voluminous purse, then plucked something from a battered box. She peeled back the packaging from a Chilcloth, activated the cooling spell on the dressing with a snap of her wrist. "Hold this here but don't put pressure on the wound." She moved the girl's hand to the Chilcloth.

Jordan coughed, bile searing her throat. "Th-Theo—"

"Mo-om!"

"Yes, it's I, child."

"This is no time for one of your snits, Medea Lee."

They were more than twenty feet from where she'd stood near the curb. A strange trail of blood led back to her original position. The farthest, largest splotch had to be where they'd first landed. Each bright red mark, the edges just starting to darken, was a spot Dillon's back had touched.

"D-D-Dil-lon?" Jordan's teeth chattered uncontrollably.

A man draped a brown jacket over her legs. "Her hands are like ice!"

—something tumbled on the sidewalk, flashing white-blue-white, smashed into the wall—

She gasped.

Strangers crowded in around her. They touched her, chafed her cold fingers, and patted her hands, forcing their memories on her.

—violet hair blown across wide brown-green eyes—

"He's unconscious, Jordan. Don't worry. An ambulance is on the way."

—something surged past in a blur of gray. Petals erupted into the air in a whirlwind of color—

The flood of thoughts battered at her, a cataract of images devoid of order and meaning. It threatened to sweep her under, into madness. *No!*

—a couple flew through the air, landed on concrete, and bounced—

—a little girl in a playsuit—

"Shanna, get me a blanket, a tarp, something to help keep him warm," Theodore snapped out.

—a woman holding a microphone—

—something white crashing into tables—

Her head throbbing to her racing pulse, Jordan moaned desperately as the onslaught continued, mind after mind without sense.

—blood on concrete—

"Where's that ambulance?"

—bodies stacked in orderly piles like so much firewood—

She could feel her hold on sanity slipping with each invasive image. She wanted to slam her barriers tight against her clairvoyance but that would leave her ignorant.

Dillon! Panting, she tried to jerk her hands free from her well-meaning assailants.

"Nonono, don't move!"

Hands clamped on her neck, pressed down on her shoulder, trapping her.

—a lurid poster advertising a video—

Jordan mewled in protest. A heavy lump landed in the pit of her queasy stomach. She tried to curl into herself.

The hands imprisoning her tightened.

"Child, you might hurt yourself," Theodore warned her in a kind but stern voice. Bony fingers pulled her hands down.

—days-old corpses lay rotting under a bright sun—humans, livestock, pets—all dead in the streets—

Her gorge threatened to rise again. Jordan wrested her hands free, pressing one on her mouth and the other to her belly, trying not to vomit. Her heart raced, thundering in her ears, as she panted.

Hands tightened on her body. The world began to shift.

"No. Don't!" Theodore again. "Not yet."

The world settled back.

The throbbing in her head eased only a little as the over-whelming torrent of images ceased. Fighting not to gag, she clung to sanity, her balance like a strand of a spider's web stretched as thin as faerie silk.

"Mom, he's still bleeding!"

Jordan froze at the cry.

Frowning, the woman in the pantsuit stopped what she was doing and got out another Chilcloth. She applied it on top of the blood-soaked one her daughter held in place.

Shanna ran up, lugging a tarp. She spread it over Dillon, worry etched across her face.

"Do you think he'll die?" the girl asked in a fearful whisper.

"No, darling. The medics will be here soon." Despite her assurance, the girl's mother pulled out another flat package, holding it in readiness.

The red splotch on the new Chilcloth grew larger.

Dillon had protected her with his own body.

Jordan's heart quailed at the cost.

CHAPTER EIGHTEEN

Dillon lay on his side sleeping, his hair clean and blood-free with no sign of the fracture the healers had sweated hours of effort and power over. It would take some time for the bones to knit fully, but his skull was intact with no stray fragments floating around his brain. So long as he didn't dash it on another hard surface, it should heal without any complications.

Standing by his bedside, Jordan stroked his bare shoulder and back lightly, needing tangible evidence he was on the mend to reassure herself what she saw through her clairvoyance wasn't false. *Smooth as a baby's. No abrasions or scars.* She smiled in relief, weakness sweeping through her. Although it looked completely healed, the new skin was probably tender and his body sore from the trauma.

He also radiated more heat than usual, running a low-grade fever. It was a natural reaction to an infection he'd picked up from his shredded back rolling all over the gritty sidewalk, and nothing to worry about, according to the healers.

Dillon had also suffered a concussion. Luckily, there'd been few emergencies that afternoon until their wailing ambulance arrived, so a surfeit of eager healers had been on hand to fix it. But they wanted to keep him under observation overnight to make sure there were no complications.

It hurt to remember he'd been injured—nearly killed—protecting her.

She, on the other hand, had suffered very little: a few cuts and bruises, possibly a mild concussion, hardly anything to merit an apprentice healer's attention, though she'd received that in abundance. She'd had worse the few times Timothy had been sick and lashed out.

Jordan bit her lip, at a loss what to do with herself. The police would probably want to talk to her about the accident—if it was an accident—but no one had come for her so far.

What to do next?

She had to inform someone that Dillon was in the hospital. He had friends who'd care. *John Atlantis, his comrade in arms.*

Reluctantly leaving the emergency ward, Jordan trudged down the crowded corridor, arguing with herself. The man was worried about his wife and babies. He doesn't need more problems. How could she even think of imposing her presence on him?

She shook her head, wiping her damp palms on the white pants of the patient gown that had replaced her stained and torn clothing. The babble of voices, clinking metal and ceramic, the squeaking of wheels and shoes on tile floors rose like a solid wall around her. *But whatever his troubles, Dillon is still his friend— more than a friend. He'd want to know Dillon's hurt, could even have been killed. Wouldn't he?*

Sidestepping a shouting match and a woman trying to pacify a screaming baby, Jordan continued on in her aimless meander, wishing Timothy were with her to talk to. For a soft-spoken cat, her pet managed to help her through many a dilemma.

Dillon and Lantis had been through combat and worse

together, had fought side by side, done unbelievable violence as comrades. *Of course he'd want to know.*

The thought of facing Dillon's teammate who embodied the danger of Dillon's job chilled her. Pressing her fist to her mouth, Jordan stopped, forcing people to walk around her. *Except it wasn't his job that landed him in the hospital, was it?* It was protecting her.

She spun around on her paper slippers, the urge to be at Dillon's side returning with tooth-grinding intensity.

Just then a miasma of blood, cleaning fluids, antiseptic, bile, and vomit washed over her, the stench nauseating and disorienting—a reminder that it wasn't Dillon's job that had nearly been the death of him. It was here, while on vacation, where he'd been laid low. From a threat to her.

It held her in place long enough for a final thought to break through: *If it had been Dan, you'd want to know.*

That was the bottom line, wasn't it?

The private room in the intensive care ward was a pool of quiet after the bedlam of the hospital corridors—a serenity probably enforced by the watchful, unobtrusive man seated just outside who'd vetted her before letting her through, another of Dillon's teammates Jordan recognized from her visions.

The woman in the bed was asleep, seemingly drained by her continuing ordeal, the red tresses fanned across her pillows making her appear paler. Dillon had said her pregnancy was posing complications for her treatment. At least from the white blanket over her rounded belly it looked like the healers were successful in their caution thus far.

The woman's frail hand clutched the darker, much larger one of a man slumped beside the bed. A pang went through Jordan at the sight, remembering that large hand stained with blood and other things.

"Mr. Atlantis?"

The seated man who turned to her warily was a far cry from the one she'd met at her exhibit just weeks past and the one she'd seen fighting beside Dillon in her visions. His wrinkled shirt looked like he'd slept in it for several days. Lines of exhaustion scored his somber face, his shoulders slumped; what sleep he'd caught hadn't been particularly restful. His skin was so ashen he could have been mistaken for a patient.

Scrubbing his hands over his eyes, he stood up, his tired gaze sharpening and his back straightening. "Ms. Kane. Jordan." He walked to her in long, smooth strides that quickly eliminated the distance between them. "Please, call me Lantis." He touched her shoulders gently. "I'm sorry for your loss."

Jordan blinked back tears. After everything he'd been through—was still going through—he still remembered Dan.

"Where's Dillon?" His deep voice wrapped around her like a warm, flannel blanket on a cold winter's day.

Her eyes widened when she registered his question. So he knew Dillon and she were . . . involved. "I— He's hurt."

Lantis frowned, his thick brows drawing together in manifest concern. "How?" He assessed her white-clad form in a swift appraising glance that told Jordan he assumed only danger to her would have resulted in Dillon's injury.

"It was a hit-and-run. He saved me."

He became infinitely still, his bright blue eyes scanning her face intently before his shoulders relaxed somewhat. "How did it happen?"

"A van nearly ran me down. He pulled me to safety and was hit instead." Just saying the words sent a cold frisson of horror through her.

"He was hit? You're sure of that?"

She nodded sharply, remembering the impact of that first blow when Dillon's body crashed into hers and knowing she'd never forget it. "We went flying. There was blood where we rolled and he hit his head." She touched the back of her head without thinking. "He had a fracture." *There was so much blood.* "I thought you'd want to know."

"Dillon?" asked a thin contralto from deeper in the room.

Lantis looked over his shoulder at Kiera, his face drawn.

"Go. I'll be fine."

"Are you sure?"

Wary of the unspoken undercurrents, Jordan held herself stock-still during the exchange between husband and wife. Lantis remained in front of her, his tension evident even in the light touch he kept on her shoulders.

"I'll feel better after you tell me Dillon's okay." His wife smiled wanly. "Besides, you know you'll worry until you've seen for yourself that he's fine."

Jordan frowned inwardly, wondering how much the pregnant woman knew about the two men. Did she know what they did for a living? She searched the other woman's drawn face, finding only concern and affection. If she knew, how had she resigned herself to the inherent danger of her husband's job?

Lantis took leave of his wife with a protracted kiss of frank carnality and a final reminder of "Remember, no strenuous activities" in a deep, velvety voice that caressed Jordan's nerve endings and left a loving smile on the other woman's face.

Wow. Jordan gulped at the sensual heat sizzling between the couple. Married life obviously hadn't dampened their ardor.

Outside, he passed the brown-haired guard with a quiet "Dillon." The other man nodded, then slipped into the room they'd just left.

Lantis put a hand on her shoulder; it was hot the way most men's hands were hot but not heavy or overbearing. Walking silently, he shortened his stride to match hers, without her asking and despite his probable impatience, subtly protective as they headed to the bank of elevators.

"Where is he?" he asked after they boarded the first car going down that arrived.

The other passengers automatically stepped back to give them room, responding instinctively to his air of authority.

"The Recovery ward on the first floor, beside Emergency." She pointed to the appropriate button, which was lit.

Lantis nodded once, his focus turning inward. Was he thinking about Dillon and their work together? Or perhaps worrying about his wife?

Jordan crossed her arms, tucking her hands against her body. Either way, she didn't want to know the answer.

She led the way back to Dillon's room, noticing how people got out of Lantis's way without a fuss. *It must be nice to have such presence.* If she had it, she wouldn't be constantly sidestepping people.

As they neared the ward, it suddenly occurred to Jordan to wonder how Dillon would take her interference. Would he resent her approaching his comrade? He hadn't liked it that she could spy on him with her clairvoyance, or had seen something of his missions with her psychometry. Would this reinforce his stance?

Stubbornness brought her chin up. Whatever happened, she was sure she'd done the right thing by not allowing her fear of his work to dictate her decision.

When they entered his room, Dillon was awake and cautiously stretching his muscles as he sat in the utilitarian bed.

His friend was at his side almost instantly, barely pausing to take in Dillon's apparent good health. "What the hell happened to your wand?"

Wand? Jordan stopped in surprise, pushing the door closed behind her.

Pausing with his arms extended forward, Dillon blinked up at his teammate. "Nothing. It's over there with the rest of my things." He gestured at a nightstand to his left.

Arms akimbo, Lantis loomed—that was the best term Jordan could think of to describe the way he stood—over Dillon. He seemed to grow larger as his blue eyes narrowed with irritation, bright sparks kindling in their depths.

Jordan frowned in confusion. Lantis had seemed so concerned for Dillon's welfare earlier. Why was he acting this way?

"Why the hell didn't you shield?" Lantis demanded in an unnervingly deep, subterranean growl she felt in her bones and made the hairs on her arms stand on end.

Shield?

Dillon's face went blank, his black eyes wide. Despite his tan, obvious color crept up his cheeks. Nonplussed, he opened then closed his mouth repeatedly without saying anything. "It didn't occur to me," he eventually choked out.

The two men exchanged speaking looks, ignoring Jordan's presence entirely. A brooding silence descended between them for long moments as they somehow conversed without words. Obviously, they knew each other so well that the muscle twitches at mouth and eyes that Jordan caught conveyed comprehensible—perhaps even pointed—meaning. Dillon looked away a few times as though Lantis's unspoken comments struck uncomfortably close to home.

Finally, Lantis rolled his knuckles on a cringing Dillon's head. "Don't let it happen again. I'd hate to have to explain to Kiera that you'd gotten yourself killed unnecessarily."

"I'm fine. The healers want to keep me overnight just to play safe." Dillon scowled, still disgruntled by the enforced bed rest he'd argued against despite his manifest need for it.

Lantis snorted, then caught the back of Dillon's head to glare at him. "I ought to—"

Her lover flinched. "Ouch. Not so hard," he groaned, grimacing in pain.

"That's where he hit his head against the post," Jordan hurriedly informed the tall man, clenching her hands against the urge to go to Dillon and soothe him.

After giving her a thoughtful look, Lantis nodded, having eased his grip even before her explanation. "Are you sure you'll be okay tomorrow?"

"I'll just be sore. It won't be the first time." Dillon shrugged smoothly. If Jordan hadn't known how he normally held himself when relaxed, she'd have thought him unhurt.

Still, Lantis frowned, mixed emotions flickering across his grave face, evidently torn between his wife and Dillon. "It'll take you a day or two to get back to passable condition after a concussion. And even more for that fracture. Maybe—"

"He'll stay with me, of course," Jordan heard herself state calmly through a red, roaring fog of possessiveness. Dillon had nearly died; she wanted him beside her where she could watch over him.

The two men turned to her in surprise as if they'd forgotten she was in the room.

Her toes curled in her paper slippers as the extent of her presumption sank in. Only the hard bite of Dillon's bloodstone ring on her little toe kept her from retracting her rash declaration.

Lantis's hand dropped to Dillon's shoulder in an oddly protective stance as he stared at her. He turned his blue gaze—so like Timothy's—to Dillon before he dipped his head and shoulders toward her in a solemn bow. "I'd appreciate that."

Jordan sagged against the door, her knees threatening to fold from under her. What had she just agreed to? It was one thing not to argue against Dillon's moving in with her when she'd been . . . unwell. But to deliberately choose to bring him into her home when she knew she could lose him so easily to his job? And yet she couldn't bring herself to turn her back on him and safeguard her heart. He was hers—would always be hers—even when he eventually left. And danger was part of him.

Was that how her mother had chosen as well?

Her stomach dropped to her knees. *Oh, for pity's sake, I've gone and fallen in love with him!*

"Ms. Kane?"

Startled, Jordan tried to raise her head off Dillon's bed, a crick in her neck protesting the sudden movement. She must have fallen asleep sometime in the early morning. The last thing she remembered was an apprentice healer coming into the room to check Dillon's condition. She'd only intended to rest for a few minutes, to give her aching mind a break from the torrent of images she received through her clairvoyance.

"Ms. Kane?" The raspy voice came again, this time a few feet closer.

She sat up slowly, rubbing her sore neck, the violent events of yesterday making themselves felt through various aches and twinges. "Yes?" Feeling at a disadvantage, she reached for her clairvoyance, afraid she might miss something by limiting herself to her four senses.

"I just heard about yesterday." The speaker was the police lieutenant who'd informed her of Dan's murder.

Jordan ushered him and his female companion out of the room, not wanting to disturb Dillon's rest. The guest lounge was vacant, so she led them there. "This isn't a homicide."

"From what we were told, it was attempted murder," the bearded lieutenant informed her bluntly in his harsh voice.

Jordan nodded reluctantly. It was hard to believe someone had tried to kill her. "A van tried to run me down. The driver jumped the curb." She clenched her fists against a surge of fear, remembering the sickening *thunk* when Dillon's and her rolling bodies came to an abrupt halt. "If Dillon hadn't been there, I'd be dead."

"What can you tell us about the incident?"

Leaning against the wall, she dug her fingers into her stiff neck. Her back felt like it was permanently hunched; straightening it took some effort. "Personally? Not much. The van came from behind."

"You didn't see anything?"

Jordan sighed. She disliked saying it. "I'm blind."

"But—" The other woman stared at her. She had a distinctive white lock that contrasted sharply with her shoulder-length black hair; when she tilted her head—as she was doing now—it flopped down like a swag across her cheek. Jordan suspected the color was natural, unlike Shanna's. She also knew she was focusing on irrelevant details to avoid facing harsh reality.

"I'm clairvoyant; that's how I'm able to get around outside the house. I was talking to Shanna at the time, so I didn't see anything." She took a deep breath. "But I'm also psychometric. If you can get me Dillon's shirt—the medics said they had to hold it for evidence—I can give you more details."

"His shirt?" Lieutenant Derwent's eyes narrowed in speculation.

"It's charged with the event. I touched it in the ambulance, on the way to the hospital. I saw what happened, then." *A van raced toward her back, the driver's narrow fingers clutched tight around the steering wheel.* She shuddered at the memory.

The bearded man exchanged a meaningful look with his companion. "That's alright. You don't have to. We have a specialist who handles that."

Chapter Nineteen

"You're a glutton for punishment," Rio commented, watching Dillon carefully extract his aching body from the car, then pick up the duffel bag of clothes and the laptop in the backseat.

"Aren't we all, to stay in our line of work?" Dillon countered lightly.

"True," the Latino conceded as his gaze swept their surroundings, on the lookout for danger. "But this isn't work."

"I can handle a few files." Perhaps something there would spark his brain. With the investigation into the kidTek bombing gone cold, he was beginning to suspect they were missing the forest. Like, were all the attempts intended for *Jordan Kane*?

"You have a woman waiting to shower you with TLC and you want to work? I don't know, that sounds like brain damage to me," Rio teased, his chocolate brown eyes twinkling. "I'd bet Brian and Lantis would think so, too, when they hear about it."

Dillon winced, remembering his former partner's reaction to

his confession about not thinking to invoke his shield spell. That blunder definitely sounded like brain damage to Dillon. How could he have forgotten something so basic?

———⦷⦷⦷———

He's here. Hovering behind the front door, Jordan still wasn't sure she'd made the right decision by insisting that Dillon stay with her. Despite her qualms, her spine stiffened in outrage at the thought of not being at his side while he was hurt. She nibbled her lip, recognizing in her behavior the way her mother had waited for her father; yet she couldn't stop herself.

Dillon made his way up the path, the slowness of his progress the only hint that he wasn't at top form.

One part of Jordan wanted to go to him and at least carry his bag for him. The other part suspected he wouldn't like the implication that he needed help; she knew she wouldn't. She rubbed her face in Timothy's fur, torn between conflicting impulses. Her pet purred soothingly, batting her hair with a gentle paw.

When Dillon got to the porch, she couldn't restrain herself any longer. Dropping Timothy to the floor, she rushed out to her lover as she shut down her clairvoyance. "You're here!"

With a laugh, Dillon embraced her, enveloping her in male warmth. While she wrapped her arms around his neck, pressing kisses on his face, he backed up and sat down. Pulling her down on his lap, he claimed her lips in a satisfying kiss that more than hinted at carnal expectations.

That would have to wait. He needed his rest.

"Your shoulders are tight." Straddling his lap, she dug her fingers into the knots she found, trying to ease them. "Is your head aching?"

"That's not the only head aching." He cupped her hip with a possessive hand, urging her closer. The hammock swung as their weight shifted.

"Dillon! Behave," Jordan ordered, fighting to keep herself from smiling at his apparent high spirits. "You just had a concussion *and* a skull fracture."

"Prrp," Timothy agreed, insinuating his body between them.

"But it'd be good for me," Dillon protested. His other hand released her to stroke the cat, judging by the purrs.

"And how do you figure that?"

"Think it through logically. Given the proposed activity, any excess blood will drain from up here." He tapped a finger on her temple. "And the endorphins released provide natural pain relief. How could it be wrong?"

She lost the battle to control her laughter, doubling over as her relief translated to giggles. Still chortling, she clung to his shirt. If he wanted to have sex, surely he couldn't be feeling that bad!

"I'll even let you do all the work," he added, a grin in his voice.

Jordan shook her head. "You're incorrigible."

"No, I just have my priorities right." He took her lips then, his kiss turning earnest. A silent request she couldn't deny, not when she'd almost lost him.

"My bedroom," she husked after long breathless moments.

Despite his lingering weakness and Timothy winding between their legs, it didn't take Dillon long to get her upstairs.

"Your bedroom," her lover announced, sighing with relief.

Jordan opened herself to her clairvoyance, knowing what could happen yet needing to touch him, feel him, *see* him. She unbuttoned his shirt slowly, taking her time pushing it off his shoulders and down his arms. Thankfully, her psychometry didn't pick up anything from the brushed cotton, unlike that time in the ambulance.

A van raced—

No! Jordan hastily suppressed the memory, stuffing it away where it couldn't ruin the moment. That was past, and Dillon was all that mattered.

She traced the hard erection behind his fly, enjoying the jerk of his hips that drove the thick ridge against her palm. If the extent of his arousal was any basis, he would be fine—she needed to believe that. Then she freed him, slowly unzipping his fly, taking care not to touch the reddened flesh she uncovered.

"You're torturing me," Dillon groaned.

Kneeling at his feet, Jordan smiled up at him. "I thought the object of the exercise was to draw the blood down here?"

"Any more blood goes down there, I'm going to pass out," he growled in teasing reply.

"Better get on the bed, then. Wouldn't want you to hurt yourself going down," she retorted in the same spirit. *That's right. Keep it light.*

Grinning, Dillon stepped out of his pants and sat on the bed. He massed the pillows behind him, nudged Timothy to the floor, then settled back like some randy eastern potentate.

Jordan flung off her clothes, resenting every second that kept her hands from him. She still couldn't accept he was alright; only the proof of her senses would convince her.

She slid on the bed. "Lie down on your side. I'm the one supposed to do all the work this time, remember?"

He stretched out with his back to her, his position dictated by his healing fracture. As much as he joked about it, he had to be hurting, but true to form, he didn't let it show. "I'm on this side."

Jordan touched his shoulder and still her psychometry remained quiescent. "Hush. I'm the one doing this," she chided, wondering how to start, worried about hurting him more. He'd taken such good care of her after her release from the hospital; now that it was him in need of cherishment, she was afraid of making things worse.

In the end, she could only go with her instincts, and they wanted—demanded—tactile proof of his well-being. She carefully kissed Dillon's back, delighting in its smooth, solid strength, and allowed her hands to explore. Broad muscles flexed under her palms, warm and resilient. She pressed harder, massaging his back with sweeping strokes.

"I love the way you feel." Jordan sighed happily, letting her tight nipples brush him, relishing the darts of excitement the contact elicited. Too bad she didn't have those oils he'd used to pamper her or something similar. Next time she'd be better prepared.

He hummed approval. "That's better."

Bending down, she licked his shoulder, nibbled gently on the meat of it.

"Wrong spot." Dillon chuckled, his body rocking hers.

"I'll get there . . . eventually," she promised him, hooking her leg over his hip. She rubbed her mound against him, the pressure sending a frisson of delight through her. "It might take all night, though," she added on a breathless whisper.

"Awww," he groaned, burying his face in the pillows. He did arch back against her, reciprocating her motion with his firm glutei maximi.

Jordan snuck a quick caress up his penis, tracing the pulsing vein along its ridge to just below the flaring crown. He was so smooth, the skin thin and fine over his hardness. "Don't tell me your blood isn't going south." Hers was.

Dillon hissed something under his breath, the words too muffled for her to catch. If it was a promise of payback, it would be worth it.

She returned to his back, the broad expanse of muscle sleek. None of the raw abrasions from the attack remained; there were no new scars. But she couldn't forget the bloody trail he'd smeared on the sidewalk. All to protect her!

Keep it light, she reminded herself. *If you think too much, you'll cry.*

Subduing her turbulent emotions, Jordan caressed her way down his back, murmuring promises of what she intended to do to him tonight.

"You're fucking with my head, you know that?" Dillon growled between clenched teeth.

She reached over to capture that velvety part of him. "And a gorgeous head it is, too." Her thumb found the spot perfectly formed for it. She rolled her pad daringly and smiled when he pulsed in her hand, firm evidence of his vitality.

"Jordan." The low rumble warned her that he might be laid low now but he wouldn't be in the future.

Returning to his back, she moved down with sweeping strokes. She could smell her scent on him, mingling with his, marking Dillon as hers. At least for now.

Palming his tight buttocks, she squeezed them the way she imagined many women had wanted to squeeze them. Marveling at his survival, she took her time exploring him, thankful she could do so. He was firm yet supple, so perfectly formed from the hollows at the base of his spine to the soft skin between his thighs. She hadn't done him justice in her psyprint.

Despite his plaints, his testicles hung low and loose—a long way from any release. She intended to make his eventual orgasm memorable.

Descending lower, she paid homage to his hard thighs, the crisp hairs rasping her nipples and the sides of her breasts when his muscles flexed beneath her attentions.

"Get up here where you belong."

His adamant tone told Jordan he might do something rash if she didn't obey. She abandoned his legs to settle in front of him, more than willing to oblige.

Dillon claimed her lips hungrily, devouring her with passionate kisses that made her melt, had heat pooling in her belly. Pushing her flat on the bed, he covered her with his body, inserting an insistent knee between hers.

Control asserted itself, struggling against the backwash of desire consuming Jordan. She managed to push him a few precious inches away. "Nonono, you're supposed to take it easy."

"Well, you're not making taking you easy." He took her mouth again, his tongue seducing her with artful licks.

She pulled free, wrestling with her own demanding libido,

wanting nothing more than to have him thrusting inside her with his usual forcefulness—but not while he was hurt. "I'll do the work."

Jordan moved down quickly so he couldn't dissuade her. If she gave him time to argue, he'd be pounding on her and she'd be screaming her ecstasy before she knew what had happened. Not that she had anything against screaming in ecstasy but that was beside the point! Dillon might exacerbate his injury.

Despite the speed of her disengagement and descent, he still managed to nibble on her neck, a single nip that stabbed her core with delight.

Womanfully ignoring the temptation to succumb to his bland-ishments, she cherished him with her hands, lips, and body, doing her utmost to pleasure him. It had its perks. The strengthening of his musk as she got lower. The heat of him like a living brand be-tween her breasts. Just the sudden tightening of his abdomen and his sharp inhalation sent a wave of gratification washing through her.

Unable to resist, she licked the smooth, straining flesh, encour-aging it to greater thickness, alternating sides as she would with a cone of ice cream. Except this was much better. His salty taste revved her appetites, as if she were coming off a yearlong fast instead of go-ing less than two days without sex. She wanted to immerse herself in his taste, his smell, his touch, and his groans of pleasure.

Over broad slabs of muscle, lush impossibly pink lips closed around a thick penis. Flushed cheeks hollowed as a pretty woman sucked on it.

Jordan stilled, startled by the vision. That was her! She'd stopped expecting one by the time she'd reached his waist. And to see herself as Dillon saw her!

Cradling him in her hands, she gave him what he obviously wanted, taking his silken thickness into her mouth, filling herself with his heat.

Dillon groaned, his hands capturing her head as his hips thrust forward.

Exultation soared through her at his reaction. She took him

deeper, sucked him harder, teasing him with flicks of her tongue. She caressed him, molding him with her hands and playing with his testicles, enjoying how he pulsed and swelled.

She drew him out to focus her tongue-lashing on his sensitive head. After all, she wanted him relaxed enough to rest and quickly. She could play with Dillon some other time—when he was fully recovered. Now, she ignored her own desires and concentrated on encouraging his release, not wanting him to do too much when his fracture was still healing.

A shudder ran through Dillon, his testicles quivering under her fingertips. "Not yet," he gasped.

Emboldened by his response, Jordan nibbled his length, then returned to play her lips on his velvety tip, kissing it and growling her approval when his penis twitched in response. Holding him in place, she teased his salty slit and swirled her tongue over the flare of his head.

"Damn it, Jordan!"

A surge of triumph washed through her at the ferocity in his voice. She took him into her mouth and sucked, inciting him to orgasm. Bucking, he came in a gush of salty sweetness, pouring his passion into her as he roared his completion.

She licked him clean, ignoring the slight bitter aftertaste. Maybe next time she'd have a glass of wine on hand, or perhaps find some of those edible massage oils he'd used on her. If not, she still had some cream in the refrigerator. But right now, she wanted nothing more than to have Dillon in her arms where he belonged.

"You . . ."

Jordan crawled up to snuggle against her lover, embracing him tightly. "Shhh, I'm fine." This time was for him.

Dillon pulled her closer, deeper into his musky warmth. "You're dangerous." He kissed her, replacing the taste of his passion with the more familiar taste of his mouth. "Thanks."

"You saved me. I'm the one who should be thanking you," she

murmured against his throat, sleepy now that worry had released its grip on her.

"That was entirely selfish on my part."

The next thing Jordan knew, she was lying alone with only a blanket around her hips. Timothy was somewhere nearby; his purr sounded like a small engine running at full speed, something he usually did when he was getting a belly rub. Which meant Dillon had to be close, even though she couldn't hear him. She couldn't smell his presence since his scent was so embedded in the sheets and in her room that she couldn't tell the difference.

She stretched slowly, refreshed by her nap. "What are you thinking?"

Dillon sighed. "Someone's trying to kill you."

Jordan froze, shocked to hear Dillon put it so bluntly. "What makes you say that?" She hadn't told him about the vision she'd gotten from his shirt.

"The investigation into the bombing that killed Dan has gone cold. They can't identify anyone with a motive to attack him or kidTek. It's too much of a coincidence that soon after, you're poisoned, then someone tries to run you down."

His logic was chilling and irrefutable. Feeling vulnerable lying down, she pushed herself into a sitting position and hugged her knees. "But why plant a bomb in Dan's car?"

The bed dipped beside her, tumbling her into Dillon's embrace. "Whoever did it didn't know it wasn't your car. It's registered in your name, parked at your house. On the surface, it's simple—if they don't know you're blind. Bomb. Poison. Hit-and-run. That's no coincidence, that's enemy action."

A van raced toward her back. "*From what we were told, it was attempted murder.*" Jordan shivered, pulling Timothy close when he butted his head against her arm.

"It's the gloves, isn't it? It has to be the gloves." Why else would someone poison her? Someone was trying to kill her and didn't care who else was hurt. She couldn't help but wonder if Dan would still be alive if she'd succeeded in probing the gloves that first time—certainly Dillon wouldn't have been hurt.

"Probably."

She had no choice. She had to overcome her revulsion of the memories charged into the gloves. Otherwise, the next attempt on her life might get her lover killed. She couldn't fool herself into thinking that Dan's murderer would just give up. "I need to face it. The memory in the gloves."

"Are you sure about this?" Dillon's concern was obvious in the deeper timbre of his voice.

"I have to." She couldn't leave it to the police; it was her failure that had gotten Dan killed. If she'd pushed through the horror then, that murderer might have been stopped already.

He stroked her back slowly, meditatively, his furnacelike heat a living blanket around her. "Can you wait a few days until I've recovered? I can't do much in my present condition."

"Can we afford to wait? The next attempt might kill you!"

His arms tightened around her. "We'll be careful."

Jordan rubbed her face against his chest, torn between Dillon's logic and her fear for him. "Okay, I'll wait. Maybe something will turn up in the police investigation in the meantime." Something that would preclude her probing the gloves? She shoved back the cowardly thought. It was wanting to avoid turmoil that had started this whole nightmare.

"Anything's possible."

"Have you heard anything about the hit-and-run?" Dillon settled deeper in the couch, trying to find a comfortable angle for his aching head. It didn't hurt as much now as before Jordan made love to him, but the endorphins were beginning to wear off. Timothy lay on top of him, eyeing his phone, obviously under the impression his mistress needed help in pinning him down.

"They found the van but it was next to spotless." Disgust hung heavy in Rio's voice, clear as shallow water around a coral reef even over the cell phone connection. "Not even sweat on the steering wheel. If it weren't for traces of your blood in the door seams and the psychic residuals from the side panel, there'd be nothing to confirm its link to the attack."

Dillon ended the call to let Rio get back to tying up loose ends. Nothing terrorism-related had turned up so far. It really pointed to something local . . . and personal. Which circled back to murder. Something he wasn't set up to investigate.

"Nothing new?" Jordan snuggled against his side. His poor darling was done in. He wasn't feeling all that great himself, but he was used to working through exhaustion.

"They found the van, thanks to their psychometrist, but the driver took precautions." He'd suggested Jordan pass the gloves to the cops, but she'd turned stubborn and refused. For some reason, it was important to her to probe the gloves herself.

Trying to jumpstart his brain, Dillon browsed through the files on his PDA.

"Do you have to do that now? You're supposed to be resting." Jordan's worried tone reminded him that his condition was why she'd put off probing the gloves.

"Prrp!" Timothy added, rolling onto his back to bat air.

Dillon grinned despite his headache. "I'm not good for much else, but I can do this." He clicked down. A recent file, tagged "From Lantis," stopped him cold, the hairs on his arms prickling with foreboding. *Lantis?* What could his friend have sent him?

The file yielded a long list of names: Jordan Kane, Timothy, Linda Danvers, Tatianna Jones . . . The flow sparked a dim memory of scrying . . . *The gloves!* With the heart-stopping events that had supervened, he'd forgotten all about it.

Chapter Twenty

Dillon slumped down, allowing his head to droop to the couch back. His head throbbed where the fracture continued to heal. Too many hours bent over the laptop cross-checking the results of kidTek's internal investigation against the names in his scrying list, on top of his injury, left his shoulders tight and his neck stiff.

Jordan had fallen asleep an hour earlier, sliding down the cushions to rest her cheek on his thigh. She looked fine and the healers assured him she'd come through the hit-and-run virtually unscathed. But her nightmares and her hovering at his bedside were telling on her.

When he thought about how nearly he'd lost her, his gut turned to ice. He grimaced. His first instinct had been to get to her side, to take her to safety, when he'd have done her more good by stopping the van with magic. *Talk about a tyro mistake.* His training and all his experience from years in the field had gone right out the window. He'd responded with his heart, not his mind, and nearly gotten her killed.

Now he was failing her again.

He brushed his hand over her short tousled hair, frustrated by his lack of progress.

A *fuumph* of a cushion warned him of Timothy's approach. Hard pads pressed down heavily on his deltoids, kneading the knots loose to the accompaniment of deep purring. The cat shifted his paws along Dillon's shoulders as if deliberately seeking out tense muscles, putting a lot of his twenty-odd pounds behind his ministrations.

"Damn. No wonder she keeps you around." Dillon closed his eyes, not protesting when the cat laid his furry chin on his forehead. With Timothy's purr like a quiet motor for background, he let his mind drift where it would.

Nothing in his investigation into Dan's activities raised any flags. The results of his scrying included most of the people the gloves had touched since their manufacture—and he couldn't find any overlap with kidTek's personnel. The subsequent attacks on Jordan indicated she was the actual target of the bomb that killed her cousin. It stretched credibility for the close timing between the poisoning and the hit-and-run to be coincidence. Two different perps totally unconnected? He shook his head slowly so as not to dislodge Timothy.

He could only hope Jordan's probe would narrow the field.

Seated at one end of the kitchen table, Jordan faced the ill-omened gloves in the afternoon sun slanting through the windows. Even punctured and scratched, it appeared nothing more than expensive black leather. No matter how close she examined it with her clairvoyance, she couldn't see any blood.

She took another breath to control her racing pulse.

"You sure you want to do this?" Dillon frowned at her from her right, concern evident in his dark eyes. In his arms, Timothy stared at her, mewing, clearly nursing his own reservations about her plan.

At her left, Dillon's beautiful friend who'd helped with her door said nothing. Rio Rafael merely waited, his pencil held in readiness over a blank unlined pad.

Jordan gave them a quick nod, her heart in her throat. "If I can see it—really *see* it—I can put it on psyprint. But I have to get the details first."

She had to do this. If Dillon was right, the murderer was the one responsible for Dan's death and the driver of the van that rammed Dillon. If they didn't stop him, Dillon might be the next to die. Her heart leaped to her throat at the thought of losing him. No matter how horrifying the images were, she had to see it through to the very end.

"Take a deep breath," Dillon instructed in a calm voice, sounding like the very soul of dispassion.

She obeyed raggedly, the gloves filling her vision as her clairvoyance responded to her growing dread. A sudden whiff of cinnamon made her gasp, then her sight showed her Dillon holding a bottle near her nose.

"Relax." She couldn't help but comply since the sweet scent evoked blissful memories.

"That's better," he murmured when her breathing slowed to a more measured pace. "Remember: breathe in and two and three, then breathe out and two and three and four. Slowly. Ready?"

This time Jordan's nod was smooth, her dread a distant cloud on the horizon, no longer a looming thunderhead that threatened to engulf her senses.

Picking up the gloves had immediate effect. *A knife slashed down.* Stiffening, she forced back her instinctive panic, then Dillon's voice tugged at her senses. "Tell me what you see."

"A gloved hand with a knife." She held the image in her mind, straining for more detail as she gulped air.

"Easy, breathe," Dillon coaxed her, his even tone drawing her back from the edge. "Describe it to me. Thick? Thin? What kind of edge? Can you see the hilt?"

Fighting down dread, Jordan rolled the gloves between her cold hands, folded the fingers of one until she approximated the grip in her vision. "It's narrow. The blade is about this wide." She placed two fingers against the edge of the glove's palm.

"Good. That's good. What else?"

The question steadied her, distanced her from the vision. She tilted her head, trying to see more detail through the shadows. "It's . . . simple. Straight edges. Bilateral symmetry. With a blade about this long." She measured the width of the gloves, then held her hands apart.

"Bilateral?" Rio muttered over the light scratching of pencil on paper.

"Probably double-edged," Dillon added. A harder, staccato sound of plastic on plastic—a stylus on a PDA?—suggested he was taking notes. "Not a kitchen knife, that's for sure."

Jordan's temples started to throb as she strained to hold the vision to that one scene. "I can't see much of the handle."

"Is there a guard? Something that protects the hand?"

Her psychometry showed her shades of gray, black on black with the barest gleam of steel. Fixing the image into memory, she shook her head. "I don't see anything."

"Go on, then."

Cuts on upraised arms. Despite knowing what followed, Jordan gasped, the scene rattling her hard-won equanimity. *The knife struck repeatedly, creating obscene mouths in white flesh.*

"Easy," Dillon cautioned from over her shoulder. He chafed her upper arms, his body heat and the scent of cinnamon surrounding her, pushing back the bone-deep chill. "Deep breaths. In and two and three, and out and two and three and four."

Jordan gulped, trying to copy his slow rhythm. His soothing croon spun a silken cocoon around her, distancing her from the brutality of her vision. Gradually, her ragged breathing slowed, her tension ebbing slightly, replaced by a veneer of calm.

"Better?" When she nodded, Dillon stepped away. "What do you see?" Wicker creaked to her right; he must have sat down.

"Stabbing." Jordan's hands rose and fell in involuntary mimicry of her vision. "Wounds on raised arms."

"Defensive injuries," Rio remarked softly.

"Can you see skin color?" Dillon prompted.

"The arms look pale, but there isn't much light."

"Maybe Caucasian or north Asian?" The muttered comment sounded like an aside to Rio.

The other man grunted in agreement.

"What else?"

"The arms look feminine."

"How so?" Rio asked.

She shrugged. "The grain of the skin, the fineness of the hairs, the shape of the muscles, they all say female to me."

"Go on."

Blood splattered black walls, spurted through the air to splash on a dark floor.

Jordan whimpered, horrified by the amount of blood, the size of the growing pool on the floor. She bit her quivering lip as her control cracked. "Oh, God!"

"Jordan?"

A feline whine of protest cut through her sobs.

"Timothy, no." Familiar hands gripped her heaving shoulders, drew her up. Hard, male heat warmed her back as a whiff of citrusy soap and cinnamon reached her nostrils. "Relax. Deep breaths. You're scaring the cat."

She leaned into his support, dark splatters filling her vision. "There's so much blood!"

Dillon's lips grazed her ear. "You can stop anytime you want. You don't have to do this."

His words yanked her from the horror, reminded her of their

present danger. *Dillon crumpled on the pavement, his shirt torn, his skin raw from the dual impact of van and concrete.*

"No." Steeling her resolution, Jordan pulled away from him and sniffed, swallowing tears. "I have to do this." She couldn't save Dan—only avenge him—but Dillon was another matter. She wouldn't let the murderer steal him from her as well. "Help me do this."

"Okay. Take your time." Once again, Dillon talked her into regaining some emotional distance from the butchery.

In and two and three, and out and two and three and four. I can do this. I have to!

Feeling as though she hung on to her control by her fingernails, Jordan returned her focus to her psychometry. "The— The walls and floor are made of wood. Wide planks." Shaking, she gulped as her queasy stomach flopped. "Blood splatters them, drips down. There's a— A window, square with small panes."

"What's outside the window?"

"It's dark. Nighttime." She strained at the shades of black filling her vision. Her temples were pounding at the effort, matched by the drumming in her ears. "I see . . . bark? Trees? I can't make out much. I don't see any leaves I recognize."

"Is that it?"

"Yes. I don't see any furniture." She fixed the image into memory. Maybe they could get more detail from the psyprint.

A mangled face trying to scream.

Jordan faltered, swallowing with difficulty to keep her gorge down. Bile seared her throat. She pressed the back of a fist to her mouth, afraid she'd throw up. "Dillon?" she whimpered, embarrassed by her weakness.

"I'm here." He wrapped his arms around her chilled body, chafing the gooseflesh on her rigid arms. "It's okay. Deep breaths. You can do it."

She gulped, feeling like she couldn't get any air. That bloody face filled her vision, a waking nightmare—one she had to imprint into memory or it would all be for nothing.

Tears spilled down her cheeks, wiped away with soft cotton.

"No, no, no. You don't want to do that," Dillon crooned against her ear. "You don't want to scare Timothy now, do you?"

Startled, Jordan snorted with amusement.

"That's better. Breathe deeply. Remember: This is past. We can only help her by finding her killer." Hers and Dan's.

She leaned back against Dillon, a solid bulwark against the horrors of her vision, a stirring reminder of her present—one she had to protect.

"I can't see much of her hair but she's—" Jordan swallowed, fighting her rising gorge. "She's blonde. Fair, clear skin. No freckles. H-high cheekbones, I think. There's a slash on the left one that's o-open to the b-b-bone. Nose looks broken. I can't tell the color of her eyes or their shape. They're—" Panting, she turned her face into Dillon's shoulder, drawing strength from his clean male scent. "They're mutilated. Pointed chin. Wide mouth with thin lips."

Dillon's embrace tightened. It felt like it was the only thing preventing her from flying apart. "Easy. Take your time."

Jordan clung to his voice, one last handhold of strength. She had to see this nightmare through to the very end.

"She's screaming. Oh, God. She's screaming." Jordan's control snapped. Dropping the gloves, she twisted in Dillon's arms, sobbing as she buried her face in his shoulder.

CHAPTER TWENTY-ONE

He'd known it would come to this point. As much as he wanted to deal with the murderer himself—for what he was doing to Jordan and had done to Kiera and Dan—he couldn't. If he went rogue, he wouldn't be any different from the terrorists he'd fought.

Besides which, it wouldn't give Jordan—or kidTek's employees for that matter—any closure if they didn't know the murderer had been caught and punished. Only Lantis, Kiera, and he would know. Only they would have that satisfaction. Still, he had to wrestle with himself to overcome that temptation.

Time to bring the cops into the picture. But first . . .

"I need to talk to Lantis." Dillon eased his cell phone out of his pocket, wondering if it was too late to call.

Jordan sat up, the cold washcloth he'd placed on her forehead to soothe her migraine falling to her lap. "Lantis?"

"He has some equipment that might come in handy," he explained as he pressed the numbers for his friend's phone, "but I don't know where he keeps them."

Jordan caught his hand before he could complete the call. "Lantis is sleeping and Kiera's watching him. Let him rest."

Wariness pricked Dillon's back with ice. "It's that easy?"

"I know them, so I can look in on them anytime." Rubbing her temples, she shrugged as if to say it was nothing unusual.

Oh, fuck. "You just have to know whom you want to see?"

"I have to know they exist and something specific about them. Take this murderer, for example. I know he exists and is probably connected with the art scene somehow, but that's not enough for me to isolate him from all the other murderers in the city. So I can't tell you where he is or who or what he's doing right now." She propped her chin on her upturned palm and pouted in dissatisfaction. "But if you ask me about your friend Rio, I can tell you that he's—" She broke off, blushed fiercely, and finished in a mumble, "otherwise occupied."

"Otherwise occupied?"

Jordan shifted abruptly on the couch, giving him her back, much like Timothy did when he didn't want to play anymore. Dipping the washcloth in the bowl of cold mint-infused water, she lay down and wadded it over her forehead.

Enlightenment dawned. "Oh." Dillon fell silent, chilled by further proof that any involvement with Jordan posed a security risk to his black ops missions. Even if she managed to refrain from asking questions, all she had to do was use her clairvoyance to get classified information. She didn't even have to work at it; the knowledge seemed to come spontaneously.

He was so fucked.

Derwent arrived at the same time Rio and Malva pulled up in a sleek sedan the following afternoon. The homicide lieutenant

practically bristled with suspicion as he stalked up the walk behind the couple.

"They're here," Dillon announced unnecessarily, stepping
away from the window as the doorbell rang. He followed Jordan
and Timothy down the stairs, hauling back on his excitement
when his heart leaped in predatory anticipation.

After greeting the new arrivals and going through the niceties
of offering drinks and snacks, Jordan excused herself, withdrawing to her studio.

Dillon was relieved. After last night's nightmare, he didn't
want to expose her to more reminders of the murder. Not that she
might not be watching them at that very moment—easy enough
to do with her clairvoyance—but he hoped she'd get some rest.

"Big of you to share your suspicions with us," Derwent remarked, his harsh voice ladled with sarcasm as he faced Dillon
across the kitchen table over the gloves.

"Jordan needed to do this herself." Dillon picked up the envelope he had waiting and pulled out the psyprints Jordan had
made just that morning. "We got these from her visions."

Pulling the picture of the probable victim closer, Rio muttered a curse under his breath, tilting the psyprint to give Malva a
better view.

Derwent gave a nearly soundless whistle as he studied the
other images. "These are psyprints?" At Dillon's nod, he shook his
head in awe. "Hell of a lot of detail." Which justified Jordan's insistence in probing the gloves.

Rio's Amazon plucked out other psyprints, her eyes hardening. "Made a thorough job of it." Surely, she meant the murderer,
although Jordan had rendered the victim's mangled face from
several different angles.

"I'm not sure this will help, but . . ." Jordan walked in with
Timothy tucked under her chin and another psyprint in hand. It
was a close-up of the knife, looking sharp enough to cut.

Dillon frowned. He hadn't expected her to be working on yet

another psyprint of the murder. Her nightmares were bad enough. Needing to touch her, he pulled her down on his lap. "How are you doing?"

Jordan leaned into him, her upper arms cold, her hands restless on her pet's fur. "It wasn't pleasant, but I just want to get this over with."

After studying the psyprints, the two cops grilled Jordan about the gloves. Dillon had to admit they did a good job of interrogation. Once they were satisfied they had all the details, they allowed him to talk Jordan into lying down.

"So what do you have in mind?" Derwent patted the tabletop restively like a quiet metronome. "Why'd you call us here?"

"I was thinking, if we can find the victim, we can identify the murderer."

"*We* meaning *you*." The older man snorted. "Just because you work security doesn't make you any less a civilian. The retrospection was one thing, this is something else altogether." He stabbed a blunt, nicotine-stained finger at Dillon.

Dillon looked at Rio, conferring silently. The police knew them as security because of Kiera's problem last year. They couldn't reveal they were actually black ops agents—not that that detail was likely to help argue their case.

The Latino stirred. "He's good at what he does—especially scrying." He smiled grimly. "And you won't have to worry about us messing up your crime scene . . . if you're with us."

A ghost of a grin crossed Malva's face and was gone.

Derwent reared back in his chair. "I ought to have you surrender those gloves. You're talking obstruction of justice," he blustered.

Dillon shook his head. "There's nothing to tie them to a crime—yet." He waved at the gory images on the table. "These don't mean anything without a body attached to them."

Scowling, the older man turned to his detective, obviously expecting her to take his side of the argument.

"They have a point, L-T." Malva tapped a psyprint. "If they're right and Ms. Kane is the target, I don't like the perp's versatility. Knife, bomb, poison, van." She ticked off the murderer's methods on slender fingers. "He doesn't care who else gets killed and the body count's already past twenty. Who knows what he'll try next?"

"That's assuming this *is* the motive for the attacks on Ms. Kane." Derwent crossed his arms over his broad chest, the scowl on his face deepening.

"What do you mean?" Feeling his shoulders tense, Dillon had to force himself to relax. They weren't adversaries, here.

"These"—the lieutenant gestured at the psyprints on the kitchen table—"don't match the perp's MO. The attacks on Ms. Kane have all been in public, impersonal."

Rio turned to Malva, surprise leaving his brown eyes wide. "Even the poisoning?"

Making a face, she nodded reluctantly. "There's been no indication the perp tried to enter the house or was even in the vicinity. The poison wasn't applied here." Meaning Jordan's attacker had somehow found out about her order and sprayed praxialle over it before it was delivered . . . otherwise there'd have been a rash of poisonings in the area.

"While this is damned personal." Derwent tapped an image of the victim's face.

Though he hated to believe in coincidence, Dillon had to concede the point. But this at least would put paid to Jordan's nightmares. "It still merits investigation."

Sitting back, Derwent ruffled his beard thoughtfully. After several heartbeats, he finally asked: "What do you propose?"

At the implicit approval, Dillon released a surreptitious breath. The police probably had specialists who could cast the same spells that he could but none of his caliber, if their scrying specialist was representative of their quality. "Essentially, there are two spells involved: blood identification and direction." He looked at Malva and Derwent, skimming over Rio seated at the foot of the table. If this led to a crime scene, the cops may have jurisdiction. "You're familiar with them?"

The older man kept his response to a sharp nod.

"Not to cast, but the theory, yes." The tall woman tilted her head, professional interest leavening her regal mien. "That's a tall order and a taxing piece of spellwork."

The homicide lieutenant raised a bushy, grizzled brow at her, clearly soliciting her expert advice.

Malva shrugged. "It's not offensive magic, but a spell is only as good as its caster." She turned critical gray eyes at Dillon. "Are you sure you're up to it? Rio said you intend to do both today." He'd asked the Latino to set up the meeting.

Dillon ran his hand over the back of his head where the skin over his fracture was still tender. "I can manage." The sooner this was done, the better for Jordan.

Derwent waved a dismissive hand. "Okay, you're on."

It didn't take Dillon long to get ready. He'd made his preparations yesterday, anticipating the lieutenant's approval.

The spell for blood identification was the simpler of the two. All it did was detect a correspondence between any dry blood on the leather and fresh blood. To do that, he first had to define the association he wanted to find.

From the floor, he picked up a potted pine and set it on the table. A cut he'd made earlier on its trunk had produced enough sap for his purposes. He collected the brownish fluid with a glass stirrer, then focusing his magic in a bowl of water, he dissolved the sap, turning the water momentarily cloudy. The pure ringing of glass filled the silence.

"Had this set up ahead of time," Derwent remarked in a harsh rasp from across the table as Dillon set the stirrer down.

Dillon shrugged, reaching for a sealed plastic bag. "I was going to do it—with or without you. If we're right, whoever's attacking Jordan won't stop unless we make him."

He spilled a pea-sized chunk of resin into a waiting mortar

and pestled it into a fine powder. The resin was produced by the same species of pine as the sap. Most mages would consider that degree of caution excessive, but he'd learned in black ops that details counted and it didn't pay to cut corners unnecessarily.

Focusing once more on the water, he poured the resin into the bowl. Cupping the glass between his spread hands, he closed his eyes and drew ambient magic into himself, then forced the prickling power down his arms to pool over the water. The glass warmed against his palms, informing him of his success even before he opened his eyes.

The water glowed a bright blue almost electric in intensity, the association made. As sap was to resin, so would he use fresh blood to identify dried.

With the first stage behind him, Dillon allowed himself a brief smile. He turned to Malva, extending a paper-wrapped lancet. "Care to donate some?"

Technically, the blood didn't have to be a woman's; Dillon could have used his own. However, since Jordan's visions indicated the victim was female, using Malva's would reduce the chance of detecting blood stains from a male source, and any risk of him getting his own blood on the leather. Not that he'd be so inept as to do so, but why run the risk?

Too, it would allay any concerns either cop might harbor that Dillon had rigged the results.

Malva accepted the lancet without hesitation. Stripping the paper wrapper, she plunged the narrow blade into the tip of her left ring finger, obviously well-versed in the theory. Squeezing the digit, she forced a couple of dark drops out.

The light from the bowl turned momentarily purple as the blood dispersed through the water. Dillon held back a sigh of relief, reminding himself they'd yet to pass the first hurdle.

When the light changed back to blue, he raised the bowl to eye level, holding the glass sides firmly, and completed the spell with a mental nudge. The glow flickered, scintillating like sunshine on gentle waves. Keeping the bowl suspended, he stepped sidewise to play the dancing rays over the gloves.

After a few seconds, brilliant blue splotches appeared on the leather, as though the light from the bowl clung to the gloves. Slowly, the splotches spread until very little of the original black remained visible.

Catching Malva's eye, Dillon jerked his chin to a pair of chopsticks on the table. "Turn them over?"

She did so with minimal fuss, handling the smooth ivory pieces easily to expose unmarked black grain. Bright blue luminescence spread across the leather, like a growing stain, as Dillon held the radiant bowl over the gloves. In less than a minute, the only black to be seen was on the fingers and upper palm of the right glove.

At the completion of the first spell, relief woke in Dillon, tempered by wariness at the results and the need to maintain the spell.

Keeping the bowl raised, he studied the shadow. *Right-handed. Underhand grip. More for stabbing than slicing.* It looked a match for the hilt of the knife in Jordan's vision.

Derwent stepped closer to the table with a grunt. "Looks premeditated."

"How so?" Malva leaned down to peer at the gloves, a lock from her white streak flopping down to curl in front of her forehead like an open quotation mark.

The homicide lieutenant used a chopstick as a pointer to indicate the spatter pattern. "Held it blade down. You don't do that in self-defense. Not normally." He raised a brow at Dillon. "Can you hold it? Gonna need documentation." He didn't wait for Dillon's nod before digging through his bag to produce a digital camera. He'd obviously come prepared despite his protests.

The scratching of pencil on paper told Dillon Rio was busy sketching, producing his own version of documentation.

Derwent photographed the gloves exhaustively with Malva

posing the gloves to highlight certain details. With his attention on holding the bowl steady while maintaining the flow of the spell, Dillon couldn't tell for certain, but it looked like the older man used a special setting to compensate for the radiance of the blue splotches. Possibly, the camera was customized police equipment. *Wonder what else it can do?*

Dillon had no difficulty maintaining control of the spell, but his arm muscles were starting to burn by the time the cops were satisfied with their documentation. There was a subtle difference between holding up a bowl for over half an hour during a spell and lying in wait for several hours to spring an ambush on a convoy carrying illegal arms and contraband spell components, he mused in a quiet corner of his mind. The latter didn't make his body ache as much, probably because he was usually seated or prone.

With the documentation requirements met, Dillon had Malva peel a strip of leather from a blooded portion, using a crystal blade, then expose the underside of the piece to his spell. The leather turned blue, proof that the blood had permeated it.

Dillon eyed the homicide lieutenant askance. "Satisfied?"

The clicking of the camera shutter filled the silence. "Yeah," the older man sighed wearily. "Damn, that must have been a bloodbath."

Dismissing his magic with a mental wave, Dillon set the bowl down, then stretched his arms and back on an explosive exhalation, allowing the built-up tension to leak away.

"That bad?" Malva's gray eyes narrowed in sympathy.

Dillon rolled his neck. While holding a pose for nearly an hour wasn't a hardship, the mere fact that it involved Jordan tied his muscles in knots. He was just grateful this was a step toward resolving her nightmares.

"Not really," he said in answer to his fellow mage. "Just draining." The blood identification spell wasn't technically difficult; at least, not for him. But to maintain it while keeping his body mostly motionless—which ran counter to his preference for deci-sive action—was something of a strain.

"Going to do the second spell now?" Derwent turned an as-sessing glance at him.

The spell for direction was fairly basic, the most difficult part was power. It had to be imbued with a lot of magic to have any sort of detection range. The more magic he used during the acti-vation, the farther the spell would reach. Many mages probably preferred to cast it when they were rested, not having expended energy in an earlier working. Evidently, the homicide lieutenant knew that.

Dillon, however, was a graduate of the rough-and-ready school of black ops. On missions, the enemy didn't care if he was rested or not. During their years as partners, Lantis had made cer-tain Dillon learned to always be ready.

"Now's as good as any." Anticipation sharpened his smile. Whatever the cops believed, he felt it was the next step to resolv-ing Jordan's problem and capturing the bomber responsible for hurting Kiera and killing Dan.

"You're sure about this?" Malva frowned, tilting her head, the white lock at her temple sliding down to brush her cheek. Beside her, Rio kept his silence; after several missions together, he knew how Dillon would answer.

"Of course." Using the crystal blade, Dillon trimmed the leather strip she'd peeled into an elongated diamond, a four-point star with a long tail. Once he cast the spell, the stubbier end would be drawn more strongly when like called to like. The imbalance of the shape would turn the piece into a directional arrow.

He dropped the piece into a small, empty bowl and added salt water until the glass globe was half full. The leather strip lay curled at the bottom like a quiescent leech.

Cupping his hands, palms down, over the bowl, Dillon closed his eyes and reached out to gather ambient magic. He stretched further to tap a nearby minor wicce line, drawing power until its electric prickle had the short hairs on his forearms standing and heat warmed his palms.

Someone hissed.

When he opened his eyes, violet energy swirled above the water, giving off so much light he could see the bones of his hands through his flesh.

He reached out for more. In this case, it was better to use too much magic than too little. Who knew how far away the victim's body lay? So long as he didn't burn out his gift, he'd be safe. And he was a long way from pushing the limits of his magic sense. The only question was his physical capability.

Squinting at the power he'd summoned, Dillon pushed his hands closer, compressing the roiling energy. It resisted his efforts like a solid cloud. His biceps bulged, his arms shaking at the effort. Slowly, in muscle-quivering degrees, he forced his hands together until his fingers touched and the violet light condensed into a brilliant ball. Weaving his shadowy digits together, he formed the rune for similitude and bound his magic into the pattern with a concentration of will.

When the power stabilized, he pushed the spell into the water and the leather strip that would serve as its focus. Since the blood on the gloves was fresher than the leather, the spell should draw the leather piece to the closest mass with DNA identical to the blood, allowing them to home in on the victim.

With magic permeating the bowl, the water fluoresced a gentle blue. The leather strip rose, floating to the surface of the glowing water, absolutely level, pointing at the gloves. Dillon tested it with a nudge of his finger. The leather piece returned to its original axis, like a compass pointing to an organic north. When he moved the gloves, the strip obediently tracked their position.

"Looks good." Dillon surrendered the gloves to the homicide lieutenant. He forced down the tension threatening to knot his shoulders. The next test would tell him if he'd succeeded in drawing enough magic.

Derwent sealed the gloves inside a plastic bag, then slid that into a silk-lined envelope. Now that they were considered evidence, Dillon wasn't likely to see them again anytime soon. With them in police custody, Dillon hoped it meant the end to Jordan's nightmares.

As soon as the older man closed the envelope, the leather strip slowly began to shift, finally settling to point steadily northwest. Dillon grinned around a rush of predatory jubilation. *Success!*

Chapter Twenty-two

"Stop the car." Frustration at their slow progress made Dillon brusque. His shoulders ached with tension, adding fuel to the slow fire burning in the base of his skull from having to maintain the homing spell for so long.

When Rio obeyed, Dillon raised the bowl of blue glowing water, moving it back and forth experimentally. Elation burst through him as the diamond-shaped leather on the water's surface quivered, its angle adjusting minutely as the bowl's position changed. "We're close, maybe within half a mile. It's around here that way." He pointed directly away from the road toward the woods; the axis of the arrow was practically perpendicular.

Rio and Malva immediately slid out, heads swiveling to study the roadside as they stretched their legs. Though they were probably less than thirty minutes from downtown, tall conifers loomed overhead, interspersed with patches of brush. It had taken them over an hour of careful driving and backtracking from Jordan's house to get this close. Despite online aid, the winding country roads hadn't been easy to navigate, frequently ending in cul-de-sacs or simply petering out—not at all conducive to quick travel.

"That's promising," Derwent remarked from beside him. The cop had been unexpectedly patient with the protracted search, accessing maps that had enabled them to get this far.

"What is?" Malva asked, scanning their sylvan surroundings with wary eyes. Apparently, she was a city girl more at home in an urban environment.

Getting out of the car, the older man indicated a stand of conifers fuzzy with young green needles a fair distance from the road. "Tamarack. You usually find them in bogs." He turned an assessing look at Dillon. "If there's a body around here, we might be in luck."

Leaning back into his seat, Dillon narrowed his eyes against the throbbing in his head as he followed Derwent's logic. A bog meant acidic, anoxic water conditions—which retarded decomposition. If they found it, the corpse was likely to be in good condition. *Hell of a thing to hope for.*

"Hard to believe there's this much nature so close to the city." Malva tucked her hands into her leather jacket pockets, her long legs flashing as she joined Rio in scouting out a path in the direction Dillon had indicated. The Latino gave her a welcoming half smile as she caught up with him.

Around them, only the gravel road and the car hinted at human presence; the woods looked pristine. Even with his concentration absorbed by keeping the spell up, Dillon was conscious of the lack of man-made noise: no traffic, no sirens, none of the subliminal hints of human occupation.

"You going to be okay?" The older man bent down to turn critical brown eyes at him through the window.

"Yeah, I just need to get this over with," Dillon muttered in reply, thankful the stop gave him time off from balancing changing levels of ambient magic.

Significant movement was difficult with active magic, especially over long distances. When reasonably stationary, a mage could tap a minor wicce line to fuel a spell. But unless one remained a constant distance from the power source, moving more than ten feet while maintaining a spell was difficult.

Unfortunately, the homing spell didn't lend itself to easy recasting since it required a high influx of power upfront. It actually took less energy to maintain than to do it over and over again. Except travel was involved.

Of course, his headache was entirely his fault. Dillon could have opted to power the spell with his own carefully hoarded cache of personal energy, but it would have left him drained if an emergency came up that required magical muscle.

Derwent took Dillon at his word and communed with his PDA, barely looking up when Rio and Malva returned to report failure. He took a reading on the leather arrow, using a digital compass and a GPS receiver, and noted the precise direction it pointed.

Irritation rose in Dillon at not being similarly equipped. Lantis probably had a military version with higher accuracy hidden in his office somewhere. But when Dillon called to ask, his friend had been occupied with helping Kiera through another healing session. Dillon wouldn't have interrupted that, short of mortal danger to Jordan.

"Let's back up a little," the older man said finally, running his hand over his thick beard. "The county map shows a fork nearly a mile back. Maybe we can triangulate."

With Rio back at the wheel, they took the other road. The leather shifted gradually until it pointed in the opposite direction.

When it looked like they'd gone past the site, Derwent had them stop to take another reading. "Hah. It looks like the site is over there, about six hundred yards in." He pointed across the road. "But the maps say it's a bog. Unused land. Nothing leads that way."

Heavy brush blocked their view, shadowed by more fuzzy conifers.

Rio brought the car around to backtrack at a crawl. As much as Dillon wanted to eyeball the woods, the homing spell was taking most of his fraying concentration. He had to leave that to the two cops.

It was Malva who spotted an overgrown track that looked like it went in the direction they wanted.

"Good eye," her lieutenant muttered.

Dillon grunted as a nerve along his nape twinged in protest. Just a little longer. Wary anticipation stirred through him as Rio turned the car onto the dirt road.

Leathery-leafed shrubs scraped against the doors as the car rolled slowly over brown needles and fallen twigs with a quiet squelch. The track wound its way through a shadowy twilight between trees nearly a hundred feet tall. Hopefully, whatever they found at the end of the trail would take them another step closer to the bastard threatening Jordan.

The thought made his headache more bearable.

The dirt road ended in front of a small cabin. Banks of short, brown needles and small, round cones covered its rough porch, giving the building an abandoned appearance.

The leather arrow swung wildly between the cabin and some point beyond it to one side, deeper into the stand of conifers spearing up from a mossy patchwork of browns, greens, and reds.

Dillon swore. That wasn't normal.

"What?" Derwent twisted away from the window to frown at him.

"It's torn between two locations," Dillon explained. "There's DNA in the cabin." Which meant they'd probably found their murder site. Blood from a simple cut wouldn't have the same effect on the spell.

The lieutenant grunted. "Where's the other spot?"

"Someplace that way." Dillon pointed into the trees. "We'll have to get some distance beyond the cabin before it'll settle down enough for a good reading."

Carrying the luminescent bowl at waist level, Dillon walked grimly behind Rio and Malva with Derwent taking the rear. Now, he was certain they'd find a corpse at the end of the trail.

The arrow continued to alternate between its two targets in a frenzied swinging that was disturbing to watch. The cabin had to be an abattoir for the homing spell to respond that way. The hairs on the back of Dillon's neck stood on end, a visceral reaction he tried to ignore since it wasn't the familiar prickle that warned him of danger. Only when they'd gone more than twenty yards past the cabin did the leather diamond train forward and slightly to the left of the path.

Derwent took another reading, gesturing at Rio and Malva to wait while he communed with his PDA. "Hah," the older man finally muttered triumphantly. "The spot should be a little over seventy yards that way."

Dillon nodded agreement, but kept his spell active. The way his head throbbed, he wasn't sure he'd be able to recast the spell any time soon if he dropped it. Better to maintain it until they found whatever they would find.

"Watch your step," Derwent warned. "There's supposed to be a small lake somewhere there, but with a bog you might not realize you're already on the water until you fall through."

"Right," Rio and Malva acknowledged simultaneously, then shared a smile. The two once more took point. They worked well together, dividing the load between themselves with minimal discussion.

It was slow going, not because there was that much by the way of underbrush, but because Rio and Malva had to test the ground several times, probing the mossy surface with sticks, before taking each step. No one wanted to break through the peat into cold water, especially given what they were hunting. Despite the lateness of the day, the air was cool, probably because of that lake Derwent mentioned.

Dillon had no qualms about following Rio. The younger man's visual acuity made him an excellent point man.

With part of his attention devoted to maintaining the homing spell, Dillon took greater care with his footing. Clumps of sphagnum made for a springy, uneven path capable of twisting the ankles of the unwary, while the slippery needles scattered between them made footing even more uncertain. The occasional sparkles of afternoon sun reflecting off the glass bowl didn't help his headache, either.

"Damn, it's so silent," Malva muttered uneasily.

She was right. Save for the little noise of their passage, all that could be heard was the soughing of the wind through the trees. What wildlife there was in the area was in hiding.

"Typical bog," Rio remarked, eyeing the dense undergrowth between some trees.

"Hang out in these places a lot, do you?" Malva returned jokingly.

Rio snorted in amusement but refrained from expanding on his statement. Was the Latino keeping his line of work a secret from his Amazon or did she know?

Behind them all, Derwent was a silent presence, hopefully one who was keeping a sharp rear guard; Dillon couldn't free up enough attention to check.

A clump of wizardwort glowed a luminous red at their approach, reacting to the presence of active magic. "Rio." When the younger man looked back, Dillon jerked his chin at the shining plant.

"Gotcha." His friend prodded the ground before the clump, then guided Malva away.

The detective caught Rio's arm. "Why?"

"Wizardwort floats on water," he explained with a finger pointed at the soft red glow.

She stared at the plant. "That's wizardwort? I've only seen the powdered form, usually for deflagration spells."

Her lieutenant snorted unexpectedly. "We don't usually get fresh ones at crime scenes."

They skirted the invisible shoreline, following a faint trail curving north. Beyond a line of black spruce, they finally saw the lake. Although it was early in the season, pink orchids bloomed near the water, bringing with them the scent of fresh red raspberries.

"We should be close," Derwent called out from the rear. "Just a matter of yards."

"Any change?" Rio asked, turning to Dillon.

"It's that way." Dillon gestured toward the lake, extending his arm along the line of the leather arrow. He ground his teeth against the pounding in his skull. Despite the shade from the trees and the refreshing breeze, the effort of maintaining the spell had sweat trickling down his back.

Malva and Rio tested the footing, prodding the moss to establish safety, while Dillon and the older cop waited. An occasional grunt and splash when they broke through to water punctuated their search. Then Rio finally waved him forward.

Walking carefully, Dillon gave the arrow most of his attention. It changed direction with each step he took along the perimeter of solid ground mapped out. Gradually, it started to twist, dipping below the surface of glowing water in the bowl.

"Whoa." Rio's voice cut through his concentration. "That's far enough."

Dillon looked down, past the bowl and his friend's outstretched arm blocking him at chest height. He'd almost gone over the edge into the water. "Thanks." He grinned at Rio. "Anyway, it should be here."

The others closed in to study the arrow, which had declined more than thirty degrees below the glowing surface.

Derwent whistled softly. "No doubt about that."

The older man's brown eyes turned flat behind a mask of cool professionalism. He had Malva mark off the area with sturdy branches, and then photographed the site and the telltale arrow from different angles. He also took a GPS reading, muttering the coordinates under his breath as he noted the location in his PDA. "Okay. That's good. We've got it."

With a sigh, Dillon dismissed his magic. He rubbed the base of his skull where the heavy throb refused to let up, the price for keeping the spell going for so long in the field. "What next?" He set the now-ordinary-seeming bowl on a convenient tussock of dark red moss. With the search for evidence localized to this end of the lake, what would follow was police business.

"Now, we'll see if we can do some preliminary work," the homicide lieutenant grunted, a fierce light in his eyes.

"Preliminary?" Malva echoed, a cell phone in her hand. "What about the techs?"

"First, we find out how deep we're looking at, what kind of equipment we might need, that sort of thing. Luckily, I brought some gear." Waving away offers of help, Derwent trudged back to the car.

"Is that wise?" Rio asked Malva softly from where he crouched at the lake's edge.

She shrugged, studying the branch markers in the water. "It'll be more efficient. The department's been putting in a lot of overtime lately. He's trying to keep it from increasing more than it has to."

"And this isn't overtime?" Rio took out a pad, propped it on his thigh, and started sketching.

"We're here anyway." Shoulders stiff, back as straight as a high adept's verge, Malva stared at the moss-shrouded lake with regal gravity, almost as though she were willing it to surrender its secrets. "Might as well do the spadework. Find out what we're dealing with." Nothing in her voice betrayed her evident unease.

Kneading his nape, Dillon filtered out their conversation.

Despite the likelihood that they'd found the victim, he couldn't help but worry about what they would discover—and it wasn't helping his headache. Just because the remains were in the bog didn't mean they'd be immediately useful in bringing an end to Jordan's problem—regardless of the homicide lieutenant's optimism.

He knew from long experience that scrying didn't pick up everything. In all probability, that applied to psychometric visions as well. Who knew what else the murderer had done after that emotionally charged scene Jordan caught from the gloves? He'd seen too many burnt and mutilated corpses in his other life not to know that what awaited them could be worse than what was depicted in the psyprints.

As Lantis would say, "So what?" They'd find whatever they would find. And whatever it was, they'd deal with it. He only hoped something about the victim would help them identify who was threatening Jordan.

Predatory eagerness rose up inside, baring razor-sharp fangs, and setting his pulse echoing in his ears. Soon they'd know one way or another.

Shifting his weight impatiently, he dug his fingers into his nape. If only his head would stop aching.

Irritated by his weakness, Dillon joined the two by the lake. Large patchworks of brightly colored moss gave it a deceptively benign appearance. What he could see of the water was murky from half-rotted vegetation and the darkening sky. Somewhere in its depths was the corpse of a murder victim. What else might it hide?

Heralded by rustling bushes, Derwent returned laden with a duffel bag of equipment and an eager—almost sprightly—bounce to his step. Like a man on a mission.

A good man to have at his side. One who wanted things done right, not just easy.

When a thorough test showed the lake was only knee-deep by

the shore, the older cop donned rubber waders and entered the water, cautiously pushing back floating mats of pale green moss as he ventured into thigh-high depths. To help his efforts, Rio held out a probe, extended in the angle and direction the arrow had indicated, while Malva picked up the camera to document the proceedings.

"A bit more to the right," Dillon directed Rio, his head still pounding from the spellwork. He winced as the low afternoon sun came out from behind a cloud to play on the water.

With a nod, Rio adjusted the probe. Despite the angle, he held it remarkably steady, as steady as if it were a rifle.

His adrenaline rising with each cautious step Derwent took toward the site, Dillon paced to work off some of his tension, not wanting to give in to the urge to plant his fist or foot in something. Unlike Lantis, he didn't have a knack for sitting still and just waiting.

Not much longer now.

Time seemed to slow until even breathing took forever.

He scanned their surroundings while he tried to stretch the tension from his tight muscles. His shoulders resisted his efforts. It was as if he couldn't believe they were close to resolving Jordan's problem. Or perhaps he didn't want to believe. Because it meant going back to black ops and leaving Jordan? Not seeing her for weeks—possibly months—at a time? His stomach churned at the thought.

He glanced at Rio and Malva. The two lovers spent as much time apart. How did his fellow agent handle it? Only a spike of pain in the base of his skull answered him.

Wrenching his attention back to the business at hand, Dillon watched the homicide lieutenant's unsteady progress, which was peppered by low curses whenever his footing gave way, leaving the cop stumbling in waist-deep water.

"It should be to your front and slightly left," Dillon called out, the throbbing in his head forgotten as excitement stirred, riding the adrenaline in his veins. He took an involuntary step forward into squelching moss in his eagerness.

The older man waved acknowledgment, then grabbed hold of a hummock to push it out of his way. On the shore, Rio used the probe like a barge pole to help.

Malva continued shooting, coolly professional in her own way. Whatever stress she'd felt earlier had apparently been banished by the need to take action.

Dillon held his breath as the cop took that last step. Disconcertingly, the scent of ripe raspberries filled his nostrils, overpowering the smell of decaying plants.

Suddenly, Derwent leaped back, cursing profusely, his arms flailing and splashing. The moss mats bobbed wildly in his wake. Sunlight sparkling on the waves made it difficult to see what had startled him. "There! Right there!" Florid color filled the older man's face as he pointed a shaking finger at the dark water a few feet in front of him.

Chapter Twenty-three

Timothy twisted under Jordan's hand, his muscular body sliding off her lap. "Prrp?" he chirped inquisitively. He'd been keeping her company while she napped, trying to recover from another night's broken sleep. At least it'd be over soon.

Dillon had called earlier to inform her they'd found the murder victim. They were just waiting for the crime scene technicians and an ambulance, but he was coming back once the body was bagged and the scene was secured. It wouldn't do to strand the cops in the middle of nowhere, he'd joked.

"What is it, Tim?" She reached out to pat his head, but he pulled away. The couch rocked, then a heavy *thud* announced the cat's departure, off to assuage his curiosity.

Jordan frowned. It couldn't be Dillon; it was too early. Besides, he'd said he'd call before leaving the scene. It couldn't be the police, either. The homicide lieutenant had arranged for a regular drive-by, but she's just heard the cruiser leave, its radio's squawking rendered unintelligible by the distance. It would be another hour or so before it returned.

Lowering her barriers, she sent her clairvoyance trailing after her pet.

Timothy prowled to the kitchen on silent feet, his head tilted inquisitively. He walked straight through without even pausing to sniff at the refrigerator, entering the pantry to stare at the door to the garage. Then his ears swiveled back to lie flat against his head, his eyes narrowing and hackles rising in an unwonted show of temper.

A shiver of apprehension swept up Jordan's spine as she willed her sight to show her what had drawn his ire.

The garage door gaped open. A monster stood silhouetted against the lamp-lit drive, more shadow and nightmare than anything else. Sprouting horns and scales and wearing a horrific scowl, it held a familiar, narrow knife in a gauntleted paw, unsheathed and ready for stabbing, and a black box in the other.

Jordan fumbled with the phone, hastily punching the buttons for speed dial. "Dillon, someone's in the garage," she hissed when her lover answered. "I think it's him. The murderer. He has the same knife."

Dillon's blood turned to ice at Jordan's words. *The murderer at her house?*

Just a few feet away, the victim's corpse gave testament to the bastard's viciousness. The brutality of the injuries—so many stab wounds the victim would have been unrecognizable even to her closest loved one—flashed before his eyes. His heart skipped a beat at Jordan's danger and his impotence.

She'd called him for help. What to tell her?

He couldn't advise her to get out of the house. If the murderer caught her outside, help might not arrive in time to do any good. Given the uneven surface of the gardens, Jordan would be at a disadvantage despite her clairvoyance, especially if the murderer wasn't alone. Without depth perception, she wouldn't be able to move at speed; a sighted person would outrun her without any difficulty. The path through the front yard was the most level, but long and winding. The shortest and most direct egress would require her to leave the path. Her only alternative was the driveway, but the gravel was noisy and made for uneasy footing. It would also bring her too close to the murderer.

"Use the darkness and stay away from him. Keep moving. Don't get stuck hiding in one place. I'll tell the cops," he gritted out through clenched teeth.

Dillon sprinted for the cabin, ignoring the startled faces of the crime scene techs kneeling beside the pale corpse laid out at the lake's edge. Past the magelights, the trail led into inky darkness. Brush became clutching hands; mossy hummocks concealed wet hollows and black waters waiting to trap unwary feet. Though he stumbled, he couldn't bring himself to go slower, not when Jordan was in danger.

So stupid! He should have asked Rio to stay behind.

Running full tilt, Dillon cursed hindsight and his acceptance of the cops' logic. *Impersonal, yeah, right.* Sure, Jordan's attacker had kept his distance; and, yes, there had been no indication of forced entry—other than Dillon's. And Derwent had gone so far as to arrange for regular drive-bys to check on Jordan.

But that hadn't been enough.

He still should have asked Rio to watch over Jordan. He'd considered it, then dismissed the notion, not wanting to piss off the homicide lieutenant just when the older man had turned cooperative and agreed to investigate. He'd accepted Jordan's assurances that she didn't intend to leave the house and her teasing reminder that he was only a phone call away.

Now, because he hadn't gone with his instincts, Jordan was at the mercy of a vicious killer.

Fear gave his legs wings. But even at his best speed, it took too bloody long to navigate the dark forest trail.

Dillon broke into the spell-lit clearing at a run. "Rio! Derwent!" Head swiveling in search of the two, he darted through the mess of official vehicles in front of the cabin, making for the sedan at the back.

Though he stood to one side, chatting with Malva, Rio responded instantly, pitching the car keys to Dillon with a quick sling of the arm even as he turned to follow.

The keys slapped into Dillon's palm with a clash of metal.

"What happened?" Derwent demanded across the clearing as Dillon rounded the hood to wrench open the driver's door.

"Intruder at Jordan's," he explained, sliding behind the steering wheel. "Same knife."

The car rocked as Rio got in, the other door slamming shut after him.

"Wait!" The homicide lieutenant abandoned the knot of techs waiting to search the cabin, scrambling for the backseat. "I'm coming with you." For an older man, he moved well. "Cyn!"

"Right." Malva gave an index-finger salute apparently in acknowledgment of instructions. To judge by her glum face, she wasn't happy at being left behind.

Dillon started the car, the engine turning over immediately if only from sheer force of will. He clenched his hand on the wheel, his knuckles turning white, forcing back the urge to drive off now! Jordan was in danger.

As soon as Derwent had most of his body inside, Dillon put the car in gear, not waiting for the cop to close the door. The wheel fought him, the soft soil and slippery needles covering the track providing little traction.

Derwent cursed, clinging to a grab bar as he wrestled with the door. A solid *thud* announced his success. "Give me details."

Jordan brushed her hand over the light pad, deactivating the spell. She'd fallen into the habit of keeping a light on when expecting Dillon, but she didn't need it. The darkness was her friend. Now, light would only aid her enemy. And activating the light spell would be impossible for the murderer without leaving proof of his identity—something his disguise was clearly intended to prevent.

The monster knelt by the pantry door, pointing the black box in his hand at the lock panel. Lights flashed and flickered, dancing across the box's face, then disappeared, leaving a lone green dot glowing. The dark anonymous figure reached confidently for the door knob.

Jordan sent her clairvoyance around the house and bit back a sigh of relief at seeing nothing else out of the ordinary. But just because the murderer was alone didn't mean he didn't have an accomplice waiting for him somewhere outside.

She retreated upstairs on bare feet, trying to move as silently as she could. Where to hide?

Timothy crouched in a corner of the pantry, his fangs bared in a snarl, thick tail lashing from side to side.

Jordan dismissed the bedrooms as quickly as they came to mind. They were dead ends with only one exit, according to her firefighter father, since she couldn't climb out the windows. She briefly considered Dan's apartment with its private access to the garage, then dismissed it as well. If she tried to escape that way, it would leave her out in the open and she couldn't be sure of outrunning the murderer or any accomplice. She had to outthink him, had to win this game of cat and mouse. If she kept the murderer here long enough, Dillon and the police would be able to catch him—Dan's killer.

The only alternative left was the library with its two entryways. She fled there, hiding between the busts of her parents as the murderer slowly searched the ground floor.

Dillon sent the car rocketing on another hellish drive, shadowed by a harrowing sense of helplessness. He couldn't shake the awful feeling of déjà vu choking him. This time they might be too late, arriving to find Jordan in a pool of her own blood.

The mangled corpse they'd found provided graphic evidence of what the murderer was capable of; the bog had kept it in good condition. The sight of it kept flashing before his eyes, translated to Jordan's slender body. His scalp throbbed, right over his healing fracture, another reminder of near failure.

If they were too late . . .

Flooring the accelerator, he gritted his teeth, rejecting the possibility. They wouldn't be too late. The alternative didn't bear thinking.

The monster prowled the darkness, probing the nooks and crannies, even behind the curtains, his sharp knife held at the ready, to slash and stab as he had at least once before. Timothy kept pace, a large, stealthy shadow pouncing at random. Soft vituperation drifted through the night, berating her pet. *They covered the ground floor, then climbed the stairs—one with deadly intent, the other with hostile wariness.*

Jordan bit her lip, hoping her pet wouldn't get bored with his game and lead the murderer to her. Down the hall, the cat crowed in triumph at yet another successful blow. How much longer would his patience last?

The monster searched the sitting area at the top of the steps, then entered the nearest door—Jordan's bedroom. Moonlight from the windows washed her empty bed in white and left no shadows large enough to hide in. The monster ransacked the closet, lashing out with his knife and spilling torn clothes and shreds of fabric—all in silence.

The sudden violence sent a frisson of fear darting through Jordan's body. *Dillon, where are you?* She withdrew to the entryway on the far side from the murderer's approach and slid into the hall, out of sight, wondering if her enemy would search the other rooms first or the library. She'd have to dodge back into the library or up the hall, depending on which one the murderer chose.

Sniffing the rags, Timothy bristled with an outraged snarl, nearly doubled in size. He chased the monster, made another lightning pass on strangely shaped legs—hopefully, a distraction to his search.

The monster paused at the entryway to the library, his grotesque silhouette a nightmare come to life. Only a thin wall stood between him and his prey. He searched the windowless room and its reminders of family with uncaring haste.

Holding her breath, Jordan slid along the wall, away from discovery. One misstep, one bit of noise could bring death slashing down on her.

The monster hissed, muttered something under his breath as he stopped in the middle of the library. He spun on his heel and crossed the hall, shoving open the door to a guest room, with Timothy chasing after him.

Jordan circled in the opposite direction, partnering the murderer in a fearful dance. She slipped into the library as her enemy continued down the hall. When the murderer disappeared into the second guest room, she fled back downstairs.

There was only that bedroom, the hall bath, and Dan's apartment left to search. What would the murderer do then? Would he leave to try another day—eluding Dillon and the police? It would be so simple for the murderer to take the stairs down to the garage and escape.

Keeping her sight open to monitor her enemy, Jordan headed for the dining room with its doors to the kitchen, hallway, and living room. There, she knelt down to catch her breath and plan.

Long minutes crawled by without any sign of her lover. What was taking Dillon so long?

"Go straight, one mile. After the bridge, turn left into the side street."

Leaving the navigation to Derwent, Dillon ran the solitary red light. As a local cop and with the maps on his PDA, the older man had the inside track on the roads. Dillon had to take the lieutenant's word for the route; streetlights were few and far between in the woods.

"There's the bridge," Rio warned.

They whipped past a patrol car parked on the shoulder. A few seconds later, a siren wound up behind them.

"Keep going!" Derwent ordered, leaning between the front seats.

Dillon hadn't intended otherwise. "Hang on." Barely slowing, he slid into the turn amid squealing tires and a flurry of gravel pinging on the undercarriage.

A shrill cry and a sudden clatter broke the silence, the thick planks of the stairs resonating bell-like in the night. Jordan tensed, pressing her back against the wall separating the dining room from the living room. A surprised squeal from Timothy. A low curse followed, then silence. Heart pounding, she risked using her sight to find out what happened.

Crouching at the foot of the steps, Timothy lashed his tail, glaring at the monster clinging to the posts beside the staircase to stay upright.

Jordan could imagine what had happened: her pet must have dashed between the murderer's legs and tripped him. She smiled, remembering the times he'd nearly done the same to her.

A growl of deadly frustration came from the hallway. *A flash of silver in moonlight. Red blood on white fur.* A wail of startled pain pierced the silence.

Timothy!

The knife slashed through the darkness at the cat, its silver blade edged black with blood.

Elemental rage boiled in Jordan's heart. This murderer had killed Dan, hurt Dillon, invaded her home. And now he was attacking *Timothy*? The injustice of it all rose up inside her in a blinding wave of fury. *How dare he!*

She scrambled into the living room, groping for a weapon, anything to smash her enemy into submission. The scent of vanilla reached her nose and she swept her arm in its direction. A large block of smooth candle wax met her questing hand, four stiff wicks scraping her palm. She grabbed it, the adrenaline coursing through her body making the hefty mass featherweight. Homing in on Timothy's cries, she flung the block high, hoping she wouldn't hit her pet. Without waiting to see the effect of her attack, she fumbled for another weapon.

A blunt *thud* and a grunt came from the foyer.

Sweet chocolate filled Jordan's nostrils. Her fingers brushed against leathery petals. Below them, she found a hard edge. Smooth ceramic, rough wicker, and damp charcoal. One of Dillon's orchids. The pot weighed less than Timothy, but it was better than nothing.

The monster sprang to his feet. Knife in hand, he rushed into the living room.

Patrol cars converged on the quiet residential street, sirens wailing in dissonant chorus, emergency lights flashing red and blue. Cops spilled out, adding to the tumult.

An ambulance appeared in the distance, racing their way—more of Derwent's handiwork, Dillon suspected, but he couldn't think about that now. Spotting a gap by the curb, he brought the sedan to a screeching halt in the open space.

Leaving the engine running, Dillon got out and vaulted the

hood. He sprinted down the garden path, cutting across its mean-
dering curves and hurdling half-seen obstacles with Rio at his
back. Jordan had to be alright. *Please, let her be safe!*

"Gavin! Leave it to us!" Derwent called out from behind,
huffing.

*Hell, no. Not when every second of delay could mean Jordan's
death.*

Her arms stinging from several cuts, Jordan lashed out wildly,
punching and kicking, trying to remember Dillon's lessons. She'd
fled the living room when she realized her danger. But in her
haste, she'd made a mistake. Instead of turning down the hall,
she'd run to her studio—and it had only one door. Before she
could slam it shut, the monster had shoved his way in.

Now, Jordan fought for her life. She'd tried to get out of reach
but failed.

The knife glinted in the dark. Slashed down.

Jordan threw herself to one side. Pain stole her breath as she
crashed into something—the psyprinter, she realized when her
hand landed on sharp pins.

The monster gave a wordless scream in a high, strange voice.
He was answered by a savage snarl as Timothy attacked, climbing
and clawing Jordan's enemy.

"Tim!" Jordan collided with the monster, desperate to protect
her pet. The monster flung off the cat, his arm catching Jordan's
cheek in a glancing blow. She caught her attacker's wrist, trying to
keep the knife away, and grunted when her back slammed against
the psyprinter. With her free hand, she clawed at anything within
reach—leather, hard plastic. Her hand slipped, skin and hair
catching on her fingers.

Bent over the tact board and trapped in place, she brought
her knee up just as Dillon taught her: a sudden jerk with her other

foot braced on the floor. She hit hard bone, sending pain shooting up her leg. *Oh, no!*

Dillon caught up with a pair of cops on the porch busy donning black body armor with painted metallic runes that gleamed softly in the half-light. They needed the protection to get past the security spells. He knew he ought to let them go first, but his gut screamed he didn't have time to waste. Then Timothy's normally soft voice rose in a piercing, maddened yowl of challenge and outrage.

Dillon's blood froze.

Ignoring the cops' preparations, he lunged for the lock panel, deactivating the door wards with one hand while gripping his wand with the other.

Pushing past him, Rio swept the entry for danger, a gun appearing in his hand as if by magic. "Clear. Go!"

Dillon didn't need any urging. With Rio and the cops at his heels, he ran toward the sounds of battle, fearing the worst. *Let her be alive!*

Two figures struggled in Jordan's studio, unidentifiable in the shadows. He hurriedly cast a magelight. Timothy clung to the back of a blond stranger, clawing and snarling like a wildcat.

Jordan's costumed attacker had her pinned against a table, above her psyprinter, a double-edged knife held ready to stab. Only Jordan's arm held the knife back.

But her arm shook, threatening to collapse.

The blond hurled the cat away, sending him crashing into a cabinet to fall to the floor in a limp heap.

Screaming furiously, Jordan twisted, thrusting her enemy to one side. The knife plunged down. Her attacker shrieked.

Dillon cast another spell, terrified he would be too late.

"Police! Don't move!"

Powered by desperation, his spell held, transforming the battle into living sculpture.

Brushing past him, the cops immediately secured Jordan's attacker. Only then did he dare to banish his magic.

Jordan lay on her desk, her arms a gory mess, a red slash on her neck. Blood stained her psyprinter, covered the raised steel pins of her tact board. It cast the knife—the last psyprint she'd worked on—in stark relief and gave it a stomach-churning appearance of realism.

"Get me a medic," Dillon ordered Derwent as he rushed to his lover. On closer inspection, none of the blood along her carotid was hers, coming from the blade that just barely missed its mark. But most of the cuts on her arms looked shallow.

So where's it from?

Timothy?

Jordan's pet lay still where he'd fallen, whole patches of his black-and-white fur matted with blood, reminding Dillon of a bad joke. As Rio knelt by the cat's side, checking his injuries, Timothy stirred weakly.

"Over here," the Latino called to the medics responding to Derwent's summons, then flashed Dillon the high sign. However badly the cat was hurt, it wasn't fatal. With immediate healing, chances were good he would recover completely.

Taking Jordan in his arms, Dillon closed his eyes against a knee-melting wave of relief. His woman didn't need another loss.

She cupped his face with quivering hands. "Dillon?"

He smiled against her palms, shaken by how nearly he'd lost her. "You shouldn't scare a man who loves you like that. If I was a cat, I'd have lost three lives at the very least."

Jordan stiffened. "Timothy?"

"He's cut up but the medics are here. They'll have him fixed up in no time." Raising a hand, he beckoned sharply to get some of their attention for Jordan, trying not to jostle her.

"Good." She closed her eyes, the tension in her slender body fading. "That's good."

Assured of Jordan's safety, Dillon turned to her attacker who was struggling in the arms of two uniformed cops, all the while screaming imprecations. Middling tall, he wore a fantastic costume, the festival mask that covered his head now lying askew and revealing blond hair and pale skin along a smooth jaw and a ragged gash on the neck.

Derwent yanked off the mask, exposing famous features marred by bloody scratches. "Lindsay Thorpe?!"

CHAPTER TWENTY-FOUR

"No, no, no," Jordan admonished, laughter in her voice as she pushed Dillon out of her bedroom. "If I let you, we'll be late."

Though he was already decked out in formal wear, Dillon conceded to himself that she probably had a point—*hell, no "probably" about it!*—but her lighthearted response convinced him to try his luck. "Oh, come on. I can make sure we're only fashionably late."

Jordan's lips twitched before she brought them back under control. "No," she repeated resolutely, closing the door in his face. "I'll just be a few minutes."

Resigning himself to defeat, he stretched out on the recliner in the sitting area outside her door to await Jordan's appearance. It had been worth it to see that twitch of her lips. She'd been withdrawn since the small memorial service for the victims of the bombing at kidTek, though he believed it had done much to help her accept Dan's death.

In the two weeks since the final brutal attack on Jordan, the whole sordid story had slowly come to light. According to Derwent, Dan's murderer, the one responsible for Jordan's poisoning, and the driver of the van that nearly killed her was actually Linda Danvers, the older sister of Lindsay Thorpe. The model herself was dead, her corpse the same one they'd found in the bog.

Danvers had been a programmer at a local defense contractor until she was made redundant in a series of cutbacks. The police were still investigating, but it looked like she'd stolen her famous younger sister's face and identity, killed her, then taken over her life.

It had been her at the exhibit trying to convince Jordan to do her portrait.

At some point, Danvers had taken off and misplaced the gloves she'd kept as a trophy. She'd witnessed Jordan's initial violent reaction to them, and suspected that Jordan had picked up on the psychic residuals of the murder. Everything that ensued she'd done to hide her crime.

Timothy took advantage of Dillon's contemplative repose to crawl onto Dillon's lap and demand a belly rub with a piteous mewl, still milking his heroism for all it was worth. His injuries were completely healed with only a few additional slashes of white in his black fur to show for them, but he still tired easily. Because of his blood loss and trauma, it would be a few more days before the cat was up to his usual antics.

Dillon couldn't begrudge Timothy his attention, not after the way Jordan's pet had leaped to her defense despite his own wounds. "Yeah, you're a real hero, aren't you?"

Furry limbs falling limp on either side, the cat accepted his praise with a rumbling purr, having come to terms with Dillon's presence in his mistress's life.

Jordan, on the other hand, seemed to be withholding judgment, despite her continued enthusiasm for his lovemaking. He'd been giving her time to recover, free from fear and confusion, and to grieve for Dan but tonight he intended to get to the bottom of it.

They hadn't been late, though if the charity auction hadn't been so important to Jordan, Dillon would have tried harder at seducing her. But this was her night and he'd finally see the psyprint she was so secretive about. He didn't want to spoil it for her and he had to admit she'd made him curious.

Shanna, sporting unusually subdued midnight-blue hair, had taken Jordan under her wing shortly after they arrived. Even better, Dillon spotted Lantis and Kiera in the crowd.

His heart sister looked radiant in her first public appearance since the bombing. Dillon studied her covertly with critical eyes, worried that she might have overextended herself. Her belly looked bigger than before but otherwise she seemed completely recovered. His former partner, however, still looked somewhat drawn, the grave lines of his face etched a little deeper after Kiera's two weeks in intensive care.

Godfather, huh? Somehow the thought didn't seem so outrageous, now.

The crowd grew denser as more guests arrived to inspect the offerings. Fabian Merellyn, the ponytailed president of the Spatha Foundation, the charity that organized the auction, kept Jordan's new psyprint under wraps until late in the evening. A consummate showman, he made its unveiling an event in itself, eliciting *oohs* and gasps of surprise.

Dillon stared at the psyprint dominating the central stage, dumbfounded by the image. Jordan had been so secretive about it, he hadn't known what to expect. But the canvas exceeded his wildest imaginings.

He turned his head to look at his lover.

Jordan stood talking with Shanna and Kiera as if nothing unusual had been revealed.

A huff beside him drew his attention from her.

Lantis stared at the psyprint, a minuscule but definite quirk to his lips, his blue eyes wider than usual, sparkling with hilarity. Deep inside, his erstwhile best friend was laughing his fool head off.

Dillon narrowed his own eyes at the taller man, glaring threats at his smirking face. He jabbed a surreptitious elbow at his not-so-former partner's ribs, which was blocked just as stealthily.

"Looks like you've been claimed and branded." Lantis arched an eloquent dark brow, clearly of the opinion that the claiming was long overdue.

Claimed?

On one hand, it was a compliment that Jordan had used him as a model. On the other, the purpose of this sort of exhibition wasn't quite on par with black ops objectives, not that he had to worry about those anymore.

Of course, if she'd used someone else— Dillon's jaw clenched, a growl starting deep in his chest, at the thought of Jordan spending even a second in the presence of another naked man. She was his, damn it. He didn't share.

Back home, Jordan continued to burble over the response to her new psyprint. Shanna had confided to Dillon that the final bid exceeded her expectations, so he understood his lover's excitement. Still, he had mixed emotions about starring in her art, especially since it looked like that psyprint would be the first of many.

Jordan's pacing eventually brought her before him. "You're quiet." She fiddled with his lapels. "Do you mind being my model?"

He drew her into his arms, savoring the contact from chest to thighs. "I'm glad you didn't use someone else. I'd have had to beat him up." Despite his droll delivery, he meant it.

She giggled, just as he expected, then bit her lip. "You're serious. You really would, wouldn't you?"

"Maybe," he temporized. "I'd be tempted."

Dillon ran his finger along Jordan's neck, the slash of red that had crossed her carotid still fresh in his mind—a chilling reminder of how nearly he'd lost her.

Catching his hand, Jordan pressed her soft cheek into his palm. "Quit stewing over it. I'm alright, thanks to you. Get over it." Despite her acerbic words, her tone was loving.

With an effort, he gave her a boyish grin. "I don't know. I think I'm traumatized for life. I'm going to have a difficult time letting you get more than ten feet away from me," he told her half-jokingly.

She stilled, her body held like a doe's poised for flight. "What about your job? Don't you have to return to it?" She tilted her head toward him, her eyes taking on a piercing quality, as if she wasn't blind—or she was using her sight.

"I'm not going back."

Beneath Dillon's fingertips, her pulse raced. "You shouldn't make decisions like that without thinking it over, you know." Tears sparkled in her eyes.

His heart clenched in trepidation. Surely, Jordan couldn't mean she didn't want him. "Too late. I turned in my resignation last week."

Her lips parted in surprise. "You really meant it when you said you love me?" she asked in a wondering tone.

The doubt in her voice stiffened Dillon's determination. Somehow, some way, he'd convince her of his sincerity. "I said so, didn't I?"

She licked her lips, a gesture of uncertainty that made him want to kiss her senseless. "I thought it was just the heat of the moment."

"Nope. I meant what I said. I want to spend my life with you, not just weeks snatched between missions."

Jordan bent her head, making him wish he had her clairvoyance so he could better read her expressions. "What will you do?"

Frustration stirred at the way she ignored his statement. He suppressed it with an effort, making sure there was no hint of it in his voice. "Private investigation—corporate security, mainly. I've been talking with Lantis about going into business with him. It looks feasible." Kiera'd said kidTek would be his first client. And it didn't hurt that he now had a good rep with the cops; Derwent was already hinting about tracking jobs. "I thought I'd settle here. It would give us more time together."

"You've really thought this out."

He tipped her chin up so he could see her face. "I wanted to have something concrete to offer you."

Jordan smiled, a seductive, naughty curve that hinted at numerous carnal possibilities. "Does that mean I get to have my hands on you all the time?" She traced her fingers over his jacket, drawing teasing circles around his nipples.

Fire stirred in his blood as his cock sprang to steel-hard attention, his precipitate response still taking him by surprise. "I'm all yours." He rubbed his erection against her belly to emphasize his sincerity.

Leaning into his motion, Jordan purred, then took a step back. "I get to take you any way I want to?"

"So long as you take me," Dillon responded huskily.

"So if I ask you to strip and wait for me here"—she patted the bed behind her—"you'd do it?"

"Of course." He suited action to agreement, watching Jordan as he doffed his formal wear. "What do you have in mind?" Nude, he lounged against the headboard.

She smiled at him just before she pulled her blouse over her head with artful sensuality. "You're supposed to be waiting."

"Call me impatient." He watched with appreciative eyes as she dropped her skirt and wriggled out of her panty, her high breasts bobbing to an eye-catching rhythm. His cock hardened even more, obedient to her siren song.

"You'll like this." Jordan opened her nightstand to pull out a set of jars and implements he recognized from his stash of toys.

She'd obviously gone raiding, but he found he didn't mind it at all.

Dillon grinned. "You want me to eat you again?" he asked, already reaching for the paintbrush.

"Uh-uh." She intercepted his hand with unerring accuracy and pushed it away, obviously using her sight. "That's for my use," she informed him with a saucy grin.

Her use? Dillon swallowed with difficulty at the images her words conjured. *On me?* His cock throbbed with eagerness.

"You're not going to run, are you?"

"Me, run?" He chuckled despite the vise constricting his lungs. "You're not getting rid of me that easily. Bring it on. I laugh in the face of danger."

With a temptress's smile on her lips, Jordan straddled his lap, placing her pink folds just a breath away from his cock. She chose the blunt powder brush with great deliberation, the tip of her tongue peeking out the corner of her mouth. The studious image she presented was adorable.

Dillon found himself wanting to bend down and give her glossy lips a lick of extremely carnal encouragement.

"Now which one . . . ?"

He checked the jars arrayed beside them. "That's for the large flat one."

She found it and unscrewed the lid. Dipping the brush inside, she applied it to his chest with a liberal hand, leaving his pecs dusted with gold.

He shivered at the grazing contact, his heart pounding at the hint of vulnerability. He was normally on the giving end of this, not receiving.

Jordan picked up another jar.

"That's the—" Dillon cleared his suddenly choked throat. "The chocolate body paint."

"Edible?" She opened it and sniffed delicately.

"Uh-huh." He forced himself to swallow as she dipped a finger into the jar, as if testing the paint's consistency.

"Hmmm . . ." She found his tight nipples unerringly, tweaked them to stiffer points and painted them, her wet finger swirling around them over and over—until he thought he'd grind his teeth to nothing. When she was done, she licked her finger, laving it with slow strokes of her tongue, then sucked it—a graphic foretaste of what he could expect.

Just watching made his heart skip a beat. "Tease. You're enjoying this."

Jordan smiled around her finger. "Of course, I am." As she bent forward to lick him, her tongue flicking across his chest, her wet sex anointed his shaft with cream. "Ummm . . . Orange honey with a dash of Man."

He lay back as she continued to lap him, his awareness torn between her wandering tongue, hard nipples stropping his belly, and the hot kiss of her sex. Damned if she was killing him! Groaning, he caught her ass, pulling her closer to get more of her buttery caress.

She giggled, then fastened her lips on his nipple, nibbled it, then drew on it hard.

Lightning scorched his balls in sync with her suction. Dillon hissed for breath, trying to ride out the suddenly scalding need coiling through his cock that threatened to wipe all thought except taking her.

Undulating over him, Jordan transferred her attentions to his other nipple, paying it the same intense regard as she had its partner. At the same time, she swiveled her hips, swirling the dewy petals of her slit over his sensitive cock head.

Under the lash of her sensual torture, his control didn't hold out for long. After a particularly sultry bump and grind, he couldn't take it anymore. As she leaned into him, her thighs squeezing his hips, he pulled her that last inch over and slid his aching cock home.

Jordan's throaty moan rewarded him even as her slick sheath enfolded him in a torrid welcome. He anchored her against him, groaning as she took him all the way in, her soft mound cushioning the final contact. "Oh, yeah."

But he couldn't stay still. She'd gotten him so wound up he couldn't draw out their lovemaking the way he preferred. When she wrapped her arms and legs around him, he started moving, lunging beneath her, taking her with powerful thrusts that sent their need spiraling to greater heights.

With her breathless encouragement, he drove them to the peak and tumbling over, ecstasy exploding through them in a blast of fiery delight. Their orgasms left them panting and boneless, floating on a wave of pure bliss.

"I love you," Jordan murmured without prompting against his heaving chest, an admission that made his heart stutter.

"Good. I won't let you forget it." Dillon sighed, his frustration burned away by their passion. He had time. Now that he was out of black ops, he had all the time in the world.

His languid stupor was broken by the touch of a rougher tongue. He cracked open an eye to see— "Timothy!"

"Prrp?" The unrepentant cat gave him a look of innocence as he continued to lick Dillon's chest.

"Shit." Dillon quickly gathered up the brushes and jars of edibles, and hid them in the nightstand where Timothy couldn't get at them.

Jordan threw back her head and laughed, her hilarity translating into breath-stealing flutters around his cock that wrenched him back to carnal attention. Then she fell silent as his cock gave another twitch. "Oooh! Do that again."

Forgetting the cat, he rolled his hips slowly, drawing out that tender, soul-searing friction. Oh, yeah, he had all the time in the world.